THE BECKETT COUNTRY

Samuel Beckett's Ireland

Eoin O'Brien

Photography
David H. Davison

Foreword
James Knowlson

Illustrations
Robert Ballagh

Design
Ted and Ursula O'Brien

The Black Cat Press
in association with
Faber and Faber

In gratitude
to
Samuel Beckett
in his eightieth year,
for enrichment as from no other.

The Beckett Country was first published in 1986 by
The Black Cat Press Limited, 9 Clifton Terrace,
Monkstown, Co. Dublin, Ireland,
in association with Faber and Faber Limited,
3 Queen Square, London WC1N 3AU.

Photography by David H. Davison
Design by Ted and Ursula O'Brien of Oben Design, Cork, Ireland
Photoset in *Tiffany* on Compugraphic® MCS8200

Reproduction of duo-tone photographs by
Colour Repro Ltd, Dublin
Printed in Italy by Arnoldo Mondadori.
Paper 125 gsm Juppiter
Limited Edition Paper 143 gsm Juppiter

British Library Cataloguing in Publication Data

O'Brien, Eoin
The Beckett Country. Samuel Beckett's Ireland

1. Beckett, Samuel — Criticism and interpretation

I. Title

828' .91209   PR6003.E2822/

ISBN 0 – 571 – 14667 – 8

ISBN 0 – 948050 – 05 – 5   Cased Edition (Ireland)

ISBN 0 – 948050 – 06 – 3   Limited Edition

CONTENTS

ACKNOWLEDGEMENTS

This book had its beginnings on walks through Dublin, and cycle rides on the Dublin mountains when, in a purposeless way, I explored the terrain of Beckett's writing. I would not have proceeded with detailed research of the subject had not Samuel Beckett encouraged me gently when I first told him of my interest. For his patience in answering my queries, and for redirecting me onto the correct path on more than one occasion, I am most grateful; our meetings in Paris were of great significance for me. For his writing, the starting point for any such venture, I express gratitude and admiration.

The Beckett Country, depends for its visual impact on photography, and I am indebted to David Davison for the great care he took in capturing the mood of this land in photography. I am indebted moreover to David for reprinting many archival photographs to maintain the photographic quality that is the hall-mark of his own work, and he provided me also with a number of photographs from his own collection. *The Beckett Country* owes much to his skills. To capture the ambience of the city of Dublin before the developers cast their dark shadow over its eloquent features, I have relied heavily on the sensitive photography of Nevill Johnson, to whom I express my thanks.

Two ambitions were foremost in writing *The Beckett Country*: that it should be produced as a tribute to Samuel Beckett in his eightieth year, and that the quality of production, especially of the photography, should be of a standard befitting so important a subject. That these aspirations have been fulfilled is due to the skill and remarkable dedication of Ted and Ursula O'Brien who worked many nights and every day over several months in guiding *The Beckett Country* through the tribulations of printing. No tribute from me can convey adequately my gratitude and admiration for their design capabilities in marrying the photography so skillfully with the text, for coping so efficiently with the conversion from word processor to typesetting, and in over-seeing in elaborate detail the quality of duo-tone reproduction of the photography and the printing of the text; in tolerating the many last minute changes which I demanded so unreasonably they demonstrated not only a profound patience but their total commitment to *The Beckett Country*.

Robert Ballagh joins a group of artists who have been associated with Beckett's writing in giving to the topographical aspects of *The Beckett Country* a simplicity that is both individualistic and informative.

Professor James Knowlson welcomed me to Reading University with a sincerity and warmth that must be unique to academic institutes. He and his wife, Elizabeth, generously gave me the hospitality of their home and ensured that all I required in the Beckett Archive at the University of Reading was at my disposal. James Knowlson has read the manuscript of the book, corrected many errors, and saved me from drawing conclusions that were based on unsound evidence. I am grateful also for the foreword which he has written for the book. It was James Knowlson's appreciation of *The Beckett Country* that led to an exhibition of photography from the book, (with its catalogue also entitled *The Beckett Country*) which was opened for the first time by Dame Peggy Ashcroft at the University of Reading on May 11th, 1986. As a gesture of gratitude and in recognition of the academic value of the Beckett Archive, the photography of *The Beckett Country* has been donated to the University of Reading. To Michael Bott, Keeper of Archives and Mss., my thanks for invaluable help in locating sources in the Archive and for proof-reading quotations. John Pilling at the Department of English at Reading gave freely of his advice which is always substantive.

To Gerry Dukes, who in his sensitive compilation from the trilogy, *Molloy, Malone Dies, The Unnamable*, for Barry McGovern's performance *I'll go on* has brought a sense of feeling and comprehension to this complex work, I am grateful for giving freely of his time to read the page-proofs of *The Beckett Country* , and for his many helpful suggestions.

Sean O Mórdha's researches for his award-winning drama-documentary, *Silence to Silence*, produced by Radio Telefis Éireann, coincided with mine for *The Beckett Country*, and he generously shared his sources with me, provided me with the script of his film, and read the manuscript making many helpful suggestions. Sean provided me with the text of Samuel Beckett's radio broadcast on Saint-Lô for which I am indebted. I acknowledge with gratitude permission from Radio Telefis Éireann to publish this broadcast. While on the subject of Saint-Lô I would like to thank Ms Mary Crowley, first Dean of The Faculty of Nursing at the Royal College of Surgeons in Ireland, who was Matron at the Irish Hospital in Saint-Lô, and who generously placed at my disposal her album of photographs, letters and memorabilia relating to the hospital. Professor Ethna Gaffney, obtained for me from her sister-in-law, Josephine Gaffney, her late husband's letters from Saint-Lô, and also a number of invaluable photographs, for which I am grateful. To Maurice Gaffney, also my thanks for helpful information. Mr. Paddy Carey and his wife Breda, both of whom were at Saint-Lô, gave generously of their time, and allowed me to copy many photographs from their albums. Mr. Marcus Thompson, kindly loaned me photographs that had belonged to his father, the late Professor Alan Thompson.

Paddy and Caroline Murphy (née Beckett) gave me not only the family photographs I sought, but also the warm hospitality of their home and beautiful gardens at *Shottery* in Killiney, for which I am most thankful. I am indebted also to Edward Beckett for his assistance.

In Foxrock I was fortunate in having the assistance of a number of people who made it possible for me to identify, and even obtain photographs of many of the personalities who feature in Beckett's prose and drama. Mrs. Sheila Brazil, former postmistress of the village was of invaluable help to me. She obtained for me a number of early photographs which are acknowledged individually later, and of these that of Bill Shannon, the whistling postman, rates as the most important. Liam Clare of the Foxrock Historical Society went to considerable trouble to obtain a number of photographs and historical information of the area, which I acknowledge with gratitude. The Reverend Cecil Hyland, Rector of Tully Parish Church, provided old photographs and historical details of the church and parish. Mr. Edward Farrell, Mr. Reggie Farrell, Mr. Fintan Flynn, Mr. Ken Gregory, Mr. Michael McGovern, Mr. P. Cronin and Mr. Eamonn Reynolds all provided me with interesting local historical information. Mr. and Mrs. Noel Hughes allowed me to visit their home, *Cooldrinagh*, on more than one occasion for photography, as did Mr. and Mrs. Peter Stapleton, the owners of *New Place*, Professor G. Doyle of *Barrington*, and the British Ambassador to Ireland, Sir Alan Goodison and his wife Lady Goodison of *Glencairn*, to all of whom I am grateful. Mr. Reginald Avery and Paul Whiteway, of the British Embassy also gave me helpful assistance.

In the National Gallery of Ireland, Dr. Michael Wynne, Keeper of the Gallery, gave me expert assistance in identifying the references to art in Beckett's writing. I am grateful to him for enlightening me on many aspects of this subject, and for facilitating my researches in the Gallery. Mr. Michael Olahan's valuable assistance in obtaining photographs of paintings in the Gallery is much appreciated. To Ms Barbara Davison, Ms Catherine de Courcy, and Ms Janet Drew, I am indebted for photographs and art history material. As always, James Geirin, Head Attendant, and his staff facilitated me in any way possible. Patrick Johnston, Curator of the Civic Museum was ever available to discuss and ponder an elusive piece of research. Not only did he provide me with some original photographs, but he directed me to a number of sources, which I would not otherwise have located. Another Dubliner to give valuable assistance was Seamus de Burca, and I would like also to acknowledge the help of Fred Dixon and Eamonn MacThomais. Brother Finbarr Murphy O.H. and Dr. Patrick Tubridy, Director of St. John of God Hospital in Stillorgan, and Dr. Michael Conway, Clinical Director and Medical Superintendant of St. Ita's Hospital at Portrane allowed me to visit their institutions, and I am indebted to them for the valuable information they gave me. I am particularly grateful to Brother Finbarr who provided me with old photographs of St. John of God's. At Portora Royal School Mr. Davison and I were made most welcome by Mr. M.R.H. Scott, the Estates Manager, to whom I am indebted for placing many interesting photographs at our disposal, and to Mr. R.L. Bennett, the headmaster for permission to publish these and material from the school archives.

Ms Anne Yeats was most generous in giving me helpful information, and allowing me to study the sketch-books and other papers of her uncle, Jack Yeats. To Liam Miller, I am grateful for help and advice in the production of *The Beckett Country*, and for his suggestion for a title.

I am grateful to John Hall and Philip Curtis of the Audio-Visual Department of the Royal College of Surgeons in Ireland, who assisted me with the preliminary photography. Mr. Patrick Tutty went to considerable effort to assist me in researching and obtaining suitable prints from the comprehensive Bord Fáilte archive. Mr. D. Ó'Luanaigh, Keeper of Printed Books, kindly allowed me to consult the photographic archives in the National Library of Ireland; I am grateful also to Mr. Martin Ryan and Mr. Eugene Hogan who facilitated me in obtaining photographs from the Library's collections, and to the Director Mr. Michael Hewson for permission to publish these. Mr. Richard Mooney, not for the first time, drew my attention to pertinent sources in the Library. John Kennedy of the Green Studio gave me valuable help in researching and obtaining prints of early railway photographs, and in this regard I would like also to thank Mr. R.C. Flewitt. In the Irish Architectural Archive, the director Mr. William Garner, assisted me in researching the extensive photographic archive, and in the Royal Society of Irish Antiquaries, Ms. Siobhan de hÓir provided similar assistance. Mr. Thomas O'Dowd, now an occupant of the top floor of no. 6 Clare Street, generously provided me with photographs of the rooms, and Mr. Ian MacMillan, successor in the firm of Beckett and Medcalf, allowed me to photograph his office and the garret above. Mr. Thomas Cranitch, Press Officer to Aer Lingus researched enthusiastically on my behalf for photographs of Ireland's first aviation meeting. Ms Geraldine Reardon and Mr. John Gibbons of Leopardstown Racecourse, kindly gave of their time to provide me with an early photograph of the course, and also directed me to local sources. Mr. Wilfred Fitzsimmons of the Royal Irish Automobile Club provided me with an early photograph of the Club and facilitated my researches in the Club's library. Ms Elish Huban kindly obtained photographs of Leopardstown racecourse, including that of William Beckett, from her aunt Mrs. Carmel Clarke.

For old photographs of Dublin I am grateful to Mr. George Duncan. To Carlton Lake of the Humanities Research Center at Austin Texas I am indebted for the photograph of Samuel Beckett as a child at his mother's knee. Grateful acknowledgement is made for photographs from The National Motor Museum, Beulieu, and the National Swedish Art Museums. To the following, whose mention by name only is a reflection on the constraints of space rather than the valuable assistance afforded to me, I express my gratitude: Dr. John de Courcy Ireland, The Maritime Institute of Ireland; Mr. Peter Pearson; Mr. Andrew Renton; Mr. Hugh O'Brien; Mr. Ulick O'Connor; William and Desiree Hayter; Ms Marion Leigh; Dr. Charles Meenan; Dr. and Mrs. J. Clinch; Mr. Sean Moore; Ms Kathleen McGrory; Mrs. Gladys McConnell; Ms J.F. Plews; Mrs. R. Steen; Dr. Desmond de Courcy Wheeler; Mr. Mark Sugden; Mr. Tony Suttle; Mr. Mark Taylor; Countess H. Viani; Mrs. S. Grimley; Mr. R. Burke, Norwich Union Insurance, Ireland; Mr. Brian Mooney, Bective Rugby Club; Mr. Brian Siggins; Mr. John Ryan; Mr. and Mrs. Kevin Crowley; Mrs. Sheila Healy; Mrs. M. Ussher; Mrs. Hilary Carey; Ms Joan Kennedy; Ms Kay Lawler; Ms Rosemary Darley; Mr. and Mrs. Hugh Delap; Mr. Seamus McGrath; Mr. Peter Matthews, Old Time Cycling; Mr. Alex McAllister; Dr. Bernard Meehan and Ms Felicity O'Mahony, The Manuscript Department, Trinity College, Dublin; Sir Gordon Wolstenholme, Harveian Librarian of the Royal College of Physicians of London; Mrs. Muriel McCarthy, Librarian of Marsh's Library, Dublin; Ms Sighle Kennedy; Mr. Kieran Hickey; Mr. Francis Evers; Mrs. W. Kennedy; Mr. D. Lawlor and Mr. P. Sommerville, the General Post Office; Miss L.A. Tunbridge, Bovril Limited; Professor Barbara Wright and Dr. Roger Little, Mr. Trevor West, Professor John McCormack, Trinity College, Dublin; Mr. Joseph Collins; Mr. Matthew Murtagh; Mr. John Gibson and Dr. David Nowlan, *The Irish Times*; Mr. Stephen Hirsch; Mr. Charles Nelson; Father Brendan Hynds; Ms Jean Davison; Mr. Kiaran Taaffe; Dr. Jean Francois Pedron; Dr. Frank Edwards, Mr. Tony Smith and Mr. James Thompson, The University of Reading; Mr. Michael Colgan, Ms Marie Rooney, Ms Sheenagh Gillen and Mr. Barry McGovern, The Gate Theatre; Mrs. Nancy Cosgrove; Ms Pauline Morrissy; Mr. Paul Bennett; Mr. Roy Hewson; Ms Carmel Daly; Mr. Harold Clarke, Easons Ltd.; Dr. Keiran O'Boyle; Ms Mary Clarke, The Irish Theatre Archive; Ms Martha Fehsenfeld; Mrs. Margo Magan and Mr. Roger Kugler.

It was in the peaceful setting of The Tyrone Guthrie Centre at Annaghmakerrig that the *The Beckett Country* was moulded into its final form and I would like to express my thanks to the two Arts Councils in Ireland which made my stay there possible; but in particular I thank and pay tribute to the Resident Director and his wife, Bernard and Mary Loughlin, to whose efficiency and hospitality the centre owes its ambience.

To Rosemary Byrne my expression of thanks cannot indicate adequately the patience and time that she has devoted without murmur to the typing and re-typing of successive drafts. Her familiarity with computer technology greatly facilitated the conversion of *The Beckett Country* from typescript to print. To her and to Paula Somers, who assisted in binding the manuscripts I am indebted. Helen Litton tackled the daunting task of indexing with customary thoroughness for which I am grateful.

The publication of *The Beckett Country* has depended greatly on the generosity and support of a number of people. Samuel Beckett generously waived all rights on quotations from his published works, and his publishers Faber and Faber Limited, John Calder (Publishers) Ltd., and Grove Press, Inc., willingly complied with his wishes in this regard. To Frank Pike, I am particularly grateful for negotiating associate publication for The Black Cat Press and Faber and Faber, and for his advice and guidance on many aspects of publication. John Calder gave freely of his advice which I am glad to acknowledge. In Ireland a group of friends came together to give not only of their experience in many areas but also to provide financial support for the publication of *The Beckett Country*, and I would like to thank the co-directors of The Black Cat Press for their support and loyalty: Kieran Taaffe, Patrick Lawlor, Tona O'Brien, Harry O'Flanagan, Ted and Ursula O'Brien and David Davison. Peter Wood has overseen the publishing negotiations with Mondadori both in London and Verona, and his expertise has been of great assistance. Greg Lokko of Colour Repro Ltd. Ireland has given the attention to detail so necessary for quality duo-tone separation. Linda Killham and Jeremy Westwood of Arnoldo Mondadori have combined courtesy and efficiency in printing *The Beckett Country*.

Tona, who devised the the de-luxe edition, supported, encouraged and advised me throughout the writing of *The Beckett Country*, a work on which she has always believed no effort should be spared, and I hope that I have not failed her; for our children Aran, Aphria, and Emmet, who have already walked much of the Beckett land, perhaps *The Beckett Country* will serve as a starting point for them to begin their exploration of the writings of Samuel Beckett.

Eoin O'Brien

SOURCES OF ILLUSTRATIONS

The source for each photograph is indicated with the title. The full addresses for photographers and museums are:

David Davison, Pieterse Davison International Ltd., 11 Small Industries Cluster, Pearse St., Dublin 2.
G.A. Duncan, Trade Press Photographer, 151 Cabra Rd., Dublin 7.
John Kennedy, The Green Studio, 58 Harcourt St., Dublin 2.
Nevill Johnson, 78 Campden House, Peel St., London W8.
The Civic Museum, South William St. Dublin 2.
The Hugh Lane Municipal Gallery of Modern Art, Parnell Sq., Dublin 1.
The Irish Architectural Archive, 63 Merrion Sq., Dublin 2.
The National Library of Ireland, Kildare St., Dublin 2.
The National Gallery of Ireland, Merrion Sq., Dublin 2.
Bord Fáilte, Irish Tourist Board, Baggot Street Bridge, Dublin 2.
The Royal Society of Antiquaries of Ireland, 63 Merrion Sq., Dublin 2.

FOREWORD

Re-reading Beckett's early prose works – the published *More Pricks than Kicks* (which is firmly set in Dublin and its environs in the late nineteen-twenties) or the unpublished novel, *Dream Of Fair to Middling Women* of the same period, or, again, some of the early Dublin poems by Beckett that were published in 1935 in *Echo's Bones and Other Precipitates*, – after one has read Eoin O'Brien's book, *The Beckett Country*, is rather like returning to these works fresh from an intensive tour of the city of Dublin and its surrounding countryside in the company of an enthusiastic, highly articulate, splendidly informed guide. With its wealth of fascinating information, *The Beckett Country* brings to life locations outside the city that figure prominently in Beckett's early writings: the Hill of Wolves, Lambay Island, Portrane Lunatic Asylum, Swords, Chapelizod, Sandymount and the Hell Fire Club or, to move closer to Beckett's family home in Foxrock, 'Cooldrinagh', Croker's Gallops or Acres and Leopardstown racecourse, the Two and Three Rock mountains, and Dun Laoghaire with its 'kindergarten of steeples' and its twin-piered harbour. By capturing something of the peaceful, rugged beauty of that part of Ireland, the striking photographs accompanying the text help to suggest why Beckett should have been so deeply influenced by his upbringing in such surroundings.

Within the city of Dublin itself, which looms so large in the stories, 'Ding-Dong', 'A Wet Night' and 'What a Misfortune' in *More Pricks than Kicks*, Pearse Street, Duke Street, the paralytic beggar from the slum area of the Coombe, the red-light district of 'the Kips', the many bridges across the Liffey, the bull-necked statue of Thomas Moore, the Bovril sign (no longer a landmark flashing over the city), the Fire Station, the Dental Hospital, and (frequently invoked by Beckett) Kennedy's Pub and Mooney's Bar, are all described with a mixture of intriguing historical and topographical detail. Fine modern photographs of the city by David Davison appear alongside some superbly evocative archival photographs.

Few readers who are acquainted with Beckett's writing will be in the least surprised that these early works which are grounded in a specific social environment should be so fruitfully illuminated by the study of places and people rediscovered from the 'real' Dublin of the 1920s. Some of Beckett's allusions even call out for Dr. O'Brien's local knowledge and explanatory comments before they make full sense to anyone but an expert on the region. But what of the more mature Beckett writing? The novel trilogy, *Molloy, Malone Dies*, and *The Unnamable*, the *Texts for Nothing* or *How It Is*, and the plays of the 'fifties, texts which were written when Beckett had already discovered the unusual territory in which he was subsequently to work? The situation here is somewhat different and certainly more complex, as Beckett's writing became less localised and more concerned with issues relating to the world of the inner self. It is with respect to these later writings that an assessment of the value of Dr. O'Brien's approach and discoveries will inevitably depend on what the reader is himself looking for in this book or even on his approach to literature in general. I doubt, for instance, whether formalist or structuralist critics will consider its findings in this area to be of more than passing biographical interest. They are, I think, in an important sense mistaken, just as I too was mistaken when I dismissed photographic representations of the 'real' Dublin of the nineteen-twenties and -thirties in my *Samuel Beckett: an exhibition* catalogue of 1971.

Considering the relationship between a writer's life and his literary texts is a difficult task since it is only too easy to produce facile equivalences under the guise of revelations and to assume that the writer must always be speaking (with or without the 'I' form) with an autobiographical voice. In the past, I must admit that I have found biography to be of little help in understanding the work of Samuel Beckett. Perhaps this has been the fault of those who have practised this approach merely by hunting out biographical sources and parallels – finding, for instance, the figures of James Joyce and Beckett in Hamm and Clov in *Endgame* or discovering behind the figures of Estragon and Vladimir in *Waiting for Godot*, Beckett himself and his wife, Suzanne, indulging in idle banter to keep each other going during the war, as they made their escape from the Gestapo down through France to Roussillon in the unoccupied zone.

But Dr. O'Brien's approach differs from this in that he concentrates far more attention on the influence of place than of people. Many readers of *The Beckett Country*, including those who are very familiar with Beckett's prose texts and plays, will be surprised, perhaps even astonished, at the frequency with which passages from his mature writings are shown by Dr. O'Brien to owe a substantial debt to Beckett's childhood memories and experiences of his native land. In this respect, he seems to me to have already achieved something different and more valid than most previous writers who have related Beckett's life to his work. I recall, for example, the description of Moran's house in *Molloy*, which, as Eoin O'Brien points out, is clearly based on Beckett's own Foxrock family home. More surprising perhaps, is the fact that Mr. Knott's house in *Watt* also owes much to Beckett's childhood memories of 'Cooldrinagh' – something which was confirmed to Dr. O'Brien by Beckett himself. I remember too how convincingly he demonstrates that the macabre climax of *Malone Dies* uses precise memories of Dalkey Island or how fully *The Beckett Country* documents incidents from works as far apart in time as the *Texts for Nothing* - the first aviation meeting, for instance, that Beckett attended with his mother at the age of four – and *Company* – in which he revisits the 'old scenes' or trudges the 'old back-roads' once again. Dr. O'Brien makes a number of what one can only call fascinating 'discoveries': he prints Beckett's unpublished 1946 broadcast script about Saint-Lô; he traces 'the consumptive postman whistling *The Roses are blooming in Picardy* of *Watt* and *Dream of Fair to Middling Women* to Bill Shannon, one of Foxrock's three postmen; he locates 'Foley's Folly' in *That Time* as 'Barrington's Tower' and tells us all about it; he identifies Mr. Barrell of *All that Fall* as Mr. Farrell, the Foxrock station-master; he explains lines like Mr. Nolan's question in *Watt* as to which end of the railway line they were speaking about, 'The round end or the square end?', as applying to Harcourt Street and Bray Stations respectively and the simile 'like a woman making to cover her breasts' as a reference to Dun Laoghaire's harbour because of the shape of its two piers; and so on. In this respect, this book admirably complements Lawrence Harvey's *Samuel Beckett: Poet and Critic,* which had already explained – under Beckett's guidance, one senses – so many of the local or difficult scholarly references in the poems.

But discoveries of such parallels and influences, however fascinating they may be in themselves, remain open to the basic objection 'so what?' – with its implication that they have actually added very little to our understanding of the literary work. There are several reasons why I think this criticism either does not apply or applies only rarely to this book. First, what *The Beckett Country* does in the widest sense is to reveal the very Irishness of much of Beckett's landscape, for if, in his mature fiction, a road, characteristically, leads to nowhere, it often meanders across hills or bogs that have features that are quite recognisable as being specific to the Dublin mountains. It soon becomes clear, in fact, from this book that, though he left it for good in the 'thirties, Ireland is present in Beckett's work not only in the localised settings of the early works or in the 'old scenes' revisited of the most recent plays or prose texts like *That Time* and *Company*, but also in some of the apparently more abstracted landscapes described in *Molloy* and *Malone Dies*, and evoked in *Not I* and *... but the clouds ...* Similarly, Dr. O'Brien restores the Irish 'feel' to some of the characters of Beckett's plays, so that, as I have argued elsewhere, in spite of Jean Anouilh's view that Estragon and Vladimir resemble the *Pensées* of Pascal played by the Fratellini clowns they probably owe more to genes inherited from John Millington Synge than they do to those coming from any French philosopher.

There is also good reason for maintaining that his book is among the most important to appear on Beckett in the past two decades because it seems likely that it might encourage a shift back in Beckett criticism to consider how Beckett deals with 'outer reality' in his mature writing, as compared with the inner world with which so many critics, particularly those adopting a philosophical approach to his work, have been concerned. This now seems to me to be eminently desirable. Moreover, the general reader often seems to have gained the impression that Beckett's prose works and plays exist in a strange kind of 'no man's land' with few connections with any real world and no links at all with their own human experiences. Nothing, I suggest, could be further from the truth.

Beckett has certainly created a fictional and dramatic world of his own in which absence, distress, impermanence and lack of fulfilment are experienced directly and where the void can always be sensed behind the meaningless routines or the web of words being woven by an Estragon, a Clov or a Winnie. But it is often forgotten that this Beckettian world is constructed with specific, often very concrete elements of an outer reality which it does a great disservice to Beckett to disregard. For what is striking is that, however strange the setting – the barren, devouring earth of *Happy Days*, the country road by a spare tree of *Waiting for Godot*, or the mud of *How It Is* – it never departs entirely or for very long from scenes, experiences, or memories that draw from an outer reality, although (as John Pilling stresses in the Foreword to the exhibition catalogue based on this book) that reality will, of course, never be other than Beckett's *own* reality. And what impresses me increasingly is that these shards of observed reality emerge with striking force and great poignancy from the barren landscape in which they exist. I think, for instance, of a phrase from *Worstward Ho* 'Hold the old holding hand' which, in its context, recalls with touching simplicity the tangible, physical contact of father and child; Winnie is at her most moving in *Happy Days* when she touches a strand of her hair and says 'Golden you called it' or recalls 'that day ... the reeds'; even Mouth in *Not I* is most poignantly human as she recounts her experiences of acute loneliness in the supermart, in court, or lying with her 'face in the grass'. It is at such moments of observed human experience that Beckett's writing seems to me to be almost unbearably moving and most truthful for it contains the fragility and ephemerality of the human experience as well as its claim to reality.

The Beckett Country provides so much detailed information about 'outer reality' as it was represented by Ireland in Beckett's early life that even the best informed reader of Beckett will find something new or of interest on every page. Dr. O'Brien certainly leaves interpretation of his findings to others. But the knowledge he displays in establishing what the influences of that outer reality were on the young Beckett seems to me to be both authoritative and suggestive of many further interesting lines of enquiry and debate.

One of the things that interests me, for instance, is what Beckett *does* with landscape in his later work. I have heard some Beckett scholars speak of a marked vein of lyricism in his writing about nature, while others have disputed whether one can speak of lyricism in the case of a writer who so drastically and so self-consciously deflates his own descriptive effects. Beckett is rarely interested *merely* in describing a scene, a person or a painting and he certainly udercuts his own descriptive passages with phrases like 'end of descriptive passage' or by stating that superlatives have 'lost most of their charm'. Yet, although Beckett self-consciously manipulates fiction within the tradition of Sterne and Diderot and is also acutely conscious of and struggles with the unreliability of language (perhaps in the wake of Mauthner), none the less a form of stark yet moving lyricism remains, as his prose strives above all to 'sing' – a term that Beckett has used to me several times, half apologetically, as being the only term that he could find appropriate to what he was trying to achieve in his prose.

Another issue that is raised implicitly by the frequency with which quotations in this book appear both from the early work and the late plays and prose texts is the place that the 'old scenes' play in the different phases of his work. The subject is obviously too large to be more than touched upon here and I shall mention briefly only one feature that interests me.

Beckett has meditated for so long on the corrosive effects of time that, when the 'old scenes' return in the writings of his old age, they are inevitably accompanied by a sense of questioning that is far more radical than the mere 'when was that?' of *That Time*. For these often apparently quite precise memories are not just subject to the doubts that arise from faulty memory. The very reality of past experience is thrown into question. It is as if the experiences of the past that are very much there within the body of the text have now been eroded by the ravages of time to the point at which the speaker in whose mind these recollections resurface (or at least the voice through which they come to be restated) cannot distinguish what is said to have occurred from what is or can be imagined. 'Ah, yesterday', sighed Nell elegiacally in *Endgame*. But the experience of 'yesterday' is as elusive as if it had belonged to some earlier life or to fiction itself. When, to take an example not from Ireland, Vladimir reflects in *Waiting for Godot* that he and Estragon had once – like Beckett and Suzanne during the war years in Roussillon – picked grapes in the Macon country, the information seems inconceivable to his companion, however forcefully he asserts its truth. Yet the presence of these memories within the text, and their contrast with the present situation in which the tramps find themselves make their dramatic impact far from negligible. Similarly, in the recent prose text, *Company*, 'real' experiences from Beckett's own early years are undermined by the context in which they appear or by the surprise with which the speaker greets their resurfacing. Yet the very sharpness of detail, as well as the beauty and economy of the language, with which these 'old scenes' are recounted exercises its own particular attraction and compels belief. In this way, the experience of reading an account of such scenes in Beckett's late work involves quite a complex set of responses.

A book like *The Beckett Country* that provides so much information and goes so far in restoring relationship between Beckett and an observed reality will, I am sure, be welcomed both by the specialist and by the general reader. If it had consisted of text and notes alone, it would have already been a fascinating and useful work of scholarship. With its hundreds of fine photographs on which so much care has been lavished at every stage, it becomes a truly remarkable book, with which it has been a great privilege to be associated.

James Knowlson

INTRODUCTION

The seeds for this book were sown, I suspect, when I read *Murphy*, my first taste of the Beckett *oeuvre*. After this, I was compelled to read everything Beckett had published. I found myself drawn back irresistibly time and again to one work after another, relishing new sensations at each visit, seeing in the prose or poetry (distinction between the two is not always possible in Beckett's writing), at one time pathos and humour, at another beauty and outrage. Then the works began to blur as the one blended into the other, so that I could no longer, and still cannot (many readings later) always determine the origins of a particular piece of prose. This no longer upsets me, for I now view Beckett's writing as a total composition, each work being a different treatment of sensation, event or emotion, originating often from a single experience. With this realisation, came another. Much of the apparently surrealistic in Beckett's writing is linked, sometimes forcefully, often only tenuously, with the reality of existence, and much of this actuality emanates from Beckett's memories of Dublin, a world which he renders almost unrecognisable as he removes reality from his landscape and its people (while also annihilating time) in his creation of the 'unreality of the real.'[1] Compelling though this reality is in Beckett's writing, an awareness of that reality serves only one function, albeit an important one, in that it marks a point of commencement for Beckett's creative art. An obsessional diligence in identifying realities, could blight the creative beauty of Beckett's imagination - the 'soul-landscape.'[2]

Samuel Beckett is an Irishman. This simple statement should be taken for what it is, a mere declaration of fact. It should not be seized upon by the patriotic purveyors of national character and genius for public display. Beckett's nationality, taken at face value is nothing more than an accident, as a consequence of which he was brought up in a small island with a people peculiar to that region. But there is more to it than that. Beckett's confinement to Ireland occurred during a period of his life when influences are formative and lasting; a period when the culture, mannerisms and eccentricities of a particular society are not only fundamental to the development of personality, but may provide also the raw material of creativity should a sensitive talent be among its youth.

It is these influences that are the concern of *The Beckett Country*. I approached my task aware, however, that artistic issues relative to place and person must be interpreted with great care and, never more so, than with Beckett.

Beckett has a justified abhorrence of anyone attributing to minutae a personal significance that does not, or did not exist, and this has greatly influenced the structure of this book which concerns itself more with topography than with personality, more with the ambience of a life-style than with those who participated in that life. *The Beckett Country* is not biographical; if it veers towards the genre of biography it is then closer to autobiography, in that it allows the story of Beckett's life to unfold, in the only way with which he would be in agreement, that is through his art. Yet, to treat Beckett's writing as a whole as autobiographical would be to reduce its artistic value, and to detract from its beauty.[3]

Proust (a figure whose technique bears a much closer resemblance to Beckett's than that of Joyce[4]), sees art 'put together out of several intercalated episodes in the life of the author,'[5] and this is certainly as true for Beckett as it was for Proust. The inspirational influences of time past on the art of Samuel Beckett constitute the dominant theme of *The Beckett Country*. The 'posse of larches' is every bit as potent as the 'madeleine' was to Proust, the granite rocks of Dun Laoghaire pier, as revelatory to Beckett's art as the granite kerbstone on the *Guermantes* pavement was in awakening in Proust the vision that inspired his masterpiece.

I believe that a knowledge of the geography and custom of a writer's habitat may enhance appreciation of his art. Indeed Sighle Kennedy goes so far as to suggest that 'entry to certain spirals of his (Beckett's) art will continue to require the possession (in sympathy at least) of a green Eire passport.'[6] I take support for this view also from Martin Esslin, who sees in Beckett's poetry a compression almost to the point of being in code, and this analogy could be extended to much of the later prose: 'A single line may carry multiple meanings, public and private allusions, description and symbol, topographic reference, snatches of overheard conversation, fragments in other languages, Provencal or German, the poet's own asides ... learned literary allusions together with brand names of cigarettes or shop signs in Dublin. Four lines may thus require four pages of elucidation, provided, that is, that the full information were at hand ...'[7] Perhaps *The Beckett Country* will provide some of that necessary information.

Twenty years ago the late Con Leventhal, Beckett's close friend and confidant, identified in Beckett scholarship the neglect of the visual, that aspect of art which Beckett himself prizes so highly: 'In parenthesis and a new paragraph may I ask when are we going to have an illustrator of B.'s work? Both Blake and Dali have interpreted Dante; it would require a mixture of both their qualities, a power of illumination plus magic.'[8] Con had a painter in mind and one of considerable genius at that; I decided instead to endow the Beckett country with a visual perspective through the art of photography. The portrayal of that land could only be achieved by an artist willing to familiarise himself with the terrain, its people and its fickle sky and light. I was fortunate in obtaining the support of David Davison, who developed an empathy with the mood of the land and the Beckettian character. Together, we walked this land, often returning many times to a particular place to catch the moment when light, sky and object were in harmony with the Beckett spirit, a harmony that was to be further enriched by the delicate manipulation of processing techniques, to create through the art of photography a series of compositions that would be a tribute to the writer who had inspired them.

In spite of a massive secondary literature, it is early days in Beckett scholarship. As is customary, the Irish academic beacon (with a few honourable exceptions), has been directed elsewhere, with the result that the specifically Irish references in Beckett's writing have, for the most part, passed unnoticed. But in the face of such few Irishmen as are aware of Beckett's Irishness, there are those who, whilst in no position to deny him the facts of his birth, nevertheless do not consider him to be truly Irish. The reasons traditionally cited are: his Anglo-Irish origins and education,[9] his prolonged absence from the homeland (though allowances seem to have been made for Joyce in this regard), his adoption of a foreign tongue, and the fact that his writings are at variance with the popular pieties of Irish literature.

Beckett's adoption of France as a homeland does not lessen the relevance of Ireland to his writing. He left Ireland for good reasons, having found himself at odds with the canons of propriety. Moreover, the inebriating ambience of Dublin had laid to rest many a budding flower, in 'lakes of boiling small-beer'.[10] Nor should his physical departure from Ireland be equated with a spiritual exodus. He brought with him to France the tools of his trade, the back-drop against which his dramas would be acted out, his models and their dialogue to be spliced on occasion to another language, their aspirations and despairs. He did not as one critic has put it, 'cast off race and genius', and thereby become 'a Frog'.[11] No, as for the protagonist of *The Calmative*, so too for Beckett, 'there was never any city but the one ... I only know the city of my childhood, I must have seen the other, but unbelieving.'[12]

Con Leventhal was one who marvelled at academe's inability to appreciate the Irish influence in Beckett's writing. The question as to whether France had the right to claim Beckett as its eleventh Nobel prize-winner in 1969 or whether the country of his birth could claim him as her third (after Yeats and Shaw) drew an interesting comment from Leventhal:[13] 'There is no one here to make the full Irish case. Few to talk of the kinship with Swift though more to tie the Dubliner in a Joycean knot. No one, however, is sufficiently aware of the background to notice the Irishness of the Godot tramps. The highest praise that the dramatist Anouilh can give to 'Waiting for Godot' is that in it we have Pascal's 'Pensées' played out by the Fratellini clowns. How could he know or be expected to recognise the Dublin lilt of the dialogue as translated by the author? How few French people were able to realise the added humour and pathos to the French version of 'Fin de Partie' when in its English form it was acted by Patrick Magee and Jack MacGowran in the author's own production! The French, ignorant of the exciting possibilities of an 'Endgame' played by the right Irish actors are likewise unfamiliar with the revelatory new touches which these two actors can give to their interpretation of a Beckett text on radio and television.'

Any discussion as to whether or not the French or the Irish can lay claim to Samuel Beckett, is of consequence only insofar as it may assist in the interpretation of his work. A squabble over national identity would be most offensive to Beckett, to whom national boundaries, geographical and cultural, have always been tiresome, and at times threatening, encumbrances. Harry Cockerham takes a refreshingly positive approach to Beckett's dual nationality: 'Arguments over whether he is properly a French or an Irish writer are therefore necessarily sterile and it may indeed be that his example and the fact of his existence as a bilingual writer will do much to break down barriers between national cultures and encourage a trend towards comparativism in literary studies.'[14] So while allowing that Beckett is Irish in origins, in manners, and at times thought, we must accept that he belongs to no nation, neither to France nor to Ireland; if any claim has validity, it is that he represents in outlook the true European, but even this tidy categorisation is excessively constraining, *Beckett is of the world.*

Topographic references to Dublin in Beckett's writing are numerous. It is widely accepted that *All That Fall* is set in Foxrock, but what is not so well known is that *Happy Days* may have had its origins in a seaside cove bearing the delightful name of Jack's Hole, that one of the climatic episodes in *Krapp's Last Tape* occurred on Dun Laoghaire pier, and that a case can be made for placing Vladimir and Estragon's vigil for Godot on the Dublin mountains. *Dream of Fair to Middling Women* and *More Pricks than Kicks* are set squarely in Dublin, whereas *Murphy* is played out in both Dublin and London. Mercier and Camier spend their time between the city of Dublin, it's canals and the Dublin mountains, and there are Dublin locales to be found in *Watt, Malone Dies, The Unnamable, Company, That Time, Eh Joe, Embers*, much of the later prose, and some of Beckett's poetry. Not all see it thus. Vivian Mercier, while freely acknowledging the influence of Dublin in a number of Beckett's novels and plays, asserts that 'Beckett had brought from his carefully insulated suburban community very little that was usable and durable.'[15] Sighle Kennedy, on the other hand, has not only appreciated that Ireland has a relevance to Beckett's writing, she is aware of its significance to his art: "But Beckett's continued and varied use of Irish materials - a usage persisting through more than forty years of his residence abroad - seems to point to some deep involvement of this material with the central working of his genius ... The Irishness in Beckett's work seems part of its vital core: that element which he himself sees as constituting in any work of art, its 'condensing spiral of need.' "[16]

She appreciates, moreover, the dangers of confusing Beckett's national background with his concept of art, or as he once called it 'the autonomy of the imagined.'[17]

An interesting feature in Beckett's writing is the recurrence of themes and scenes with the same people and the same places, most especially in Dublin, being introduced and reintroduced repeatedly. Beckett is not unaware of this as the end of *The Expelled* indicates: 'I don't know why I told this story. I could just as well have told another. Perhaps some other time I'll be able to tell another. Living souls you will see how alike they are.'[18] But no two treatments are the same. The style, mood, composition and technique are so varied as to make memorable each in itself. What has inevitably changed, however, is the age of the artist and, with it, his mood, sensibility and most important perhaps, his power of evocation. When Beckett writes from an experience, he often does so from the moment of that experience and the sensations are of that moment be they those of the foetus, of childhood or of aging man. If, for instance, Beckett writes of a small boy, he does so seeing and feeling as did that small boy. When the small boy writes of an old man we should not necessarily permit our imagination to bring before us a picture of senility, but rather that of a man closer to his prime, for such men appear 'old' to small boys. Or when the child speaks of hills of 'extraordinary steepness' we should not be too surprised as adults to find that the reality is an incline of modest proportions. When Beckett writes of the womb experience he is, I believe, writing out of the reality of his experience which few of us are capable of appreciating because our memories simply do not permit us to do so and we duly designate such writing as surrealistic.

A few words on the structure of *The Beckett Country* may be helpful. Chronological threads may be identified, but a chronological imposition is not possible, if for no reason other than Beckett writing in his seventies is as likely, indeed more likely, to evoke memories from his first year as from his sixth decade. None the less an obvious point of commencement is a consideration of the early influences of *Home, Foxrock and Environs*. The heart of the Beckett country lies in the Dublin mountains and the coast of Dublin Bay, each of which is considered in Chapters 2 and 3. The influence of education on Beckett is not readily apparent in his writing (unless, of course, one takes his talent as being a consequence of the educational process), but Portora Royal School may have had more influence than is first apparent and Chapter 4 is devoted to this institute and to Trinity College. In Chapter 5, the relevance of Dublin's streetscape and its institutes, most notably the National Gallery of Ireland, are considered. Also within this context, Chapter 6, bearing the title *The River Circle*, encompasses a circuitous odyssey along the Grand Canal and the river Liffey, that is depicted in the poems, *Enueg I* and *Serena III*. Chapter 7, devoted in its entirety to two Dublin lunatic asylums, that at Portrane, and the House of St. John of God, is a measure of Beckett's esteem for the mentally deranged. The mannerisms, dialect, beliefs, prejudices, and some of the day-to-day preoccupations of Dubliners are touched upon in Chapter 8, where brief reference is also made to Dublin literary personalities, such as Denis Devlin and Thomas MacGreevy, who feature in Beckett's criticism, to the artist Jack Yeats, and to others as varied as the Brothers Boot and Billy in the Bowl. In Chapter 9, the country of Ireland outside of the close reaches of Dublin, *Beyond the Pale*, is considered. The point of Beckett's physical departure from Ireland, presented in the closing chapter, may in reality have been Dun Laoghaire pier, or the Liffey's North Wall, but his spiritual exodus, if I am not mistaken, was at the devastated town of Saint-Lô in Normandy, where, with a few Irish friends, he helped to establish the *Hôpital de la Croix Rouge Irlandaise de Saint-Lô* in 1945.

I make no claim to having identified all the references to Ireland in Beckett's writing. There were passages which I considered almost certainly to have Irish origins, but as these were numerous, I had to be selective. I have confined myself, with one or two exceptions, to the published writings in English, but there is a field for further study in the early manuscripts and in the translations in which topographical identification is often more apparent than in the final 'stripped' work.[19] There have been times when I was unable to locate unreferenced Irish locations in writings on Beckett.[20]

After nearly half a century of exile, Beckett has developed and perfected his talent through selfless dedication to his art, so that the despairing cry in *Watt* now has no meaning for Beckett: 'for all the good that frequent deportations out of Ireland had done him, he might just as well have stayed there.'[21] Beckett left Ireland, but he has revisited Dublin with the same intensity that Proust returned to Combray. Even in his recent writing, he depends upon the sea, the sky, the mountains and the islands that pulsate in 'a mighty systole.'[22] Here, in the Dublin mountains and on the seashore of Dublin Bay, lies the real Beckett country, the country that was fundamental to the early novels, faded (but never quite disappeared) from the drama and prose of the middle years, until in his seventh decade - 'the old haunts were never more present'. 'I walk those backroads', he tells us 'with closed eyes',[23] but it is those roads and mountains that he sees in his mind.

June 1986

Eoin O'Brien,
Monkstown,
Co. Dublin.

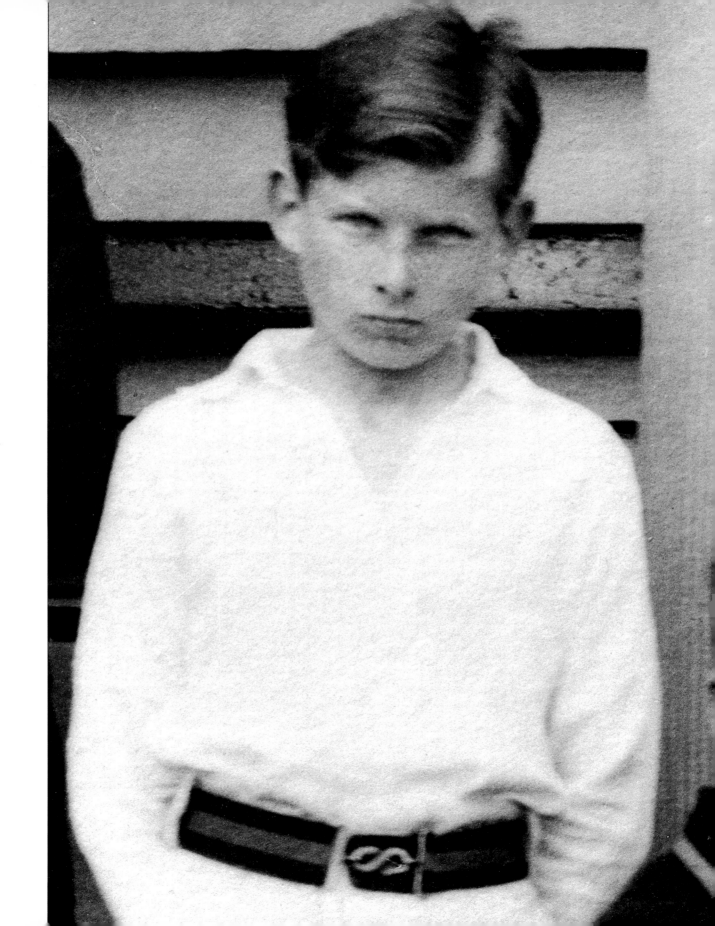

Samuel Beckett aged 14
(From a photograph of the
Cricket team at Portora, 1920.
By permission, the Headmaster,
Portora Royal School)

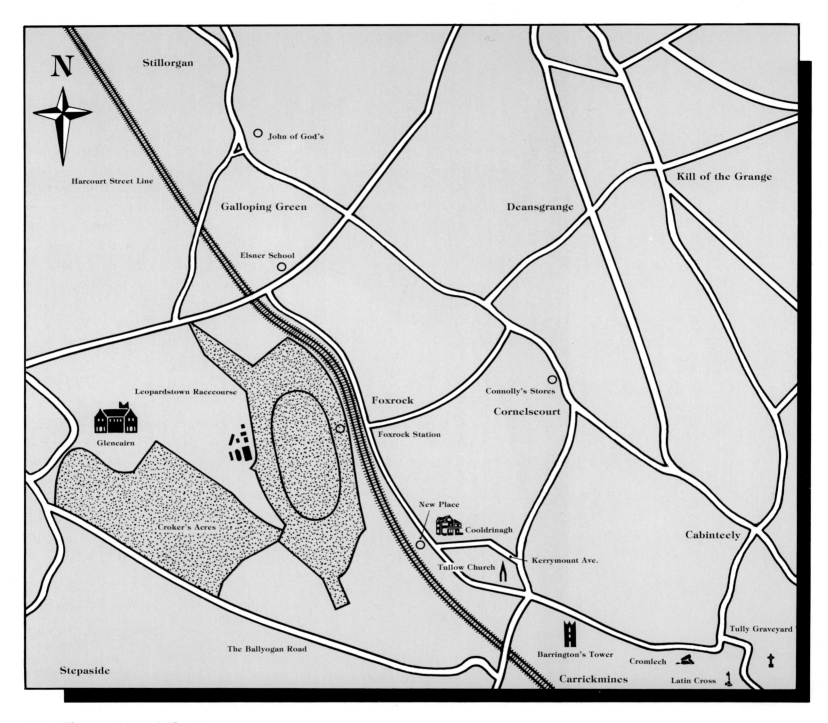

1:1 Foxrock and Environs

Chapter One

EARLY INFLUENCES: Home, Foxrock and Environs

Beckett has scoured human experience and presented a statement of existence, stripped of pretence and affectation, that is vibrant and compelling, even if, at times, it may seem repugnant in its honesty. To express the human predicament, by which is meant the development of personality, the influence of experience and habit on emotion, the subtle behavioural changes that are part of the failing biological system that is man, in a language that is persuasive and true, demands an extraordinary analysis of self. Proust, Joyce and Descartes were among those who enriched our understanding of existence in this way. Beckett, ever aware of the ephemerality of existance, has approached his task with urgency and intense dedication. The seven ages are each entered and exited but once; Beckett's analysis reaches back desperately and at times despairingly to the earliest post-natal sensations, and, on occasion, even further.

Samuel Beckett was born at *Cooldrinagh*, the family home in the Dublin suburb of Foxrock, (1:1) on Good Friday, April 13th, 1906. This date is accepted internationally as Beckett's birthday, because it is the day on which he says he was born. The authenticity of the date has, however, been questioned because his birth certificate entry is dated a month later[1](1:2). As the birth was not registered by his father until June 14th, 1906, two months after the event, it is likely that he mistakenly entered the month of May instead of that of April. Beckett himself leaves us in no doubt, he can remember the event![2] -

> You were born on an Easter Friday after long labour. Yes I remember. The sun had not long sunk behind the larches. Yes I remember.
>
> *(Company, pp. 46-47)*

Nor, does the coincidence of his arrival with the celebration of an auspicious departure pass unnoticed[3] -

> Or if only, You first saw the light and cried at the close of the day when in darkness Christ at the ninth hour cried and died.
>
> *(Company, p. 77)*

Uimh. 84

Breith a Cláraíodh i gCeantar
Birth Registered in the District of .... Stillorgan

i gCeantar an Chláraitheora Maoirseachta do
in the Superintendent Registrar's District of .... Rathdown

i gContae
.... in the County of .... Dublin

Uimh. / No. (1)	Dáta agus Ionad Breithe / Date and Place of Birth (2)	Ainm (má tugadh) / Name (if any) (3)	Gnéas / Sex (4)	Ainm Sloinne agus Ionad Chónaithe an Athar / Name and Surname and Dwelling Place of Father (5)	Ainm agus Sloinne na Máthar agus a Sloinne roimh phosadh di / Name and Surname and Maiden Surname of Mother (6)	Céim nó Gairm Bheatha an Athar / Rank or Profession of Father (7)	Síniú, Cáilíocht agus Ionad Chónaithe an Fháisnéiseora / Signature, Qualification and Residence of Informant (8)	An Dáta a Cláraíodh / When Registered (9)	Síniú an Chláraitheora / Signature of Registrar (10)	Ainm Baiste, má tugadh é tar éis Chlárú na Breithe, agus an Dáta / Baptismal Name, if added after Registration of Birth, and Date (11)
87	1906 Thirteenth May Cooldrinagh Foxrock	Samuel Barclay	m.	William Frank Beckett Cooldrinagh Foxrock	Mary Beckett Iníon Formerly Roe	Civil Engineer	William F. Beckett father Cooldrinagh Foxrock	Fourteenth June 1906	C. Sargison Cláraitheoir asst.Registrar	

Deimhnítear gur fíor Chóip í seo de thaifead atá i gClár-leabhar na mBreitheanna in Oifrg an Ard-Chláraitheora i mBaile Átha Cliath.
Certified to be a true copy taken from the Certified Copies of Births in Oifig an Ard-Chláraitheora, Dublin.

Arna Thabhairt faoi Shéala Oifige an Ard-Chláraitheora
Given under the Seal of Oifig an Ard-Chláraitheora

an
this .... Tenth

lá so de
day of .... July 19 8

Is é Bliain na Breithe sa Chóip deimhnithe thuas ná
The Year of Birth shown in the above Certified Copy is

Mile gCéad
One Thousand .... Nine .... Hundred and .... Six

Ath-Scríofa
Copied .... A

Scrúdaithe
Examined .... MS

1:2   Samuel Beckett's Birth Certificate
(A copy from Births, Deaths and
Marriages General Register
Office, Dublin)

Breith a Cláraíodh i gCeantar
Birth Registered in the District of .... Stillorgan

Uimh. / No. (1)	Dáta agus Ionad Breithe / Date and Place of Birth (2)	Ainm (má tugadh) / Name (if any) (3)	Gnéas / Sex (4)
87	1906 Thirteenth May Cooldrinagh Foxrock	Samuel Barclay	m.

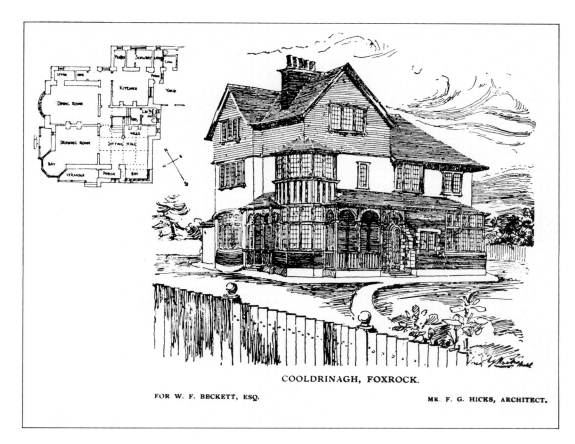

COOLDRINAGH, FOXROCK.

FOR W. F. BECKETT, ESQ.   MR. F. G. HICKS, ARCHITECT.

1:3 Architectural drawing and plan
of *Cooldrinagh*
(From *The Irish Builder*.
Supplement. February 26, 1903.
By courtesy National Library
of Ireland)

Cooldrinagh

Cooldrinagh[4] was built by William Beckett at the junction of Kerrymount Avenue and Brighton Road in the affluent suburb of Foxrock. Its architectural features were deemed worthy of illustration in the prestigious *Irish Builder* in 1903.[5](1:3) *Cooldrinagh* is a solid, comfortable family home set in mature, spacious gardens circled by a variety of tall trees, among which is a plantation of larches. The interior of the house is cosy, if somewhat dark, an impression that is heightened by the mahogany panelling of the hall and stairway on which the surreptitiously carved signature of the young Samuel Beckett may be discerned. The tiled porch, smothered in verbena, promises an atmosphere of warmth which pervades the upper-floor bedrooms as well as the ground-floor reception rooms.[6] *Cooldrinagh* serves as the model for Moran's house in *Molloy*, and for Mr. Knott's house in *Watt*.

Page 3

The sensations of light, image and sound flowing from the Dublin mountains and first perceived in *Cooldrinagh*, are destined later to become potent evocations -

> You first saw the light in the room you most likely were conceived in. The big bow window looked west to the mountains. Mainly west. For being bow it looked also a little south and a little north. Necessarily. A little south to more mountain and a little north to foothill and plain.
>
> *(Company, pp. 15-16)*

The bow window on the first floor of *Cooldrinagh* looks west towards the Dublin mountains, which sweep around to the south, whereas, to the north, the view was towards level terrain and some foothills intervening between the house and the city (1:4). A small plantation of larches[7] at *Cooldrinagh* is as dear to Samuel Beckett as the madeleine was to Marcel Proust -

> Born dead of night. Sun long sunk behind the larches. New needles turning green.
> *(A Piece of Monologue, p. 265)*

1:4 *Cooldrinagh*: Samuel Beckett was born in the second-floor room with the bay-window (Photograph by D. Davison)

The larch tree was to remain a favourite tree, perhaps, if only because it was the one tree that was readily identified in childhood -

> This country lad, he could not tell an oak from an elm. Larches however he knew, from having climbed them as a little fat boy, and a young plantation of these, of a very poignant reseda, caught his eye now on the hillside.
>
> *(More Pricks than Kicks p. 110)*

In the poem, *Serena II*, Beckett recalls early scenes of childhood with his mother at *Cooldrinagh*.

> she took me up on to a watershed
> whence like the rubrics of a childhood
> behold Meath shining through a chink in the hills
> posses of larches there is no going back on
> a rout of tracks and streams fleeing to the sea
> kindergartens of steeples and then the harbour
> like a woman making to cover her breasts
> and left me
>
> *(Serena II, p. 24)*

From the watershed, it would indeed have been possible to glimpse the county of Meath adjoining that of Dublin through the ever-present 'posses of larches'. From the heights of the Dublin mountains, streams and rivulets flow down to the sea at Dun Laoghaire, a town notable for its many steeples and its two-piered harbour.

Moran's house in *Molloy* is based on *Cooldrinagh*, where the scene is idyllic but threatened -

> None but tranquil sounds, the clicking of mallet and ball, a rake on pebbles, a distant lawn-mower, the bell of my beloved church. And birds of course, blackbird and thrush, their song sadly dying, vanquished by the heat, and leaving dawn's high boughs for the bushes' gloom. Contentedly I inhaled the scent of my lemon-verbena.
>
> In such surroundings slipped away my last moments of peace and happiness.
>
> *(Molloy p. 93)*

The small wood, the wicket gate, the main chimney-stack with its four flues and the garden with its croquet lawn are all to be found at *Cooldrinagh* (1:5) -

> So we came to the little wicket-gate. It was locked. I unlocked it and stood aside, to let my son precede me. I turned back to look at my house. It was partly hidden by the little wood. The roof's serrated ridge, the single chimney-stack with its four flues, stood out faintly against the sky spattered with a few dim stars.
>
> *(Molloy, p. 128)*

1:5 *Cooldrinagh*: wooded gardens, croquet-lawn, serrated roof-edge and chimney-stack
(Photograph by D. Davison)

Mr. Knott's strange establishment in *Watt* is also modelled on *Cooldrinagh*. Watt left Dublin from Harcourt Street Station and travelled along the Harcourt Street Line to reach Foxrock Station, from where he proceeded east; soon the chimneys of Mr. Knott's house became visible in the moonlight. The front-door of the house was locked, and Watt was admitted through the back-door leading into the red-tiled kitchen that was once a feature of *Cooldrinagh* -

> When Watt reached this light he sat down beside it, on a chair. He set down his bags beside him, on the beautiful red floor, and he took off his hat, for he had reached his destination, discovering his scant red hair, and laid it on the table beside him. And a pretty picture they made, Watt's scalp and red-grey tufts, and the floor burning up from below.
>
> *(Watt, p. 36)*

The room allocated to Watt in Mr. Knott's mansion 'commanded a very fine view of a racecourse' in reality Leopardstown racecourse, which is visible from the west-facing windows of *Cooldrinagh*. Mr. Knott's establishment, like *Cooldrinagh*, is close to Foxrock railway station from the elevated platform of which the chimneys might be seen on a clear day -

> The chimneys of Mr. Knott's house were not visible, in spite of the excellent visibility. On fine days they could be discerned, from the station. But on fine nights apparently not.
>
> *(Watt, p. 224)*

However, there are some features of Mr. Knott's house that are not to be found in *Cooldrinagh*, namely a conservatory, an American Bar, an oratory, a cellar, and a dairy. It is in these locations, among others, that the parlour maid, Mary, leaves evidence of her obsessional craving for food -

> ... morsels of meat, fruit, bread, vegetables, nuts and pastry I have frequently found in places as remote in space, and distinct in purpose, as the coal-hole, the conservatory, the American Bar, the oratory, the cellar, the attic, the dairy and, I say it with shame, the servants' W.C., ...
>
> *(Watt, p. 53)*

Glencairn, the mansion of the millionaire, Boss Croker in nearby Sandyford, did boast a conservatory, oratory, dairy and almost certainly an American Bar, and Beckett who was familiar with the house incorporated some of its more extravagant features into Mr. Knott's abode.

From his bedroom in *Cooldrinagh*, the young Beckett listened to the sounds of country and mountain -

> The sound I liked best had nothing noble about it. It was the barking of the dogs, at night, in the clusters of hovels up in the hills, where the stone-cutters lived, like generations of stone-cutters before them.
>
> *(Malone Dies, p. 206)*

Cooldrinagh emerges in Beckett's writings as a house of comfort, of peace and of fragrant sensations, an abode to which a young man would appreciate returning after a sojourn of deprivation abroad, as indeed did Belacqua in *Dream of Fair to Middling Women* -

> Belacqua was heartily glad to get back to his parents' comfortable private residence, ineffably detached and situated and so on, and his first act, once spent the passion of greeting after so long and bitter a separation, was to plunge his

prodigal head into the lush of verbena that clustered about the old porch (wonderful bush it was to be sure, even making every due allowance for the kind southern aspect it enjoyed, it never had been known to miss a summer since first it was reared from a tiny seedling) and longly to swim and swoon on the rich bosom of its fragrance, a fragrance in which the least of his childish joys and sorrows were and would for ever be embalmed.

(Dream of Fair to Middling Women, p. 128)

Even the privies, indeed perhaps especially the privies, were as close to heaven as a prodigal son could hope to get -

It was really wonderful to get back to the home comforts. Belacqua tried all the armchairs in the house he poltrooned in all the poltrone. Then he went and tried both privies. The seats were in rosewood. Douceurs ...

(Dream of Fair to Middling Women, p. 129)

William Frank Beckett (1871-1933)

ah father father that art in heaven

(Serena I, p. 21)

William Frank Beckett was a successful quantity surveyor with offices at no. 6 Clare Street in Dublin city, the house where Samuel Beckett was later to write his first major work, *More Pricks than Kicks*. William Beckett emerges from his son's writings as a jovial ebullient character. He was prepared to listen to a growing boy's opinions and problems, and earned his son's lasting affection (1:6). A touching scene in *Company*, which occurred in reality in the summer house at *Cooldrinagh*, illustrates the bond that existed between father and son[8] -

There on summer Sundays after his midday meal your father loved to retreat with Punch and a cushion. The waist of his trousers unbuttoned he sat on the one ledge turning the pages. You on the other with your feet dangling. When he chuckled you tried to chuckle too. When his chuckle died yours too.

(Company, pp. 53-54)

Beckett is never critical of his father, and his failings, if such they be, become for Beckett traits of endearment. He sympathises with the plight of his father who, not wishing to witness the labour of his wife at his son's birth, took himself off to his mountain retreat -

But he was moved also to take himself off and out of the way by his aversion to the pains and general unpleasantness of labour and delivery. Hence the sandwiches which he relished at noon looking out to sea from the lee of a great rock on the first summit scaled. You may imagine his thoughts before and after as he strode through the gorse and heather.

(Company, pp. 16-17).

Dismayed to find, ten hours later, that the event had not yet occurred, his father sought sanctuary in the coachhouse, where he contemplated a further moonlight foray to his beloved mountains, those mountains, which in time would become a land of solace and inspiration for his son -

> He at once hastened to the coachhouse some twenty yards distant where he housed his De Dion Bouton. He shut the doors behind him and climbed into the driver's seat. You may imagine his thoughts as he sat there in the dark not knowing what to think. Though footsore and weary he was on the point of setting out anew across the fields in the young moonlight when the maid came running to tell him it was over at last. Over!
>
> *(Company, pp. 17-18)*

William Beckett may actually have owned a De Dion Bouton. Certainly the car driven by Sir Horace Plunkett (1:7) in Foxrock would have been legendary in the neighbourhood.[9]

Though not a scholarly man, Bill Beckett may have recognised his son's intellectual worth, and encouraged him gently as with the narrator's father in *From an Abandoned Work* -

> Fortunately my father died when I was a boy, otherwise I might have been a professor, he had set his heart on it. A very fair scholar I was too, no thought, but a great memory. One day I told him about Milton's cosmology, away up in the mountains we were, resting against a huge rock looking out to sea, that impressed him greatly.
>
> *(From an Abandoned Work, p. 131)*

1:6   William Frank Beckett
(A photograph taken on the steps of the stand at Leopardstown Races, by courtesy Mrs. C. Clarke)

1:7   Sir Horace Plunkett in a De Dion Bouton
(From a photograph in *Seventy Years Young. Memories of Elizabeth Countess of Fingal Told to Pamela Hinkson.*Collins, London. 1938. Facing page 227)

Lacking perhaps in ambition, William Beckett had, nonetheless, achieved an admirable state of blissful contentment -

> He sat motionless in the armchair under the singing lamp, absorbed and null. The pipes went out, one after another. For long spells he heard nothing that was said in the room, whether to him or not. If you asked him next day what his book was like he could not tell you.
>
> *(Dream of Fair to Middling Women, p. 47)*

The story of Joe Breem, the son of a lighthouse-keeper, left a lasting impression on his son, and the fable, recalled many times by Beckett, remained a source of wonderment in youth, and solace in later years[10] -

> Yes, this evening it has to be as in the story my father used to read to me, evening after evening, when I was small, and he had all his health, to calm me, evening after evening, year after year it seems to me this evening, which I don't remember much about, except that it was the adventures of one Joe Breem, or Breen, the son of a lighthouse-keeper, a strong muscular lad of fifteen, those were the words, who swam for miles in the night, a knife between his teeth, after a shark, I forget why, out of sheer heroism. He might have simply told me the story, he knew it by heart, so did I, but that wouldn't have calmed me, he had to read it to me, evening after evening, or pretend to read it to me, turning the pages and explaining the pictures that were of me already, evening after evening the same pictures till I dozed off on his shoulder. If he had skipped a single word I would have hit him, with my little fist, in his big belly bursting out of the old cardigan and unbuttoned trousers that rested him from his office canonicals.
>
> *(The Calmative, p. 37)*

Bill and Sam Beckett shared a love of nature and the invigorating pleasures of Dublin's mountains and sea. Together they walked the summits of the mountains, and swam in the Forty Foot. In the unpublished dramatic piece *The Gloaming* we find them together fishing in a boat far out at sea in Dublin bay where so many Beckettian characters find themselves[11] -

> Bring me back to the hot summer evening out in the Bay with my father in the little rowboat, fishing for mackerel with a spinner. To the time when it was still time. 'Do you remember what they look like?' 'Yes, father, all blue and silver.'
>
> *(Reading University Library, MS. 16)*

The death of Beckett's father left a void that still remains -

> I was not sure where I was. I looked among the stars and constellations for the Wains, but could not find them. And yet they must have been there. My father was the first to show them to me. He had shown me others, but alone, without him beside me, I could never find any but the Wains.
>
> *(First Love, p. 19)*

May Beckett (1871-1950)

As with most Irish sons, Beckett's relationship with his mother appears to have been more complex than that with his father, and there is not the same warmth and affection for May Beckett in her son's writing as for her husband. Nonetheless, her influence is unmistakable and dominant. The earliest known photograph of Samuel Beckett is as a child at his mother's knee (1:8), though from the description of photographs in *Film*, it is reasonable to assume that there was an earlier photograph fulfilling the following details -

> 1. Male infant. 6 Months. His mother holds him in her arms. Infant smiles front. Mother's big hands. Her severe eyes devouring him. Her big old-fashioned beflowered hat.
>
> *(Film, p. 43)*

The photograph of Beckett at his mother's knee is described in brief but accurate detail in *Film* -

> 2. The same. 4 years. On a veranda, dressed in loose nightshirt, kneeling on a cushion, attitude of prayer, hands clasped, head bowed, eyes closed. Half profile. Mother on chair beside him, big hands on knees, head bowed towards him, severe eyes, similar hat to 1.
>
> *(Film p. 43)*

The provenance of this now famous photograph is given by Lady Beatrice Glenavy in her memoir *Today we will only gossip*.[12] Her sister, Dorothy, a keen amateur painter wished to enter for the Taylor Art Scholarship, the subject chosen for the year in question being 'Bedtime'. Sam Beckett, 'just the right size and age', was made to pose at his mother's knees for a photograph on the verbena-covered porch of *Cooldrinagh*. Whether or not the painting was ever executed is not recorded. This photograph is portrayed in even greater depth in *How It Is* -

> next another image yet another so soon again the third perhaps they'll soon cease it's me all of me and my mother's face I see it from below it's like nothing I ever saw
>
> we are on a veranda smothered in verbena the scented sun dapples the red tiles yes I assure you
>
> the huge head hatted with birds and flowers is bowed down over my curls the eyes burn with severe love I offer her mine pale upcast to the sky whence cometh our help and which I know perhaps even then with time shall pass away
>
> in a word bolt upright on a cushion on my knees whelmed in a nightshirt I pray according to her instructions

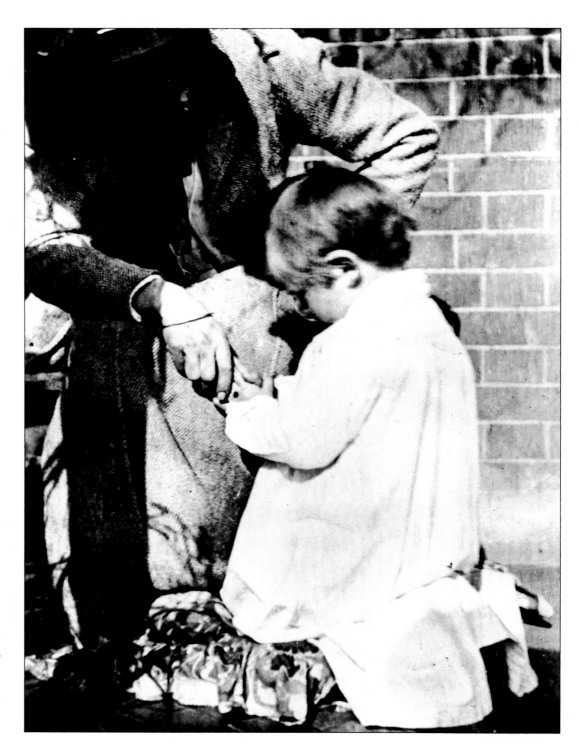

1:8 Samuel Beckett at his mother's
knee on the porch of *Cooldrinagh*
(By courtesy Carlton Lake,
Humanities Research Center,
The University of Texas
at Austin)

that's not all she closes her eyes and drones a snatch of the so-called Apostles'
Creed I steal a look at her lips

she stops her eyes burn down on me again I cast up mine in haste and repeat awry

the air thrills with the hum of insects

(How It Is, pp. 16-17)

In the poem, *Serena II*, the photograph inspires the theme of the
inevitability of death, Beckett's mother's knees becoming a cairn in the
Dublin mountains at which her son kneels for evening prayer[13] -

the toads abroad again on their rounds
sidling up to their snares
the fairy-tales of Meath ended
so say your prayers now and go to bed
your prayers before the lamps start to sing behind the larches
here at these knees of stone
then to bye-bye on the bones

(Serena II, p. 24)

May Beckett's love of animals was shared by her son, who later wrote
with affection of his Kerry Blue terrier, though many Beckettian figures
find animals quite irritating. She kept hens, donkey's and dogs (1:9), and

1:9   May Beckett and Sheila Page,
with Christy, the gardener, in the
garden of *Cooldrinagh*
(By courtesy Caroline Murphy)

1:10 May Beckett with her pomeranian
      (By courtesy Caroline Murphy)

no doubt the description of another photograph in *Malone Dies* has its origins in reality[14] -

> My photograph. It is not a photograph of me, but I am perhaps at hand. It is an ass, taken from in front and close up, at the edge of the ocean, it is not the ocean, but for me it is the ocean. They naturally tried to make it raise its head, so that its beautiful eyes might be impressed on the celluloid, but it holds it lowered.
>
> *(Malone Dies, p. 252)*

The photograph of Beckett's stern-faced mother with her pomeranian (1:10) serves to remind that this little breed crops up on more than one occasion in Beckett's writing. In *Endgame*, Hamm's dog is 'a kind of pomeranian',[15] and in *Molloy* the breed receives elaborate attention -

> A little dog followed him, a pomeranian I think, but I don't think so. I wasn't sure at the time and I'm still not sure, though I've hardly thought about it. The little dog followed wretchedly, after the fashion of pomeranians, stopping, turning in slow circles, giving up and then, a little further on, beginning all over again. Constipation is a sign of good health in pomeranians. At a given moment, pre-established if you like, I don't much mind, the gentleman turned back, took the little creature in his arms, drew the cigar from his lips and buried his face in the orange fleece, for it was a gentleman, that was obvious. Yes, it was an orange pomeranian, the less I think of it the more certain I am.
>
> *(Molloy, p. 12)*

May Beckett was a strict mother to a son who did not take kindly to rigid discipline.[16] The preparations for a visitor to *Cooldrinagh* are watched with interest by a growing boy, banned from company because of boldness-

> You are alone in the garden. Your mother is in the kitchen making ready for afternoon tea with Mrs Coote. Making the wafer-thin bread and butter. From behind a bush you watch Mrs Coote arrive. A small thin sour woman. Your mother answers her saying, He is playing in the garden. You climb to near the top of a great fir. You sit a little listening to all the sounds. Then throw yourself off. The great boughs break your fall. The needles. You lie a little with your face to the ground. Then climb the tree again. Your mother answers Mrs Coote again saying, He has been a very naughty boy.
>
> *(Company, p. 28)*

May Beckett outlived her husband by sixteen years; the tenuity of existence and the ephemerality of survival are evoked forcibly by Beckett in the contrasting qualities of a shaving-mirror's material durability and the transience of its reflected imagery -

> I can see me still, with those of now, sealed this long time, staring with those of then, I must have been twelve, because of the glass, a round shaving-glass, double-faced, faithful and magnifying, staring into one of the others, the true ones, true then, and seeing me there, imagining I saw me there, lurking behind the bluey

veils, staring back sightlessly, at the age of twelve, because of the glass, on its pivot, because of my father, if it was my father, in the bathroom, with its view of the sea, the lightships at night, the red harbour light, if these memories concern me, at the age of twelve, or at the age of forty, for the mirror remained, my father went but the mirror remained, in which he had so greatly changed, my mother did her hair in it, with twitching hands, in another house, with no view of the sea, with a view of the mountains, if it was my mother, what a refreshing whiff of life on earth.

(Texts for Nothing, pp. 90-91).

The sea, the lightships at night, and the red harbour light were all visible in the distance from the bathroom window of *Cooldrinagh*, but not from the bathroom of nearby *New Place*, the house to which May Beckett moved after her husband's death.[17] *New Place*, with its splendid view of the Dublin mountains (1:11) is situated just across Brighton Road within a few minutes walk of *Cooldrinagh*.

1:11   The Dublin mountains from *New Place*
(Photograph by D. Davison)

Childhood Personalities

There were, of course, other influences in the happy childhood ambience that emanated from *Cooldrinagh*.[18] The friends of the family who visited *Cooldrinagh*, and, presumably there were many, receive scant attention from Beckett, but his kindergarten teachers, and the tradesmen of the area have been endowed with literary immortality.

At the age of five years, Samuel Beckett joined his older brother Frank at a kindergarten in Foxrock (1:12) that was run by two German ladies, the Elsner sisters. According to Sheila Brazil[19], the Elsner sisters were colourful and odd. One, a spinster known as 'Jack' Elsner, was quite a character. She rode a bicycle in a manner in keeping with her domineering personality. The other, Mrs. Stewart, of whom no Mr. Stewart is recalled, was quieter and more reserved. The father of this strange pair, Herr Elsner, taught music, as did his daughters, and Lady Glenavy has left an interesting account of their teaching technique in *Today we will only gossip*.[20] Whatever these early educational influences may have been

1:12   The kindergarten school of the
       Elsner sisters
       (Photograph by D. Davison)

on Samuel Beckett, the Elsner sisters, their cook, Hannah, and dog 'Zulu' remained in his memory as dominant personalities -

> There she would call Hannah, the old cook of the Elsner sisters, and they would whisper together for a long time, through the railings. Hannah never went out, she did not like going out. The Elsner sisters were not bad neighbours, as neighbours go. They made a little too much music, that was the only fault I could find with them ... I thought a little of the Elsner sisters. Everything remained to be planned and there I was thinking of the Elsner sisters. They had an aberdeen called Zulu. People called it Zulu. Sometimes, when I was in a good humour, I called, Zulu! Little Zulu! and he would come and talk to me, through the railings.
>
> *(Molloy, pp. 105-106)*

During his long odyssey Moran wonders about the fate of the sisters -

> Zulu, the Elsner sisters, were they still living?
>
> *(Molloy, p. 168)*

The Foxrock postmen, of whom there were three, were an interesting lot. First, there was a moustached one, a shy but charming man, who has been identified as John Thompson[21](1:13) -

> The postman flew up with letters, he skidded up the drive on his bicycle, scattering the loose gravel. He was more pleased than he could say, but compounded with his aphasia to the extent anyhow of 'Welcome home' in the attractive accent and the old familiar smile there under the noble moustache 'master Bel'. Yes, yes, évidemment.
>
> *(Dream of Fair to Middling Women, p. 129)*

However, it was another, the musical one, identified as Bill Shannon[22](1:14), who receives Beckett's unreserved admiration, no mean feat indeed. *In Dream of Fair to Middling Women* his rise along the social ladder is applauded -

> But where was the slender one, where was he, that was the question, as thin and fine as the greyhounds he tended, the musical one, a most respectable and industrious young fellow he was, by sheer industry, my dear, plus personal charm, those were the two sides of the ladder on which this man had mounted, had he not raised himself above his station, out of the horrible slum of the cottages, did he not play on the violin, own an evening suit of his own and dance fleetly with the gentry, and, as he lay as a child wide awake long after he should have been fast alseep at the top of the house on a midsummer's night Belacqua would hear him, the light nervous step on the road as he danced home after his rounds, the keen loud whistling *The Roses are Blooming in Picardy*. No man had ever whistled like that, and of course women can't. That was the original, the only, the unforgettable banquet of music. There was no music after - only, if one were lucky, the signet of rubies and the pleasant wine. He whistled the Roses are Blooming and danced home down the road under the moon, in the light of the moon, with perhaps a greyhound or two to set him off, and the dew descending.

Now he was dead, we thought it more reverent to put that into a paragraph by itself, dead, grinning up at the lid. The dead fart, says the Preacher, vanity of vanities, and the quick whistle. Blessed be the name of Thanatos.

(Dream of Fair to Middling Women, p. 129)

This remarkable figure retains his place in Beckett's heart and emerges again in a more refined piece of prose, one of Beckett's most alluring pastoral compositions, in *Watt*.[23] In this we learn that tuberculosis, the 'galloping consumption' so prevalent in Ireland in the early part of the century, was the probable cause of Bill Shannon's death -

The crocuses and the larch turning green every year a week before the others and the pastures red with uneaten sheep's placentas and the long summer days and the new-mown hay and the wood-pigeon in the morning and the cuckoo in the afternoon and the corncrake in the evening and the wasps in the jam and the smell of the gorse and the look of the gorse and the apples falling and the children walking in the dead leaves and the larch turning brown a week before the others[24] and the chestnuts falling and the howling winds and the sea breaking over the pier and the first fires and the hooves on the road and the consumptive postman whistling *The Roses Are Blooming in Picardy* and the standard oil-lamp and of course the snow and to be sure the sleet and bless your heart the slush and every fourth year the February débâcle and the endless April showers and the crocuses and then the whole bloody business starting all over again.

(Watt, pp. 45-46)

Nor was Bill Shannon the only caller with melodic tendencies; the milkboy from the small dairy owned by Mr. Tully close to *Cooldrinagh* contributed to the pastoral cacophony[25] -

It was to the sound of bells, of chapel bells, of church bells. It was on a morning that the milkboy came singing to the door, shrilly to the door his tuneless song, and went singing away, having measured out the milk, from his can, to the jug, with all his usual liberality.

(Watt, p. 148)

Nannys were a part of every well-to-do household in Dublin in the first half of this century, and the Beckett family was no exception. Nanny was given the pet name, Bibby, and, as such, appears in many of Beckett's writings[26] -

God bless dear Daddy, he prayed vaguely that night for no particular reason before getting into bed. Mummy Johnny Bibby (quondam Nanny, now mother of thousands by a gardener) and all that I love and make me a good boy for Jesus Christ sake Armen.

(Dream of Fair to Middling Women, p. 6)

Beckett's fascination and admiration for tramps and beggars is evident in much of his work. In *More Pricks than Kicks*, joxers on the dole, the poor woman selling seats in heaven, the beggar girl of Mark Street, the newspaper sloven, the wheel-chair beggar from the Coombe and the 'complete down and out' are all very dear to Beckett.[27] His empathy with those less privileged than himself begins in early childhood -

> An old beggar woman is fumbling at a big garden gate. Half blind. You know the place well. Stone deaf and not in her right mind the woman of the house is a crony of your mother. She was sure she could fly once in the air. So one day she launched herself from a first floor window. On the way home from kindergarten on your tiny cycle you see the poor old beggar woman trying to get in. You dismount and open the gate for her. She blesses you. What were her words? God reward you little master. Some such words. God save you little master.
>
> *(Company, pp. 21-22)*

The gardens of *Cooldrinagh*, though not large, were tended with great care by one of the many gardeners of Foxrock. So plentiful were these gentlemen in this affluent neighbourhood in the early years of the century that there was a 'Gardeners Band'! Led by none other than Bill Shannon, it played regularly at the crossroads in Foxrock.[28] The gardens of *Cooldrinagh* were tended for many years by one named Christy (1:19) -

> My trees, my bushes, my flower-beds, my tiny lawns, I used to think I loved them. If I sometimes cut a branch, a flower, it was solely for their good, that they might increase in strength and happiness. And I never did it without a pang. Indeed if the truth were known, I did not do it at all, I got Christy to do it.
>
> *(Molloy, p. 128)*

Earliest childhood memories are of the home; in Beckett's case the secure and comfortable environment of *Cooldrinagh*. From there he was introduced by his mother to the tranquil village of Foxrock, its shops, its people, and its church. Later, as an adventurous, and somewhat rebellious youth, he began to explore the neighbourhood for himself, the cromlech at Glen Druid, the ancient church and graveyard at Tully, the racecourse at Leopardstown. He sought peace in the solitude of Barrington's Tower, and was calmed by the peaceful beauty of the foothills of Dublin's mountains, and the lamb-laden gallops of 'Boss Croker's Acres'. Further afield lay the mountains themselves for walking hand in hand with his father, or alone, and the sea within reach by bicycle. The Dublin and South Eastern Railway was the link, the placental cord ultimately to be severed, between the home and the city of Dublin and the world beyond. Foxrock Station and its train, the 'Slow and Easy', were to leave lasting memories with Beckett, memories that are emerging again in his latest writings.

Foxrock Village

Foxrock is now one of Dublin's most fashionable residential areas.[29] The name may derive from the days when the Kilruddery Hunt chased across the countryside.[30] When William Beckett built Cooldrinagh in the area of Kerrymount in 1903, the village was an undeveloped hamlet in picturesque countryside within ten miles of the city. It had, nonetheless, a number of desirable facilities: the Dublin mountains for walks and picnics, the beautiful coast of Killiney was only a few miles away, as was the harbour of Kingstown, the gateway to England, and there was Leopardstown racecourse and Carrickmines Golf Club within a few minutes walk of the Beckett home. The village itself did not (and still does not) amount to much. Beckett may well have had it in mind as the destination of Mercier and Camier -

> A village just one long street, everything lined up in a row, dwellings, shops, bars, the two stations, railway and petrol, the two churches, graveyard and so on. A strait.
>
> *(Mercier and Camier, p. 42)*

1:15 Connolly's store and public house, later named 'The Cornelscourt Arms' (By courtesy Mr. & Mrs. K. Crowley)

If the village of Foxrock proved unsatisfactory for the needs of the Beckett household, there was the nearby village of Cornelscourt,[31] almost as close to *Cooldrinagh* as was Foxrock itself. Here there was a most efficient store run by William Connolly.[32](1:15) May Beckett was a regular customer -

> A small boy you come out of Connolly's Stores holding your mother by the hand. You turn right and advance in silence southward along the highway.
>
> *(Company, p. 12)*

Connolly's, as was customary for the time, delivered goods which might be ordered by telephone - 'Heavens here comes Connolly's van'- exclaims Mrs. Rooney in *All That Fall*.[33] This establishment had a distinct advantage over many general stores; it provided also that institution so essential to every Irish hamlet, a public house.

Tullow Parish Church

> **Midnight struck, from the steeple of my beloved church**
>
> *(Molloy, p. 130)*

1:16 Tullow Parish Church in
the 'twenties
(By courtesy Rev. C. Hyland)

Just as pubs are fundamental institutions in all Irish villages, so too are churches, of which there must be two, one to serve the Catholic majority, the other to cater for the spiritual needs of a Protestant community. Foxrock was no exception: the Catholic church of Our Lady of Perpetual Succour is situated a mile or so from the village of Foxrock, and the Church of Ireland parish church of Tullow built in 1864, where the Beckett family worshipped (1:16), was within five minutes walk of the Beckett home. The parish formerly embraced the town lands of Loughenstowne (now Loughlinstown), Brenanstowne (now Brenanstown), Carrickmaine (from the Irish Carraig-maighin, the Little Plain of Rocks, and now Carrickmines), Slanamuck (from the Irish Glean na muc, the valley of the pigs,now Glenamuck), Leperstowne (now Leopardstown, formerly the site of a hospital for lepers), Ticknock (from the Irish Tigh Cnuic, the House on the Hill), Jamestown, Ballyogan,[34] Kerrymount, Blackthorn, and Murphystown.[35] The magic of these ancient names could not but fascinate the fertile imagination of the young Beckett, and the rich ancestry of the area was evident in the cromlech near Brenanstown, the ruined Church of Tully, and the remains of the Castles of Carrickmines and Murphystown. In the mountains, the mysticism of a primitive folklore emanated from the fairy cairns and dolmens.[36]

1:17   The interior of Tullow Parish Church from the Becketts' pew (Photograph by D. Davison)

Religious service did not inspire the aged Krapp, anymore than it did the youthful Beckett in Tullow Church (1:17) -

> Went to Vespers once, like when I was in short trousers.
> *(Pause. Sings.)*
>   Now the day is over,
>   Night is drawing nigh-igh,
>   Shadows - *(coughing, then almost inaudible)* -
>   of the evening
>   Steal across the sky.
> *(Gasping.)* Went to sleep and fell off the pew.

(Krapp's Last Tape, pp. 62-63)

Though Beckett found religion irksome and therefore let it go,[37] there are profoundly religious undertones in even his most despairing prose, which is often not devoid of one of the fundamentals of religion, hope -

> I notice one thing, the others have vanished, completely, I don't like it. Notice, I notice nothing, I go on as best I can, if it begins to mean something I can't help it, I have passed by here, this has passed by me, thousands of times, its turn has come again, it will pass on and something else will be there, another instant of my old instant, there it is, the old meaning that I'll give myself, that I won't be

able to give myself, there's a god for the damned, as on the first day, today is the first day, it begins, I know it well, I'll remember it as I go along, all adown it I'll be born and born, births for nothing, and come to night without having been.
(The Unnamable, p. 404)

One of Beckett's most evocative scenes is set in Tullow Church.[38] The utterances of the religiously fanatic Miss Fitt in *All That Fall* belong in dialect to the minority religion, but her sanctimonious mysticism is shared by more than a few of the regular attenders at Catholic parish churches throughout Ireland -

Oh but in church, Mrs Rooney, in church I am alone with my Maker. Are not you? *(Pause.)* Why even the sexton himself, you know, when he takes up the collection, knows it is useless to pause before me. I simply do not see the plate, or bag, whatever it is they use, how could I? *(Pause.)* Why even when all is over and I go out into the sweet fresh air, why even then for the first furlong or so I stumble in a kind of daze as you might say, oblivious to my co-religionists. And they are very kind I must admit - the vast majority - very kind and understanding. They know me now and take no umbrage. There she goes, they say, there goes the dark Miss Fitt, alone with her Maker, take no notice of her. And they step down off the path to avoid my running into them.

(All That Fall, p. 22)

1:18   The ancient church and
         graveyard at Tully
         (Photograph by D. Davison)

1:19 The Celtic high-cross at Tully
(By courtesy Mr. M. McGovern)

Tullow Church does not have a graveyard but the ancient ruin of the church of An Tulaigh or Tully (1:18), dating from the sixth century[39] with its graveyard lies on a quiet country road within twenty minutes walk of *Cooldrinagh* and was often visited by Beckett. The name derives from *Tulach-na-nespuc*, or the hill of the bishops, the celebrated location in the *Book of Lismore* from which seven bishops set out to visit St. Bridgid in Kildare.[40] The remains of the church's chancel, which is of Anglo-Norman construction, with its choir arch and round-headed window still stand. The chancel was probably attached to an early Celtic church which formed the nave. Two very early Christian grave slabs or leacs are to be found within the ruins of the church and in the graveyard there are a number of ancient tombstones, the earliest of which is dated 1712. As the graveyard is approached, two crosses come into view, one which stands on the road is a Celtic high-cross (1:19), bearing an inscription dated 1897 - 'Inscribed by his friends to the memory of James F. Grehan who saved this Celtic cross'. The other, standing some distance from the road in a field, is a Latin cross (1:20) bearing in relief a figure, possibly a female representation of St. Bridgid, the patron saint of the church. Both crosses date from between the 8th and 12th century,[41] though it is probable that the Latin cross was sculpted before its neighbour.[42]

It was this graveyard that Moran chose for his final resting place -

> Some twenty paces from my wicket-gate the lane skirts the graveyard wall. The lane descends, the wall rises, higher and higher. Soon you are faring below the dead. It is there I have my plot in perpetuity. As long as the earth endures that spot is mine, in theory. Sometimes I went and looked at my grave. The stone was up already. It was a simple Latin cross, white. I wanted to have my name put on it, with the here lies and the date of my birth. Then all it would have wanted was the date of my death. They would not let me. Sometimes I smiled, as if I were dead already.
>
> *(Molloy, p. 135)*

Beckett has even gone so far as to write an epitaph, at least for the narrator of *First Love* -

> Mine I composed long since and am still pleased with it, tolerably pleased. My other writings are no sooner dry than they revolt me, but my epitaph still meets with my approval. There is little chance unfortunately of its ever being reared

1:20   The Latin cross at Tully
(Photograph by D. Davison)

above the skull that conceived it, unless the State takes up the matter. But to be unearthed I must first be found, and I greatly fear those gentlemen will have as much trouble finding me dead as alive. So I hasten to record it here and now, while there is yet time:

> Hereunder lies the above who up below
> So hourly died that he lived on till now

The second and last or rather latter line limps a little perhaps, but that is no great matter, I'll be forgiven more than that when I'm forgotten.

(First Love, p. 2)

'Foley's Folly'

Beckett, like his father before him had a retreat close to *Cooldrinagh*. The ruin named 'Foley's Folly', which features in a number of Beckett's writings, was in fact *Barrington's Tower* (1:21), situated in the foothills of the Dublin mountains, a mile or so from *Cooldrinagh* and close to Tully graveyard.[43] Just beneath this tower, the cromlech of Glen Druid (1:22), one of the finest in the neighbourhood of Dublin, rests in majestic isolation in a wooded vale beside a stream. The tablestone of this portal cromlech measuring thirty square feet, has been estimated to weigh between forty and sixty tons. None of the many dolmens on the Dublin foothills and mountains is mentioned specifically in Beckett's poetry or prose, but their influence is unmistakable, as in Arsene's farewell speech -

> ... and often I turn, tears blinding my eyes, haw! without however pausing in my career (no easy matter), perhaps longing to be turned into a stone pillar or a cromlech in the middle of a field or on the mountain-side for succeeding generations to admire and for cows and horses and sheep and goats to come and scratch themselves against and for men and dogs to make their water against and for learned men to speculate regarding and for disappointed men to inscribe with party slogans and indelicate graffiti and for lovers to scratch their names on, in a heart, with the date, and for now and then a lonely man like myself to sit down with his back against and fall asleep, in the sun, if the sun happened to be shining.

(Watt, pp. 47-48)

From his hideout in Foley's Folly, Beckett had a commanding view of the Wicklow mountains, and, to the east, the sea coast of Killiney; on a clear day Wales could be sighted -

> The light there was then. On your back in the dark the light there was then. Sunless cloudless brightness. You slip away at break of day and climb to your hiding place on the hillside. A nook in the gorse. East beyond the sea the faint shape of high mountain. Seventy miles away according to your Longman.

(Company, pp. 32-33)

1:21 Barrington's Tower
(Foley's Folly)
(By courtesy Prof. G. Doyle)

The blue of sea and sky, viewed from Foley's Folly, are ever changing in hue and shade, and, at the end of day, continued to enthral the errant youth committed to an early bed, no doubt as a punishment for his lengthy wandering -

> Back home at nightfall supperless to bed. You lie in the dark and are back in that light. Straining out from your nest in the gorse with your eyes across the water till they ache.
>
> *(Company, p. 33)*

The memories of this childhood retreat are relived in *The Calmative* -

> I see a kind of den littered with empty tins. And yet we are not in the country. Perhaps it's just ruins, a ruined folly, on the skirts of the town, in a field, for the fields come right up to our walls, their walls, and the cows lie down at night in the lee of the ramparts. I have changed refuge so often, in the course of my rout, that now I can't tell between dens and ruins.
>
> *(The Calmative, p. 35)*

In *That Time*, the voice creation of an older Beckett revisits the Folly, but has difficulty remembering its name, though not the derelict solitude of the place -

> straight off the ferry and up with the nightbag to the high street neither right nor left not a curse for the old scenes the old names straight up the rise from

1:22 The Cromlech at Glen Druid
(Photograph by E. O'Brien)

the wharf to the high street and there not a wire to be seen only the old rails all rust when was that was your mother ah for God's sake all gone long ago that time you went back that last time to look was the ruin still there where you hid as a child someone's folly ...

Foley was it Foley's Folly bit of a tower still standing all the rest rubble and nettles ...

or talking to yourself who else out loud imaginary conversations there was childhood for you ten or eleven on a stone among the giant nettles making it up now one voice now another till you were hoarse and they all sounded the same ...

(That Time, pp. 228-230)

The picture portrayed is one of a defiant child at peace with his picture book in the moonlit ruin overlooking Dublin Bay, not displeased by the anxiety that he may be causing his concerned parents -

none ever came but the child on the stone among the giant nettles with the light coming in where the wall had crumbled away poring on his book well into the night some moods the moonlight and they all out on the roads looking for him or making up talk breaking up two or more talking to himself being together that way where none ever came.

(That Time, p. 233)

1:23 Foxrock Railway Station
(By courtesy Mr. L. Clare)

'The Slow and Easy':
The Dublin and South Eastern Railway

Woe is us, said Mercier, we're in the slow and easy.
(Mercier and Camier, p. 39)

The railway station at Foxrock is the setting for a number of important scenes in Beckett's writings. As a small boy he travelled from this station on the Dublin and South Eastern line to Harcourt Street Station beside the Earlsfort House School, and later as a student and lecturer at Trinity College, the 'Slow and Easy' was his means of entry to and egress from the city. He came to know the passengers and staff and delighted in their many eccentricities. Foxrock was one of several small stations on the Dublin and South Eastern line, which ran from the Harcourt Street terminus to Shankill where it joined the line from Dublin to Wexford. The first train ran on the line on Monday, 7th February 1859, and, after just short of a century of service the last train ran at 4.25 p.m. on December 31st, 1958,[44] when the line was closed and the tracks removed in one of the most short-sighted and regrettable decisions ever made by a city transport authority.

Dublin city railway stations are masterpieces of Victorian architecture, and the rural and suburban stations had a unique charm and intimacy that persists in many stations even today.[45] Foxrock station was simple, pleasing and comfortable (1:23). Moreover it commanded wonderful views for the waiting passengers: to the south the racecourse and the mountains, to the north-east the sea, to the south-east the coast and Wicklow. The beauty of the countryside around the station in moonlight impressed Watt greatly -

> He admired the permanent way, stretching away on either hand, in the moonlight, and the starlight, as far as the eye could reach, as far as Watt's eye could have reached, if it had been inside the station. He contemplated with wonder also the ample recession of the plain, its flow so free and simple to the mountains, the crumpled umbers of its verge.
>
> *(Watt, p. 223)*

Mrs. Rooney, in *All That Fall*, is also spellbound by the station and the neighbouring Leopardstown racecourse -

> The entire scene, the hills, the plain, the racecourse with its miles and miles of white rails and three red stands, the pretty little wayside station ...
>
> *(All That Fall, p. 25)*

In fact, the pastoral elegance of the station is such that the novel *Watt* ends on a note of hope -

> And so they stayed a little while, Mr. Case and Mr. Nolan looking at Mr. Gorman, and Mr. Gorman looking straight before him, at nothing in particular, though the sky falling to the hills, and the hills falling to the plain, made as pretty a picture, in the early morning light, as a man could hope to meet with, in a day's march.
>
> *(Watt, p. 246)*

1:24   Thomas Farrell,
         Station-master of Foxrock
         (By courtesy Mr. R. Farrell)

1:25   Great Southern Railways
         Diploma
         (By courtesy Mr. R. Farrell)

The station-master of Foxrock was Thomas Farrell (1:24), alias Mr. Barrell in *All That Fall* and Gorman in *Watt*.[46] He managed his station with unusual efficiency often taking first prize for the best-kept station on the line (1:25). Beckett satirises this achievement in *Watt* with a description of Mr. Gorman's ambition to leave his station unique in at least one detail, its system of locks.[47] Mr. Farrell was assisted by a signal-man and a station foreman.

Foxrock station is the setting for the radio-play *All That Fall*, in which it is renamed *Boghill*[48]. Beckett's stipulations for atmosphere demand the rural sounds of sheep, bird, cow and cock.[49] The opening scene is on the road from *Cooldrinagh* to the station. Mrs. Rooney, who knows her trains, cannot understand how the mail-train could be passing so early: 'Hist! Surely to goodness that cannot be the up mail I hear already.'[50] The lot of the station-master under trying circumstances is not made any the easier by the caustic erudition of Mrs. Rooney who sarcastically ridicules his award-winning efficiency -

> Before you slink away, Mr Barrell, please, a statement of some kind, I insist. Even the slowest train on this brief line is not ten minutes and more behind its scheduled time without good cause, one imagines. *(Pause.)* We all know your station is the best kept of the entire network, but there are times when that is not enough, just not enough. *(Pause.)* Now, Mr Barrell, leave off chewing your whiskers, we are waiting to hear from you - we the unfortunate ticket-holders' nearest if not dearest.
>
> *(All That Fall, pp. 26-27)*

Beckett exploits skilfully the auditory potential of a railway station to create atmosphere for radio -

> *(Excitedly, in the distance.)* She's coming. *(Pause. Nearer.)* She's at the level-crossing! *(Immediately exaggerated station sounds. Falling signals. Bells. Whistles. Crescendo of train whistle approaching. Sound of train rushing through station.)*
>
> *(All That Fall, p. 27)*

For the comic drama in *Watt*, the setting is again the station where Watt spends the night in the waiting-room. The waiting-rooms of many suburban and rural railway stations in Ireland have, even today, something of the atmosphere of a converted drawing-room. Many possess fireplaces which sometimes boast an open fire. The waiting-room of Foxrock station had a number of peculiarities, all of which were of interest to Watt. There was a high chair and the remains of an open fire -

> It was a high, narrow, black, wooden chair, with arms, and castors.

> One of its feet was screwed to the floor, by means of a clamp. Not one of the remaining feet, but all, carried similar, if not identical irons. Not one, but all! But the screws, which no doubt had once fixed these to the floor, had very kindly been removed. Through the bars, which were vertical, of the back, Watt saw portions of a grate, heaped high with ashes, and cinders, of a beautiful grey colour.
> *(Watt, p. 235)*

1:26   Orby, winner of the Epsom Derby in 1907

But the strangest object was a picture of a wretched horse named Joss[51] which serves as a reflection of the decrepit figure of Watt gazing upon it. The presence of 'a large coloured print' of this horse, if such existed in reality, may be explained in two ways. First, the proximity of Leopardstown racecourse to the station might seem sufficient to account for the picture's presence, but it is more likely that the print was that of Boss Croker's famous Derby winning Orby, whose name Beckett confused with that of Joss. It is probable that prints of this animal, whose achievements on the turf did so much for the fortunes of the inhabitants of the area, would have been widely circulated, and one might well have graced the waiting-room of the station (1:26). The fact that the 'horse seemed hardly able to stand, let alone run' must be taken more as an assessment of the condition of the viewer Watt, whose decrepitude is reflected in his vision of the beast. It is unlikely that a horse in this near-state of decay would attract an artist or photographer, and should one with such an eye be so drawn it is certain that the station-master of Foxrock station would not have purchased the final product.

Watt, awaiting release from the waiting-room after a peaceful night, suffered a dramatic setback at the foot of ebullient porter, Nolan, who kicked the waiting-room door open with such force that -

> The innumerable semicircles thus brilliantly begun did not end, as on all previous mornings, in the bang that Mr. Nolan loved, no, but they were all cut short, all without exception, at the same point. And the reason for that was this, that Watt,

where he stood, swaying, murmuring, was nearer the waiting-room door than the waiting-room door was wide.

(Watt, p. 237)

The scene ends with Watt purchasing for one shilling and threepence a third-class single ticket to the round end of the line, that is Harcourt Street terminus which, unlike Bray terminus, ends on a turntable (1:27) -

> He wants a ticket to the end of the line, cried Mr. Nolan.
> Is it a white man? said Lady McCann.
> Which end? said Mr. Gorman.
> What end? said Mr. Nolan.
> Watt did not reply.
> The round end or the square end? said Mr. Nolan.

(Watt, p. 244)

Foxrock Station, as well as being the scene for the major dramas in *Watt* and *All That Fall*, is probably also the landmark that heralds the end of Mercier and Camier's journey out of the city -

> Cheer up, said Camier, we are coming to the station of the damned, I can see the steeple.

(Mercier and Camier, p. 67)

The passengers on the 'Slow and Easy' were a motley crew; on Sundays there were the 'trippers' - 'Golfers and tennis players, yea, even the dashing croquet-eer go forth'[52]. Then there were 'the regulars' who travelled daily to the city. The first-class carriages catered for the well-to-do, mostly Protestant commuters, whose conversation would be of 'rockplants, plain and purl, and the number of stitches to be set up, politics and golf - each to his or her taste.' The snobbery of this affluent line did not pass unnoticed by Beckett -

> Come, Dolly darling, let us take up our stand before the first class smokers. Give me your hand and hold me tight, one can be sucked under.

(All That Fall, p. 25)

The eccentricities of the regular passengers were observed by the station staff, who, with characteristic native wit, applied appropriate sobriquets to each. One of these actual passengers on the line kept himself to himself,[53] and may have had much in common with another traveller on the 'Slow and Easy', Samuel Beckett-

> Cack-faced Miller arrived. Cack-faced Miller never greeted anyone, orally or otherwise, and few people ever greeted Cack-faced Miller.

(Watt, p. 243)

1:27 A steam engine on the turntable at Harcourt Street Station (Photograph by N. Johnson)

One of the most delightful fictional characters to travel the line was Mr. Spiro, the editor of *Crux*[54] -

> Mr. Spiro had been drinking, but not more than was good for him.
>
> I edit *Crux*, said Mr. Spiro, the popular catholic monthly. We do not pay our contributors, but they benefit in other ways. Our advertisements are extraordinary. We keep our tonsure above water. Our prize competitions are very nice. Times are hard, water in every wine. Of a devout twist, they do more good than harm.
>
> *(Watt, p. 25)*

The 'Slow and Easy', beginning its journey at Bray, progressed to Foxrock, and, passing through the stations of Leopardstown, Stillorgan, and Dundrum, eventually reached the terminus at Harcourt Street.

Harcourt Street Station (1:28), like Foxrock, is of major importance in Beckett's works. It is an interesting and architecturally fine station (alas no longer a railway terminus but still in existence at least). It was the last of the city termini to be built. Designed by George Wilkinson, it was opened at a cost of £8,502 in 1859. Possessing 'a little piazza of sixteen Tuscan pillars, broken in the middle by a large round arch surmounted by a pediment',[55] it was the pillars that caught Beckett's attention -

> But tut there I am far again from that terminus and its pretty neo-Doric colonnade, and far from that heap of flesh, rind, bones and bristles waiting to depart it knows not where, somewhere south, perhaps asleep, its ticket between finger and thumb for the sake of appearances, or let fall to the ground in the great limpness of sleep, perhaps dreaming it's in heaven, alit in heaven, or better still the dawn, waiting for the dawn and the joy of being able to say, I've the whole day before me, to go wrong, to go right, to calm down, to give up, I've nothing to fear, my ticket is valid for life.
>
> *(Texts for Nothing, p. 94)*

The station was not without its peculiarities. "It has one platform only, so that incoming and outgoing trains have to play at 'Box and Cox' perpetually. On most occasions indeed, it is truer to say that trains come in merely to go out again."[56] If waiting, expectancy and motion characterise much of man's existence, the desultory atmosphere of the waiting room of the Harcourt Street terminus permitted motionless contemplation without the threat of action -

> And what if all this time I had not stirred hand or foot from the third class waiting-room of the South-Eastern Railway Terminus, I never dared wait first on a third class ticket, and were still there waiting to leave, for the south-east, the south rather, east lay the sea, all along the track, wondering where on earth to alight, or my mind absent, elsewhere. The last train went at twenty-three thirty, then they closed the station for the night. What thronging memories, that's to make me think I'm dead, I've said it a million times.
>
> *(Texts for Nothing, p. 94)*

1:28   Harcourt Street Railway
       Station
       (By courtesy National Library of
       Ireland. Eason 1718)

1:29　Carriages on the closed
Harcourt Street Line
(Photograph by N. Johnson)

In the Harcourt Street terminus, as in Foxrock Station, it was the staff who gave the place its character -

> Watt bumped into a porter wheeling a milkcan. Watt fell and his hat and bags were scattered ...
> The devil raise a hump on you, said the porter.
> He was a handsome if dirty fellow. It is so difficult for railway porters to keep sweet and clean, with the work they have to do.
>
> *(Watt, p. 22)*

And the newsagent Evans merits detailed description, not only because of his saturnine temperament, but for his ability to master a bicycle despite deformity, a talent not unusual in the Beckettian character -

> He seemed a man of more than usual acerbity, and to suffer from unremitting mental, moral and perhaps even physical pain ... But one thought of him as the man who, among other things, never left off his cap, a plain blue cloth cap, with a peak and knob. For he never left off his bicycle-clips either. These were a kind that caused his trouser-ends to stick out wide, on either side. He was short and limped dreadfully. When he got started he moved rapidly, in a series of aborted genuflexions.
>
> *(Watt, pp. 23-24)*

One passenger, Mercier, was not at ease on the 'Slow and Easy' -

> You remain strangely calm, said Mercier. Am I right in thinking you took advantage of my condition to substitute this hearse for the express we agreed on?
>
> *(Mercier and Camier, p. 41)*

His pessimism was not unfounded. Some extraordinary events had befallen the locomotives of the Dublin and South Eastern Railway. In 1900 the up-train went too far and crashed through the end-wall of Harcourt Street station. Some twenty years later 'somebody, from sheer wantonness, sent an engine going just outside the station. Full of the joy of liberty, it puffed forth. For ages it had longed for an excuse to get away from those shining tracks - anywhere, anywhere, off these black tracks - it pointed, and flung itself wildly into an astonished backyard somewhere in Albert place.'[57]

Beckett's sadness at finding the station closed on a visit to Dublin is reflected in the poignant voice of *That Time* (1:29) -

> no getting out to it that way so what next no question of asking not another word to the living as long as you lived so foot it up in the end to the station bowed half double get out to it that way all closed down and boarded up Doric terminus of the Great Southern and Eastern all closed down and the colonnade crumbling away so what next
>
> *(That Time, p. 231)*

Page 37

Dubliners bemoan the loss of the Harcourt Street line, and suggestions abound for the use of the railway route. Perhaps some day the citizens of the city will once again pass by the pillars of Harcourt Street Station with the abandon that appealed to one contemporary commentator: 'The station building itself is gloomy and pretentious, but many really care-free human beings have passed its portals – and the really care-free are few in this world.'[58]

Leopardstown Racecourse

Another feature adding to the uniqueness of the Dublin and South Eastern line was the racecourse at Leopardstown with Foxrock railway station a few minutes walk away. On race-days, special trains ran to and from Harcourt Street Station, and there was a separate siding for the race-train at Foxrock (1:30). The racecourse, oval in shape with a track of two miles to the round,[59] was the first in Europe to use the starting-gate (1:31).

1:30 Leopardstown Racecourse from Foxrock Railway Station (By courtesy Mr. J. Kennedy)

1:31 A race-meeting at Leopardstown Racecourse (By courtesy Mrs. C. Clarke)

The events in *All that Fall*, the original title of which was *A Lovely Day for the Races*,[60] take place on the day of a race-meeting; Christy greets Mrs. Rooney with - 'Nice day for the races, Ma'am.'[61] Mr. Slocum, the Clerk of the Racecourse, who was in reality Mr. Fred Clarke[62](1.32), is seen approaching by Mrs. Rooney -

> Well if it isn't my old admirer the Clerk of the Course, in his limousine.
>
> *(All That Fall, p. 17)*

Wild tips are a part of all race-meetings; the Leopardstown meeting in *All That Fall* is no exception -

> TOMMY: *(Hurriedly.)* You wouldn't have something for the Ladies Plate, sir? I was given Flash Harry.
> MR. SLOCUM: *(Scornfully.)* Flash Harry! That carthorse!
>
> *(All That Fall, p. 20)*

1:32 Mr. Fred Clarke, Clerk of Leopardstown Racecourse seated on the steps of the stands with William Beckett (father of Samuel Beckett) holding a folded umbrella (By courtesy Mrs. C. Clarke)

1:33 A group of aviators and officials at the Leopardstown aviation meeting. From left to right: Harold Perrin, Secretary, Aero Club of the United Kingdom, Armstrong Drexel, Harry Delacombe, W.F. McArdle and Cecil Grace
(By courtesy T. Cranitch, Press Officer, Aer Lingus)

Beckett's writings, however, dwell more on the scenic beauty of the course than on equine achievements there -

> The racecourse now appearing, with its beautiful white railing, in the fleeing lights, warned Watt that he was drawing near, and that when the train stopped next, then he must leave it. He could not see the stands, the grand, the members', the people's, so   ?   when empty with their white and red, for they were too far off.

(Watt, p. 27)

Few places are more beautiful in spring -

> we are if I may believe the colours that deck the emerald grass if I may believe them we are old dream of flowers and seasons we are in April or in May and certain accessories if I may believe them white rails a grandstand colour of old rose we are on a racecourse in April or in May.

(How It Is, p. 32)

On August 29th and 30th 1910, Leopardstown racecourse was the scene of an historic event when Ireland's first aviation meeting was sponsored there by the Aero Club of Ireland. The first flight in Ireland had taken place on Newcastle Beach the previous year. Three well-known aviators (1:33) were brought to Dublin for this spectacular event: Captain Bertram Dickson gave a demonstration of 'Circular Flying' in his Farman Biplane (for which he was paid £500); Armstrong Drexel, an American, demonstrated high flying in his Bleriot Monoplane, and Cecil Grace, an American of Irish extraction, performed in his Farman Biplane (1:34).[63] The event received extensive publicity -

It must have been a very surprising, and indeed unwelcome, experience for racing men to see Leopardstown Course crowded yesterday as probably it has never been before and not by an assembly expecting to see an Orby or a Persimmon pass the post, but to witness instead a Drexel and a Grace controlling a motor engine between earth and heaven. It was the first occasion on which Ireland was brought face to face with the new wonder of the world, and Ireland, as represented by Dublin, and the Horse Show visitors to Dublin, went in thousands to see the marvel. Far back in the period of myth and legend Irish heroes and heroines sported in chariots over the hills and dales of what we now call Leopardstown. In later times, the fleetest coursers of the Irish turf carried colours to victory in what racing men call the same venue. But now, for the first time, there were seen men careering far beyond racing speed over Leopardstown Racecourse; between old Killiney Hill with its Obelisk and Ballycoras Tower, under the shadow of the Three Rock Mountains - famed in prose and verse - and speeding at a pace that equalled, nay frightened, the birds and made a sporting crowd speculate not on the future of the racing track, but on the possibilities of man in the high heavens.[64]

Mr. Farrell, the station-master at Foxrock who handled the event with customary efficiency and was commended by the press for so doing, had his hands full – 'There was a remarkable scene at Foxrock Railway Station during Mr. Drexel's flight. A crowded train from Dublin had just

1:34   A group of officials around a
Farman biplane
(By courtesy T. Cranitch, Press
Officer, Aer Lingus)

stopped at the station. The passengers tumbled out en masse to see the flying man of whom they had a good view ... They stood on the platform and swarmed on the bridge and as Drexel passed a second time they raised a loud cheer. It was some time before the empty train could be filled up again and the passengers swept on their way.'[65]

The meeting was a great success with large crowds travelling to Leopardstown for the two-day event to see their first aeroplane. Among these was the four-year old Samuel Beckett -

> But I have heard aeroplanes elsewhere and have even seen them in flight, I saw the very first in flight and then in the end the latest models, oh not the very latest, the very second latest, the very antepenultimate. I was present at one of the first loopings of the loop, so help me God. I was not afraid. It was above a racecourse, my mother held me by the hand. She kept saying, It's a miracle, a miracle. Then I changed my mind. We were not often of the same mind. One day we were walking along the road, up a hill of extraordinary steepness, near home I imagine, my memory is full of steep hills, I get them confused. I said, The sky is further away than you think, is it not, mama? It was without malice, I was simply thinking of all the leagues that separated me from it.[66] She replied, to me her son, It is precisely as far away as it appears to be. She was right. But at the time I was aghast. I can still see the spot, opposite Tyler's gate.[67] A market-gardener, he had only one eye and wore side-whiskers. That's the idea, rattle on. You could see the sea, the islands, the headlands, the isthmuses, the coast stretching away to north and south and the crooked moles of the harbour. We were on our way home from the butcher's.
>
> *(Malone Dies, pp. 269-270)*

This maternal retort shattered Beckett. Though wounded by its terseness, the wisdom of the statement, conveyed so effectively with startling brevity, later excited the admiration of a son, himself a master in the economy of expression -

> Looking up at the blue sky and then at your mother's face you break the silence asking her if it is not in reality much more distant than it appears. The sky that is. The blue sky. Receiving no answer you mentally reframe your question and some hundred paces later look up at her face again and ask her if it does not appear much less distant than in reality it is. For some reason you could never fathom this question must have angered her exceedingly. For she shook off your little hand and made you a cutting retort you have never forgotten.
>
> *(Company, p. 12-13.)*

Beckett, in an earlier version, strips the occasion of all ornament to endow it with a humorous brevity that is most effective -

> A small boy, stretching out his hands and looking up at the blue sky, asked his mother how such a thing was possible. Fuck off, she said.
>
> *(The End, p. 53)*

1:35 Richard Webster Croker
with his wife Beulah at
Leopardstown Races
(By courtesy Mrs. C. Clarke)

Boss Croker's Gallops

> One fateful fine Spring evening he paused, not so much in order to rest as to have the scene soak through him, out in the middle of the late Boss Croker's Gallops, where no horses were to be seen any more.
>
> *(More Pricks than Kicks, p. 109)*

Boss Croker's Gallops or Acres feature in a number of Beckett's writings.[68] The Gallops were used very successfully by Boss Croker[69] to train his horses, and, until recently, by the trainer Seamus McGrath. Richard Webster Croker (1:35), who emigrated from Cork to America just before the Great Famine, rose from poverty to sizable wealth as the 'Boss' of Tammany Hall. On returning to Ireland he became a highly successful horse-trainer. Beckett often trod the Ballyogan Road to the Gallops, situated some fifteen minutes walk from *Cooldrinagh*. If he continued climbing the Ballyogan Road, he came to the hamlet of Stepaside on the foothills of the Dublin mountains -

> Nowhere in particular on the way from A to Z. Or say for verisimilitude the Ballyogan Road. That dear old back road. Somewhere on the Ballyogan Road in lieu of nowhere in particular. Where no truck any more. Somewhere on the Ballyogan Road on the way from A to Z. Head sunk totting up the tally on the verge of the ditch. Foothills to left. Croker's Acres ahead. Father's shade to right and a little to the rear. So many times already round the earth. Topcoat once green stiff with age and grime from chin to insteps. Battered once buff block hat and quarter boots still a match. No other garments if any to be seen. Out since break of day and night now falling. Reckoning ended on together from nought anew. As if bound for Stepaside. When suddenly you cut through the hedge and vanish hobbling east across the gallops.
>
> *(Company, p. 30-31)*

Boss Croker spent much of his fortune building the mansion *Glencairn*, (now the residence of the British Ambassador) with its adjoining stables and gallops so ideally suited to training his horses (1:36).[70] The Boss's success on the track reflected also on his followers, most especially the gamblers of the neighbourhood clamouring at the bookmaker's door -

> And the obligations! I have in mind particularly the appointments at ten in the morning, hail rain or shine, in front of Duggan's, thronged already with sporting men fevering to get their bets out of harm's way before the bars open.
>
> *(Texts for Nothing, p. 80)*

In 1907 Boss Croker established a racing record. He won the Epsom Derby with Orby, a horse which he had bred and trained privately at

1:36 *Glencairn*
(Photograph by D. Davison)

Glencairn (1:37), and Orby also won the Baldoyle Plate and the Irish Derby. The winning of the Epsom caused a sensation in Ireland and particularly in the environs of Foxrock and Sandyford. The English press had given him no chance: 'The Turf in Ireland has no spring in it, the climate is too depressing and no Irish trainer knows enough to even dare to compete for the greatest race in the world.'[71] The bookmakers were of the same mind, despite the fact that every Irishman who ever saw a race, and probably even those few who never did, backed the horse heavily bringing the odds down from 66 to 1 to 100 to 9 at which price it won. "When the news came through that he had actually won, the announcement was followed by scenes of extraordinary enthusiasm. Bonfires were lit everywhere, one in the streets of Dublin by the students of Trinity College, and when the horse came home a brass band and many hundreds of people turned out to meet the astonished horse... and one old lady, referring to the fact that Mr. Croker belonged to the Faith of the majority in Ireland, said 'Thank God ... we have lived to see a *Catholic* horse win the Derby'."[72] Orby was laid to rest at *Glencairn*, but in the story, 'Walking Out', Beckett mistakes the burial place of Pretty Polly (a famous Irish filly who won 22 out of 24 races including three classics[73]) for that of Orby, and as we have noted earlier he had also mistaken Orby for a horse named Joss[74] -

> Pretty Polly that great-hearted mare was buried in the vicinity. To stroll over this expanse in fine weather, these acres of bright green grass, was almost as good as to cross the race-course of Chantilly with one's face towards the Castle.
>
> *(More Pricks than Kicks, p. 109)*

Not all Irishmen share the national passion for horse, one such being Molloy who found the presence of quadrupeds highly distasteful (1:38) -

> Good God, what a land of breeders, you see quadrupeds everywhere. And it's not over yet, there are still horses and goats, to mention only them, I feel them watching out for me, to get in my path.
>
> *(Molloy, p. 29)*

The Irish obsession with racing, matched only in fervour by religion and alcoholic refreshment, can with justification be accused of diverting the national intellect from more gainful pursuits -

> The sport of kings is our passion, the dogs too, we have no political opinions, simply limply republican. But we also have a soft spot for the Windsors, the Hanoverians, I forget, the Hohenzollerns is it. Nothing human is foreign to us, once we have digested the racing news.
>
> *(Texts for Nothing, p. 80)*

1:37 'Boss' Croker's horses, Orby and Rhoda B, on the gallops with *Glencairn* in the background
(From a print by courtesy Sir Alan Goodison)

Boss Croker died in 1922 'full of years, honours and troubles', and, like Orby, was buried in the vicinity of the gallops in a lake-side mausoleum within sight of *Glencairn*. His pallbearers included Oliver St. John Gogarty, 'Alfie' Byrne and Arthur Griffith.[75]   When the British Embassy bought *Glencairn*, the body of the Boss had to be removed in the interests of legal niceties and he was reinterred in Kilgobbin Cemetery closeby.[76]

Boss Croker's Gallops were situated in beautiful countryside, of such beauty, in fact, that it is difficult to withhold at least some credit from the creator -

> Leaning now on his stick, between Leopardstown down the hill to the north and the heights of Two Rock and Three Rock to the south, Belacqua regretted the horses of the good old days, for they would have given to the landscape something that the legions of sheep and lambs could not give. These latter were springing into the world every minute, the grass was spangled with scarlet after-births, the larks were singing, the hedges were breaking, the sun was shining, the sky was Mary's cloak, the daisies were there, everything was in order. Only the cuckoo was wanting. It was one of those Spring evenings when it is a matter of some difficulty to keep God out of one's meditations.
>
> *(More Pricks than Kicks, p. 109)*

1:38 'Quadrupeds everywhere:'
A Dublin street-scene
(Photograph by N. Johnson)

1:39 Lambs on the Dublin foothills
(Photograph by D. Davison)

Fifty years on, the Gallops, strewn with sheeps' placentae and frolicking lambs, are still a vivid memory for Beckett -

> Next thing you are on your way across the white pasture afrolic with lambs in spring and strewn with red placentae.
>
> *(Company, p. 48)*

The lamb (1:39) is a recurring allegorical image for Beckett -

> There had to be lambs. Rightly or wrongly. A moor would have allowed of them. Lambs for their whiteness. And for other reasons as yet obscure. Another reason. And so that there may be none. At lambing time. That from one moment to the next she may raise her eyes to find them gone. A moor would have allowed of them. In any case too late. And what lambs. No trace of frolic. White splotches in the grass. Aloof from the unheeding ewes. Still. Then a moment straying. Then still again. To think there is still life in this age. Gently gently.
>
> *(Ill Seen Ill Said, p. 11)*

Without the lamb, a symbol of life, all is desolation -

> It was lambing time. But there were no lambs ... She remarks with surprise the absence of lambs in great numbers here at this time of year. She is wearing the black she took on when widowed young. It is to reflower the grave she strays in search of the flowers he had loved.
>
> *(One Evening, pp. 209-211)*

The acceptance of human suffering, glorified in sacrificial ceremonial in the Bible, is given a simpler and more profound allegorical expression by Beckett -

> One evening she was followed by a lamb. Reared for slaughter like the others it left them to follow her. In the present to conclude. All so bygone. Slaughter apart it is not like the others. Hanging to the ground in matted coils its fleece hides the little shanks. Rather than walk it seems to glide like a toy in tow. It halts at the same instant as she. At the same instant as she strays on. Stockstill as she it waits with head like hers extravagantly bowed. Clash of black and white that far from muting the last rays amplify. It is now her puniness leaps to the eye. Thanks it would seem to the lowly creature next her.
>
> *(Ill Seen Ill Said, p.36)*

In *Not I*, Mouth's agony begins in the peaceful pastoral atmosphere of Croker's acres, 'wandering in a field... looking aimlessly for cowslips...',[77] but she is soon faced with the reality of her situation[78] -

> ... where was it? .. Croker's Acres ... one evening on the way home ... home! .. a little mound in Croker's Acres ... dusk ... sitting staring at her hand ... there in her lap ...
>
> *(Not I, p. 220)*

Boss Croker's house, visible from the adjoining gallops, and well known to Beckett, lends some of its features, notably the conservatory, American Bar, and oratory to the extraordinary establishment run by Mr. Knott in *Watt*[79]. Indeed, the blasphemy (if such it be), of Arthur in the garden, when he addresses the almighty as 'Boss'[80] might even be taken to suggest that Mr. Knott had his origins in Boss Croker -

> Halting, he contemplated the grass, at his feet.
> This dewy sward is not yours, he said. He clasped his hands to his breast. He lifted them towards the maker, and giver, of all things, of him, of the daisies, of the grass. Thanks, Boss, he said. He stood easy. He moved on.
>
> *(Watt, p. 252)*

1:40   A Kerry Blue bitch

On the gallops at the foot of Dublin's mountains, communion with nature is heightened by the company of animals: birds, sheep and lambs, and the faithful companion of the young Beckett, his Kerry Blue bitch (1:40) -

> Belacqua leaned all his spare weight on the stick and took in the scene, in a sightless passionate kind of way, and his Kerry Blue bitch sat on the emerald floor beside him. She was getting old now, she could not be bothered hunting any more. She could tree a cat, that was no bother, but beyond that she did not care to go. So she just remained seated, knowing perfectly well that there were no cats in Croker's Gallops, and did not care very much what happened. The bleating of the lambs excited her slightly.
>
> *(More Pricks than Kicks, p. 109)*

Without his father to accompany him on his long walks, the Kerry Blue was a comforting companion. The finest tribute to a loved one is a poem, and in *Serena II* his pregnant bitch, dreaming back to her days in the West of Ireland, conveys poignantly the tenuous separation between procreation and death[81] -

> in a hag she drops her young
> the whales in Blacksod Bay are dancing
> the asphodels coming running the flags after
> she thinks she is dying she is ashamed ...
>
> with whatever trust of panic we went out
> with so much shall we return
> there shall be no loss of panic between a man and his dog
> bitch though he be
>
> *(Serena II, pp. 23-24)*

Of all the personalities that compose life's motley cast, none ranks higher in Beckett's philosophy than the tramp. This majestic figure makes his entrance in the environs of Leopardstown in the story 'Walking Out' which was published in 1934 (1:41) -

> In the ditch on the far side of the road a strange equipage was installed: an old high-wheeled cart, hung with rags. Belacqua looked round for something in the nature of a team, the crazy yoke could scarcely have fallen from the sky, but nothing in the least resembling a draught-beast was to be seen, not even a cow. Squatting under the cart a complete down-and-out was very busy with something or other. The sun beamed down on this as though it were a new-born lamb. Belacqua took in the whole outfit at a glance and felt, the wretched bourgeois, a paroxysm of shame for his capon belly.
>
> *(More Pricks than Kicks, p. 111)*

Beckett's affection for purity and generosity, so often a quality of the deprived (and indeed deranged), is apparent in the tramp's reaction when Belacqua's bitch wets his 'throusers' -

> A smile proof against all adversity transformed the sad face of the man under the cart. He was most handsome with his thick, if unkempt, black hair and moustache.
> 'Game ball' he said.
> After that further comment was impossible. The question of apology or compensation simply did not arise. The instinctive nobility of this splendid creature for whom private life, his joys and chagrins at evening under the cart, was not acquired, as Belacqua one day if he were lucky might acquire his, but antecedent, disarmed all the pot-hooks and hangers of civility.
>
> *(More Pricks than Kicks, p. 112)*

Though Beckett, himself, may have been unaware at the time of writing *More Pricks than Kicks* what course his future writing would take, he is already identifying with the disadvantaged and deprived, who even at this early stage in his writings are beginning to claim the centre stage. *More Pricks than Kicks* and the earlier *Dream of Fair to Middling Women* embody many of the characteristics that were to achieve acclaim for his later writing.

1:41 A tramp at the wheel of his caravan (By courtesy National Library of Ireland, Valentine 1604)

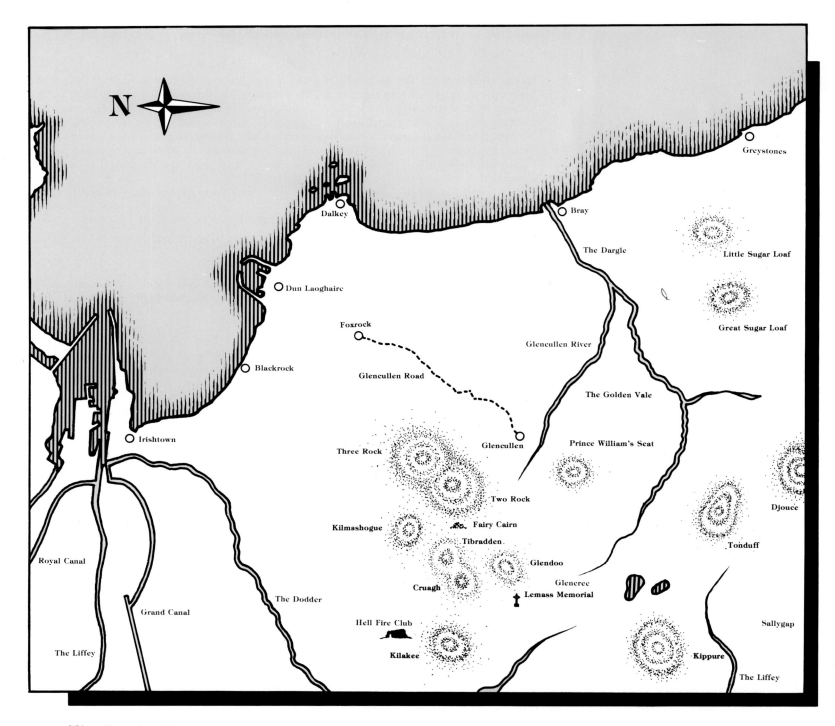

2:1 The Dublin Mountains and Dublin Bay

Chapter Two

THE DUBLIN MOUNTAINS

The city of Dublin dates from the ninth-century when a Danish settlement was founded on the banks of the river Liffey, which rising on Tonduff South, a Wicklow mountain, divides the city before entering the sea at Dublin Bay.[1] The spread of the city has been confined, to some extent, within these two natural boundaries, the sea to the east and the mountains of Dublin to the west and of Wicklow to the south (2:1). The Dublin and Wicklow mountains are part of a great granite chain that extends some 70 miles from Dalkey to Wexford and is reputed to be the longest mass of granite in the islands of Ireland and Britain. That this range influenced history is evident from the portal dolmens and cairns of the earliest inhabitants, the churches of the Christian era, the castles of the medieval period, the chain of nineteenth century Martello towers, and the massive piers of the harbours.[2] Regrettably, modern technology is enabling incompetent city planners to breach these barriers and the city is now creeping up the foothills of the mountains. The natural beauty of the city's unique setting has been further compromised by a futile policy of filling in the bay as though the sea of right belonged to the land. None-the-less, Dubliners still have at their doorsteps two precious amenities, mountain and sea, both valued highly by William Beckett who introduced his son to each at an early age. Together they spent many happy hours roaming the peaks of the Dublin mountains (2:2). Old Henry, in *Embers*, is haunted by the sea, the mountains, and the ghost of his father -

> Father! *(Pause.)* Tired of talking to you. *(Pause.)* That was always the way, walk all over the mountains with you talking and talking and then suddenly mum and home in misery and not a word to a soul for weeks, sulky little bastard, better off dead.
>
> *(Embers, p. 96)*

Beckett has remarked that his father walked himself to death on the Dublin mountains,[3] and after his father's death Beckett went on walking the mountains, not always quite alone[4] -

> Out no more to walk the little winding back roads and interjacent pastures now alive with flocks and now deserted. With at your elbow for long years your father's shade in his old tramping rags and then for long years alone.
>
> *(Company, pp. 85-86)*

2:2   Father and son on a
      mountain road to nowhere
      (Photograph by D. Davison)

The power of Beckett's childhood memories, most especially of the mountain walks with his father, is stronger, more searching in his later writings -

Where then but there see now another. Bit by bit an old man and child. In the dim void bit by bit an old man and child. Any other would do as ill.

Hand in hand with equal plod they go. In the free hands - no. Free empty hands. Backs turned both bowed with equal plod they go. The child hand raised to reach the holding hand. Hold the old holding hand. Hold and be held. Plod on and never recede. Slowly with never a pause plod on and never recede. Backs turned. Both bowed. Joined by held holding hands. Plod on as one. One shade. Another shade.

(Worstward Ho, pp. 12-13)

Ascent

From *Cooldrinagh*, father and son would climb the Glencullen Road with its views of the Wicklow mountains in the south on their left-hand side, the Two and Three Rock mountains ahead and to the right, and looking back the sea with Howth and Lambay Island – a beautiful walk or cycle. From the Glencullen Cross, the Dublin mountains were theirs to choose: to the left the shorter walk to Prince William's Seat; ahead, the turf-clad peaks of Glencree accessible either by the Pine Forest or Devil's Elbow. For a day's trek there was the splendid isolation of Sally Gap, or the peaks of Two Rock, Three Rock, Tibradden, Glendoo and Killakee.[5] The land at the foothills of the mountains, though amply coated with grass, hedge and shrub, and throwing up here and there denuded trees of often indeterminate variety, yields a living begrudgingly to those who inhabit the region. Camier descending from Glencree saw it all at a glance -

> But to have done with these inanities, at the first fork Camier stopped and his heart beat fast with the thought of what to pack into a last long salute gravid to bursting with unprecedented delicacy. It was true countryside at last, quickset hedgerows, mud, liquid manure, rocks, wallows, cow-shit, hovels, and here and there a form unmistakably human scratching at his plot since the first scabs of dawn, or shifting his dung, with a spade, having lost his shovel and his fork being broken. A giant tree, jumble of black boughs, stands between the branching roads.
> *(Mercier and Camier, p. 106)*

As one ascends the vegetation becomes sparser, the roads narrower and barer, lonely, often seemingly endless roads leading nowhere. Beckett walked these roads in childhood and youth, finding in the mountains a peace that was not be be had in the city -

> ...until the time came, with break of day, to issue forth again, void my little sanctum, shed robe and skull, resume my hat and greatcoat, and issue forth again, to walk the roads. *(Pause.)* The back roads.
> *(...but the clouds ... pp. 261-262)*

The skies over the Dublin mountains, vivid and majestic in their restlessness, often threatening, are characteristic of the Molloy country (2:3)-

> Yes, the great cloud was ravelling, discovering here and there a pale and dying sky, and the sun, already down, was manifest in the livid tongues of fire darting towards the zenith, falling and darting again, ever more pale and languid, and doomed no sooner lit to be extinguished. This phenomenon, if I remember rightly was characteristic of my region.
> *(Molloy, p. 65)*

2:3 '...but the clouds...' Sky over the Dublin mountains: a plantation of larches lies to the right
(Photograph by D. Davison)

The sky, full of light and movement, is all that the prostitute Celia in *Murphy* can remember of her homeland, which she left at the age of four[6]-

> He let her go. She rose and went to the window. The sky, cool, bright, full of movement, anointed her eyes, reminded her of Ireland.
>
> *(Murphy, p. 32)*

In a quotation borrowed by Beckett from W.B. Yeats's poem, *The Tower*[7], the birds of the mountains add a poetic dimension to the visual beauty -

> '... but the clouds of the sky ... when the horizon fades ... or a bird's sleepy cry ... among the deepening shades ...'
>
> *(... but the clouds... p. 262)*

The weather on the Dublin mountains is generally settled in summer -

> The weather, though often inclement (but they knew no better), never exceeded the limits of the temperate, that is to say what could still be borne, without danger if not without discomfort, by the average native fittingly clad and shod.
>
> *(Mercier and Camier, p. 7)*

Rain, however, is never far away in Ireland, and the wetness of the landscape is a recurring feature in Beckett's writing -

> What's the weather like now, said Mercier, if I look up I'll fall down.
> Like what it's always like, said Camier, with this slight difference, that we're beginning to get used to it.
> I thought I felt drops on my cheeks, said Mercier.
>
> *(Mercier and Camier, p. 67)*

In winter, the mountain mood can be both beautiful and treacherous. Mists descend without warning, isolating the unwary traveller and shrouding the mountain tops, obscure all view of the lands beneath -

> The top, very flat, of a mountain, no, a hill, but so wild, so wild, enough. Quag, heath up to the knees, faint sheeptracks, troughs scooped deep by the rains. It was far down in one of these I was lying, out of the wind. Glorious prospect, but for the mist that blotted out everything, valleys, loughs, plain and sea.
>
> *(Texts for Nothing, p. 71)*

The snow, which covers the summits for much of winter, bestows a silent beauty on the mountains (2:4) -

> And sure enough, soon after, the snow. In other words the night was black, when it fell at last, but no, strange, it wasn't, in spite of the buried sky. The way was long that led back to the den, over the fields, a winding way, it must still be there. When it comes to the top of the cliff it springs, some might think blindly, but no, wilily, like a goat, in hairpin zigzags towards the shore. Never had the sea so thundered from afar, the sea beneath the snow, though superlatives have lost most of their charm.
>
> *(Texts for Nothing, p. 77)*

The summits of Dublin's mountains are devoid of trees, but the slopes are richly forested with a variety of tree and plant. The plantations of larches, so beloved by Beckett, thrive in the mountain valleys -

> To the west in the valley a plantation of larches nearly brought tears to the eyes of Belacqua...
>
> *(More Pricks than Kicks, p. 100)*

Heather and fern abound on the upper reaches of the mountains, being the only vegetation that can survive the weather and the bog-soil. In *Malone Dies*, the 'hot yellow bells' of the ling and furze are objects of

2:4   Glencree in Snow
(By courtesy Bord Fáilte
No. WI 24/55)

2:5　A gorse fire on the Dublin
mountains
(Photograph by D. Davison)

nostalgic poignancy[8]. To Belacqua and the heroine, Ruby, climbing Tibradden mountain, in the love story 'Love and Lethe', the 'ling and whortleberry' impede their progress, but not without reward as Ruby abandons her skirt, much to the hero's approval.[9] On less romantic occasions, the fern-cloaked slopes provoke baser sentiment -

> Well once out on the road and free of the property what then, I really do not know, the next thing I was up in the bracken lashing about with my stick making the drops fly and cursing, filthy language, the same words over and over, I hope nobody heard me.
>
> *(From an Abandoned Work, p. 136)*

The gorse of the mountains often ignites in summer, not always spontaneously, illuminating the peaks at night with pockets of smouldering furze[10](2:5) -

> And on the slopes of the mountain, now rearing its unbroken bulk behind the town, the fires turned from gold to red, from red to gold. I knew what it was, it was the gorse burning. How often I had set a match to it myself, as a child. And hours later, back in my home, before I climbed into bed, I watched from my high window the fires I had lit.
>
> *(The End, p. 69)*

There are a number of small granite quarries in Glencullen and the neighbouring areas, and the music of the stone-cutters' hammers, ringing 'all day like bells',[11] was familiar to Beckett -

> I saw the mountain, impassable, cavernous, secret, where from morning to night I'd hear nothing but the wind, the curlews, the clink like distant silver of the stone-cutters' hammers. I'd come out in the daytime to the heather and gorse, all warmth and scent, and watch at night the distant city lights, if I chose, and the other lights, the lighthouses and lightships my father had named for me, when I was small, and whose names I could find again, in my memory, if I chose, that I knew.
>
> *(First Love, p. 18)*

Specific locations are only rarely given in Beckett's writings;[12] one such is the reference to Glencullen and the quarry on the slopes of the mountain known as Prince William's Seat[13](2:6) in the humorous conversation between Mr. Hackett and the Nixons in *Watt* -

> Nothing to the Glencullen Hacketts, I suppose, said Tetty.
> It was there I fell off the ladder, said Mr. Hackett.
> What age were you then? said Tetty.
> One, said Mr. Hackett.
> And where was your dear mother? said Tetty.
> She was out somewhere, said Mr. Hackett.
> And your papa? said Tetty.
> Papa was out breaking stones on Prince William's Seat, said Mr. Hackett.
>
> *(Watt, p. 13)*

2:6   View of the neighbouring Dublin mountain summits from Prince William's Seat: Upper Lough Bray is in the centre foreground (Photograph by D. Davison)

The Summits

A climb to the summit of any of the Dublin mountains is a rewarding experience. Not only are there spectacular views but each mountain peak has its own particular charm and personality.[14] The giant granite tors, surmounting the Two Rock and Three Rock mountains (2:7), are slabs of granite stripped of the peat and bracken blanket that covers the peaks. From these summits, or the higher neighbouring peaks of Djouce and the Sugarloaf in Wicklow, the eye can see as far as Wales on a clear day -

> Standing on the Big Sugarloaf, it may well be objected, or Djouce, or even a low eminence like the Three Rock, the Welsh Hills are frequently plainly to be discerned.
>
> *(Dream of Fair to Middling Women, p. 213)*

On Two Rock and Tibradden, there are fairy cairns marking ancient passage tombs[15]-

> They pushed on and soon the summit, complete with fairy rath, came into view, howbeit still at a considerable distance.
>
> *(More Pricks than Kicks, p. 99)*

The summit of Tibradden[16] features in the poem, *Serena II* -

> sodden packet of Churchman
> muzzling the cairn
>
> *(Serena II, p. 24)*

2:7 The granite tors on the summit of the Three Rock Mountain
(Photograph by D. Davison)

In the poem 'Return to the Vestry', in which Beckett bemoans the despoliation of the chapel in the burial ground of the poet, Pierre de Ronsard at the Prieuré de Saint-Cosme near Tours, he makes mention of the ancient custom of placing a stone on burial cairns[17](2:8) -

> So
> Swell the cairn and spill the doings.
>
> *(Return to the Vestry, pp. 308-312)*

Tibradden is the peak chosen for the love scene in 'Love and Lethe'. As Belacqua's driving skills had been strained well beyond their limits in the drive from the city, it is likely that the lovers ascended from the Kilmashogue side rather than driving further to the Pine Forest ascent -

> The pup and slut drove on and on and there was dead silence between them. Not a syllable did they exchange until the car was safely stowed at the foot of a mountain.
>
> *(More Pricks than Kicks, p. 98)*

As they climbed, the summit of Montpelier Hill with its celebrated ruin, the Hell Fire Club, would have been visible (2:9). This ruin, well known to Beckett, is alluded to in the poem *Serena III*, when the narrator glimpses the mountains with the Hell Fire ruin from Sandymount -

> Irishtown Sandymount puzzle find the Hell Fire
>
> *(Serena III, p. 25)*

2:8 A summit fairy cairn with Dublin city and bay in the background
(Photograph by D. Davison)

2:9 The Hell Fire Club on the summit of Killakee mountain (Photograph by D. Davison)

Built originally as a hunting lodge by William Connolly, the Speaker of the Irish House of Parliament and Lord Justice in 1716, it became a rendezvous for members of the notorious Hell Fire Club in 1735. The hedonistic gentlemen of this establishment usually met in the Eagle Tavern in Dublin, but, for their more extreme debauches they rode out to the secluded and more romantic ambience of Connolly's Lodge. Lord Rosse, one of the founders of the Club, received when lying on his death bed, a letter from the rector of St. Ann's urging him to repent while there was still time. Rosse noticing with amusement that the letter began simply 'My Lord', re-sealed it and addressed it to Lord Kildare, 'well known for his piety and integrity of life.' Rosse would have greatly enjoyed the encounter between his lordship and the hapless parson, but, as Maurice Craig suggests 'by this time he had passed on to another, and perhaps a warmer, climate.'[18]

Glencree mountain is 1716 feet above sea level.[19] Unlike the neighbouring peaks, the sea is not visible from much of Glencree, and its absence heightens the sense of solitude and isolation. The flat bog-land of Glencree is bare, desolate and enthralling. None inhabit this inhospitable terrain. Here and there turf-cutters from the city work their plots. Strange ruins (2:10), cairns and the occasional memorial, silhouetted against a darkening sky, make it a lonesome and at times an eerie spot. The magic of Glencree and the beauty of the neighbouring summits were well known to Beckett -

A road still carriageable climbs over the high moorland. It cuts across vast turfbogs, a thousand feet above sea-level, two thousand if you prefer. It leads to nothing any more. A few ruined forts, a few ruined dwellings. The sea is not far, just visible beyond the valleys dipping eastward, pale plinth as pale as the pale wall of sky. Tarns lie hidden in the folds of the moor, invisible from the road, reached by faint paths, under high over-hanging crags. All seems flat, or gently undulating, and there at a stone's throw these high crags, all unsuspected by the wayfarer. Of granite what is more. In the west the chain is at its highest, its peaks exalt even the most downcast eyes, peaks commanding the vast champaign land, the celebrated pastures, the golden vale. Before the travellers, as far as eye can reach, the road winds on into the south, uphill, but imperceptibly. None ever pass this way but beauty-spot hogs and fanatical trampers. Under its heather mask the quag allures, with an allurement not all mortals can resist. Then it swallows them up or the mist comes down. The city is not far either, from certain points its lights can be seen by night, its light rather, and by day its haze. Even the piers of the harbour can be distinguished, on very clear days, of the two harbours, tiny arms in the glassy sea outflung, known flat, seen raised. And the islands and promontories, one has only to stop and turn at the right place, and of course by

2:10   A deserted ruin on the slopes of Prince William's Seat (Photograph by D. Davison)

night the beacon lights, both flashing and revolving. It is here one would lie down, in a hollow bedded with dry heather, and fall asleep, for the last time, on an afternoon, in the sun, head down among the minute life of stems and bells, and fast fall asleep, fast farewell to charming things. It's a birdless sky, the odd raptor, no song. End of descriptive passage.

(Mercier and Camier, pp. 97-98)

West from Glencree, towards Wicklow on the road to Sally Gap, there are two lakes, Lough Bray lower and upper,[20] the latter a deep, black lake in the bogland (2:11).

The bogland of Glencree is divided in plots. For some Dubliners, turf-cutting is a means of obtaining fuel cheaply, and for others, using the slane is a skill to be enjoyed [21](2:12). The bog was not without its fascination for Camier -

> How beautiful the bog, said Camier.
> Most beautiful, said Mercier.
> Will you look at that heather, said Camier.
> Mercier looked with ostentation at the heather and whistled incredulously.
> Underneath there is turf, said Camier.
> One would never think so, said Mercier.

(Mercier and Camier, p. 99)

2:11 Upper Lough Bray from
the mountain summit
(Photograph by D. Davison)

2:12 A family of turf-cutters
on Glencree
(Photograph by G.A. Duncan,
No. 35AN2)

During the Civil War between the Free State Government and the Republicans in 1922-23, the former executed Republican prisoners in retaliation for each 'assassination' perpetrated on the Free State forces. This was one of the bloodiest phases of Ireland's turbulent history.[22] One Republican, Noel Lemass, who was seized by Government forces on July 3rd 1923,[23] disappeared and was not heard of again until his body was discovered on the deserted Glencree peak, where a memorial (of which the plinth less its cross still stands), marks the lonely spot[24] (2:13) -

> What is that cross? said Camier.
> There they go again.
> Planted in the bog, not far from the road, but too far for the inscription to be visible, a plain cross stood.
> I once knew, said Mercier, but no longer.
> I too once knew, said Camier, I'm almost sure.
> But he was not quite sure.
> It was the grave of a nationalist, brought here in the night by the enemy and executed, or perhaps only the corpse brought here, to be dumped. He was buried long after, with a minimum of formality. His name was Masse, perhaps Massey. No great store was set by him now, in patriotic circles. It was true he had done little for the cause. But he still had this monument. All that, and no doubt much more, Mercier and perhaps Camier had once known, and all forgotten.
> *(Mercier and Camier, p. 98)*

The simple inscription on the memorial quotes Terence MacSwiney,[25] who had also paid the ultimate sacrifice in his country's cause; it reads -

In proud and loving memory
of
Captain Noel Lemass
3rd Batt. Dublin City Brigade I.R.A.
who died that the Republic might live.
His murdered body was found
on this spot 13th Oct. 1923
R.I.P.

He has lived a beautiful life and has
left a beautiful field. He has sacrificed
the hour to give service for all time.
He has entered the company of the great
and with them he will be remembered for ever.

Terance McSwiney (sic)

2:13 The Lemass Memorial
on Glencree
(Photograph by D. Davison)

Terence MacSwiney was Lord Mayor of Cork in August 1919, when he was arrested by forces of the Crown, on the charge of 'being in possession of a document containing statements likely to cause disaffection of His Majesty.'[26] MacSwiney went on hunger strike to draw the world's attention to Ireland's claim to independence, and died on October 25th in Brixton jail, after seventy-three days without food -

> That reminds me, how long can one fast with impunity? The Lord Mayor of Cork lasted for ages, but he was young, and then he had political convictions, human ones too probably, just plain human convictions. And he allowed himself a sip of water from time to time, sweetened probably.
>
> *(Malone Dies, p. 275)*

There is, to say the least, a lack of enthusiasm for the Irish patriot's penchant for martyrdom in Beckett's writing.[27] Some would regard his sentiments as little short of treason, but many would welcome the realism of his detached analysis -

> Yes, that's what I like about me, at least one of the things, that I can say, Up the Republic! for example, or Sweetheart!, for example, without having to wonder if I should not rather have cut my tongue out, or said something else.
>
> *(Malone Dies, p. 236)*

Beckett put an old phrase to good use when a broadside headed 'The Question' was addressed to the 'Writers and Poets of England, Scotland, Ireland and Wales,' asking: 'Are you for or against the legal Government and the People of Republican Spain?'[28] This was signed in Paris in June 1937 by Beckett, Aragon, Auden, Nancy Cunard, Heinrich Mann, Pablo Neruda, Stephen Spender and Tristan Tzara among others. The writers addressed were asked for 'a statement in not more than 6 lines.' Some complied with the request, many exceeded the limit; Beckett's statement was the briefest: 'UPTHEREPUBLIC'.

Indeed, the Irishman's preoccupation with political history often perpetuates sectarian discord, and so firmly shackled does he become with the past that he is blinded to the inevitable changes of time, and incapable of looking towards the near, to say nothing of the distant, future -

> What constitutes the charm of our country, apart of course from its scant population, and this without help of the meanest contraceptive, is that all is derelict, with the sole exception of history's ancient faeces. These are ardently sought after, stuffed and carried in procession. Wherever nauseated time has dropped a nice fat turd you will find our patriots, sniffing it up on all fours, their faces on fire.
>
> *(First Love, pp. 8-9)*

2:14 The summit of Glencree
(Photograph by D. Davison)

Waiting for Godot is a timeless play. No detail dates the drama or its message to any age. It will adapt to the theatre of the future as readily as it has done to the twentieth century stage. As it is timeless, so too, it is placeless, demanding little more for its setting than a strange tree, a country road and desolation. Beckett removed most, but not quite all, detail that might permit identification of place in *Godot*. He wished to create, as Con Leventhal so aptly put it, 'a cosmic state, a world condition in which all humanity is involved.'[29]. He sought to free us from the restrictions that a specific location would place on interpretation. Beckett did not wish us to see the tramps as 'a pair of Joxers in a Limbo of the Dublin Liberties,'[30] or a couple of peasants on a country road in Roussillon. Perhaps then one should desist from even suggesting an influence in Beckett's setting for *Godot*. Might it be better to refrain from touching something so precious for fear of damaging it? And yet ...! Walking the summits of the Dublin mountains, in certain weathers the mood of *Godot* is so palpable, that though the urge emphatically to locate the drama there might be resisted, a director in search of inspiration for the ideal setting for *Godot* could not find better than the lonely summit of Glencree (2:14), with its occasional threatened tree (2:15). Here, Estragon and Vladimir might have settled as did Mercier and Camier before them.[31] The tree defies accurate description -

> VLADIMIR: He said by the tree. *(They look at the tree.)* Do you see any others?
> ESTRAGON: What is it?
> VLADIMIR: I don't know. A willow.
> ESTRAGON: Where are the leaves?
> VLADIMIR: It must be dead.
> ESTRAGON: No more weeping.
> VLADIMIR: Or perhaps it's not the season.
> ESTRAGON: Looks to me more like a bush.
> VLADIMIR: A shrub.
> ESTRAGON: A bush.
>
> *(Waiting for Godot, p. 14)*

From the summits of Dublin's mountains there are magnificent views of the neighbouring peaks, the mountains and valleys of Wicklow to the south, the plains of Meath to the north-west, the city to the north-east (2:16), and to the east the harbour of Dun Laoghaire, Dublin Bay, Howth, Ireland's Eye, Lambay Island, and further east, Wales (2:17) -

> The first thing they had to do of course when they got to the top was admire the view, with special reference to Dun Laoghaire framed to perfection in the

2:15 A tree on Glencree
(Photograph by D. Davison)

shoulders of Three Rock and Kilmashogue, the long arms of the harbour like an entreaty in the blue sea. Young priests were singing in a wood on the hillside. They heard them and they saw the smoke of their fire. To the west in the valley a plantation of larches nearly brought tears to the eyes of Belacqua, till raising those unruly members to the slopes of Glendoo, mottled like a leopard, that lay beyond, he thought of Synge and recovered his spirits.

(More Pricks than Kicks, p. 100)

Synge, like Beckett, knew the mountains of Dublin and Wicklow well and wrote about them with feeling and affection -

I have gone on, mile after mile, of the road to Sally Gap, between brown dikes and chasms in the turf, with broken foot-bridges across them, or between sheets of sickly moss and bog-cotton that is unable to thrive. The road is caked with moss that breaks like pie-crust under my feet, and in corners where there is shelter there are sheep loitering, or a few straggling grouse ... The fog has come down in places; I am meeting multitudes of hares that run round me at a little distance - looking enormous in the mists - or sit up on their ends against the sky line to watch me going by. When I sit down for a moment the sense of loneliness has no equal. I can hear nothing but the slow running of water and the grouse crowing and chuckling underneath the band of cloud. Then the fog lifts and shows the white empty roads winding everywhere, with the added sense of desolation one gets passing an empty house on the side of a road.[32]

2:16　The city of Dublin and the plains of Meath from Tibradden summit (Photograph by D. Davison)

2:17 The neighbouring Dublin mountain peaks from the rath on Tibradden; Three Rock is to the right, Kilmashogue to the left and between these summits lies the sea with Dun Laoghaire harbour, and on the horizon Lambay Island
(Photograph by D. Davison)

The Wicklow mountains to the south did not have the same appeal as the Dublin peaks for the lovers in 'Love and Lethe'[33] (2:18) -

Wicklow, full of breasts with pimples, he refused to consider. Ruby agreed.
(More Pricks than Kicks, p. 100)

Though in *Krapp's Last Tape*, the aged Krapp recalls the happier days of his youth when he walked Croghan, one of the Wicklow mountains, with his Kerry Blue terrier and listened to the Sunday church bells in the town beneath -

Be again on Croghan on a Sunday morning, in the haze, with the bitch, stop and listen to the bells.

(Krapp's Last Tape, p. 63)

The rich pasture-land of the Wicklow valleys, often called the 'Garden of Erin', contrasts with the bleakness of the Dublin mountain summits -

I had heard tell, I must have heard tell of the view, the distant sea in hammered lead, the so-called golden vale so often sung, the double valleys, the glacial loughs, the city in its haze, it was all on every tongue.

(Texts for Nothing, p. 72)

Looking south from the Dublin peaks there is the pastoral elegance of Wicklow, and to the north, the city, and the plains of Meath beyond are visible[34] -

> Sometimes it's the sea, other times the mountains, often it was the forest, the city, the plain too, I've flirted with the plain too.
>
> *(Texts for Nothing, p. 73)*

But for Beckett, much of the magic of the Dublin mountains is in the ever-changing view of the sea to the east. Dublin Bay with its ships, islands, promontories, and most importantly Dun Laoghaire harbour with its granite piers reaching out to sea 'like a woman making to cover her breasts',[35] is commented on many times. In *How It Is*, the scene for the lovers is the summit of a Dublin mountain peak with the city haze, and the towers and steeples of Dun Laoghaire in the distance -

> brief black and there we are again on the summit the dog askew on its hunkers in the heather it lowers its snout to its black and pink penis too tired to lick it we on the contrary again about turn introrse fleeting face to face transfer of things swinging of arms silent relishing of sea and isles heads pivoting as one to the city fumes silent location of steeples and towers heads back front as though on an axle.
>
> *(How It Is, p. 33)*

At night the Dublin mountains are cloaked in a silent blackness, softened by the light of the moon and stars above, and, in the distance, the blue-black of the sky blends with the purple sea from which it would be indistinguishable were it not for the distinctive lights of the city, its beacons and lighthouses, familiar to Beckett, as to his father -

> I saw the beacons, four in all, including a lightship. I knew them well, even as a child I had known them well. It was evening, I was with my father on a height, he held my hand. I would have liked him to draw me close with a gesture of protective love, but his mind was on other things. He also taught me the names of the mountains.
>
> *(The End, p. 69)*

2:18 The Wicklow mountains, 'full of breasts and pimples', as seen from near Tibradden with the 'golden vale' in the centre foreground (Photograph by D. Davison)

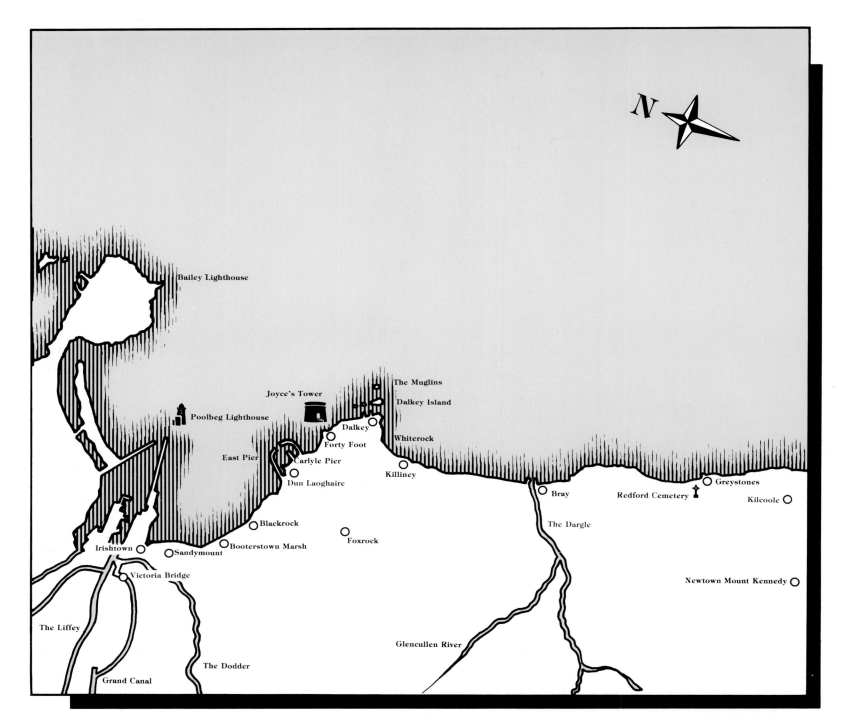

3:1 Dublin Bay and the coast

Page 74

Chapter Three

THE SEA

To Dublin's east lies the sea. Its influence is ever-present; it frames the city's skyline from every vantage point, most notably from the mountains. Dubliners take the sea, its sounds and smells for granted, but removed from it, their sense of loss can be profound, as with Henry in *Embers* -

> I'm like you in that, can't stay away from it,
> but I never go in...
>
> *(Embers, p. 94)*

The bathing areas of Sanydcove and Killiney, a short distance from Foxrock, were the seas in which Beckett swam. For topographical convenience, the sea and coast of the south-side of the city will be introduced as if a visitor to the area was travelling southwards from the city-centre to Wicklow[1](3:1). The north-city coastal areas of Malahide and Portrane that feature in the Fingal story in *More Pricks than Kicks* are considered in Chapter 8.

From Ringsend to Blackrock

In the story 'Love and Lethe', Belacqua prepares himself for a drive to the mountains, via the coast, with his girl of the day. This he does by fortifying himself with food and wine in a popular hostelry, probably the *Bailey* or *Davy Byrnes*, in Duke Street.[2] Our hero may be excused imbibing excessively as he anticipates the execution of a suicide pact for which he has already made the necessary preparations. Departing eventually the Duke Street pits for Irishtown, where Ruby resides, he terrorises the city's inhabitants 'in a swagger sports roadster'[3] of unstated pedigree -

> So fiercely indeed did he do this, though so far from being insured against third-party risks he was not even the holder of a driving-licence, that he scored a wake of objurgation as he sped through the traffic. The better-class pedestrians and cyclists turned and stared after him. 'These stream-lined Juggernauts' they said, shaking their heads, 'are a positive menace.' Civic Guards at various points of the city and suburbs took his number. In Pearse Street he smote off the wheel of a growler as cleanly as Peter Malchus's ear after the agony, but did not stop.
> *(More Pricks than Kicks, p. 96)*

To relish Belacqua's taste in motor cars, we must digress momentarily to a later chapter, where we meet his best man Hairy, also the worse for a pause in Duke Street, unable to locate the solitary hind-wheel Morgan (3:3) selected by Belacqua for his honeymoon[4] -

The best man had received instructions to collect in Molesworth Street the Morgan, fast but noisy, lent for the period of the high-time journey by a friend of the bboggses. Needless to say some eejit had parked it so far up towards the arty end that luckless Hairy, coming from the west upon the stand after the usual Duke Street complications, hastening along the shady southern pavement because he felt there was not a moment to lose, was almost in despair of ever finding the solitary hind-wheel that he had been advised to look out for.

(More Pricks than Kicks, p. 144)

Trodding on the gas for Irishtown, Belacqua encountered serious difficulties at the old Victoria Bridge over the Ringsend basin of the Royal Canal[5] (3:2) -

But before the terrible humped Victoria Bridge, its implacable bisection, in a sudden panic at his own temerity he stopped the car, got out and pushed her across with the help of a bystander. Then he drove quietly on through the afternoon and came in due course without further mishap to the house of his accomplice.

(More Pricks than Kicks, p. 96)

3:2   The Victoria Bridge
      (By courtesy *The Irish Times*)

3:3   A Morgan with a solitary
       hind-wheel
       (From an advertisement in
       The Irish Cyclist and Motor Cyclist,
       June 23, 1926)

After negotiating the Victoria Bridge, the level Ringsend Bridge over the river Dodder presented no difficulty and Belacqua reached Irishtown safely, where his paramour awaited him (3:4) -

> The Toughs, consisting of Mr and Mrs and their one and only Ruby, lived in a small house in Irishtown.
>
> *(More Pricks than Kicks, p. 91)*

Ringsend and Irishtown, once seaside villages on the outskirts of Dublin, have now been absorbed by the city's growth, and the encroachment of the city on the sea has removed them from the ocean they once enjoyed. Both areas have unusual personality, attributable in part to their seafaring traditions going back many centuries.[6] Belacqua enters Irishtown just as the public houses close for the 'Holy Hour', that dreadful hour after lunch, when the barmen are freed to rest and feed themselves in preparation for the evening[7] -

> It struck the half-hour in the hall. It was half-past two, that zero hour, in Irishtown.
>
> *(More Pricks than Kicks, p. 92)*

Departing abruptly from the Toughs, Ruby and Belacqua speed along

3:4   Irishtown: The open tram is
       going from Nelson's Pillar
       to Sandymount
       (By courtesy National Library of
       Ireland, Lawrence, Royal, 10963).

the coast by Sandymount (3:5) towards their destination, Tibradden mountain. The journey is given an urgent rhythm in the poem *Serena III* [8] -

> whereas dart away through the cavorting scapes
> bucket o'er Victoria Bridge that's the idea
> slow down slink down the Ringsend Road
> Irishtown Sandymount puzzle find the Hell Fire
> the Merrion Flats scored with a thrillion sigmas
> Jesus Christ Son of God Saviour His Finger
> girls taken strippin that's the idea
> on the Bootersgrad breakwind and water
> the tide making the dun gulls in a panic
> the sands quicken in your hot heart
> hide yourself not in the Rock keep on the move
> keep on the move

(Serena III, p. 25)

The 'Hell Fire' Club situated, as noted earlier, in the Dublin mountains is visible from Sandymount on a clear day. The 'Merrion Flats' are the sandy stretches at Merrion, the next suburb to Sandymount. When the tide is out, the sands rippled with 'a thrillion sigmas', extend for miles to the water-line. The irreverent reference to 'Jesus Christ Son of God

3:5 The strand at Sandymount Martello Tower; the rectangular structure in the foreground is an open sea swimming bath (Photograph by D. Davison)

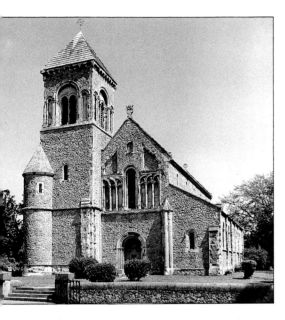

3:6 The Church of St. John the Evangelist, Sandymount (Photograph by E. O'Brien)

3:7 Sandymount Tower and Tram terminus (By courtesy National Library of Ireland, Lawrence, Royal 10956)

3:8 Booterstown marsh and bird sanctuary (Photograph by D. Davison)

Saviour His Finger/girls taken strippin' may be to the Church of John the Evangelist in Sandymount, the phallic round tower of which is visible from the coast road (3:6). There is also a Martello Tower at Sandymount which once served as a terminus for trams and buses (3:7) -

> The trams, the Blackrock, the Dun Laoghaire, the Dalkey, one Donnybrook and a little single-decker bound for Sandymount Tower, cried up to him from the causeway of Nassau Street, and passed.
>
> *(Dream of Fair to Middling Women, p 47)*

At Booterstown there is a small marsh[9] - 'on the Bootersgrad breakwind and water' (3:8). To the westward side of this marsh is the coast road from the city, and on the eastward or seaside, the railway from the city was built as a viaduct. Most of the marsh-land intervening between the sea and the mainland has been reclaimed, but the Booterstown marsh has been preserved as a sea-bird sanctuary.

Blackrock (3:9) - 'Hide yourself not in the Rock' - is a suburb of Dublin that had changed little over the years, but recently the erection of a large office and shopping development altered its character irrevocably.[10] However, in Beckett's day, Belacqua would have been free to speed down

its main street in his roadster without fear of impediment. Beyond Blackrock, he would have veered west to reach the Dublin mountains, but this narrative will continue along the coast road to visit other seaside locations that form part of the Beckett Country.

Dun Laoghaire

The coast-road from Blackrock continues through the Victorian sea-side resort areas of Monkstown and Salthill to Dun Loaghaire, where the churches and the town-hall, with their 'kindergartens of steeples',[11] dominate the Victorian architecture of the town(3:10). But it is the two large granite piers, the West and the East, enclosing the harbour of Dun Laoghaire, that give this seaside town its individual character.[12] The harbour, with its three yacht clubs, is a haven for the yachting fraternity. Within the harbour, enclosed by the mighty east and west piers, there is a smaller wooden jetty, the Carlyle pier[13]. From here, the mail-boat

3:9 Blackrock Village: the main street with a No.8 Tram travelling from Dalkey to Nelson's Pillar (By courtesy National Library of Ireland, Lawrence, Royal 9115)

once departed for Holyhead[14](3:11). It was here on a stanchion[15] that Belacqua's love got the better of him in a moment of passion after the departure of his once-beloved on the mail-boat (3:12) -

> Belacqua sat on the stanchion at the end of the Carlyle Pier in the mizzle in love from the girdle up with a slob of girl called Smeraldina-Rima whom he had encountered one evening when as luck would have it he happened to be tired and her face more beautiful than stupid. So he now sagged on the stanchion in the grateful mizzle after the supreme adieu, his hands in a jelly in his lap, his head drooped over his hands, pumping up the little blirt. He sat working himself up to the little gush of tears that would exonerate him.
>
> *(Dream of Fair to Middling Women, p. 2)*

The piers of Dun Laoghaire have acquired a place of immense significance in literary history; it was on the east pier, one fateful night, that Beckett saw the course he would pursue in his literature (3:13). Carlton Lake has written of this moment: 'Like Saul on the road to Damascus, like Paul Valéry during his *nuit de Gênes*, Beckett had his

3:10 Dun Laoghaire Harbour with the steeple of St. Michael's Church to the left and that of the Town Hall to the right
(By courtesy Bord Fáilte, No. D 58/517)

Page 82

blinding revelation one stormy postwar night as he wandered around the Dublin harbor area. He suddenly realised he had one subject - himself - and henceforward he would tell that story, with all its dark side, directly, through a narrator whose voice would always be his own. What he had recorded over the years, he would now play back.'[16]

This revelation, for such is the word that Beckett applies, however reticently,[17] to the event, is portrayed vividly and poignantly in the play, *Krapp's Last Tape.* [18] An early draft version of the play in the Humanities Research Center at Austin is of particular interest as it identifies, not only the pier, the East Pier, but also locates precisely the spot on this 3,500 foot granite pier where the event occurred -

> Intellectually a year of profound gloom until that wonderful night in March, at the end of the pier, in the high wind, when suddenly I saw the whole thing. The turning-point, at last. This, I imagine, is what I have chiefly to set down this evening, against the day when my work will be done and perhaps no place in my memory, and no thankfulness, for the miracle - *(pause)* - for the fire that set it alight. What I saw was that the assumption I had been going on all my life, namely - *(He switches off machine impatiently, winds tape forward, switches on again)* - granite rocks the foam flying up in the light of the beacon and the anemometer spinning like a propeller, clear to me at last that the dark I have struggled to keep at bay
> ~~out of my work~~ is in reality my most valuable - *(He curses, switches off, winds tape forward, switches on again)* - strange association till my dying day of storm and night with the light of understanding and the - *(He curses louder, switches off, winds tape forward, switches on again.)* [19]

The delicate anemometer (3:14), some 600 feet from the lighthouse beacon at the end of the pier (3:15), perched on top of a granite building of Greco-Egyptian style, has recorded wind speed and direction since 1852.[20] In the published version of *Krapp's Last Tape* the words 'beacon' and 'anemometer' have been changed to 'lighthouse' and 'wind-guage.'[21]

The episode on the East Pier of Dun Laoghaire is of interest, not only for the profundity of the revelation, but also because Beckett alludes, for the first time, to motivating influences in his literature,[22] even if later he excuses the indulgence -

> Sneers at what he calls his youth and thanks to God that its over. *(Pause.)* False ring there. *(Pause.)* Shadows of the opus ... magnum. Closing with a - *(brief laugh.)* - yelp to Providence.

(Krapp's Last Tape, p. 58)

3:11   The mail-boat *Connaught* at the Carlyle Pier; stanchions are to right, a train is ready to pull away and the East Pier with its anemometer and bandstand is in the background (Photograph: William Cavanagh; by courtesy James Fitzgibbon)

The Forty Foot

The young Becketts, like most Dubliners, were brought to the sea at an early age. Many coves and strands were within easy reach of *Cooldrinagh*, and at Dun Laoghaire there were the Victorian sea-water baths. However, it would seem that William Beckett, who swam in the all-male preserve known as the Forty Foot (3:16) at Sandycove deemed it a fitting place to introduce his children to the water[23] -

> You stand at the tip of the high board. High above the sea. In it your father's upturned face. Upturned to you. You look down to the loved trusted face. He calls to you to jump. He calls, Be a brave boy. The red round face. The thick moustache. The greying hair. The swell sways it under and sways it up again. The far call again, Be a brave boy. Many eyes upon you. From the water and from the bathing place.
>
> *(Company, p. 23-24)*

A high diving board and water feature again in the poem *For Future*

3:12 The Carlyle Pier and railway siding with passengers disembarking from the mail-boat
(By courtesy National Library of Ireland)

3:13 The East Pier, Dun Laoghaire
(Photograph by D. Davison)

Page 86

Reference, in which disdain and fear for a school-teacher at Portora are expressed -

> And then the bright waters
> beneath the broad board
> the trembling blade of the streamlined divers
> and down to our waiting
> to my enforced buoyancy ...

(For Future Reference, p. 299)

Beckett's childhood experiences in the Forty Foot with his father were to leave lasting impressions on him. According to Laurence Harvey, Beckett was 'plagued by a recurring nightmare in which he was required to dive into a small and distant pool closely ringed by jagged rocks'[24] -

> But his fatigue was so great, at the end of this long day, and his bedtime so long past, and the desire for rest so strong in consequence, and the desire for warmth, that he stooped, very likely with the intention of setting down his bags, on the floor, and of shutting the door, and of sitting down at the table, and of putting his arms on the table, and of burying yes of burying his head in his arms, and who knows perhaps even of falling, after a moment or two, into an uneasy sleep, lacerated by dreams, by dives from dreadful heights into rocky waters, before a numerous public.

(Watt, pp. 220-221)

The Beckett children, however, soon came to terms with the sea and became strong swimmers, as is evident from Samuel Beckett's sporting achievements at Portora Royal School which are considered in Chapter 4.

The Forty Foot is a deep water cove situated on a granite promontory at Sandycove. An early morning plunge in the cold deep waters of the Forty Foot brings a sense of vitality and tranquility, that elevates thought above the babble of the world (3:17). As Mervyn Wall has observed - 'Nearly everyone of note in Dublin who swims at all, has at one time or another bathed in the Forty Foot'.[25] The derivation of the name is uncertain, and theories abound: some say it denotes the depth of water, others the diameter of the swimming area, and yet others attribute the name to the Fortieth Foot Regiment which may have been stationed in the Battery or Martello Tower dominating the cove, or to a road known as The Forty Foot Road (Marine Road) in the vicinity. Whatever the origin of the name, its place in literature has been well established by L.A.G. Strong, Oliver Gogarty and Mervyn Wall. The most illustrious occupant of the Martello Tower which overlooks the Forty Foot was James Joyce, who chose the setting to open *Ulysses*.[26]

3:14 The Anemometer on the East Pier at Dun Laoghaire (Photograph by D. Davison)

3:15 The beacon on the
East Pier at Dun Laoghaire
(Photograph by D. Davison)

3:16 A lone diver at the
Forty Foot at Sandycove;
Howth is in the distance
(Photograph by D. Davison)

Coliemore and Dalkey Island

From Sandycove the coast road south takes one through the small
harbour of Bullock, and on to another fishing harbour, Coliemore[27] across
from which lies Dalkey Island. This is the setting for the macabre climax
in *Malone Dies*. A local lady of kindly disposition takes a group of lunatics
on an outing from the mental institute, the House of Saint John of God -

> Lady Pedal was not the only one to take an interest in the inmates of Saint John
> of God's, known pleasantly locally as the Johnny Goddams, or the Goddam
> Johnnies, not the only one to treat them on an average once every two years to
> excursions by land and sea through scenery renowned for its beauty or grandeur
> and even to entertainments on the premises such as whole evenings of
> prestidigitation and ventriloquism in the moonlight on the terrace, no, but she
> was seconded by other ladies sharing her way of thinking and similarly blessed
> in means and leisure.
>
> *(Malone Dies p. 282)*

From Coliemore Harbour, the ill-fated group set out for Dalkey Island
in a boat (3:18) -

> The boat. Room, as in the waggonette, for twice as many, three times, four times,
> at a pinch. A land receding, another approaching, big and little islands
>
> *(Malone Dies p. 287)*

3:17 Morning sun at the
Forty Foot
(Photograph by D. Davison)

3:18   Coliemore Harbour and
        Dalkey Island
        (By courtesy National Library
        of Ireland, Lawrence, 8919)

3:19   Killiney and the Wicklow
        mountains from Dalkey Sound
        (Photograph by D. Davison)

As the boat crosses Dalkey Sound, Malone imagining the receding shore and the Dublin mountains in the distance (3:19) is reminded of his childhood, of the gorse and the stonecutters hammers -

> Lemuel watches the mountains rising behind the steeples beyond the harbour, no they are no more
>
> No, they are no more than hills, they raise themselves gently, faintly blue, out of the confused plain. It was there somewhere he was born, in a fine house, of loving parents. Their slopes are covered with ling and furze, its hot yellow bells, better known as gorse. The hammers of the stone-cutters ring all day like bells.
> *(Malone Dies, p. 287-288)*

Dalkey Island (3:20), comprising an area of about 29 acres, is the largest of a group of small islands connected to each other by a reef.[28] Next to Dalkey Island lies Lamb Island, partially covered with grass, and adjoining which are two granite islets covered with sea-wrack, Clare Rock and Maiden Rock, (the latter deriving its name from an old tale of young girls from the mainland who were surrounded by the tide and perished in view of their parents). To the north are the Muglin Rocks, the famous execution site of two notorious eighteenth-century pirates[29] -

> The island. A last effort. The islet. The shore facing the open sea is jagged with creeks. One could live there, perhaps happy, if life was a possible thing, but nobody lives there. The deep water comes washing into its heart, between high

walls of rock. One day nothing will remain of it but two islands, separated by a gulf, narrow at first, then wider and wider as the centuries slip by, two islands, two reefs.

(Malone Dies, p. 288)

The only life on the island now is a herd of goat, but it has served many unusual functions in its history. In 1575, during an epidemic of plague in the city of Dublin, many of the well-to-do citizens took refuge on the island. In the late nineteenth century it was proposed to make the island a lazaretto for vessels coming from countries subject to quarantine. The Government took possession of the island and erected a battery, but the plan for a sanatorium never materialised.[30] The island has a number of wells and three buildings: a Martello Tower, built in 1804 in anticipation of the threatened Napoleonic invasion, (unique in that is entered from the top),[31] a ruined battery and an ancient church, dedicated to the patron saint of Dalkey, St. Begnet (3:21) -

> Suddenly she turned and said, You know, on the island, there are Druid remains.
>
> *(Malone Dies, p. 288)*

The ruined church, considered by Wakeman to be an example of an early Christian church, has been much modified over the years. Near the church there is a sacred well, and on one of these rocks a curious cross is engraved.[32] It may be to this that Lady Pedal was referring, or she may have mistaken the location of the 'Druids Chair' in Killiney. Among other strange uses to which the island has been put over the years few can have been more colourful than the election of the King of Dalkey who bore the proud title:

> 'His facetious Majesty, Stephen the First, King of Dalkey, Emperor of the Muglins, Prince of the Holy Island of Magee, Elector of Lambay and Ireland's Eye, Defender of his own faith and Respecter of all others, Sovereign of the illustrious Order of the Lobster and Periwinkle.'[33]

Hopefully, the island's history cannot match the carnage committed by Lemuel from the House of John of God, who having slaughtered the sailors and left the injured Lady Pedal to her fate, at length put to sea with his companions[34](3:22) -

3:20   Dalkey Island with its Martello Tower and St. Begnet's Church (Photograph by D. Davison)

> They are far out in the bay. Lemuel has shipped his oars, the oars trail in the water. The night is strewn with absurd
>
>   absurd lights, the stars, the beacons, the buoys, the lights of earth and in the hills the faint fires of the blazing gorse.
>
> *(Malone Dies, p. 289)*

3:21 St: Begnet's Church and
the Martello Tower on
Dalkey Island
(Photograph by D. Davison)

Killiney

Further south along the coast from Coliemore and visible from Dalkey Island is the beautiful bay at Killiney, likened by many to the bay of Naples (3:23). This bay is overlooked by a gorse-covered hill on top of which is an obelisk to Queen Victoria.[35] There is excellent bathing at Whiterock, a small cove on the bay, and on the long beach of Killiney, which is stony rather than sandy. It may have been here that Molloy collected the sucking stones, which 'abound on our beaches'[36]. The sucking of these stones - 'appeases, soothes, makes you forget your hunger, forget your thirst.'[37] They were also useful as ballast -

> I took advantage of being at the seaside to lay in a store of sucking-stones. They were pebbles but I call them stones. Yes, on this occasion I laid in a considerable store. I distributed them equally between my four pockets, and sucked them turn and turn about.

(Molloy, p. 69)

Perhaps Beckett's fascination with sucking stones derived from his observations of a Dublin eccentric, known as 'Stoney Pockets' who "walked round the Dublin streets with a pronounced tilt to one side, keeping his right-hand pocket filled with stones to straighten himself up, or as he sometimes claimed 'to keep his head from flying away."[38]

3:22　The Dublin coast-line and the Wicklow mountains from the sea at Dalkey Island (Photograph by D. Davison)

3:23　Killiney beach and bay; the Sugar Loaf mountain is to the right and Bray Head to the left (By courtesy Bord Fáilte, No. D 125/54)

At Whiterock there is a cave which would have been familiar to Beckett as it is to most children from the area[39] -

> These are some of the advantages and disadvantages of the seaside. Or perhaps it was I who was changing, why not? And in the morning, in my cave, and even sometimes at night, when the storm raged, I felt reasonably secure from the elements and mankind.
>
> *(Molloy, p. 75)*

To some the sea is a temptation, a temptation not easily resisted by many of Beckett's characters -

> ... perhaps he'll drown, he always wanted to drown, he didn't want them to find him, he can't want now any more, but he used to want to drown, he usen't to want them to find him ...
>
> *(I gave up before birth, p. 197)*

The sea is the setting for death in a number of Beckett's writings[40]. In *Embers*, the sound of the sea permeates the conscience of Henry -

> *(Rough sea. ADA cries out. Cry and sea amplified ,*
> *cut off. End of evocation. Pause. Sea calm. He*
> *goes back up deeply shelving beach. Boots laborious on shingle*
> *He halts. Pause. He moves on. He halts. Pause. Sea calm and faint.)*
>
> *(Embers, p. 100)*

The death by drowning of Henry's father is the pervading theme to the play *Embers*[41]. The location for the play is Killiney strand, though the main event, the father's death, took place at Howth, a peninsular promontory across the bay. The play opens with Henry telling his father's spirit that, though it is not long past noon, 'all the shore' and 'the sea out as far as the island'[42] are in shadow. His father lived on the other side of the bay so that he could have 'the sun on the water for that evening bathe' he took once too often. After his father's death, Henry moved residence to the Killiney side of the Bay - 'when I got your money I moved across ...' [43] That the location of his father's drowning was Howth is confirmed when Ada takes the old Howth tram:[44] '... then on down path to tram, up on open top and sits down in front'[45]. The statuesque posture of Henry's father, prior to his death, possibly by suicide, is one that Ada has observed also in his son (3:24) -

> He was sitting on a rock looking out to sea. I never forgot his posture. And yet it was a common one. You used to have it sometimes. Perhaps just the stillness, as if he had been turned to stone.
>
> *(Embers, p. 102)*

The location of another seaside suicide, in *Eh Joe*, is not clear,[46] but the mention of 'the viaduct' and 'the Rock' is suggestive of Whiterock. The railway from Dublin to the south courses along the coast and there are many low viaducts providing access to the strand (3:25) -

> All right ... Warm summer night ... All sleeping ... Sitting on the edge of her bed in her lavender slip ... You know the one ... Ah she knew you, heavenly powers! ... Faint lap of sea through open window ... Gets up in the end and slips out as she is ... Moon ... Stock ... Down the garden and under the viaduct ... Sees from the seaweed the tide is flowing ... Goes on down to the edge and lies down with her face in the wash ...
>
> *(Eh Joe, p. 20)*

The imagery of the mists and flowing sand, between the shingle and the dune, in a poem written in French in 1948,[47] has its origins in Killiney -

> my way is in the sand flowing
> between the shingle and the dune
> the summer rain rains on my life
> on me my life harrying fleeing
> to its beginning to its end
>
> my peace is there in the receding mist
> when I may cease from treading these long shifting
> thresholds
> and live the space of a door
> that opens and shuts
>
> *(Collected Poems, p. 59)*

3:24 A man in statuesque pose gazes on Dalkey Island and the Muglins beyond
(By courtesy National Library of Ireland, Lawrence 2183)

3:25 Whiterock Cove; the railway viaduct is in the background
(Photograph by D. Davison)

The Wicklow Coast

Continuing further south along the coast from Dublin to Wicklow County, the seaside village of Bray is reached (3:26). Once a popular and thriving resort, it has not fared well in recent years, and is mentioned only once in Beckett's work -

> 'But if it is merely a matter of getting me out of the way,' said Neary, 'while you work up Miss Counihan, why need I go to London? Why not Bray?'
>
> *(Murphy, p. 45)*

Greystones

> **'the bone-yard by the sea'**
> *(More Pricks than Kicks, p. 203)*

Beckett was greatly attracted by graveyards. One of his favourites was the ancient burial ground at Tully, but all graveyards had a certain appeal -

> Or I wander, hands clasped behind my back, among the slabs, the flat, the leaning and the upright, culling the inscriptions. Of these I never weary, there are always three or four of such drollery that I have to hold on to the cross, or the stele, or the angel, so as not to fall.
>
> *(First Love, p. 2)*

Samuel Beckett's parents are buried in the small seaside cemetery of Redford, near Greystones (3:27), a fishing village within easy reach of Foxrock. As a graveyard it does not rank highly in Beckett's estimation -

> But my father's yard was not amongst my favourite. To begin with it was too remote, way out in the wilds of the country on the side of a hill, and too small, far too small, to go on with. Indeed it was almost full, a few more widows and they'd be turning them away.
>
> *(First Love, pp. 2-3)*

Nevertheless it was this little graveyard that Beckett chose for the climax of Belacqua's love cycle in the story 'Draff' (3:28) -

> In the cemetery the light was failing, the sea moonstone washing the countless toes turned up, the mountains swarthy Uccello behind the headstones. The loveliest little lap of earth you ever saw.
>
> *(More Pricks than Kicks, p. 195)*

Here, the moonlight shining on the headstones, and the sea of Greystones provided a romantic setting -

> What with the company of headstones sighing and gleaming like bones, the moon on the job, the sea tossing in her dreams and panting, and the hills observing their Attic vigil in the background, he was at a loss to determine off-hand whether the scene was of the kind that is termed romantic or whether it should not with

3:26 Bray in its hey-day
(By courtesy National Library
of Ireland, Eason 3869)

3:27 Redford Cemetery, Greystones
(Photograph by D. Davison)

3:28 The sea and Greystones
Village from Redford Cemetery
(Photograph by D. Davison)

more justice be deemed classical. Both elements were present, that was indisputable. Perhaps classico-romantic would be the fairest estimate. A classico-romantic scene.

(More Pricks than Kicks, p. 204)

The Wicklow mountains (3:29) in the distance, with a Paul Henry look about them, added the final touches -

Hairy, gazing straight before him through the anti-dazzle windscreen, whose effect by the way on the mountains was to make them look not unlike the picture by Paul Henry, was inclined to think that it was about time they started to make a move.

(More Pricks than Kicks p. 203)

Paul Henry (1877-1958), one of Ireland's best known landscape artists, was renowned for his interpretation of the light and colour so unique to the Irish landscape.

At Redford, with its view of the sea, the hero Belacqua was laid to rest by his beloved Smeraldina, the obsequies being performed by the undertaker Malacoda (3:30) -

Malacoda and Co. turned up bright and early with their six cylinder hearse, black as Ulysses's cruiser.

(More Pricks than Kicks, p. 198)

3:29 The Wicklow hills from
Redford Cemetery
(Photograph by D. Davison)

3:30 A grave-digger at
Redford Cemetery
(Photograph by E. O'Brien)

After his father's death in 1933, Beckett wrote the poem, *Malacoda*, in which he depicted, with ruthless economy, the functional efficiency of the undertaker that makes such a mockery of life -

> thrice he came
> the undertaker's man
> impassible behind his scutal bowler
> to measure
> is he not paid to measure
> this incorruptible in the vestibule
> this malebranca knee-deep in the lilies
> Malacoda knee-deep in the lilies
> Malacoda for all the expert awe
> that felts his perineum mutes his signal
> sighing up through the heavy air
> must it be it must be it must be
> find the weeds engage them in the garden
> hear she may see she need not
>
> to coffin
> with assistant ungulata
> find the weeds engage their attention
> hear she must see she need not
>
> to cover
> to be sure cover cover all over
> your targe allow me hold your sulphur
> divine dogday glass set fair

(Malacoda, p. 26)

When his mother moved to live in Greystones, the little cemetery of Redford was close-by. Here, perhaps, she found solace in being close to her husband, and was able to contemplate the approaching day when she must join him, as did the old woman in *Worstward Ho* [48] -

> Nothing and yet a woman. Old and yet old. On unseen knees. Stooped as loving memory some old gravestones stoop. In that old graveyard. Names gone and when to when. Stoop mute over the graves of none.

(Worstward Ho, p. 45)

Like his mother, and the narrator of *First Love*, Beckett probably visited his father's grave from time to time (3:31), and on such visits, he no doubt took the opportunity of picnicking -

> I visited, not so long ago, my father's grave, that I do know, and noted the date of his death, of his death alone, for that of his birth had no interest for me, on that particular day. I set out in the morning and was back by night, having lunched lightly in the graveyard. But some days later, wishing to know his age at death, I had to return to the grave, to note the date of his birth.

(First Love, p. 1)

3:31 The Beckett tombstone at
Redford Cemetery
(Photograph by D. Davison)

As always there was contentment in his father's company -

> Personally I have no bone to pick with graveyards, I take the air there willingly, perhaps more willingly than elsewhere, when take the air I must. The smell of corpses, distinctly perceptible under those of grass and humus mingled, I do not find unpleasant, a trifle on the sweet side perhaps, a trifle heady, but how infinitely preferable to what the living emit, their feet, teeth, armpits, arses, sticky foreskins and frustrated ovules. And when my father's remains join in, however modestly, I can almost shed a tear. The living wash in vain, in vain perfume themselves, they stink. Yes, as a place for an outing, when out I must, leave me my graveyards and keep - you - to your public parks and beauty-spots. My sandwich, my banana, taste sweeter when I'm sitting on a tomb, and when the time comes to piss again, as it so often does, I have my pick.
>
> *(First Love, pp. 1-2)*

Beckett was not alone among the Irish in favouring a graveyard for a picnic, as a delightful nineteenth century photograph shows (3:32). Redford cemetery and the old graveyard at Tully are small burial grounds of which only the former is now in use. Neither are well-known. Glasnevin cemetry, however, where the Great Liberator, Daniel O'Connell rests, is one of Dublin's largest cemeteries.[49] It receives mention in the original French version of *Malone Meurt* as 'nom d'un cimetière local très estimé', but not in the subsequent English translation -

> C'est l'amour qui nous conduit
> La main dans la main vers Glasnevin
> C'est le meilleur du chemin
> A mon avis au tien aussi
> Mais oui
> A notre avis.
>
> *(Malone Meurt, p. 148)*

Dublin obsequies have been carefully observed and recorded by Beckett. In 'What a Misfortune', Hairy, in pursuit of his duties as Belacqua's best man, encountered a cortege on Parliament Street, where he declined to observe a long-established Irish custom[50] -

> In Parliament Street a funeral passed and Hairy did not uncover. Many of the chief mourners, consoling themselves in no small measure with the reverence expressed by every section of the community, noticed with rage in their hearts that he did not, though to be sure they made no allusion to it at the time. Let this be a lesson to young men, strangers perhaps to sorrow, to uncover whenever a funeral passes, less in act of respect towards the defunct than in sympathetic acknowledgement of the survivors. One of these fine days Hairy will observe, from where he sits bearing up bravely behind the hearse in a family knot, a labourer let go of his pick with one hand, or gay dandy snatch both his out of his pockets, in a gesture of more value and comfort than a ton of lilies. Take the case of Belacqua, who ever since the commitment of his Lucy wears a hat, contrary to his inclination, on the off chance of his encountering a cortège.
>
> *(More Pricks than Kicks, p. 144)*

3:32 A graveside picnic at
Clonmacnois
(By courtesy National Library of
Ireland, Lawrence, Royal 5149)

Kilcoole

Further south along the Wicklow coast from Redford cemetery and
Greystones is the small village of Kilcoole. Kilcoole does not feature in
Beckett's published writing, but a seaside village named 'Kilcool'[51] is to
be found in an unpublished fragment of a dramatic monologue[52] which
is of importance both as a precursor to *Not I* and *That Time*, and as an
example of the relevance of the reality of childhood experience to
Beckett's creative technique.[53] Kilcoole is a small village lying about a
mile inland from the coast. The village itself possesses little of note,
but its coastal aspect offers an expanse of pebbled beach which is in
contrast to the more secluded coves of Dublin Bay. Kilcoole became
fashionable as a seaside resort for Dubliners in the early part of the
century, and among those who rented a summer house for his family
at Kilcoole was William Beckett.[54] The Wicklow/Dublin railway line runs
along the western aspect of Kilcoole strand and a lone signal box on this
stark but beautiful strip of coast represents what passes for a railway
station in this part of the Beckett Country.[55]

The reality that emerges from the 'Kilcool' monologue is that of an orphaned girl recalling her journey from Dublin to 'Kilcool' to live with her 'widowed childless Aunt'. She travels to Bray on 'the Slow and Easy' (the Dublin and South Eastern third class coast line) and onwards along the coast with its 'beautiful view all bare and glitter'. The railway passes through the promontory of Bray Head -'tunnels through the Head'- and after passing the graveyard -'Redford by the sea'- reaches Kilcoole[56](3:33).

The Silver Strand and Jack's Hole

There are a number of popular sandy beaches in County Wicklow. Two of these, the Silver Strand and Jack's Hole, merit mention in the unpublished *Dream of Fair to Middling Women*. These locations are of considerable interest because it can be deduced from the Alba's possessions, and her behaviour, that the love scene in Jack's Hole has some similarities to the later drama, *Happy Days*. Like Winnie, who has a nailfile among the many possessions in her fathomless bag,[57] so too does the Alba's bag contain such an instrument -

> Side by side, touching, they recline in the shadow of a great rock, chosen by him for the shadow it gave, on the Silver Strand. She has rummaged in her fathomless

3:33   The beach and railway halt
at Kilcoole
(Photograph by D. Davison)

3:34 The Silver Strand, Co. Wicklow
(Photograph by D. Davison)

bag, she has taken out from it scissors and file, she is beautifying his fingers, hurting him slightly in her determination to leave not one lunula undiscovered, pleasantly aware that she is causing him a little pain, grousing *Avalen* this time, the refrain over and over again, swallowing from time to time little flaws of saliva, born of her absorption. They are entrenched behind a low palissade of bottles driven into the pale sand. Beyond the palissade two gulls skirmishing for a sandwich fascinate the wincing lover.

(Dream of Fair to Middling Women, p. 166)

At first it seems that the location for this love scene is the Silver Strand (3:34), a golden strip of sand and sea to the south of Wicklow town, but on deeper scrutiny we find it is the small cove known as Jack's Hole (3:35), further south again, closer to the popular resort of Brittas Bay[58] -

Not that the Silver Strand - looking back through our notes we are aghast to find that it was Jack's Hole; but we cannot use that, that would be quite out of place in what threatens to come down a love passage - not that it were (mood of Fall indispensable) by any manner of means definitely hostile as atmosphere and soape to the Olympian romance that may break over it now at any moment....

(Dream of Fair to Middling Women, p. 168)

This once quiet cove, with its stretch of golden sand, its dunes, its sea-wrack, its rock rising in sea-sculpted majesty, and over all a sky of

3:35 Jack's Hole, Co. Wicklow
(Photograph by D. Davison)

inconstant mood, offers as picturesque a variety of seascape as any to be found in Ireland (3:36) -

> The rock was there, crumbling beyond a shadow of doubt, into dust; the wind was on the job, exfoliating the wrack; the inconstance of the sky was incontestable. And, over and above all these conditions, the fickle sea and sand. Lying there to a casual eye so calm between its headlands this little beach, without being the Bride of the Adriatic or anything of that kind and in spite of its leaving a few trees to be desired, furnished as neat a natural comment on the ephemeral sophism as any to be had in the Free State. Which is saying the hell of a lot.
> *(Dream of Fair to Middling Women, pp. 168-169)*

3:36 Rock formation at Jack's Hole
(Photograph by D. Davison)

Chapter Four

EDUCATION

They loaded me down with their trappings
and stoned me through the carnival.
(The Unnamable, p. 327)

There are few references in Samuel Beckett's writings to the institutes in which he received his education. Those comments that he does make can be revealing and are often humorous. His education began at the age of five in the kindergarten of the Misses Elsner in Foxrock.[1] The influence of these ladies may have been more one of personality than of learning, but they did make a lasting impression on Beckett and their place in his literature has been considered in Chapter 1. After the Elsner kindergarten, Beckett went with his brother Frank to a primary school, the Earlsfort House School, then to Portora Royal School in Enniskillen. For his undergraduate university education, Beckett attended Trinity College, Dublin.

The Earlsfort House School

The Earlsfort House School was situated at Nos. 3 and 4 Earlsfort Place (the original building has been demolished and the address is now no. 63, Adelaide Road), just a few minutes walk from Harcourt Street Station. This school was run by a Frenchman named Monsieur Alfred Le Peton, described in *Thom's Directory* as 'Professor of French'.[2]

Samuel Beckett attended this school, with his brother Frank, from about 1915 to 1920, an important period in Irish history; the Irish Free State was born out of the Easter Rising of 1916 and the execution of its leaders. How much effect this event was to have on Beckett we do not know. His distaste for Irish politics has already been alluded to. The sacrifice of life cannot, none the less, have been without effect on the boys of the Earlsfort House School.

Portora Royal School

4:1 Portora Royal School, Enniskillen, overlooking Lough Erne (By courtesy National Library of Ireland, Lawrence 4961)

Portora Royal School situated high on a hill overlooking Lough Erne (4:1) and the town of Enniskillen, Co. Fermanagh, in the province of Ulster, Northern Ireland, has educated the sons of Protestant gentlemen from all parts of Ireland for over three and a half centuries.[3] Ecumenical today in outlook, and more relaxed, no doubt, in the application of the disciplinary tradition of past centuries, the school, nevertheless, conveys to the visitor mounting the rising tree-bordered drive from the imposing memorial gates, a sense of austerity and pride that many a young newcomer might find forbidding (4:2). Founded in 1618, it should by right have celebrated its tercentenary in 1918, but 'in face of the tremendous crisis that convulses Europe and turns the fair plains of France and Flanders into a shambles ... no great celebrations in keeping with the dignity and prestige of the school' were held that year. So declared that most valuable of archives, the schoolboys' own magazine, *Portora*, in the Trinity term issue for 1918.[4]

The earliest record of a Beckett presence in the *Portora* is that of Frank, Samuel Beckett's older brother, who is listed twice among the forwards on the rugby team of 1919 which, incidentally, lost both games.[5] This issue of *Portora* is unique in publishing a photograph of the Christmas schoolplay, the name of which is not given. Frank Beckett, occupies a prominent place in this picture and from his royal costume and crown, and his position beside the leading 'lady', it can be assumed that his was the title 'male' role (4:3). Frank's theatrical ability is in evidence again

4:2   The main building of
Portora Royal School
(Photograph by D. Davison)

in a Hallow E'en concert in 1920[6], but his stay at Portora was most notable for his sporting achievements on the cricket and rugby fields.[7] In recognition of these, he was appointed Head of the House in 1919,[8] and Captain of the School Cricket X1 in 1920.[9]

Samuel Beckett joined his successful brother at Portora in the Easter (Hilary) term of 1920. We can only wonder at his impressions as he passed through the great door firmly set between Ionic pillars of Portland stone (4:3) and entered the austere school building. The school has, of course, changed considerably since Beckett's day, but there is still the atmosphere, almost an aroma, of a distant past reaching further back than most schoolboys care even to contemplate. The hallway and the dining-hall, in which classes were once held, are little changed (4:5).

Samuel Beckett seems to have settled in quickly and he does not appear to have been daunted by Frank's reputation. We find him playing well at half-back for the rugby team against Sligo Grammar School in his first term.[10] At the age of fifteen (4:6) young Samuel Beckett's place on the Cricket XI was firmly established–

3. The same. 15 years. Bareheaded. School blazer. Smiling.

(Film, Eh Joe, and other writings, p. 43)

4:3   The cast of the school play, Christmas 1918
Standing: Morton, G.; Allen, iii, C.F.; Killingley, ii, S.; Wilson, W.C.; Babington, A.O.; Jones, H.R.
Seated: Taylor, i, W.; Bor, i, G.T.; *Beckett, F.E.*; Warrington, ii, G.; Vaughan, V. St.G.; Graham, H.G.
(The numerals indicate brothers at the school. From *Portora*, 1919: *XIII*, No. 2 Facing p. 1. By courtesy the Headmaster, Portora)

4:4 The entrance hall of
Portora Royal School
(Photograph by D. Davison)

4:5 A school-class at Portora in the
early 'twenties
(By courtesy the Headmaster,
Portora)

4:6 Samuel Beckett (standing on
right) in the School Cricket XI
in 1921
(By courtesy the Headmaster,
Portora)

Like his brother, Samuel Beckett soon began to feature prominently in the *Portora* in rugby, swimming, boxing, and cricket.[11] These achievements were duly rewarded by caps in both rugby and cricket[12] (4:7), and appointment as a Junior Prefect, with his friend A.G. Thompson, in 1923.[13] Beckett may have had some misgivings about his schoolboy commitment to sport, if his feelings on the subject are those of the narrator in *Horn Came Always* -

> What ruined me at bottom was athletics. With all that jumping and running when I was young, and even long after in the case of certain events, I wore out the machine before its time. My fortieth year had come and gone and I still throwing the javelin.
>
> *(Horn Came Always, p. 194)*

The school archives at Portora have preserved a selection of photographs showing Samuel Beckett's achievements in sport (4:8, 4:9). However, of all the sporting activities in which Beckett indulged at Portora, the one of greatest relevance to his writing is swimming. As the Misses Elsner were to be remembered from early childhood, so too did a teacher from

4:7   Samuel Beckett wearing his
      cricket blazer and cap in 1923
      (By courtesy the Headmaster,
      Portora)

Portora, Mr. W. N. Tetley[14] (4:10), the mathematics and science master, who was also the swimming coach, make a lasting, if not very favourable impression, on Beckett -

> The hair shall be grey
> above the left temple
> the hair shall be grey there
>   abracadabra!
>   sweet wedge of birds faithless!
> God blast you yes it is we see
> God bless you professor
> we can't clap or we'd sink
> three cheers for the perhaps pitiful professor
> next per shaving? next per sh. . . . .?
> Well of all the . . . .!
> that little bullet-headed bristle-cropped
> red-faced rat of a pure mathematician
> that I thought was experimenting with barbed wire in
>   the Punjab,
> up he comes surging to the landing steps
> and tells me I'm putting no guts in my kick.[15]

(For Future Reference, pp. 299-301)

The unfortunate Tetley may also have contributed to the creation of Basil, later Mahood, in *The Unnamable* [16] -

> One in particular, Basil I think he was called, filled me with hatred. Without opening his mouth, fastening on me his eyes like cinders with all their seeing,

4:8   Samuel Beckett in the School
      Rugby XV, 1922-23
      (By courtesy the Headmaster,
      Portora)·

he changed me a little more each time into what he wanted me to be. Is he still glaring at me, from the shadows? Is he still usurping my name, the one they foisted on me, up there in their world, patiently, from season to season?

(The Unnamable, p. 300)

Vivian Mercier, who attended Portora after Beckett, has written of the surrounding countryside and lakes: 'Portora Royal School stands on a steep little hill just on the northern edge of the county town of Enniskillen. From the cricket pitch behind the School you can see Lower Lough Erne and all its islands, stretching away out of sight northwards. Hidden behind the slope of the hill on your right is the Narrows, a kind of strait through which the Erne passes on its way from Enniskillen to the lower lake. The river broadens out just beyond Portora, and the lake proper does not begin for a mile or so yet. Over to the west the horizon is bounded by the long whale's back of Mount Belmore.'[17] The boys from Portora swam in Lough Erne, usually in the Narrows[18] In 1920 the swimming facilities were greatly improved with the provision of a shed for changing, and the erection of a diving board on a stone parapet across the water of the Narrows[19](4:11). From the *Portora* it is apparent that the acquisition of a certificate of competence in swimming was no mean achievement: 'The definite swimming test which was enforced last

4:9   Samuel Beckett on the School
Cricket XI, 1923
(Each of the team has signed
his name on the caption to the
photograph. By courtesy the
Headmaster, Portora)

summer was again enforced this term and only those who have passed it satisfactorily have had their names placed upon the swimmers list.'[20] Whatever Beckett's later memories of the swimming test may have been, he seems to have passed it with ease in his first term at Portora[21]. Moreover, in 1921, he went on to win the Junior Long Race, the Junior Sprint Race, and the Junior Cup for swimming[22]. In 1923, he came second in the Senior Sprint Race across the Narrows, but had to abandon the Senior Long Race because of 'lack of training'.[23]

Of Beckett's academic progress at Portora, there is no record. It is possible that the quatrain, popular in the school during his latter years, is an example of a burgeoning wit, again at the expense of poor Tetley[24] -

> Tetley has gone
> To the mountains of Wales,
> Leaving behind
> His balance and Scales.

The piece was published in an unofficial student magazine *The Philiparabolic Adjudicator*, a parody of Enniskillen's *Impartial Recorder*, to commemorate Tetley's departure for Wales, and his replacement by a Mr. Scales as mathematics and science teacher.

4:10   Mr W.N. Tetley From *Portora*, Michaelmas 1925. Vol XIX No. 3. page 1. (By courtesy the Headmaster, Portora)

4:11   'The Narrows' on Lough Erne; the stone parapet from which the boys once dived is across the water (Photograph by D. Davison)

4:12 Portora Royal School and Lough Erne from the town of Enniskillen
(By courtesy National Library of Ireland, Eason 2133)

As all the prose and verse contributions to the *Portora* appear anonymously, it is not possible to attribute with certainty any of the contributions to Beckett. This, however, has not deterred Deirdre Bair [25] from doing so, even in the face of Beckett's denial of being the author of a piece of nonsense about Caesar,[26] which bears none of Beckett's literary characteristics. This attribution may have been encouraged by a note of doubtful credibility in the Beckett file at Portora, which states incorrectly that Beckett wrote for the School magazine under the pseudonym 'BAT'.

One contribution, however, does have some features of Beckett's literary style, and there is a reference in it, moreover, to Dante. This is a sonnet entitled *To the Toy Symphony.*[27] Signed by 'John Peel', it was written to commemorate the school orchestra's performance of Haydn's *Toy Symphony* in 1922. That Beckett was, at least, a contributor to this musical cacophony is confirmed by his contemporary, the late Dr. J.A. Wallace[28]: 'My main recollections of him at Portora (this is being honest, and excluding extrapolations from memories of him at T.C.D.) is of his cricketing ability, being a member of the small group of regular morning cold bathers, and of *playing some sort of bird-call in a prize day performance of Haydn's Toy Symphony* (my italics). He must have been one of the few boys in V or VI in my time who took music lessons.'

TO THE TOY SYMPHONY

(Being an effort in mangled metre after hearing the first practice.)

A crash, a shuddering cataclysm of sound
Which trembling hovers round on discord's brink;
And then it rises once again, to sink
To weird chaotic murmurings which wound
The poor, numb, jangled senses. While around
The tympanum they cluster, one would think
Such noises are the one surviving link
Between this world and that where Dante found
His wild exotic phantoms. Now the strain
Of fiddles rises through the din, now drums
Conquer the rest, and now to us amain
The treble squawking of the cuckoo comes.
But human words, though strong, can ne'er express
This unsymphonic clamour's awfulness.

JOHN PEEL

We can surmise that Beckett's school days at Portora were, on the whole happy, if for no other reason than because of his successful participation in sport. It is to be hoped, however, that Portora Royal School, high on its hill above Enniskillen (4:12), did not always influence Beckett's comments on an educational background -

> They gave me courses on love, on intelligence, most precious, most precious. They also taught me to count, and even to reason. Some of this rubbish has come in handy on occasions, I don't deny it, on occasions which would never have arisen if they had left me in peace. I use it still, to scratch my arse with. Low types they must have been, their pockets full of poison and antidote.
>
> *(The Unnamable, p. 300)*

Trinity College, Dublin

> **Spend the years of learning squandering**
> **Courage for the years of wandering**
> **Through a world politely turning**
> **From the loutishness of learning.**
>
> *(Gnome, p. 7)*

Samuel Beckett entered the Elizabethan University of Dublin in October 1923 at the age of seventeen to study arts, and later modern languages[29](4:13). He graduated with outstanding scholarship in 1927. Trinity College has an unique city centre location. The campus, secluded from the city by its high walls and railing, and surrounded by some of the finest architecture in Dublin, has an atmosphere of considerable charm. As an undergraduate, Beckett lived in rooms on the campus at 39, New Square (4:14), and when he returned to Trinity as lecturer in modern languages after two years at the Ecole Normale Superieure, he occupied no. 40, New Square. His quarters looked out on one of the College's peaceful squares -

> I had to ask her sister and she closed me the vowel. I wonder did I do well to leave my notes at home, in 39 under the east wind, weind please.
>
> *(Dream of Fair to Middling Women, p. 64)*[30]

Trinity College, was dominantly Protestant when Beckett was a student there. In fact, until recently Catholics were forbidden to enter the College, under pain of excommunication, unless granted a special dispensation by the Archbishop of Dublin[31] -

> 'Might I see him?' he whispered, like a priest asking for a book in the Trinity College Library.
>
> *(More Pricks than Kicks p. 194)*

4:13 Trinity College Dublin from
College Green
(By courtesy National Library
of Ireland, Eason 1744)

4:14 No 39, New Square,
Trinity College
(Photograph by E O'Brien)

Through photography, ageing man can view the milestones of his development. In *Film*, photographs of childhood and adult-life are used to depict ageing and maturation (4:15), in much the same way as Beckett adapted the tape-recorder in *Krapp's Last Tape* -

> The Same. 20 years. Graduation day. Academic gown. Mortar-board under arm. On a platform, receiving scroll from Rector. Smiling. Section of public watching.
>
> *(Film, pp. 43-44)*

Beckett's undergraduate days at Trinity were probably reasonably content,[32] but, as a lecturer with the academic potential that would lead to a chair, the decision to abandon the university for literature cannot have been an easy one. Academe, however, did not attract him and he later turned his humour and wit on the Fellows of the College, especially Senior Fellows (4:16) -

> Buttered toast was all right for Senior Fellows and Salvationists, for such as had nothing but false teeth in their heads. It was no good at all to a fairly strong young rose like Belacqua.
>
> *(More Pricks than Kicks, p. 12)*

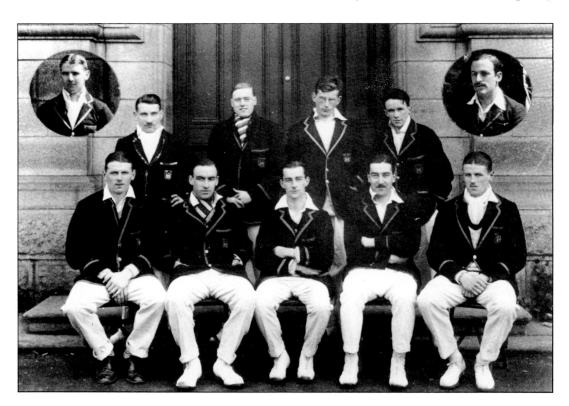

4:15 Samuel Beckett on the Cricket XI at Trinity College (By courtesy Trinity College, Dublin)

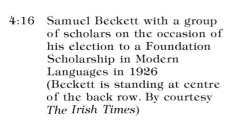

4:16 Samuel Beckett with a group of scholars on the occasion of his election to a Foundation Scholarship in Modern Languages in 1926 (Beckett is standing at centre of the back row. By courtesy *The Irish Times*)

Junior Fellows did not escape his invective either[33] -

> When Wylie called the following afternoon, four or five hours late, Neary's hair was white as snow, but he felt better in himself.
> 'A curious feeling came over me,' he said, 'just as you were leaving, that I was going to start dying.'
> 'So you have,' said Wylie. 'You look like a Junior Fellow already.'
>
> *(Murphy, p. 153)*

In the Fellows Garden, an idyllic reserve on the campus, great intellectual happenings might be witnessed -

> A divine creature, native of Leipzig, to whom Belacqua, round about the following Epiphany, had occasion to quote the rainfall for December as cooked in the Dublin University Fellows' Garden ejaculated:
> 'himmisacrakruzidirkenjesusmariaundjosefundblutigeskreuz'
>
> *(More Pricks than Kicks, p. 87)*

In a piece of satirical writing in *Watt*, Beckett ridiculed the academic administration of the College in what must rate as one of the wittiest pieces of farce ever written on academe. Ernest Louit seeking support for his dissertation demonstrates that the financial niceties of research are not necessarily related to the academic worth of the project -

> The title of his dissertation I well remember was The Mathematical Intuitions of the Visicelts, a subject on which he professed the strongest views, for he was a close companion of the College Bursar, their association (for it was nothing less) being founded on a community of tastes, and even I fear practices, all too common in academic circles, and of which perhaps the most endearing was brandy on awakening, which they did habitually in each other's society.
>
> *(Watt, p. 169)*

Page 123

The end result of the scholar Louit's association with the bursar was that the latter provided Louit with fifty pounds for a six-months 'Research expedition, in the County Clare.' When Louit, on his return, was called upon by the College Committee to produce the fruits of his academic endeavours he is at a loss to do so, as he had mislaid -

> ...on the very morning of his departure from the west, between the hours of eleven and midday, in the gentlemen's cloakroom of Ennis railway-station, the one hundred and five loose sheets closely covered on both sides with shorthand notes embracing the entire period in question.
>
> *(Watt, p. 171)*

Louit had not, however, returned empty handed. He produced a primitive capable of uttering on demand the square root of anything -

> The day and hour having been appointed, Louit was seen advancing, leading by the hand an old man dressed in kilt, plaid, brogues and, in spite of the cold, a pair of silk socks made fast to the purple calves by an unpretentious pair of narrow mauve suspenders, and holding a large black felt hat under his arm. Louit said, This, gentlemen, is Mr. Thomas Nackybal, native of Burren.
>
> *(Watt, p. 172)*

The farce concludes with the committee assembling in the examination hall to study the phenomenal Nackybal from Burren, in much the same manner as their equivalents in the discipline of psychology had tested the mathematical capabilities of the horse Hans.[34]

The examination hall in which the farce is set, and where Beckett would have sat many examinations and received his degree, has an architectural majesty heightened by the effect of light, a feature that not every student may have had time to notice (4:17) -

> Through the western windows of the vast hall shone the low red winter sun, stirring the air, the chambered air, with its angry farewell shining, whilst via the opposite or oriental apertures or lights the murmur rose, appeasing, of the myriad faint clarions of light.
>
> *(Watt, pp. 190-191)*

4:17   Graduation ceremony in the Examination Hall, Trinity College (By courtesy L. O'Connor, No74A)

An obscure reference to Trinity College has been noted by Rubin Rabinovitz[35]. Samuel Madden (1696-1765) left a bequest to Trinity College to establish a scholarly award, to which Beckett refers in the Addenda to *Watt* [36] - 'the maddened prizeman' - thereby suggesting, perhaps, that Watt's odyssey of suffering was an intellectual quest.

Trinity College, with its campus in the very heart of Dublin, was an ideal vantage point from where Samuel Beckett might observe the happenings in the surrounding city.

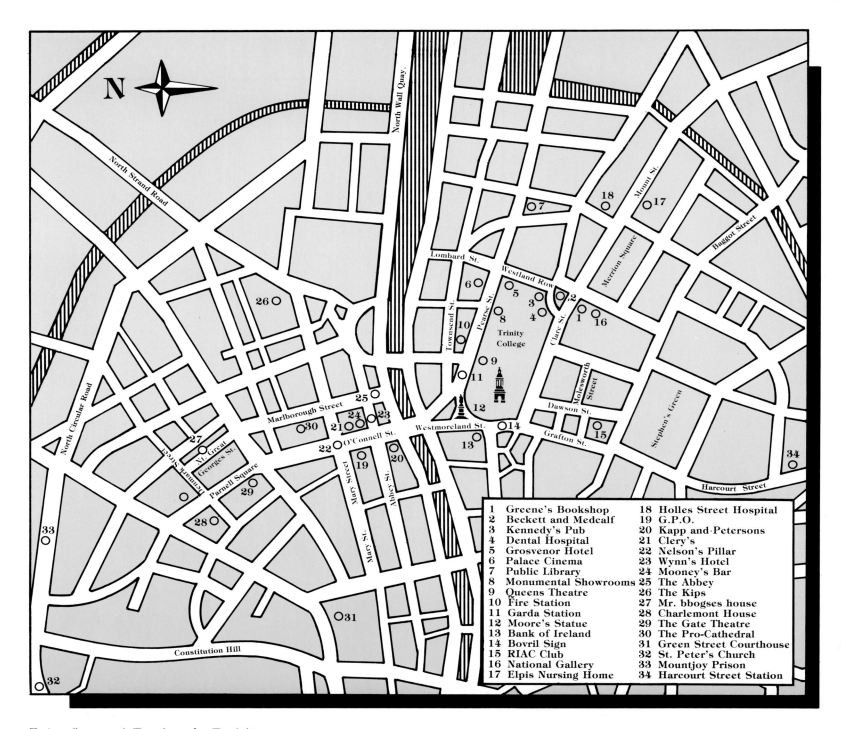

5:1   Samuel Beckett's Dublin.

Chapter Five

THE CITY

Dublin changed but little in structure or character in the first half of the twentieth century. Bloom's universe differed only in time from Beckett's city. The intimacy, lack of pretence, the Dubliner's humour and stoicism (some would say faith) that elevated drudgery to near happiness, the harmony of scale in all things, save, of course, prosperity, which held man's ambition within the realms of reasonable possibility, all contributed to making Dublin the largest village in Europe. And what village is without intrigue and hypocrisy? On the small stage of this theatre the emotions of life's pageant were enacted daily for anyone who cared to stop and look. Beckett was one who did, and the city is the stage on which he plays many of his dramas. Dublin's influence pervades his writings in mood and dialogue, and in the humour and personality of his characters.

The Dublin atmosphere emerges most strongly in *More Pricks than Kicks*. The vignettes in this novel are best not disturbed, but I have imposed a topographical order on Belacqua's peregrinations through the city (5:1), so that the reader, unfamiliar with Dublin, can revisit his haunts; in so doing it is well to bear in mind that Belacqua[1] did not suffer company kindly. Within this scheme references to Dublin in Beckett's other works are indicated as appropriate.

Merrion Square and Environs
Clare Street

To the west of Trinity College lies Merrion Square with its handsome Georgian buildings. Its southern boundary continues into a small street, Clare Street, which boasts a fine old book-shop, Greene's Library (5:2), which has been in existence many years.[2] It is a convenient meeting place, if for no other reason than everyone knows where it is, a point well made

5:2   Greene's Library and Bookshop
(Photograph by D. Davison)

by the 'Polar Bear' in an amusing scene on a tram in the unpublished *Dream of Fair to Middling Women* -

> 'Can't the bloody thing be stopped?' he cried.
> 'Next stop the Green' said the conductor.
> 'Damn the Green' cried the P.B. 'damn you and your damn Green.'
> He drew his plump hand's glabrous crown across his raw mouth.
> Three nouns, three adjectives.
> 'The Dublin United Tramways Bloody Company' he vociferated 'seems to exist for the sole purpose of dragging its clients forcibly out of their way to Greens. Isn't there enough green in this merdific island? I get on to your accursed bolide at the risk of my life at the College Green and get fired out at the next of your verminous plaguespots whether I like it or not. If it's not the Steven's (sic) Green it's Green's (sic) bloody library. What we want' he screamed from the sidewalk 'in this pestiferous country is red for a change and plenty of it.'
> *(Dream of Fair to Middling Women, p. 140)*

College Green[3] is the area in front of Trinity College where Grafton Street Lower, Dame Street, Westmoreland Street, and College Street have their origins. St. Stephen's Green[4] is a park in central Dublin, once frequented by nannies and their charges from the Georgian residences of Fitzwilliam Street and Square (5:3). It was, and still is, a popular rendezvous for lovers -

> ... Like those summer evenings in the Green ... In the early days ... Of our idyll ... When we sat watching the ducks ... Holding hands exchanging vows ... How you admired my elocution! ...
> *(Eh Joe, p. 18)*

How right the Polar Bear was! Dublin is awash with green, but even more than the P.B. had realised -

> Alas the conductor was slow, he was Irish, his name was Hudson, he had not the Cockney gift of repartee. He might have made a very nice use of Green St. and he did not, he missed his chance. Very much later in the day, brooding over this incident, the right answer came to him, or one of the answers that would have done, and from that moment forth he had at least a presentable anecdote for his colleagues at the depot. But too late. Once again the Polar Bear had been let go unscathed.
> *(Dream of Fair to Middling Women, p. 140)*

The reference to Green Street is to Green Street Courthouse (5:4), an establishment with a long history in the administration of justice.[5]

On the opposite side of Clare Street to Greene's bookshop, at No. 6., are the offices of Beckett and Medcalf (5:5), the family firm of quantity surveyors, founded by Beckett's father.[6] Beckett lived in the top floor of this house in the early 'thirties. Here he wrote his first novel, *More*

5:3 St. Stephen's Green
(By courtesy Bord Fáilte.
No. D 11/44)

5:4 Green Street Courthouse
(By courtesy Bord Fáilte.
No. D 1/50)

5:5 The offices of Beckett and
Medcalf, No. 6, Clare Street
(Photograph by D. Davison)

Pricks than Kicks, (published in 1934) and some of the later novel, *Murphy* (published in 1938). The period of each novel can be calculated from the occurrence of certain events.[7] On the top floor of No. 6. there is a spacious front room overlooking Greene's bookshop, where we may presume Beckett did his writing (5:6). A small backroom served as a kitchenette, where Belacqua's culinary eccentricities were probably indulged -

> He must be left strictly alone, he must have complete quiet and privacy, to prepare the food for his lunch.
> The first thing to do was to lock the door. Now nobody could come at him.
>
> *(More Pricks than Kicks, p. 10)*

A bathroom is tucked into a return on the stairs, and above all this was a garret, a physical and spiritual retreat from the meddlesome world below. In *Murphy*, the garret in the Magdalen Mental Mercyseat is chosen with great care for the climax of the novel. Such is the undisturbed solitude of the garret in Clare Street, the opalescence of light from the skylight, and the paraphernalia of oddments, almost undisturbed since Beckett's tenure, that the scene demands a rocking Murphy for completion[8] (5:7, 5:8) -

> But the garret that he now saw was not an attic, nor yet a mansard, but a genuine garret, not half, but twice as good as the one in Hanover, because half as large. The ceiling and the outer wall were one, a superb surge of white, pitched at the perfect angle of farthest trajectory, pierced by a small frosted skylight, ideal for closing against the sun by day and opening by night to the stars. The bed, so low and gone in the springs that even unfreighted the middle grazed the ground, was wedged lengthways into the cleft of floor and ceiling, so that Murphy was saved the trouble of moving it into that position. The garret contained, in addition to the bed, one chair and one chest, not of drawers. An immense candle, stuck to the floor by its own tallow, pointed its snuff to heaven at the head of the bed. This the only means of light, was more than enough for Murphy, a strict non-reader.
>
> *(Murphy, p. 113)*

In *More Pricks than Kicks*, the theme of death, on which the novel ends, is introduced early with the execution of Henry McCabe. As Belacqua prepares his frugal lunch the details of the trial which shocked the city are brought vividly to his attention on the ageing pages of a daily paper, the *Evening Herald* [9] -

> He deployed an old Herald and smoothed it out on the table. The rather handsome face of McCabe the assassin stared up at him.
>
> *(More Pricks than Kicks, p. 10)*

Page 132

On 31st March 1926, a house named *La Mancha*, at Malahide in County Dublin, was found in flames, and six bodies were recovered from the blaze: the owners Peter and Joseph McDonnell, brothers, their sisters Annie and Alice, and two servants. There was only one survivor from the household, the gardener, Henry McCabe, who raised the alarm. A number of inconsistencies in McCabe's account of the event led to his arrest and he was tried for the murder of six people and arson on 8th November, 1926. The trial lasted six days and, after an absence of fifty minutes, the jury returned the verdict of guilty. The death sentence was passed by Mr. Justice John O'Byrne with the advice: 'I can hold out no hope of mercy to you in this world. I advise and implore you to spend the remainder of the time allocated to you in this world, preparing to meet your Maker.'[10] When asked by the Clerk of the Peace "if he had anything to say why the sentence of death and execution should not be awarded, the prisoner in a hoarse and almost inaudible voice, said: 'I can only say God forgive you and the people who swore falsely against me.'"[11] McCabe's fate haunts Belacqua through the pages of *More Pricks than Kicks*,[12] and he is disturbed to learn of the rejection of an appeal -

> Then the food had been further spiced by the intelligence, transmitted in a low tragic voice across the counter by Oliver the improver, that the Malahide murderer's petition for mercy, signed by half the land, having been rejected, the man must swing at dawn in Mountjoy and nothing could save him. Ellis the hangman was even now on his way. Belacqua, tearing at the sandwich and swilling the precious stout, pondered on McCabe in his cell.[13]
>
> (*More Pricks than Kicks, p. 17*)

The theme of death, sudden death, in 'Dante and the Lobster', links McCabe's execution with the merciless despatch of the unfortunate gesticulating lobster into a cauldron of boiling water by Belacqua's Aunt-

> She lifted the lobster clear of the table. It had about thirty seconds to live. Well, thought Belacqua, it's a quick death, God help us all.
> It is not.
>
> (*More Pricks than Kicks, p. 21*)

Elsewhere a more grisly death sentence has been enacted. Henry McCabe was hanged by Pierpoint on Thursday, December 9th, 1926 in Mountjoy Prison.[14] The event cast a gloom over a city preparing for the Christmas festivities, and there was much sympathy for McCabe's widow and nine children. Beckett's fascination with McCabe's execution is not merely because of its brutality and inevitability, fixing so precisely the hour of

5:6 The front-room on the top floor of No. 6 Clare Street (Photograph by D. Davison)

5:7 The garret of No. 6 Clare Street
(Photograph by D. Davison)

5:8 The garret skylight
(Photograph by D. Davison)

departure from life for one accursed man; he is disturbed by the self-righteous attitude of a society prepared to accept without question a judgement that left unanswered so many questions of importance, as to leave at least some doubt about McCabe's guilt.[15] But, what troubles Beckett's sensitivity most is the paucity of mercy in the land; only the women of the city of Dublin were prepared to make a demonstration of concern and a gesture of forgiveness (5:9) -

> Why not piety and pity both, even down below? Why not mercy and Godliness together? A little mercy in the stress of sacrifice, a little mercy to rejoice against judgement. He thought of Jonah and the gourd and the pity of a jealous God on Nineveh. And poor McCabe, he would get it in the neck at dawn. What was he doing now, how was he feeling? He would relish one more meal, one more night.
> *(More Pricks than Kicks, p. 20)*

McCabe's crime is incorporated in part by Beckett, in the later story, 'Draff', in which a demented gardener rapes a maidservant and then sets the house alight -

> On their return they found the house in flames, the home to which Belacqua had brought three brides a raging furnace. It transpired that during their absence something had snapped in the brain of the gardener, who had ravished the servant girl and then set the premises on fire. He had neither given himself up nor tried to escape, he had shut himself up in the tool-shed and awaited arrest.
> *(More Pricks than Kicks, p. 202)*

5:9   Women kneeling in prayer outside Mountjoy Prison (The *Evening Herald*, Thursday, December 9, 1926. By courtesy National Library of Ireland)

From his Clare Street lodgings, Beckett was within easy reach of shops and pubs. Belacqua's tastes, though of necessity frugal (as indeed would those of his creator have been), were nevertheless demanding. The ripe cheese so essential to lunch was not to be acquired without difficulty.

The hapless victualler chosen for this transaction may have been Mr. Kennedy, who ran a family grocery (5:10) attached to a public house, of which more later -

> He threaded his way rapidly, his head bowed, through a familiar labyrinth of lanes and suddenly dived into a little family grocery.
>
> *(More Pricks than Kicks, p. 13)*

The cheese safely stowed between the burnt boards of toast, the next port of call was a lowly pub of which there were many in the area -

> Stumbling along by devious ways towards the lowly public where he was expected, in the sense that the entry of his grotesque person would provoke no comment or laughter, Belacqua gradually got the upper hand of his choler.
>
> *(More Pricks than Kicks, p. 15)*

At lunch Belacqua contemplated the none too-arduous duties of the afternoon. The pub would close for the holy hour at half-past two, giving him just enough time to purchase the lobster for his aunt, before presenting himself for his Italian lesson. The Italian Lesson was a source of particular joy to him, because of the delightful Signorina Ottolenghi[16]-

> Signorina Adriana Ottolenghi was waiting in the little front room off the hall, which Belacqua was naturally inclined to think of rather as the vestibule. That was her room, the Italian room. On the same side, but at the back was the French room. God knows where the German room was. Who cared about the German room anyway?
>
> *(More Pricks than Kicks, pp. 17-18)*

After the Italian lesson, Belacqua's destination was the house of his aunt, where he was to dine on the ill-fated lobster now in his possession. On his way there he encountered two street scenes that are characteristic of the period. A horse had fallen under its cart and Belacqua wondered at the wisdom of the custom then prevailing that required a man to sit on the horse's head, while awaiting its executioner -

> At the corner of the street a horse was down and a man sat on its head. I know, thought Belacqua, that that is considered the right thing to do. But why?
>
> *(More Pricks than Kicks, p. 20)*

5:10 Kennedy's grocery and public-house, Westland Row. The Dental Hospital is in the background
(Photograph by D. Davison)

He also observed a lamplighter,[17] one of those creatures of the distant past,[18] flying through the dusk of the evening city -

> A lamplighter flew by on his bike, tilting with his pole at the standards, jousting a little yellow light into the evening.
>
> *(More Pricks than Kicks, p.20)*

Another Dublin figure of the past, the dustman with his two-wheeled push cart, is brought to mind in *Murphy* -

> In Dublin he need only have sat down on the nearest bench and waited. Soon one of the gloomy dustmen would have come, wheeling his cart marked, 'Post your litter here.'
>
> *(Murphy, p. 187)*

The National Gallery

Beckett's writing contains within it many references to the visual arts. Sometimes these are obvious, even stated, but more often they are obscure allegorical associations, emanating from the mind of a writer with a deep knowledge of art, both ancient and contemporary, and many would test the ingenuity of the most astute art historian. At times the influence of a painting on Beckett's writing is only apparent because he says it is so. It is likely, for example, that Caravaggio's, *Decollation of St. John*, in Valetta Cathedral, was, at least in part, the inspirational spark for the drama, *Not I*.[19] Though there are some scholarly essays[20] on the visual arts in Beckett's literature, a comprehensive dissertation is not available. This section is concerned with references to paintings in the National Gallery of Ireland, or to paintings and painters in Ireland.

Beckett often enhances his description of a person or place by drawing the reader to a painting, or to an artist's style and technique. Though there are some direct references to specific artists and works of art, there are also obscure allusions which utilise the technique of painting to expand literary expression, and these cannot always be identified with any certainty.

More Pricks than Kicks was written in Dublin and many of the art references in this early novel are to paintings in the National Gallery of Ireland,[21] to which Beckett often retreated on cold winter days. Later, his interest in Dublin's gallery and his association with it continued when his friend, Thomas MacGreevy, was appointed its Director.

The National Gallery of Ireland was built between 1858 and 1864 to commemorate William Dargan, engineer and financier, who gave to

Dublin and much of Ireland, its railway system. Dargan's statue, sculpted by Thomas Farrell, stands in front of the Gallery[22](5:11). For Beckett, impecunious and lost in uncertainty, the National Gallery in Dublin provided sanctuary on lonely wet days, as did the National Portrait Gallery in London in later years -

> when you went in out of the rain always winter then always raining that time in the Portrait Gallery in off the street out of the cold and rain slipped in when no one was looking and through the rooms shivering and dripping till you found a seat marble slab and sat down to rest and dry off and on to hell out of there when was that

(That Time, p. 228)

Here, the warmth and a solitude was disturbed only by the odd shuffling attendant -

> ... huddled up on the slab in the old green greatcoat with your arms round you whose else hugging you for a bit of warmth to dry off and on to hell out of there and on to the next not a living soul in the place only yourself and the odd attendant drowsing around in his felt shufflers not a sound to be heard only every now and then a shuffle of felt drawing near then dying away

(That Time, p. 229)

5:11   The National Gallery of
       Ireland with William Dargan's
       statue in the foreground.
       (Photograph by D. Davison)

5:12   Interior of the National Gallery
       of Ireland
       (By courtesy Bord Fáilte.
       No. D 12/54)

5:13 *A Portrait of an Old Lady* by
the Master of the Tired Eyes
(By courtesy National Gallery of
Ireland No. 903)

5:14 *The Pietà* by Perugino
(By courtesy National Gallery of
Ireland, No. 942)

Alone, he absorbed the details of the ancient portraiture that gazed down on him (5:12), and became familiar with the Gallery's collection of masterpieces from many schools -

> till you hoisted your head and there before your eyes when they opened a vast oil black with age and dirt someone famous in his time some famous man or woman or even child such as a young prince or princess some young prince or princess of the blood black with age behind the glass where gradually as you peered trying to make it out gradually of all things a face appeared had you swivel on the slab to see who it was there at your elbow ... or was that another time there alone with the portraits of the dead black with dirt and antiquity and the dates on the frames in case you might get the century wrong not believing it could be you till they put you out in the rain at closing-time.
>
> *(That Time, pp. 229 & 231)*

Some of these portraits find their way into Becketts's works. In 'Ding Dong', the beggar woman in the pub is respectable and vivacious, but the tranquil sadness in her eyes is reminiscent of *A Portrait of an Old Lady,* painted by the Master of the Tired Eyes[23](5:13) -

> But her face, ah her face, was what Belacqua had rather refer to as her countenance, it was so full of light. This she lifted up upon him and no error. Brimful of light and serene, serenissime, it bore no trace of suffering, and in this alone it might be said to be a notable face. Yet like tormented faces that he had seen, like the face in the National Gallery in Merrion Square by the Master of Tired Eyes, it seemed to have come a long way and subtend an infinitely narrow angle of affliction, as eyes focus a star.
>
> *(More Pricks than Kicks, p. 47)*

In 'Love and Lethe', Belacqua's girlfriend is one named Ruby Tough from Irishtown. The reader wishing to ascertain Ruby's looks has no choice but to visit the National Gallery of Ireland,[24] unless it is more convenient to go to the Uffizi in Florence where a more vivid portrayal of Ruby's beauty may be seen, not only in the *Pietà* there, but more especially in *La Maddalena* [25] -

> Those who are in the least curious to know what she looked like at the time in which we have chosen to cull her we venture to refer to the Magdalene in the Perugino Pietà in the National Gallery of Dublin, always bearing in mind that the hair of our heroine is black and not ginger.
>
> *(More Pricks than Kicks, p. 93)*

The latter directive draws attention immediately to the woman supporting Christ on one knee (5:14).

Beckett sometimes uses art to augment his verbal portrayal of women. The physical beauty of the Smeraldina, Belacqua's sixth and last love,

is evoked through the art of Botticelli -

> Bodies don't matter but hers went something like this: big enormous breasts, big breech, Botticelli thighs, knock-knees, square ankles, wobbly, popputa, mammose slobbery - blubbery, bubbubbubbub, the real button-bursting Weib, ripe.
> *(More Pricks than Kicks, pp. 189-190)*

In the 'twenties two paintings in the National Gallery in Dublin were attributed to Botticelli.[26] Of these, not even *The Story of Lucretia* (5:15) is likely to have inspired the above passage, and the *Allegory of Spring* in the Uffizi would seem to suit Beckett's luscious portrayal more adequately. Botticelli is evoked again to portray the muscular thighs of the cyclist in the poem *Sanies I*: 'Botticelli from the fork down ....'[27]

On another occasion reference to the fifteenth century artist Masaccio brings to mind a Florentine masterpiece by Uccello in Dublin -

> It was just a vague impression, it was merely that she looked, with that strange limey hobnailed texture of complexion, so frescosa, from the waist up, my dear, with that distempered cobalt modesty-piece, a positive gem of ravished Quattrocento, a positive jewel, my dear, of sweaty Big Tom.
> *(More Pricks than Kicks, p. 67)*

Uccello's magnificent *Virgin and Child* (5:16), acquired by the Gallery in 1909, was regarded by Tom MacGreevy as one of its most treasured acquisitions.[28]

Uccello, renowned for his study of perspective, is again evoked in *More Pricks than Kicks*, this time to magnify a graveyard scene -

> In the cemetery the light was failing, the sea moonstone washing the countless toes turned up, the mountains swarthy Uccello behind the headstones.
> *(More Pricks than Kicks, p. 195)*

Two Florentine panels in the National Gallery of Ireland, *The Battle of Anghiari* (5:17) and *The Taking of Pisa*, which were attributed to Uccello by MacGreevy, may have provided the swarthy mountain background evoked by Beckett.[29]

Among Tom MacGreevy's many achievements, during his term as Director of the Gallery, was the re-attribution of Titian's, *Ecce Homo*[30] (5:18), which was correctly attributed at the time Beckett wrote *More Pricks than Kicks*. As McMillan has observed, Hairy's hiss of *Ecce*, brings 'the whole visual tradition - Christian architecture and the *Ecce Homo*' into 'ironic juxtaposition with Belacqua's fate'[31] -

> 'Ecce' hissed Hairy, according to plan, and Belacqua's heart made a hopeless dash

5:15 Detail from *The Story of Lucretia* by the Master of Marradi
(By courtesy National Gallery of Ireland, No. 110)

5:16 *The Virgin and Child* by Uccello
(By courtesy National Gallery of Ireland, No. 603)

5:17 Detail from *The Battle of Anghiari*, Florentine School
(By courtesy National Gallery of Ireland, No. 778)

5:18 *Ecce Homo* by Titian
(By courtesy National Gallery of Ireland, No. 75)

against the wall of its box, the church suddenly cruciform cage, the bulldogs of heaven holding the chancel, the procession about to give tongue in the porch, the transepts culs-de-sac.

(More Pricks than Kicks, p. 148)

These references to painting demonstrate Beckett's familiarity with art, particularly with the Italian School of painting, but, more importantly, his growing fascination with art in his early writings leads eventually to a remarkable symbiosis of literature and painting. The exploitation of painting to convey in writing a symbolism, that words alone fail to achieve, is evident in the poem *Malacoda*, written after the death of his father in 1933 -

> to cover
> to be sure cover cover all over
> your targe allow me hold your sulphur
> divine dogday glass set fair
> stay Scarmilion stay stay
> lay this Huysum on the box
> mind the imago it is he
> hear she must see she must
> all aboard all souls
> half-mast aye aye

(Malacoda, p. 26)

Laurence Harvey has analysed this poem in detail.[32] 'The natural plant,' he writes, 'that will meet the fate of all natural things, as the mother must follow the father to the grave, contrasts sharply with the Huysum that is laid by the son on the coffin.' Jan van Huysum, was the most famous floral artist in the eighteenth century Dutch School,[33] and *A Bouquet of Flowers* (5:19) in the National Gallery is an excellent example of his mastery. Reproductions of his paintings of bouquets and butterflies were often placed on coffins.[34] By incorporating Van Huysum's painting in this poem Beckett adorns and enriches his tribute to his father. The line, 'mind the imago it is he', is a pledge from Beckett himself, to preserve (and perhaps elevate) the memory of his cherished father, thereby giving to his existence a form of permanence, of immortality. Beckett's source for the 'imago' Harvey writes, was 'a butterfly poised on a flower in the Huysum painting. As the insect, in the beauty of its finished form, finds its eternity among the fading flowers of art, so the father has his immortality in the idealising memory of his son, in the son's poem, and among the incorruptible figures created by the most enduring of poets, Dante Alighieri.'[35] There is in fact, no

5:19 *A Bouquet of Flowers*
by Jan van Huysum
(By courtesy National Gallery
of Ireland, No. 50)

butterfly in the Huysum painting in the National Gallery of Ireland, and Beckett probably had another painting by the same artist in mind.

In the early *Dream of Fair to Middling Women*, Beckett makes reference to Rembrandt's portrait of his brother and reminds himself that he must develop further his thoughts on the work of this artist. This he does with vigour a little later in the novel, when he discusses not only Rembrandt's portrait of his brother, but also Rembrandt's painting of St. Matthew in the Louvre. Beckett's introduction to Rembrandt may well have been with his masterpiece *Rest on the Flight into Egypt* [36](5:20) in the National Gallery of Ireland -

> I shall state silences more competently than ever a better man spangled the butterflies of vertigo. I think now ... of the dehiscing, the dynamic décousu, of a Rembrandt, the implication lurking behind the pictorial pretext threatening to invade pigment and oscuro; I think of the Selbstbildnis, in the toque and the golden chain, of his portrait of his brother, of the cute little Saint Matthew angel that I swear van Ryn never saw the day he painted, in all of which canvases during lunch on many a Sunday I have discerned a disfaction, a désuni, an Ungebund, a flottement, a tremblement, a tremor, a tremolo, a disaggregating, a disintegrating, an effloresence, a breaking down and multiplication of tissue, the

5:20 *Rest on the Flight into Egypt* by Rembrandt van Ryn (By courtesy National Gallery of Ireland, No. 215)

corrosive ground-swell of Art. It is the Pauline (God forgive him for he knew not what he said) *cupio dissolvi.*

(Dream of Fair to Middling Women, p. 123)

The image of truthfulness and even holiness, unlikely attributes in the Neary persona, is conveyed most effectively through the creation of a fictional painting, which Beckett attributes to the artist, St. Luke -

Neary began to speak, or, as it rather sounded, be spoken through. For the voice was flat, the eyes closed and the body bowed and rigid, as though he were kneeling before a priest instead of sitting before two sinners. Altogether he had a great look of Luke's portrait of Matthew, with the angel perched like a parrot on his shoulder.

(Murphy, p. 147)

It is possible that Beckett's use of St. Luke as the artist was influenced by the painting in the National Gallery of Ireland of *St. Luke Drawing the Virgin* (5:21), and that the St. Matthew he had in mind, was, as suggested to me by James Knowlson, Rembrandt's painting of *Saint Matthew* in the Louvre where Beckett, no doubt, spent many a lunchtime.[37]

Beckett is drawn towards a self-portrait in the story 'What a Misfortune', when he allows himself to emerge in the persona of the cicisbeo, Walter Draffin, author of the 'promising' *Dream of Fair to Middling Women.* But, if we seek to pursue further the comparison of subject and creator by a study of the former's physiognomy, it becomes apparant that Draffin bears no physical resemblance to the young Beckett, as he was portrayed, for example, by Sean O'Sullivan[38](5:22) -

.... the dimpled chin, the bright brown doggy eyes that were so appealing, the unrippled surface of vast white brow whose area was at least double that of the nether face, and anchored there for all eternity the sodden cowlick that looked as though it were secreting macassar to discharge into his eye.

(More Pricks than Kicks, p. 130)

Useful though these references to known paintings are to Beckett, he is confined somewhat within the limits of another artists imagination as expressed on canvas. However, he manages to escape this restriction, while continuing to use the device, by creating imaginary or near-imaginary artists and works of art. The reader is thus no longer permitted the facility of direct recourse to a particular painting or statue, but is freed to broaden the allusion, within certain meticulously planned strategies that direct the imagination towards a school of painters or

5:21 *St. Luke Drawing the Virgin* after Rogier van der Weyden (By courtesy National Gallery of Ireland, No. 4)

5:22 *Samuel Beckett* by Seán O'Sullivan

a genre of art. In *Watt*, for example, Beckett creates an artist, who appears at first glance to be fictitious. However, when we look more closely at Art Conn O'Connery, otherwise known as 'Black Velvet O'Connery, product of the great Chinnery-Slattery tradition'[39] it becomes apparent that though no such artist ever existed, the traditions that influenced O'Connery are none-the-less identifiable. By thus invoking different schools of painting, Beckett is enabled to commit to paper, rather than canvas, his vision of a nude man seated at a piano with an effect that may be every bit as compelling and durable as a framed portrait. There may exist somewhere a portrait of a nude pianist, but it is more likely that the composition is a creation of Beckett's imagination which, if he were a painter, would be committed to canvas, but is instead described in critical detail as if it did indeed have a material existence. If we look closely at the traditions out of which Art Conn 'Black Velvet' O'Connery was created, we find these well represented in the National Gallery of Ireland.

5:23 *A View of the Devil's Glen* by James Arthur O'Connor (By courtesy National Gallery of Ireland, No. 825)

5:24 *Christ in the House of Martha and Mary* by Peter Paul Ruebens with Jan 'Velvet' Brueghal (By courtesy National Gallery of Ireland, No. 513)

James Arthur O'Connor[40] was one of Ireland's most famous landscape painters, and there are fifteen of his paintings in the Gallery. *The View of the Devil's Glen* (5:23), is a good example of the depth of texture O'Connor gave to his landscapes, and in its deep darknesses there is a suggestion of velvet texture to which Beckett may have been alluding in the 'Black Velvet' cognomen. Alternatively, Beckett may have had Jan 'Velvet' Brueghel (the elder) in mind who[41] is represented in the National Gallery by an ink and wash drawing, *Antwerp from the City Walls*.[42] A

5:25   *A Self-Portrait* by
Roderic O'Conor
(By courtesy National Gallery of
Ireland, No. 922)

5:26   *A Portrait of a Mandarin* by
George Chinnery
(By courtesy National Gallery of
Ireland, No. 785)

painting by his son, Jan Brueghel the Younger (who was influenced greatly by his father,[43] with Peter Paul Ruebens, *Christ in the House of Martha and Mary* (5:24), with which Beckett would have been familiar,[44] was attributed to Jan 'Velvet' Brueghel until 1985.

Roderic O'Conor,[45] another Irish artist, would have been capable of executing the painting devised by Beckett, and it is likely that Beckett would have been familiar with *A Self Portrait* (5:25) by O'Conor which was acquired by the Gallery in 1919, and to which six of the paintings of this much sought-after artist have since been added.[46] It is possible, of course, that Art Conn O'Connery earned the sobriquet, 'Black Velvet', not by virtue of his artistic capabilities, but from a penchant, perhaps leading to over-indulgence, for that strangest of Irish beverages, an elixer of champagne and Guinness Stout, known as 'black velvet'.

Another possible influence in the creation of Art Conn O'Connery is the Con O'Donnell[47] portrait of *Art O'Neill, Harper (1737-1816),* which, as McMillan points out, Beckett might not have been familiar with as it was not acquired by the Gallery until 1951. However, had he been aware of its existence, this portrayal of the blind harpist with its Homeric overtones, would have had appeal for him.[48]

Looking to the 'great Chinnery-Slattery tradition' of which Art Conn O'Connery is a product, we find a common bond between Beckett, who created a portrait of a mandarin[49] in *Dream of Fair to Middling Women* and George Chinnery,[50] a famous Irish artist, whose *A Portrait of a Mandarin* (5:26), hangs in the National Gallery of Ireland. The Slattery tradition is a reference to John Slattery,[51] a nineteenth century portrait painter of modest merit, whose only painting in the National Gallery, a portrait of *William Carleton, Novelist, (1798-1869)*[52] brings this hybrid creation back from painting to literature (5:27).

The portrait by Art Conn O'Connery is described in meticulous detail in *Watt* -

> Second picture in Erskine's room, representing gentleman seated at piano, full length, receding profile right, naked save for stave-paper resting on lap. With his right hand he sustains a chord which Watt has no difficulty in identifying as that of C major in its second inversion, while with other he prolongs pavilion of left ear. His right foot, assisted from above by its fellow, depresses with force the sustaining pedal. On muscles of brawny neck, arm, torso, abdomen, loin, thigh and calf, standing out like cords in stress of effort, Mr. O'Connery had lavished

all the resources of Jesuit tactility. Beads of sweat, realized with a finish that would have done credit to Heem, were plentifully distributed over pectoral, subaxillary and hypogastrical surfaces. The right nipple, from which sprang a long red solitary hair, was in a state of manifest tumescence, a charming touch. The bust was bowed over the keyboard and the face, turned slightly towards the spectator, wore expression of man about to be delivered, after many days, of particularly hard stool, that is to say the brow was furrowed, the eyes tight closed, the nostrils dilated, the lips parted and the jaw fallen, as pretty a synthesis as one could wish of anguish, concentration, strain, transport and self-abandon, illustrating extraordinary effect produced on musical nature by faint cacophony of remote harmonics stealing over dying accord. Mr. O'Connery's love of significant detail appeared further in treatment of toenails, of remarkable luxuriance and caked with what seemed to be dirt. Feet also could have done with a wash, legs not what you could call fresh and sweet, buttocks and belly cried out for hipbath at least, chest in disgusting condition, neck positively filthy, and seeds might have been scattered in ears with every prospect of early germination.

That however a damp cloth had been rapidly passed at a recent date over more prominent portions of facies (Latin word, meaning face) seemed not improbable.
(Latin quote.)
Moustache, pale red save where discoloured by tobacco, advancing years, nervous chewing, family worries, nasal slaver and buccal froth, tumbled over ripe rid lips, and forth from out ripe red jaw, and forth in same way from out ripe red dewlap, sprouted, palely red, doomed beginnings of bushy pale red beard.

(Watt, p. 251-252)

From earlier manuscripts of *Watt* it is apparent that the subject of this paining is Mr. Knott's father who possessed a degree of Bachelor of Music (Kentucky).[53]

In his creation of Art Conn O'Connery, Beckett has made available for his use an extravagant array of techniques with which to create, through verbal imagery, O'Connery's masterpiece. But it is not quite enough. Suddenly, Beckett pulls away from the traditions and partly fictional influences that moulded his artist, to depict in his writing a more telling visual image through the painting of an artist renowned for his ability to render the minutest detail onto canvas with refreshing clarity. In Jan de Heem's,[54] *A Fruit Piece, with Skull, Crucifix and Serpent* (5:28), in the National Gallery, objects are presented in exquisite detail within a composition of deep symbolic content.

In his manipulation of the techniques of painting in his writing, Beckett creates, as we have seen, fictional subjects executed by known artists, or artists whose techniques are identifiable within a particular art tradition. In *Watt*, the work in which he experiments most frequently

5:27 *William Carleton, Novelist, (1798 – 1869)* by John Slattery (By courtesy National Gallery of Ireland, No. 224)

5:28 *A Fruit Piece, with Skull, Crucifix and Serpent* by Jan de Heem (By courtesy National Gallery of Ireland, No. 11)

with this device, he goes one inevitable step further; he dispenses with the artist altogether, and though he stops short (as far as we know) of actually taking up a palette himself,[55] he creates with potent imagery, an abstraction fascinating in its reality and philosophical symbolism. This is the painting in Erskine's room which so bemused and intrigued Watt -

> The only other object of note in Erskine's room was a picture, hanging on the wall, from a nail. A circle, obviously described by a compass, and broken at its lowest point, occupied the middle foreground, of this picture. Was it receding? Watt had that impression. In the eastern back-ground appeared a point, or dot. The circumference was black. The point was blue, but blue! The rest was white.
>
> *(Watt, p. 126)*

Fascinated by this painting, Watt ponders the concept of a circle in search of its centre, which brings him to conclude: 'It is by the nadir that we come ... and it is by the nadir that we go, whatever that means.'[56] Watt's deliberations on the circle, with undertones of Bruno's philosophy,[57] has attracted the attention of a number of scholars.[58] There is certainly no painting in the National Gallery of Ireland that might have inspired the startling composition in Watt's room, which if based at all on reality, is more likely to have association with an abstraction, such as *Alcuni cerchi*, painted by Vasily Kandinsky in 1926.[59]

In the 'Addenda' to *Watt* the sentence 'the Master of the Leopardstown Halflengths'[60] suggests either a horse with a record number of wins over a certain distance on Leopardstown racecourse, or perhaps, as Rubin Rabinovitz suggests, a minor racing official.[61] The phrase refers to neither. The Master of the Female Half-Lengths was an unknown sixteenth century painter who painted female half-length portraiture with a particular style.[62] We need to go back to the earlier manuscripts of *Watt* to discover that Knott's mother (Knott's name was then Quinn) had her portrait painted by the 'Master of the Leopardstown Halflengths'.[63] As it would clearly have been impossible for a sixteenth century artist to paint a nineteenth century portrait, we can only assume that Beckett had parodied the title by applying it to a painter who either lived in Leopardstown, or attracted many of his sitters from that affluent area. The retention of the phrase in the 'Addenda' of the final version of *Watt* serves, perhaps, only to draw attention to the replacement of the portrait by the circle abstraction in Erskine's room, which leads

5:29 *A Lady and Two Gentlemen*
by Jean Antoine Watteau
(By courtesy National Gallery of
Ireland, No. 2300)

inevitably to a comparative analysis of the merits of abstract and realistic art, a subject beyond the scope of this discussion.

Before departing the subject of Irish art in Beckett's writing, the significant influence of the work of Jack Yeats must be considered. His place in Beckett's literature is dealt with in more detail in Chapter 8. Of his painting, Beckett had this to say -

> It is difficult to formulate what it is one likes in Mr Yeats's painting, or indeed what it is one likes in anything, but it is a labour, not easily lost, and a relationship once started not likely to fail, between such a knower and such an unknown.
> (*MacGreevy on Yeats. p. 95*)

Beckett rates Yeats with Kandinsky and Klee, Ballmer and Bram van Velde, Rouault and Braque, because like them, he illuminated existence.[64] He saw, moreover, in Yeats's treatment of the object, an integrity of vision which he likened to Watteau.[65] The drawing *A Lady and Two Gentlemen* (5:29) in the National Gallery of Ireland may have suggested this comparison.[66]

In Yeats's painting, Beckett perceived in the simplistic beauty of, for example, *In the Tram* (5:30), a majesty every bit as profound as the mysticism of *A Race in Hy-Brasil*, or the expression of existence threatened with apocalyptic vividness in the allegorical masterpiece, *The*

5:30 *In the Tram* by Jack B. Yeats (By courtesy National Library of Ireland, No. 1408)

Tinker's Encampment, the Blood of Abel (5:31).[67] It is of interest to note that Beckett kept Jack Yeats's painting *Morning* with him, when he was forced to leave Paris and go into hiding in Roussillon during the war.[68]

Merrion Square

Merrion Square West, boasts not only the National Gallery but also Leinster House, the home of the Irish parliament, Dáil Éireann, and the National Museum.[69] The square continues southwards to Merrion Street on which stand the offices of the Land Commission. In these stately quarters worked one, named Walter Draffin, whose close liaison with Belacqua's future mother-in-law cast a shadow of doubt on the legitimacy of the hero's intended bride, Thelma -

> Mrs bboggs had a lover in the Land Commission, so much so in fact that certain ill-intentioned ladies of her acquaintance lost no occasion to insist on the remarkable disparity, in respect not only of physique but of temperament, between Mr bboggs and Thelma ...

(More Pricks than Kicks, p. 130)

Mount Street

The death of Belacqua in the final sequence of *More Pricks than Kicks*, 'Yellow', occurs in a nursing home in Lower Mount Street, named the Elpis Nursing Home[70](5:32), close to Merrion Square -

> When she was gone he thought what an all but flawless brunette, so spick and span too after having been on the go all night, at the beck and call of the first lousy old squaw who let fall her book or could not sleep for the roar of the traffic in Merrion Row. What the hell did anything matter anyway!
>
> Pale wales in the east beyond the Land Commission. The day was going along nicely.
>
> *(More Pricks than Kicks, p. 177)*

Belacqua's premature demise was the doing of the anaesthetist, who 'had clean forgotten to auscultate him',[71] and who, moreover, may have been drunk into the bargain (5:33) -

> The surgeon was washing his invaluable hands as Belacqua swaggered through the antechamber. He that hath clean hands shall be stronger. Belacqua cut the surgeon. But he flashed a dazzling smile at the Wincarnis. She would not forget that in a hurry.
> He bounced up on to the table like a bridegroom. The local doc was in great form,

5:32   The Elpis Nursing Home
        Nos. 17-21, Lower Mount Street
        (Photograph by D. Davison)

he had just come from standing best man, he was all togged up under his vestments. He recited his exhortation and clapped on the nozzle.

(More Pricks than Kicks, p. 186)

For the departure of the hero, Belacqua, Beckett chose the nursing home in which John Millington Synge died -

He (Synge) used to speak of *Deirdre* as his last disappointment; but another awaited him. An hour before he died he asked the nurse to wheel his bed into a room whence he could see the Wicklow mountains, the hills where he used to go for long solitary walks, and he was wheeled into the room, but the mountains could not be seen from the windows; to see them it was necessary to stand up, and Synge couldn't stand or sit up in his bed, so his last wish remained ungratified and he died with tears in his eyes.[72]

Dawson Street

Also in the vicinity of Merrion Square is Dawson Street, which receives mention three times in *Dream of Fair to Middling Women*. In the first, the ebullient Polar Bear makes reference to a poulterer on Dawson Street[73] -

'Where' the P.B., inexpressibly relieved now that he had the oil safe and sound in his pocket, would be interested to know 'is it possible to acquire a chicken

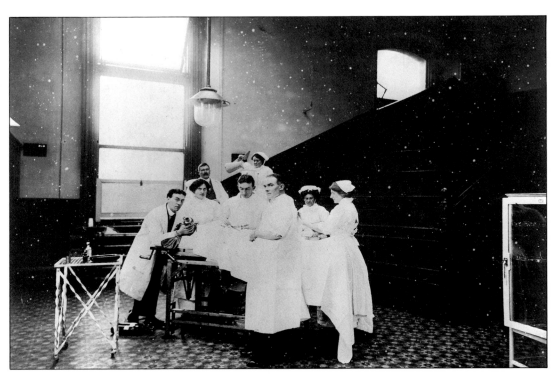

5:33 An operation in a Dublin
theatre in the 'twenties
(By courtesy Ms. B. Walsh)

for the sum of two shillings? At the great poulterer's of D'Olier Street, at Brady's of Dawson Street, or in the Market?'

(Dream of Fair to Middling Women, p. 133)

The market referred to is Smithfield Market where fruit, vegetables, poultry, meat and fish is sold to the city's suppliers each morning.

The Irish Automobile Club (5:34), (now the Royal Irish Automobile Club)[74] on Dawson Street is a further obstacle to the progress of the irate Polar Bear -

Fiercely now retracing his steps, weighed down by the bag, he had occasion most bitterly to upbraid a wall-eyed employee of the R.A.C., a little mousy ex-service creature known to the members as Dick Deadeye. With a courtly gesture Dick motioned back the pedestrians that the cars for whose comings and goings he was responsible might issue forth unimpeded from the garage. It was the rush hour for the little man.

(Dream of Fair to Middling Women, p. 140)

Jem Higgins, the rugby player in *Dream*, writes a love letter to the Alba suggesting a rendezvous at one of two popular tea-shops, Fuller's of Grafton Street, or the Bon Bouche in Dawson Street[75] -

May I send you a touchline seat? I lead the forwards you know. It should be a good game. We could meet after for tea at Fuller's or if you prefer that Bon Bouche place in Dawson St.

(Dream of Fair to Middling Women, p. 136)

5:34 The Irish Automobile Club, Dawson Street. The Reliability Trial 13-16th June, 1906. Mr. R.W. Morris in a 6 cylinder 40 h.p. Ariel Simplex. (Presented to the R.A.C. by J.C. Millard. By courtesy Mr. W. Fitzsimmons)

Pearse Street and Environs

Thomas Moore's Statue

The events in two chapters in *More Pricks than Kicks* take place in or around Pearse Street, an historic thoroughfare to be sure, but one which has not before received the affectionate treatment meted to it by Beckett. Belacqua's adventures in both 'Ding Dong' and 'A Wet Night' are suffered in pursuit of pleasures, lubricous and bibulous. Both stories may be taken together as constituting a debauch of no small measure, and are illustrative of the singular dedication of the hero of the piece to his hedonistic goal. Each opens with Belacqua emerging from the depths of College Street to contemplate future progress in the shadow of Thomas Moore's statue. In 'Ding Dong', he has walked from the Park Gate at the Phoenix Park along the Liffey to O'Connell Bridge, and then up Westmoreland Street to a public convenience on College Street where he relieved himself of essences imbibed *en route* -

> He had experienced little or no trouble coming back from the Park Gate along the north quay, he had taken the Bridge and Westmoreland Street in his stride, and now he suddenly found himself good for nothing but to loll against the plinth of this bull-necked bard, and wait for a sign.
>
> *(More Pricks than Kicks, pp. 41-42)*

The events in 'A Wet Night' take place in December 1926, and the streets of Dublin are preparing for Christmas. Hyam's, a Jewish tailors and outfitters, on Westmoreland Street, was no exception[76](5:35) -

> Hark, it is the season of festivity and goodwill. Shopping is in full swing, the streets are thronged with revellers, the Corporation has offered a prize for the best-dressed window, Hyam's trousers are down again.
>
> *(More Pricks than Kicks, p. 53)*

The colours of the sky at sunset over the Liffey, noted by Belacqua as he walked down the quays, were worthy of contemplation as he climbed the steps from the depths of the underground public privy[77] -

> Emerging, on the particular evening in question, from the underground convenience in the maw of College Street, with a vague impression that he had come from following the sunset up the Liffey till all the colour had been harried from the sky, all the tulips and aerugo expunged, he squatted, not that he had too much drink taken but simply that for the moment there were no grounds for his favouring one direction rather than another, against Tommy Moore's plinth.
>
> *(More Pricks than Kicks, p. 41)*

5:35 Westmoreland Street from O'Connell Bridge. The photograph also features O'Connell's Monument, the Ballast Office, Trinity College, the Bovril Sign and in the distance, the Dublin mountains
(By courtesy National Library of Ireland, Valentine, R.1679)

In 'A Wet Night', Belacqua makes his appearance, not from the underground privy, but from close by McLoughlin's public house -

> Emerging happy body from the hot bowels of McLoughlin's he looked up and admired the fitness of Moore's bull neck, not a whit too short, with all due respect to the critics.
>
> *(More Pricks than Kicks, p. 53)*

The pub from which the happy Belacqua broke, and to which Beckett gave the name 'McLoughlin's', was probably the licensed premises[78] formerly known as Crampton House. This building still stands at the intersection of D'Olier Street, College Street and Pearse Street, a spot then ornamented by a leafy memorial to Sir Philip Crampton, a Victorian surgeon (5:36), whose boast it was that he could swim across Lough Bray, ride into town, and amputate a limb before breakfast.[79]

In Dublin rugby circles there is a tall story told of Beckett, the College Street toilets and one named Jammy Clinch (5:37) whose exploits both on and off the rugby field were legendary.[80] Jammy, then an impecunious medical student, had been given a tip for a 'certainty' in the 2.30 at the

5:36 The Crampton Memorial with the columns of the Bank of Ireland in the background. (Photograph by G.A. Duncan, No. PX1518)

5:37 Jammy Clinch (second on right)
on the playing fields of
Trinity College
(By courtesy
Dr. and Mrs. J. Clinch)

Curragh races, but an absence of cash prevented him from investing in the animal. Pondering his predicament, he met Beckett outside Trinity College. Beckett was also broke but Clinch, not one to be easily dismissed, had observed that his prey was clad in a 'set of good Protestant tweeds'. The story goes that Clinch persuaded Beckett to divest himself, temporarily, of his suit in the gentleman's convenience, were he was to await the happy return of his partner complete with a share of the spoils and the tweeds, redeemed safely from the pawn shop where they would rest just long enough for the certainty to pass the post. Legend has it that the horse is running yet and that Beckett languishes still in the underground latrine in College Street (5:38).

The siting of this convenience, with its facilities for both 'Fir' (Men) and 'Mná' (Women), in such close proximity to the statue of the famous poet Thomas Moore, is not without irony. The location most associated with Moore is the Vale of Avoca in Arklow, where the bard's tree stands at the 'Meeting of the Waters'.[81] Belacqua's concern about the critics opinion of Moore's statue (5:39), reflects Beckett's knowledge of his city. The sculptor, whose name, by coincidence and not relationship, was Christopher Moore, had to complete the statue of the poet out of his own funds, which may account for some of the shortcomings. It is described by Strickland, as a 'Grotesque effigy ... and unfortunate memorial to the poet.'[82]

The Bank of Ireland

From Moore's statue Belacqua looks across to the arcade of the former House of Parliament, now the Bank of Ireland,[83] and observes the comings and goings of a blind beggar -

> Turning aside from this and other no less futile emblems, his attention was arrested by a wheel-chair being pushed rapidly under the arcade of the Bank, in the direction of Dame Street. It moved in and out of sight behind the bars of the columns. This was the blind paralytic who sat all day near to the corner of Fleet Street, and in bad weather under the shelter of the arcade, the same being wheeled home to his home in the Coombe.[84]
>
> *(More Pricks than Kicks, p. 42)*

The beggar's home was in 'the Coombe', a slum-area of Dublin (5:40), now largely cleared and rebuilt.[85] It was famous for its Dublin 'characters' such as the blind paralytic, and for its maternity hospital - The Coombe Lying-in Hospital, now demolished, and referred to in *Murphy* -

> 'Dear old indelible Dublin,' said the coroner. 'Our only female link passed peacefully away in the Coombe, a month and a half before her time, under the second George ...'
>
> *(Murphy, p. 182)*

5:38   The underground convenience
on College Street
(By courtesy National Library of
Ireland, Eason 1767)

5:39 Thomas Moore's statue,
      College Street
      (By courtesy National Library of
      Ireland, Lawrence, Royal, 4717)

5:40 Slums in the Coombe, Dublin
      (Photograph by N. Johnson)

Another well known maternity hospital in Dublin is the National Maternity Hospital, situated in Holles Street and referred to in the poem, *Sanies I-*

> get along with you now take the six the seven the eight or
> the little single-decker
> take a bus for all I care walk cadge a lift
> home to the cob of your web in Holles Street

(Sanies I, p. 18)

The Bovril Sign

The bright lights of the Bovril sign,[86] above Fox the tobacconist, on College Green were once a well-known landmark to all Dubliners. Beckett by endowing this rainbow mirage with celestial powers has given it an indelible place in Dublin history (5:41). In 'Ding-Dong', the sign fails him -

> There were signs on all hands. There was the big Bovril sign to begin with, flaring beyond the Green. But it was useless. Faith, Hope and - what was it? - Love, Eden missed, every ebb derided, all the tides ebbing from the shingle of Ego Maximus, little me. Itself it went nowhere, only round and round, like the spheres, but mutely. It could not dislodge him now, it could only put ideas into his head.
>
> *(More Pricks than Kicks, p. 42)*

But, in 'A Wet Night', Belacqua is guided firmly on his nefarious path -

> Bright and cheery above the strom of the Green, as though coached by the Star of Bethlehem, the Bovril sign danced and danced through its seven phases.
>
> The lemon of faith jaundiced, annunciating the series, was in a fungus of hopeless green reduced to shingles and abolished. Whereupon the light went out, in homage to the slain. A sly ooze of gules, carmine of solicitation, lifting the skirts of green that the prophecy might be fulfilled, shocking Gabriel into cherry, flooded the sign. But the long skirts came rattling down, darkness covered their shame, the cycle was at an end. Da capo.
>
> Bovril into Salome, thought Belacqua, and Tommy Moore there with his head on his shoulders. Doubt, Despair and Scrounging, shall I hitch my bath-chair to the greatest of these?
>
> *(More Pricks than Kicks, p. 53)*

And, what was the iridescent message from the celestial sign? To proceed to a drinking establishment, a command not to be gainsaid -

> Belacqua had been proffered a sign, Bovril had made him a sign.
>
> *(More Pricks than Kicks, p. 54)*

5.41 The Bovril Sign.
Oliver Goldsmith's statue by
John Foley stands in the
grounds of Trinity College
(By courtesy Bovril Limited)

Pearse Street

Pearse Street, running along the northerly perimeter of Trinity College, is an ideal setting for many of Beckett's street events so typical of Dublin life. Characteristically, Beckett chose a street abounding in common comings and goings rather than one representing the fashionable aspects of city life. Pearse Street in the 'twenties and 'thirties was bustling with commercial life: there were shops of all sorts, coal-merchants serving the adjacent docks, grocers, tobacconists, a theatre, a cinema, a police-station, a fire-station, a marble works, coffee and tea shops, and of course, public houses.[87] All were of interest to Beckett and he writes of the street with great affection -

> Long straight Pearse Street, it permitted of a simple cantilena in his mind, its footway peopled with the tranquil and detached in fatigue, its highway dehumanised in a tumult of buses.
>
> *(More Pricks than Kicks, p. 54)*

Originally named Brunswick Street, it was renamed Pearse Street in 1920 in memory of the Pearse brothers, Willie and Padraic, sons of an ecclesiastical sculptor of some renown, whose shop, that of Pearse and Sharp, stood on the street.[88] Padraic Pearse, executed after the Easter Rising of 1916, was a teacher, Irish scholar, and poet.[89] After the moment of torpor at Moore's plinth, Belacqua walks along Pearse Street coming first to the Police Barracks, built of granite from Glencullen in the mountains he knew so well (5:42) -

> Down Pearse Street, that is to say, long straight Pearse Street, its vast Barrack of Glencullen granite.
>
> *(More Pricks than Kicks, pp. 42-43)*

The unusual fire-station,[90] built in 1907, at the corner of Pearse and Tara Street, with its Florentine look-out tower (5:43), transports Belacqua to the banks of the Arno[91] -

> For there Florence would slip into the song, the Piazza della Signoria and the No 1 tram and the Feast of St John, when they lit the torches of resin on the towers and the children, while the rockets at nightfall above the Cascine were still flagrant in their memory, opened the little cages to the glutted cicadae after their long confinement and stayed out with their young parents long after their usual bedtime. Then slowly in his mind down the sinister Uffizi to the parapets of Arno, and so on and so forth. This pleasure was dispensed by the Fire Station opposite which seemed to have been copied here and there from the Palazzo Vecchio. In deference to Savonarola? Ha! Ha!
>
> *(More Pricks than Kicks, pp. 54-55)*

5:42　The Garda Station on Pearse Street (Photograph by D. Davison)

Later in the novel, in the Story 'Draff', the firemen of Tara Street are called upon in vain (5:44) -

'Where are the heroes of the fire-brigade' said Hairy, entering into the spirit of the thing, 'the boys of the old brigade, the Tara Street Cossacks? May we expect them to-day? They would act as a kind of antiphlogistic.'
(More Pricks than Kicks, pp. 202-203)

Opposite the fire-station, the Queen's Theatre once stood (5:45) -

Then to pass by the Queens, home of tragedy, was charming at that hour, to pass between the old theatre and the long line of the poor and lowly queued up for thruppence worth of pictures.
(More Pricks than Kicks, p. 54)

Opened in 1829 as the Adelphi, it became the Queen's Royal Theatre in 1844.[92] It was remodelled and reopened in 1909 without the 'Royal' prefix, an event referred to by Beckett: '… its home of tragedy restored and enlarged.'[93] When the original Abbey Theatre[94] in Abbey Street (5:46) was destroyed by fire in 1951, it moved to the Queen's, where it remained until the new Abbey reopened on its original site in 1966. The Queen's remained empty until its demolition three years later.

Other theatrical references, which we may note in passing, are perhaps surprisingly few in Beckett's writings. The Abbey Theatre (5:47), and the Gate[95](5:48) receive mention but once, and neither is quite honourable -

'With regard to the disposal of these my body, mind and soul, I desire that they be burnt and placed in a paper bag and brought to the Abbey Theatre, Lr. Abbey Street, Dublin, and without pause into what the great and good Lord Chesterfield calls the necessary house, where their happiest hours have been spent, on the right as one goes down into the pit, and I desire that the chain be there pulled upon them, if possible during the performance of a piece, the whole to be executed without ceremony or show of grief.'
(Murphy, p.183)

'Didn't I have the dishonour once in Dublin,' he said. 'Can it have been at the Gate?'
(Murphy, p. 61)

Pearse Street is crossed by a bridge carrying the Dublin-Dun Laoghaire railway line. Beneath the viaduct, a poignant tragedy is witnessed by Belacqua -

It was a most pleasant street, despite its name, to be abroad in, full as it always was with shabby substance and honest-to-God coming and going. All day the roadway was a tumult of buses, red and blue and silver. By one of these a little girl was run down, just as Belacqua drew near to the railway viaduct. She had

5:43   The fire-station on
       Pearse Street
       (Photograph by D. Davison)

5:44   The 'Tara Street Cossacks'
       (By courtesy The Civic Museum,
       Dublin)

5:45 The Queen's Theatre,
Pearse Street
(By courtesy G.A. Duncan.
Folder 1, Sleeve 87)

been to the Hibernian Dairies for milk and bread and then she had plunged out into the roadway, she was in such a childish fever to get back in record time with her treasure to the tenement in Mark Street where she lived. The good milk was all over the road and the loaf, which had sustained no injury, was sitting up against the kerb, for all the world as though a pair of hands had taken it up and set it down there. The queue standing for the Palace Cinema was torn between conflicting desires: to keep their places and to see the excitement. They craned their necks and called out to know the worst, but they stood firm. Only one girl, debauched in appearance and swathed in a black blanket, fell out near the sting of the queue and secured the loaf. With the loaf under her blanket she sidled unchallenged down Mark Street and turned into Mark Lane. When she got back to the queue her place had been taken of course. But her sally had not cost her more than a couple of yards.

(More Pricks than Kicks, p. 43)

The poor girl, wearing a blanket, was not an uncommon sight. She had come from the tenements in Mark Street just around the corner from this unhappy occurrence (5:49). The Palace Cinema (5:50) then occupied the building of the Ancient Concert Rooms, one of Dublin's oldest music halls.

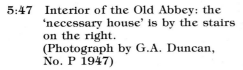

5:46 The Old Abbey Theatre,
Abbey Street
(Photograph by G.A. Duncan,
No. P 1944)

5:47 Interior of the Old Abbey: the
'necessary house' is by the stairs
on the right.
(Photograph by G.A. Duncan,
No. P 1947)

Let us not forget that Pearse Street, apart from its shops, its coal merchants and monumental sculptors, also boasted along its south side, Trinity College -

> ... and implicit behind the whole length of its southern frontage the College. Perpetuis futuris temporibus duraturum. It was to be hoped so, indeed.
>
> *(More Pricks than Kicks, p. 43)*

In the shadow of the College, Belacqua's progress along Pearse Street, which had gone exceptionally well, was rudely threatened -

> Painfully then under the College ramparts, past the smart taxis, he set off, clearing his mind for its song. The Fire Station worked without a hitch and all was going as well as could be expected considering what the evening held in pickle for him when the blow fell.
>
> *(More Pricks than Kicks, p. 55)*

The showrooms of the sculptor, W. Harrison and Sons (5:51), were situated below the viaduct and it was here that Belacqua came to grief -

5:48 The Gate Theatre,
Cavendish Row

He was run plump into by one Chas, a highbrow bromide of French nationality with a diabolical countenance compound of Skeat's and Paganini's and a mind like a tattered concordance ...

In the lee of the Monumental Showroom Belacqua was obliged to pause and face this machine. It carried butter and eggs from the Hibernian Dairy. Belacqua however was not to be drawn.

(More Pricks than Kicks, p. 55)

The 'Hibernian Dairy' was one of a number of similarly named shops in the city which dispensed fresh dairy produce. The obstacle to progress eventually circumvented, Belacqua was free to return to the serious matter of deciding on which public house would best suit his mood. The choice is not always an easy one in a city which has made an art of purveying drink. Placed strategically as he was at the crossroads of Westland Row and Pearse Street, a bewildering selection was within easy reach. He decided against heading for a more distant hostelry in Merrion Row because of his antipathy to jarveys and poets -

Of the two houses that appealed spontaneously to these exigencies the one, situate in Merrion Row, was a home from home for jarveys. As some folk from hens, so Belacqua shrank from jarveys. Rough, gritty, almost verminous men. From Moore to Merrion Row, moreover, was a perilous way, beset at this hour with poets and peasants and politicians. The other lay in Lincoln Place ...

(More Pricks than Kicks, p. 54)

5:49　A tenament in Mark Street
(Photograph by N. Johnson)

Page 172

5:50 The Palace Cinema,
Pearse Street
(From *The Joyce Country*, by
William York Tindall, Schocken
Books, New York. 1976. p. 85)

5:51 The monumental showrooms of
W. Harrison & Sons.
(By courtesy E. MacThomáis)

He could simply have turned left into Lombard Street, which Beckett has called 'the street of the sanitary engineers'[96] because of its many suppliers of sanitary ware. The street also housed three public houses,[97] of which one may have been Belacqua's haunt -

> Here he was known, in the sense that his grotesque exterior had long ceased to alienate the curates and make them giggle, and to the extent that he was served with his drink without having to call for it. This did not always seem a privilege. He was tolerated, what was more, and let alone by the rough but kindly habitués of the house, recruited for the most part from among dockers, railwaymen and vague joxers on the dole. Here also art and love, scrabbling in dispute or staggering home, were barred, or perhaps better, unknown. The aesthetes and the impotent were far away.
>
> *(More Pricks than Kicks, pp. 43-44)*

Westland Row

Belacqua's choice of direction in 'A Wet Night' is, however, away from the docks towards Westland Row, on this occasion a bad error of judgement -

> ... from out the Grosvenor sprang the homespun Poet wiping his mouth and a little saprophile of an anonymous politico-ploughboy setting him off. The Poet sucked his teeth over this unexpected pleasure. The golden eastern lay of his bullet head was muted by no covering. Beneath the Wally Whitmaneen of his Donegal tweeds a body was to be presumed. He gave the impression of having lost a harrow and found a figure of speech. Belacqua was numbed.
>
> *(More Pricks than Kicks, p. 57)*

Page 173

This time Belacqua was not so successful in shaking off a persuasive representative of Dublin's intelligentsia, whom he had to follow reluctantly into the Grosvenor Hotel (5.52)-

> Belacqua slunk at his heels into the Grosvenor, the gimlet eyes of the saprophile probed his loins
>
> *(More Pricks than Kicks, p. 57)*

The Grosvenor,[98] a fashionable hotel in the early part of the century, was well know to tourists from Britain who arrived on the English mail from Westland Row station across the road. Renowned for Eblana whisky, and its elegant smoking room where the best cigars were to be had, it had little appeal for Belacqua, who, unable to tolerate the poet's company any longer, made a run for freedom -

> 'Pardon me' stuttered Belacqua 'just a moment, will you be so kind.' He waddled out of the bar and into the street and up it at all speed and into the lowly public through the groceries door like a bit of dirt into a Hoover.
>
> *(More Pricks than Kicks, p. 57)*

The 'lowly public' to which Belacqua fled was Kennedy's of Westland Row, where earlier he had purchased the cheese for his lunch in the grocery department (5:53). Kennedy's Pub was situated on the corner of Lincoln Place and Westland Row. Formerly owned by a Mr. Conway, it gains mention in *Ulysses* as 'Conway's Corner',[99] and was bought by Mr. Kennedy in 1907. It had a grocer's shop attached to it until it was renovated in 1941, and the letter-head on its notepaper boasted this facility until Mr. Kennedy sold his business recently.[100] Safe in Kennedy's all that Belacqua lacked for contentment was an evening paper, not to be long denied him as the newspaper boys were in and out like yo-yos (5:54) -

> He bought a paper of a charming little sloven, no but a truly exquisite little page, a freelance clearly, he would not menace him, he skipped in on his miry bare feet with only three or four under his oxter for sale. Belacqua gave him a thrupenny bit and a cigarette picture.
>
> *(More Pricks than Kicks, p. 57)*

These bare-footed lads were extraordinarily vocal in proclaiming their wares -

> What lacerated me most was the din of the newspaper boys. They went pounding by every day at the same hours, their heels thudding on the sidewalk, crying the names of their papers and even the headlines.
>
> *(The End, p. 57)*

5:52 The Grosvenor Hotel, Westland Row (From *The Joyce Country*, by William York Tindall, Schocken Books, New York. 1976. p. 87)

5:53 The back entrance to Kennedy's Public House on the corner of Westland Row and Lincoln Place (Photograph by D. Davison)

5:54 A barefooted newspaper boy by Jack Yeats (By courtesy Anne Yeats)

Once paper and beverage had been acquired, consideration could be given to posture, a prerequisite to some serious drinking (5:55) -

> He sat to himself on a stool in the central leaf of the main triptych, his feet on a round so high that his knees topped the curb of the counter (admirable posture for man with weak bladder and tendency to ptosis of viscera), drank despondent porter (but he dared not budge) and devoured the paper.
> *(More Pricks than Kicks, pp. 57-58)*

Leaving our hero on his stool for the moment, we may consider alternative entertainments that were within easy reach of Westland Row. On other days when mood and finances were not as auspicious, there was the Public Library housed in its large Georgian mansion (5:56) in Pearse Street,[101] a welcome shelter on inclement days -

> always winter then always raining always slipping in somewhere when no one would be looking in off the street out of the cold and rain in the old green holeproof coat your father left you places you hadn't to pay to get in like the Public Library that was another great thing free culture far from home or the Post Office that was another another place another time.
> *(That Time, p. 232)*

On other occasions, a less intellectual ambience was called for. To consort with female company, after a pleasant night's drinking, was not an unreasonable nor uncharacteristic epilogue to a night on the town. In the 'twenties, the decision was whether to take one's chances with the professional ladies or trust to romance at a social gathering. In 'Ding Dong' the former option is taken -

> Now the woman went away and her countenance lighted her to her room in Townsend Street.
> But Belacqua tarried a little to listen to the music. Then he also departed, but for Railway Street, beyond the river.
> *(More Pricks than Kicks, p. 49)*

'The Kips', Dublin's red-light district, was situated at Railway Street (formerly Tyrone Street, and before that Mecklenburgh Street Lower), and Montgomery Street (now Foley Street) from which came the popular name for the area 'Monto'[102](5:57). In this locale, described as 'one of the most dreadful dens of immorality in Europe,' the city police permitted prostitution. It was to this area that Mercier and Camier probably strayed after their mountain sojourn -

> They paced on a little way in silence. Then Mercier said:
> I smell kips.
> *(Mercier and Camier, p. 91)*

5:55 The interior of a Dublin pub
(Photograph by N. Johnson)

5:56 The Public Library,
Pearse Street
(Photograph by D. Davison)

There were a number of famous madames in the area: Mrs. Meg Arnott, Mrs. Annie Mack who operated eight houses on the street, Bella Cohen, who featured in the 'night-town' episode of *Ulysses* [103] and May Oblong. [104]

A police raid in March 1925, during which 120 persons, including a country deputy to Dáil Éireann, were arrested, heralded the end of 'Monto'. Oliver St. John Gogarty, who, in the company of Joyce, had passed many pleasant hours in 'Monto', was so incensed by the impending closure of the brothels that he composed a sonnet entitled 'When the Clearance was intended to the Kips.' [105] However, it was in 'The Hay Hotel' that he expressed most eloquently the activities of the area -

> Shall Becky Cooper be forgot
> Have I forgotten Liverpool Kate
> And all the foam she used to frot
> Were she for one night celebrate?
> I often tried to dam that spate
> When 'Fuck me like a horse!' she'd yell
> And who was I to remonstrate
> Before I sought the Hay Hotel. [106]

Becky Cooper is also commemorated by Beckett in the poem, *Sanies II* -

> upon the saloon a terrible hush
> a shiver convulses Madame de la Motte
> it courses it peals down her collops
> the great bottom foams into stillness
> quick quick the cavaletto supplejacks for mumbo-jumbo
> vivas puellas mortui incurrrrrsant boves
> oh subito subito ere she recover the cang bamboo for
>   bastinado
> a bitter moon fessade à la mode
> oh Becky spare me I have done thee no wrong spare me
>   damn thee
> spare me good Becky
> call off thine adders Becky I will compensate thee in full
> Lord have mercy upon us
> Christ have mercy upon us
>
> Lord have mercy upon us

(Sanies II, p. 20)

5:57 'The Kips', Railway Street
(By courtesy Seamus de Burca)

But let us return to the night in question, to Kennedy's pub where Belacqua, now well oiled, contemplates an amorous engagement with the promise, perhaps, of spiritual as well as carnal satisfaction if all

Page 179

goes well. With a naggin of whiskey safely stowed away, he emerges from Kennedy's into a wet world -

> Half-past nine. It was raining bitterly when Belacqua, keyed up to take his bearings, issued forth into the unintelligible world of Lincoln Place. But he had bought a bottle, it was like a breast in the pocket of his reefer.
>
> *(More Pricks than Kicks, p. 75)*

When it rains in Dublin, it does so persistently and penetratingly[107](5:58) -

> But the wind had dropped, as it so often does in Dublin when all the respectable men and women whom it delights to annoy have gone to bed, and the rain fell in a uniform untroubled manner. It fell upon the bay, the littoral, the mountains and the plains, and notably upon the Central Bog it fell with a rather desolate uniformity.
>
> *(More Pricks than Kicks, p. 87)*

Lincoln Place to Baggot Street

Much the worse for drink as he emerged from Kennedy's, Belacqua's childhood memories of the Dental Hospital (5:59) came flooding through his mind, and feeling weak he leaned against one of the many small iron gateways that permit access to Trinity College to the privileged few who hold a key -

> He set off unsteadily by the Dental Hospital. As a child he had dreaded its facade, its sheets of blood-red glass. Now they were black, which was worse again, he having put aside a childish thing or two. Feeling suddenly white and clammy he leaned against the iron wicket set in the College wall and looked at Johnston, Mooney and O'Brien's clocks. Something to ten by the whirligig and he disinclined to stand, let alone walk.
>
> *(More Pricks than Kicks, p. 75)*

Johnston, Mooney and O'Brien's was a popular bakery and confectionery shop on Leinster Street that sported a fine pair of clocks. Suddenly Belacqua was summoned from his drunken world -

> The next thing was his hands dragged roughly down from his eyes, which he opened on the vast crimson face of an ogre. For a moment it was still, plush gargoyle, then it moved, it was convulsed. This, he thought, is the face of some person talking. It was. It was that part of a Civic Guard pouring abuse upon him. Belacqua closed his eyes, there was no other way of ceasing to see it. Subduing a great desire to visit the pavement he catted, with undemonstrative abundance, all over the boots and trouser-ends of the Guard, in return for which incontinence he received such a dunch on the breast that he fell hip and thigh into the outskirts of his own offal.
>
> *(More Pricks than Kicks, pp. 75-76)*

5:59 The Dental Hospital,
Lincoln Place
(Photograph by D. Davison)

The policeman's mighty boots having been duly cleansed by the repentant inebriate, Belacqua tottered off, via Kildare Street, for his destination in Baggot Street. Feeling 'extraordinarily light and limber and haeres caeli', he philosophised on the state of inebriation, the 'bumless eight of the drink figure.'[108]

The Kildare Street Club, the Royal College of Physicians, the National Library, Leinster House the home of Dáil Éireann, and the National Museum, all on Kildare Street cost Belacqua not a thought. From Kildare Street, he made his way along Baggot Street to Baggot Street Bridge over the Grand Canal, where he paused for a time -

> He stopped on the crown of Baggot Street bridge, took off his reefer, laid it on the parapet and sat down beside it.
>
> *(More Pricks than Kicks, p. 78)*

At the party in 'Casa Frica', somewhere close to the canal, a number of Dublin eccentrics were gathered for an evening's entertainment and conversation. The city's most fashionable thoroughfare, Grafton Street

5:60 Grafton Street
(By courtesy National Library of
Ireland, Eason E1763)

(5:60), is mentioned sparingly for only the second time in all Beckett's writing -

.. a chorus of playwrights, the inevitable envoy of the Fourth Estate, a phalanx of Grafton Street Stürmers and Jemmy Higgins arrived now in a body.

(More Pricks than Kicks, p. 70)

One of the guests, Jem Higgins, 'a weight-lifter, a Rugby man, a pugilist, not even a shinty or camogie man, a feller of ladies with the pillard muscle-fluted thighs bulging behind the stuff'[109] played for a well-known rugby club in Donnybrook, the Bective Rangers (5:61).[110] His skills were duly put to good use at the soirée -

Mr. Higgins, who kicked up his heels in the scrum for the Rangers, made short work of the nuisance.

(More Pricks than Kicks, p. 72)

Belacqua, homeward bound after an amorous night with his beloved Alba, meets the canal once again at Hubband Bridge. The Grand Canal, a waterway of some importance in Beckett's writing, is considered further in Chapter 7.

5:61   Bective Rangers, 1st. XV, Season 1927-28
Backrow: T.E. Murphy *(Hon. Sec.)*; M.A. Sheehan; T.J. Little; M. Deering; C. Carroll; J.J. Sheehan; J.J. Robinson; P.E. Dunn *(President)*. Middle Row: T. Dowd; D.J. O'Connor; J.J. Fitzsimons; J.L. Farrell *(capt)*; J.J. Fitzsimons; P.J. Keane; J. Delany. Front Seated: N. Cuddy; J.C. Arigho.
(By courtesy of Mr. B. Mooney, Bective Rugby Club, Donnybrook)

O'Connell Street and Environs

O'Connell Street, formerly Sackville Street, and now named after Daniel O'Connell, the Great Liberator,[111] whose statue overlooks O'Connell Bridge, is Dublin's main thoroughfare. A number of institutes on this street feature in Beckett's writing.

The General Post Office

Not far from O'Connell Bridge is the General Post Office, an imposing building designed by Francis Johnston in 1814-18 (5:62). Its interior was badly damaged when it was used by Pearse and Connolly as the Republican headquarters in the 1916 Easter rising, but the main facade escaped serious damage.[112] The interior was rebuilt and a statue of Cuchulain,[113] an Irish folk hero, was erected symbolising the martyrdom of the signatories to the proclamation of the Republic, all seven of whom were executed in 1916.[114] Always thronged with people, the Post Office

5:62 The General Post Office,
O'Connell Street
(By courtesy National Library of
Ireland, Eason E1743)

was another of many public refuges frequented by a tired wanderer -

> always winter then endless winter year after year as if it couldn't end the old year never end like time could go no further that time in the Post Office all bustle Christmas bustle in off the street when no one was looking out of the cold and rain pushed open the door like anyone else and straight for the table neither right nor left with all the forms and the pens on their chains sat down first vacant seat and were taking a look round for a change before drowsing away.
>
> *(That Time, p. 233)*

The statue of Ireland's legendary hero (5:63) is called upon to fulfil an unlikely role in one of the funniest moments in *Murphy* -

> In Dublin a week later, that would be September 19th, Neary minus his whiskers was recognized by a former pupil called Wylie, in the General Post Office, contemplating from behind the statue of Cuchulain. Neary had bared his head, as though the holy ground meant something to him. Suddenly he flung aside his hat, sprang forward, seized the dying hero by the thighs and began to dash his head against his buttocks, such as they are.
>
> *(Murphy, p. 33)*

5:63 *The Fall of Cuchulain* by Oliver Sheppard in the General Post Office
(Photograph by D. Davison)

But for the intervention of the inevitable policeman, and the even quicker action by Neary's friend Wylie, Cuchulain's athletic rump would have provided Neary with the means for his extinction.[115]

Nelson's Pillar

Wylie effected Neary's escape by hurrying him onto a Dalkey tram at Nelson's Pillar, the turnabout point for the south-bound trams (5:64) -

> Wylie rushed him into the street and into a Dalkey tram that had just come in.
>
> *(Murphy, p. 34)*

Trams were the city's main form of transport until 1949 when they were discontinued,[116] an event acknowledged in nostalgic tones by Beckett in *That Time* -

> straight off the ferry and up with the nightbag to the high street neither right nor left not a curse for the old scenes the old names straight up the rise from the wharf to the high street and there not a wire to be seen only the old rails all rust...
>
> *(That Time, pp. 228-229)*

Belacqua preferred buses to trams -

> Trams were monsters, moaning along beneath the wild gesture of the trolley. But buses were pleasant, tyres and glass and clash and no more.
>
> *(More Pricks than Kicks, p. 54)*

5:64 Nelson's Pillar, O'Connell Street with the tram turnabout at the base
(By courtesy National Library of Ireland, Eason 1758)

Beckett bestows on the tram life and feelings, albeit those of a monster,[117] in *Dream of Fair to Middling Women*. -

> At the end of the street they parted. The Alba boarded a tram and like a Cézanne monster it carried her off, it moaned down Nassau Street into the darkness, little thinking what a royal and fragile tuppenny fare it had in keeping.
>
> *(Dream of Fair to Middling Women, p. 149)*

Nelson's Pillar or Column, one of the city's best known landmarks, was blasted to earth in 1966 by extremists whose motives are unknown to this day.[118] This memorial rising to a height of 134 feet, and surmounted by a statue of Nelson by Kirk was erected in 1808. It contained a spiral stairway by which, for a few pence, one could climb to the top to stand 'dizzily on the doric abacus, overlooking the G.P.O. and O'Connell Street',[119] and of course, the mountains (5:65) -

> The treacherous hills where fearfully he ventured were no doubt only known to him from afar, seen perhaps from his bedroom window or from the summit of a monument which, one black day, having nothing in particular to do and turning

5:65 View of O'Connell Street, and the Dublin mountains from the top of Nelson's Pillar (Photograph by G.A. Duncan)

to height for solace, he had paid his few coppers to climb, slower and slower, up the winding stones. From there he must have seen it all, the plain, the sea, and then these selfsame hills that some call mountains, indigo in places in the evening light, their serried ranges crowding to the skyline, cloven with hidden valleys that the eye divines from sudden shifts of colour and then from other signs for which there are no words, nor even thoughts. But all are not divined, even from that height, and often where only one escarpment is discerned, and one crest, in reality there are two, two escarpments, two crests, riven by a valley.

(Molloy, p. 10)

It was the railings surrounding the plinth of the Pillar that supported Neary when he realised the accursed holy hour was upon him -

'But by Mooney's clock,' said Wylie, 'the sad news is two-thirty-three.'
Neary leaned against the Pillar railings and cursed, first the day in which he was born, then – in a bold flash-back – the night in which he was conceived.

(Murphy, p. 35)

Nelson's Pillar occupied a site in the centre of O'Connell Street, with the General Post Office to one side, and one of the city's largest stores, Clerys,[120] on the other (5:66) -

The crone was as fond of the P.B. as though she had bought him in Clery's toy fair.
(More Pricks than Kicks, p. 68)

5:66   Clery's Store, O'Connell Street
with Nelson's Pillar to the left
(By courtesy National Library of
Ireland, Valentine, 215097)

Abbey Street

A short distance from the Pillar, O'Connell Street is crossed by Abbey Street where four institutes feature in Beckett's works. On Middle Abbey Street there is the Oval Bar, where one named Sproule, assistant to Hairy, Belacqua's best man, is rewarded for his services in *More Pricks than Kicks* -

> Sproule raised his sad eyes to the sky and saw the day, its outstanding hours that could not be numbered, in the form of a beautiful Girl Guide galante, reclining among the clouds. She beckoned to him with her second finger, like one preparing a certificate in pianoforte, Junior Grade, at the Leinster School of Music. Closing his mind softly on this delicious vision, feeling it in his mind like a sponge of toilet vinegar on a fever, he advanved into the Oval towards it.
>
> *(More Pricks than Kicks, p. 142)*

5:67 Wynn's Hotel,
Lower Abbey Street
(From the *Irish Builder and
Engineer*. Feb. 5, 1927. Vol. 69,
p. 76. By courtesy National
Library of Ireland)

5:68 Mooney's Bar,
Lower Abbey Street
(Photograph by G.A. Duncan,
No. NB140063)

The Leinster School of Music was situated at No. 43, Harcourt Street. On Lower Abbey Street we find the Abbey Theatre, Wynn's Hotel[121](5:67), and Mooney's Bar (5:68). In the latter hostelries, Neary, Miss Counihan and Wylie plotted their trip to London to reunite Murphy with Miss Counihan -

> While Cooper was combing London, where he would stay at the usual stew, Neary would be working a line of his own in Dublin, where Wynn's Hotel would always find him.
>
> *(Murphy, p. 41)*

In Mooney's public house across the road from Wynn's Hotel, Neary succumbed to love-sickness in a manner as strange as it was original -

> He instructed the hall porter in Wynn's to send any telegrams addressed to him from London across the street to Mooney's, where he would always be found. There he sat all day, moving slowly from one stool to another until he had completed the circuit of the counters, when he would start all over again in the reverse direction. He did not speak to the curates, he did not drink the endless half-pints of porter that he had to buy, he did nothing but move slowly round the ring of counters, first in one direction, then in the other, thinking of Miss Counihan.
>
> *(Murphy, p. 42)*

We may, in passing, note the physical attributes of the beautiful Miss Counihan, the contemporary embodiment of Cathleen ní Houlihan -

> For an Irish girl Miss Counihan was quite exceptionally anthropoid. Wylie was not sure that he cared altogether for her mouth, which was a large one. The kissing surface was greater than the rosebud's, but less highly toned. Otherwise she did. It is superfluous to describe her, she was just like any other beautiful Irish girl, except, as noted, more markedly anthropoid. How far this constitutes an advantage is what every man must decide for himself.
>
> *(Murphy, p. 83)*

Mary Street

Henry Street leads directly from the site of Nelson's Pillar past Moore Street to Mary Street (5:69) where Belacqua's best man, Hairy, in the company of Capper Quin, purchased flowers for Belacqua's wedding-

> He led the way to a florist's off Mary Street. The proprietress, having just discovered among her stock an antirrhinum with the rudiment of a fifth stamen, was highly delighted.
>
> *(More Pricks than Kicks, p. 140)*

Mary Street is situated in a part of the city that might not be expected to command the prices readily realised in the more fashionable Grafton Street area, at the lower end of which may be found Nassau Street[122] -

> She now mentioned a sum that caused the buyer great amusement. He appealed to Hairy.
> 'Mr. Quin' he said, 'do I wake or sleep?'
> She not merely made good her figures but mentioned that she had to live. Sproule could not see the connexion. He pinched his cheek to make sure he was not in Nassau Street. 'My dear madam' he said, 'we do not have to live in Nassau Street.'
> *(More Pricks than Kicks, p. 141)*

The Neighbourhood of North Great George's Street

In the story 'What a Misfortune' in *More Pricks than Kicks,* Belacqua is destined to marry one named Thelma bboggs, younger daughter of Mr. and Mrs. Otto Olaf bboggs who resided at 55 North Great George's Street[123](5:70). This street was once one of Dublin's finest Georgian streets, but, sadly, at the time of our hero's courtship it had fallen into considerable decay, a fact which no doubt influenced Mrs. bboggs to attempt to persuade her husband, Olaf, to move to the more salubrious environs of the Beckett home -

> He was said to have the finest and most comprehensive collection of choice furniture in North Great George's Street, from which lousy locality, notwithstanding the prayers of his wife and first-born for a home of their own very own in Foxrock, he refused coarsely to remove.
> *(More Pricks than Kicks, p. 128)*

Olaf, having worked hard to aquire his home on North Great George's Street, was not easily influenced (5:71) -

> ... all the ups and downs of a strenuous career instituted in the meanest household fixture and closing now in the glories of Hepplewhites and bombé commodes,

were bound up in good old grand old North Great George's Street, in consideration of which he had pleasure in referring his wife and first-born to that portion of himself which he never desired any person to kick nor volunteered to kiss in another.

(More Pricks than Kicks, p. 128)

There is also mention of North Great George's Street in the early prose piece *Sedendo et Quiesciendo* -

Crémieux hold your Saliva and you Curtius, I have a note somewhere on Anteros I believe, in fact I seem to remember I once wrote a poem (Nth. Gt. Georges St. diphthong Captain Duncan if you please) on him or to hom cogged from the lecherous laypriest's Magic Ode and if I don't forget I'll have the good taste to use the little duckydiver as a kind of contrapuntal compensation do you comprehend me and in deference to your Pisan penchants for literary stress and strain.

5:69 Mary Street, The Cinematograph Theatre (Photograph by N. Johnson)

5:70 The Hall-door of No. 38 North Great George's Street (By courtesy Irish Architectural Archive, No. 10/4 x 1)

5:71 Interior of a North Great George's Street drawing-room (By courtesy Irish Architectural Archive, No. 10/7Y2)

5:72   St. Peter's Church, Phibsboro
       (By courtesy National Library of
       Ireland, Eason 1876)

5:73   Denmark Street
       (By courtesy Royal Society of
       Antiquaries of Ireland. No. 9.
       'Darkest Dublin' Collection)

Dublin in the 'twenties and 'thirties was one of the finest examples of a Georgian city, and its architecture was appreciated and recalled by Beckett in the minutest detail -

> I have always greatly admired the door of this house, up on top of its little flight of steps. How describe it? It was a massive green door, encased in summer in a kind of green and white striped housing, with a hole for the thunderous wrought-iron knocker and a slit for letters, this latter closed to dust, flies and tits by a brass flap fitted with springs.
>
> *(The Expelled, p. 23)*

Belacqua's wedding in 'What a Misfortune', takes place in the Church of Saint Tamar which does not exist, but that its spire was 'pointed almost to the point of indecency', suggests St. Peter's Church in Phibsboro[124] (5:72). The wedding, predictably, is a fiasco, from which Belaqua effected an early departure -

> 'Slip out quick' said Belacqua 'and run her behind into the lane off Denmark Street.'
> *(More Pricks than Kicks, p. 158)*

Denmark Street (5:73) is at one end of North Great George's Street and a lane from it runs behind the houses, on the southern side of the street. Having bolted the feast, the bride and groom head for Galway in a Morgan three-wheeler. Four other guests retreat to Charlemont House, (now the Hugh Lane Municipal Gallery of Modern Art) on Parnell Square[125] (5:74) -

> As for the other four, they did not feel safe until they reached the Capella Lane, superb cenotheca, in Charlemont House. Nobody would ever think of looking for them there.
>
> *(More Pricks than Kicks, p. 159)*

5:74 Charlemont House,
Parnell Square.
(By courtesy National Library of
Ireland, Eason 1721)

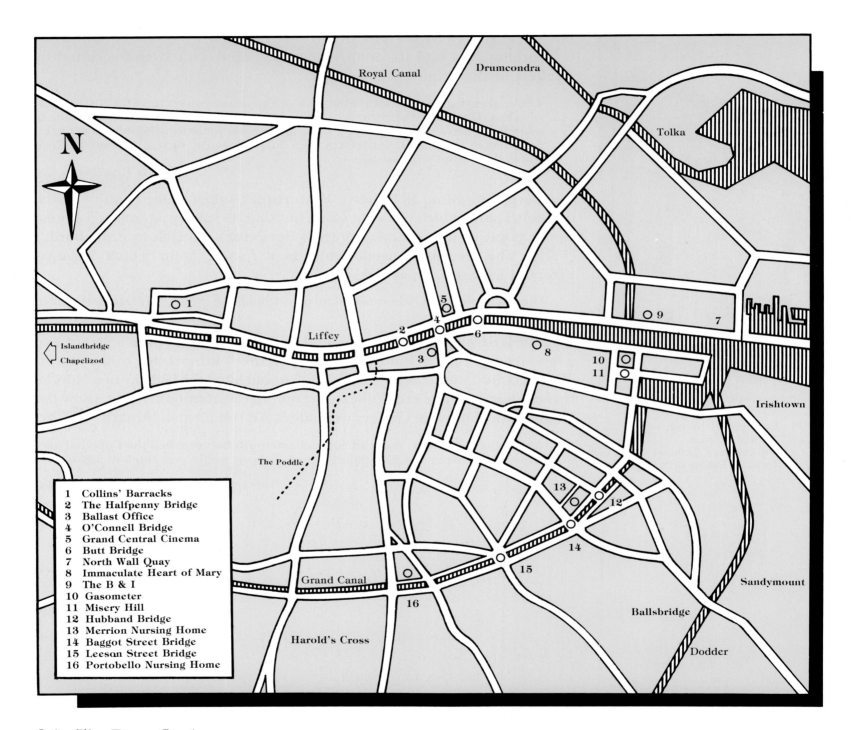

6:1 The River Circle

Chapter Six

THE RIVER CIRCLE

Dublin is divided by two canals, the Grand and the Royal, and a number of rivers of which the Liffey, flowing from the Dublin mountains to the sea, is the largest. The Grand Canal and the Liffey encircle a part of the city that was well known to Beckett (6:1). Though this route does not feature as a sequence in Beckett's writings, it is convenient to consider the river references in topographical order progressing from the Grand Canal at Ringsend to Chapelizod, and from Chapelizod back along the Liffey, as it bisects the city, to its entry at the sea near Ringsend.

The Huband Bridge

Proceeding from the canal basin along the Grand Canal, the first bridge to be encountered in Beckett's Dublin was the dreaded Victoria Bridge, (now McMahon Bridge) at which Belacqua had had such difficulty in crossing by motor car (see Chapter 3). The next bridge on the Canal to feature in Beckett's writing is the attractive Huband Bridge (6:2). Belacqua's drunken peregrinations through the city in 'A Wet Night' have been traced in Chapter 5, where we left the hero in the arms of the Alba, in a house somewhere in the locality of Baggot Street and the Canal. Departing the Alba in the small hours of the morning to wend his way home, he came to an abrupt halt on the Huband Bridge[1] -

> When he came to the bridge over the canal, not Baggot Street, not Leeson Street, but another nearer the sea, he gave in and disposed himself in the knee-and-elbow position on the pavement.
>
> *(More Pricks than Kicks, p. 87-88)*

Huband Bridge has relevance in the Beckett canon for another reason. Beckett's mother died, on August 25th 1950, in the Merrion Nursing Home,[2] No. 21 Herbert Street, overlooking the Huband Bridge[3] -

> ... there is of course the house on the canal where mother lay a-dying, in the late autumn, after her long viduity ...
>
> *(Krapp's Last Tape, p. 59)*

Beckett nursed his mother during her last illness,[4] and from a bench on the canal gazed at the window of her room (6:3) -

> – bench by the weir from where I could see her window. There I sat, in the biting wind, wishing she were gone. *(Pause.)* Hardly a soul, just a few regulars, nursemaids, infants, old men, dogs.
>
> *(Krapp's Last Tape, p. 59)*

A drawn blind, an old custom signifying death, announced his mother's departure -

> – the blind went down, one of those dirty brown roller affairs, throwing a ball for a little white dog as chance would have it. I happened to look up and there it was. All over and done with, at last. I sat on for a few moments with the ball in my hand and the dog yelping and pawing at me. *(Pause.)* Moments. Her moments, my moments. *(Pause.)* The dog's moments.
>
> *(Krapp's Last Tape, p. 60)*

6:2 The Huband Bridge and Upper Mount Street (Photograph by N. Johnson)

6:3 The top window of The Merrion Nursing Home from the bank of the Grand Canal (Photograph by D. Davison)

This profound experience may also be sensed in *Rockaby* -

> so in the end
> close of a long day
> went down
> in the end went down
> down the steep stair
> let down the blind and down
> right down
> into the old rocker
> mother rocker
> where mother rocked
> all the years
> all in black
> best black
> sat and rocked
> rocked
> till her end came
> in the end came

(Rockaby, p. 280)

6:4   The Grand Canal from
Baggot Street Bridge
(Photograph by D. Davison)

Baggot and Leeson Street Bridges

It was on Baggot Street Bridge that Belacqua stopped en route to 'Casa Frica' for his rendezvous with the Alba (6:4). Sitting precariously on the parapet of the bridge, he viewed the distant lights of Leeson Street Bridge (6:5) to the west[5] -

> Next, resolved to get full value from the bitter nor'wester that was blowing, he slewed himself right round. His feet dangled over the canal and he saw, lurching across the remote hump of Leeson Street bridge, trams like hiccups-o'-the-wisp. Distant lights on a dirty night, how he loved them, the dirty low-church Protestant!
>
> *(More Pricks than Kicks, p. 78)*

Beckett is not the only Irish writer to have found peace and inspiration on the Grand Canal at Baggot Street Bridge. Patrick Kavanagh loved the spot and his prayer for a simple memorial was answered, on St. Patrick's Day 1968, with the erection of a seat from which the casual passer-by may contemplate the shimmering waters flowing beneath the trees[6] -

6:5   Leeson Street Bridge
(Photograph by N. Johnson)

> O COMMEMORATE me where there is water,
> Canal water preferably, so stilly
> Greeny at the heart of summer. Brother
> Commemorate me thus beautifully.
> Where by a lock Niagariously roars
> The falls for those who sit in the tremendous silence
> Of mid-July. No one will speak in prose
> Who finds his way to these Parnassian islands.
> A swan goes by head low with many apologies,
> Fantastic light looks through the eye of bridges –
> And look! a barge comes bringing from Athy
> And other far-flung towns mythologies.
> O commemorate me with no hero-courageous
> Tomb – just a canal-bank seat for the passer-by.
>
> (Patrick Kavanagh. *Lines written on a seat on the Grand Canal,*
> *Dublin, 'Erected to the memory of Mrs Dermot O'Brien')*

Charlemont Street Bridge

After Leeson Street Bridge there is Charlemont Street Bridge,[7] on which Mr. Hackett and the Nixons observed Watt on his way to Harcourt Street Station -

> There he is now, on the bridge, said Mrs. Nixon.
> He stood with his back towards them, from the waist up faintly outlined against the last wisps of day.
>
> *(Watt, p. 16)*

Portobello Bridge

Moving in a westerly direction along the Canal, Portobello Bridge[8] is reached. This bridge with its adjacent nursing home[9](6:6) features in the poem *Enueg I*, which evokes a walk along the banks of the Grand Canal and the River Liffey. This poem laments the impending death of a young woman from tuberculosis in Portobello Nursing Home[10] -

> Exeo in a spasm
> tired of my darling's red sputum
> from the Portobello Private Nursing Home
> its secret things
> and toil to the crest of the surge of the steep perilous bridge
> and lapse down blankly under the scream of the hoarding
> round the bright stiff banner of the hoarding
> into a black west
> throttled with clouds.

(Enueg I, p. 10)

The steep perilous footbridge (6:7), and the hoarding are still there, though the advertisments have changed. The hoarding seems to have impressed itself on Beckett's memory, as we find it mentioned again

6:6 Portobello Bridge with a barge in the lock; Portobello Nursing Home is on the left
(By courtesy Bord Failte, D8/46)

6:7 The 'perilous footbridge' at Portobello Lock; the advertising hoarding is in the background (By courtesy Bord Failte, No. D56/51)

in the early short story, *A Case in a Thousand*, in which a young boy dies in hospital -

> He stood with Surgeon Bor at the end window of the long ward and looked out. Canal, bridge, lock and bright hoarding composed the scene. Three groups had gathered, one on the bridge and one on either bank, to watch a barge pass through the lock.
>
> *(A Case in a Thousand, p. 241)*

Tall trees skirt the canal in many places (6:8), and in the distance the Dublin mountains beckon to the distressed narrator -

> Above the mansions the algum-trees
> the mountains
> my skull sullenly
> clot of anger
> skewered aloft strangled in the cang of the wind
> bites like a dog against its chastisement.
>
> *(Enueg I, p. 10)*

Parnell Bridge

At Parnell Bridge,[11] a dying barge may still be found (6:9) -

> I trundle along rapidly now on my ruined feet
> flush with the livid canal;
> at Parnell Bridge a dying barge
> carrying a cargo of nails and timber
> rocks itself softly in the foaming cloister of the lock;
> on the far bank a gang of down and outs would seem to
>   be mending a beam.
>
> *(Enueg I, p. 10)*

A similar scene is recounted in *Molloy* -

> I got down, I put my foot to the ground the better to see the approaching barge, so gently approaching that the water was unruffled. It was a cargo of nails and timber, on its way to some carpenter I suppose. My eyes caught a donkey's eyes, they fell to his little feet, their brave fastidious tread. The boatman rested his elbow on his knee, his head on his hand. He had a long white beard. Every three or four puffs, without taking his pipe from his mouth, he spat into the water.
>
> *(Molloy, pp. 26-27)*

The canal soon leaves the city and leads to the country and the Dublin mountains claim attention to the south -

> Then for miles only wind
> and the weals creeping alongside on the water
> and the world opening up to the south
> across a travesty of champaign to the mountains
>
> *(Enueg I, p. 11)*

But the pastoral tranquility of the canal can easily be disturbed by a variety of animals -

> Next:
> a lamentable family of grey verminous hens,
> perishing out in the sunk field,
> trembling, half asleep, against the closed door of a shed,
> with no means of roosting.
>
> *(Enueg I, p. 12)*

Indeed, the banks of Dublin's canals (of which there are two, the Royal, and the Grand), are frequented more by animals than by humans (6:10) -

> There I am then, before I knew I had left the town, on the canal-bank. The canal goes through the town, I know I know, there are even two. But then these hedges, these fields? Don't torment yourself, Molloy. Suddenly I see, it was my right leg the stiff one, then. Toiling towards me along the tow-path I saw a team of little grey donkeys, on the far bank, and I heard angry cries and dull blows.
>
> *(Molloy, p. 26)*

6:8   Trees along the bank of the Grand Canal
(Photograph by N. Johnson)

6:9   Parnell Bridge with a 'dying barge'
(Photograph by E. O'Brien)

6:10   Horses and a donkey on the
canal bank
(Photograph by E. O'Brien)

In *First Love*, the canal bank is the scene of an amorous encounter -

> I met her on a bench, on the bank of the canal, one of the canals, for our town
> boasts two, though I never knew which was which.
>
> *(First Love, p. 5)*

As the Grand Canal departs the city, the pavements are replaced by
undulating green-verged towpaths[12] -

> ... alone on the towpath with the ghosts of the mules the drowned rat or bird or
> whatever it was floating off into the sunset till you could see it no more nothing
> stirring only the water and the sun going down till it went down and you vanished
> all vanished.
>
> *(That Time, p. 233)*

Even Mercier and Camier, neither of whom is inclined to pass
compliment on man or place, acknowledge the charm of the canal -

> The little bridges slip by, said Camier, ever fewer and farther between. We pore
> over the locks, trying to understand. From the barges made fast to the bank waft
> the watermen's voices, bidding us good-night. Their day is done, they smoke a
> last pipe before turning in.
>
> *(Mercier and Camier, p. 22)*

The Liffey

In the poem, *Enueg I*, Beckett follows the Grand Canal as far as the locality known as the Fox and Geese before turning down a steep hill away from the Grand Canal into the village of Chapelizod on the river Liffey (6:11) -

> Next:
> on the hill down from the Fox and Geese into Chapelizod...
>
> *(Enueg I, p. 12)*

The name of Chapelizod is said to derive from the lovely princess, *la belle Iseult* or Isolde, the daughter of King Anguisshe, King of Ireland, who flourished in the days of King Arthur.[13] In Chapelizod, Beckett's attention is arrested by a gathering of men who have been watching a Sunday game of hurling in the nearby locality of Kilmainham -

> the Isolde Stores a great perturbation of sweaty heros,
> in their Sunday best,
> come hastening down for a pint of nepenthe or moly or
> half and half
> from watching the hurlers above in Kilmainham.
>
> *(Enueg I, p. 12)*

6:11   Chapelizod on the Liffey
(By courtesy National Library of
Ireland, Lawrence, 678)

This scene is first presented in *Dream of Fair to Middling Women*,[14] where in addition to the Islode Stores and the Kilmainham hurlers there is mention of the 'Park Gates' guarding one of the entrances to the Phoenix Park opposite the bridge across the Liffey, known as Island Bridge[15] (6:12) -

> Belacqua took cognisance of this corpulent reportage on his way home from the Fox and Geese over cheese and porter in the tabernacle of a wayfarer's public near the Island Bridge that has since been destroyed and consumed utterly by brimstone the bishops all say.
>
> *(Dream of Fair to Middling Women, p. 163)*

The 'public' that provided sustenance for a tiring Belacqua was probably *The Mullingar Hotel*, so named not by virtue of its proximity to Mullingar, which is all of fifty miles distant, but as an indication to the thirsty traveller that he is either at the start or the end of his journey, either event being a just cause for contemplation.

If, instead of following the Liffey back into the city of Dublin as we shall do, we were to proceed along its banks in a westerly direction, we would come to the picturesque riverside village of Leixlip with its famed Salmon Leap (6:13), at which Nemo finally meets his nemesis -

> C.J. Nicholas Nemo saltabat sobrius and in amore sapebat and had in consequence in the prepuscular gloom of Good Friday's or was it Lady Day's autumnal cetava been withdrawn more dead than alive from under the stairs of the Salmon Leap at Leixlip by Adam of St. Victor most notorious poacher who on being interrogated turned a little yellow as well he might and was understood to depose that Ireland was a Paradise for women and a Hell for hosses and that he had no doubt at all in his own mind that the Lord would have mercy on whom he would have mercy.
>
> *(Dream of Fair to Middling Women, p. 162)*

Beside Leixlip, there is the village of Lucan, overlooked by its Spa Hotel[16] (6:14), to which establishment the drowned Nemo was being rushed in a jaunting car -

> ... the poor young gentleman before coughing up and commending in a vague general way his spirit in the well of the jaunting-car that was bearing them post-haste to the Stillorgan Sunshine Home or was it the Lucan Spa Hotel, had embraced him with a wild Spanish light in his dusked eyes...
>
> *(Dream of Fair to Middling Women, p. 163)*

In *The End*, the narrator spends his last days on a private estate close to the banks of a river. It is not possible to locate this river precisely, but the occurrence of a barracks and its playground suggests the Liffey -

> From the last quays beyond the water the eyes rose to a confusion of low houses, wasteland, hoardings, chimneys, steeples and towers. A kind of parade ground was also to be seen, where soldiers played football all the year round.
>
> *(The End, p. 66)*

6:12   Island Bridge
       (By courtesy *Collection Ireland*)

6:13   Salmon Leap at Leixlip
       (By courtesy National Library of
       Ireland, Lawrence, 6811)

6:14   The Spa Hotel, Lucan
       (By courtesy National Library of
       Ireland, Lawrence, Royal 9106)

6:15 Collins' Barracks and playing fields from Wolfe Tone Quay (Photograph by D. Davison)

6:16 The 'fingers' of a ladder on the Liffey parapet (Photograph by D. Davison)

The barracks was probably Collins' Barracks,[17] situated on Benburb Street, which has playing fields fronting on to the quays (6:15). From here, the narrator in *The End* paddles a boat down the Liffey to its mouth, and on out to the sea of Dublin Bay and oblivion.

The Liffey, rising in the Dublin mountains in the west, bisects Dublin as it flows towards the sea. It is crossed by a number of bridges, and is joined by two small rivers, the Camac and the Poddle,[18] which running underground for most of their courses, are heavily polluted with sewage and industrial waste. At Capel Street Bridge, the Poddle makes its underground exit into the Liffey -

> His back is turned to the river, but perhaps it appears to him in the dreadful cries of the gulls that evening assembles, in paroxysms of hunger, round the outflow of the sewers, opposite the Bellevue Hotel. Yes, they too, in a last frenzy before night and its high crags, swoop ravening about the offal.
>
> *(Malone Dies, p. 230)*

This scene is depicted again in the poem *Enueg I*, with the additional feature of the Liffey ladders clasping the granite parapet[19] (6:16) -

> Blotches of doomed yellow in the pit of the Liffey;
> the fingers of the ladders hooked over the parapet,
> soliciting;
> a slush of vigilant gulls in the grey spew of the sewer.
>
> *(Enueg I, p. 12)*

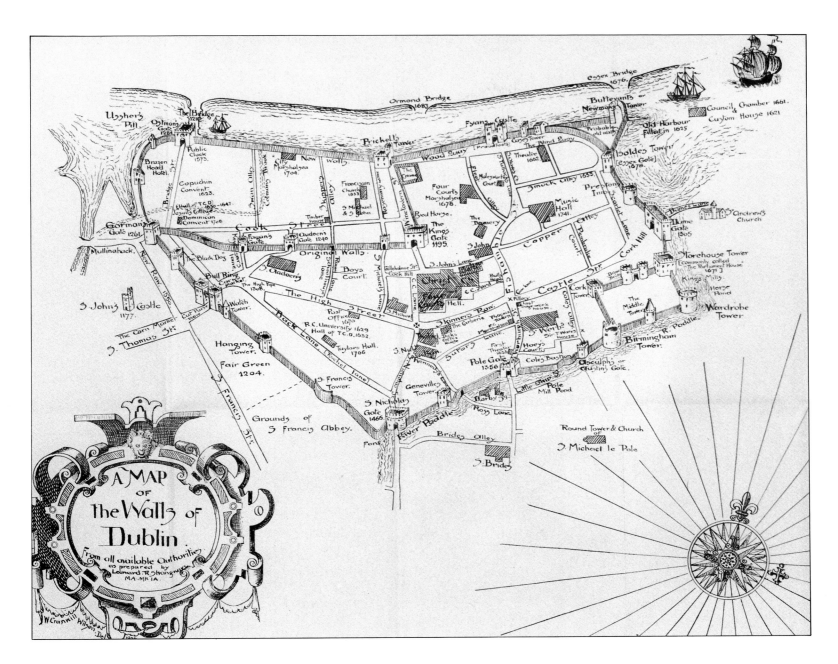

6:17   Map of the Poddle with the old
       walls of Dublin City
       (*Dublin Main Drainage Scheme
       Souvenir Handbook* Sealy, Bryers
       and Walker, Dublin 1906.
       facing p. 10)

The name of the Bellevue Hotel is fictitious, but a well-known Dublin hotel, *The Clarence,* does exist above the point where the Poddle enters the Liffey. The Poddle flows through the 'Liberties', the old walled city of Dublin once entered only through its historic gates, of which only one, St. Audoen's, now stands.[20] The references to the 'Sheppard's Gate' in *The Calmative*[21] may be to the Cornmarket Gate leading to the Bull Ring and Cornmarket (6:17). The Poddle receives further brief mention in *More Pricks than Kicks,*[22] along with another city river the Tolka[23](6:18) which also features in the earlier story *Sedendo et Quiesciendo -*

> ... or crossed the Seine or the Tolka or the Pegnitz or the Fulda as the case might be and it never for one single solitary instant occurring to me that he was on all such and similar occasions (which we are sorry to say lack of space obliges us regretfully to exclude from this chronicle) indulging in the pandering to the vilest and basest excesses of sublimation of a certain kind.
>
> *(Sedendo et Quiesciendo, p. 16)*

The Liffey at sunset, drawing colour from the reddening sky, creates pools of vibrant hue[24](6:19) -

> The water cradles already the distant fires of the sunset, orange, rose and green, quenches them in its ruffles and then in trembling pools spreads them bright again.
>
> *(Malone Dies, p. 230)*

6:18   Tolka Bridge, Drumcondra
       (By courtesy National Library of
       Ireland, Lawrence, Royal 10528)

6:19　The Liffey Quays at sunset
(Photograph by N. Johnson)

6:20 A city drinking trough
for horses
(Photograph by N. Johnson)

Many of the Liffey's unique features have disappeared, and the personality and character of this river traversing the capital, which it once so endowed with unique grace and charm, have now been dissipated. Mrs. Maxwell's watering trough for the horses of the city may never have existed, but there were many such conveniences erected by The London Metropolitan Drinking Trough Association, most of which have long since disappeared[25](6:20) -

> Yes, the river still gave the impression it was flowing in the wrong direction. That's all a pack of lies I feel. My bench was still there. It was shaped to fit the curves of the seated body. It stood beside a watering trough, gift of a Mrs. Maxwell to the city horses, according to the inscription. During the short time I rested there several horses took advantage of this monument.
>
> *(The End, p. 54)*

Many of the Liffey warehouses are also now gone (6:21) -

> But for Macmann, thank God, he's still there, for Macmann it is a true spring evening, an equinoctial gale howls along the quays bordered by high red houses, many of which are warehouses.
>
> *(Malone Dies, p. 232)*

The Guinness barges,[26] ferrying their precious cargo from the brewery to far-flung destinations, are also of the past -

> The tugs, their black funnels striped with red, tow to their moorings the last barges, freighted with empty barrels.
>
> *(Malone Dies, p. 230)*

6:21 Houses and warehouses on
Arran Quay
(Photograph by N. Johnson)

The Metal Bridge

Between Capel Street Bridge and O'Connell Bridge is the Wellington Bridge,[27] known by Dubliners as the Metal or Halfpenny Bridge, the latter appellation deriving from its original use as a toll bridge (6:22). It is a graceful, single-span, cast-iron footbridge on which Dubliners 'converse and friendly meet.' Belacqua's best-man in *More Pricks than Kicks* meets the egotistical Walter Draffin upon this bridge -

> Whom should Hairy meet on the crest of the Metal Bridge but Walter Draffin, fresh from his effeminate ablutions and as spruce and keen as a new-ground hatchet in his miniature tails and stripes.
>
> *(More Pricks than Kicks, p. 142)*

The Bridge has always been and still is a favourite spot for beggars (6:23), an occasion made use of by the passing humorist who drops a coin in the best-man's outstretched top-hat -

> Hairy, with a sudden feeling that he was wasting his client's time and his own precarious energies on a kind of rubber Stalin, took his departure with a more than boorish abruptness, leaving Walter to enjoy the great central agency and hang out as it were his cowlick to air or dry. A passing humorist dropped a penny into the empty hat, it fell on the rich wadding without a sound, and so the joke was lost.
>
> *(More Pricks than Kicks, p. 144)*

6:22   The Halfpenny Bridge
(Photograph by N. Johnson)

6:23 A beggar-woman on the
Halfpenny Bridge
(Photograph by N. Johnson)

The Metal Bridge also features prominently in *Dream of Fair to Middling Women*[28] -

> There the wind was big and he was wise who stirred not at all, came not abroad. The man, Nemo to be precise, was on his bridge, curved over the western parapet. High over the black water he leaned out, he let fall a foaming spit, it fell plumb to the top of the arch, then was scattered, by the Wild West Wind. He moved off left to the end of the bridge, he lapsed down blankly on to the quay where the bus rank is, he set off sullenly, his head sullenly, clot of anger, skewered aloft, strangled in the cang of the wind, biting like a dog against its chastisement.
>
> *(Dream of Fair to Middling Women, p. 48)*

The quay with the bus rank is Aston Quay, which joins O'Connell bridge on the southern side (6:24). There is a subtle pun in Walter Draffin's remark to Hairy on the Metal Bridge -

> 'This is where I stand' said the little creature, with a sigh that made Hairy look nervously round for prisons and palaces, 'and watch the Liffey swim.'
>
> *(More Pricks than Kicks, p. 143)*

This reference is to the Annual Liffey Swim or Race, a popular event attracting as many as eighty competitors and a large crowd of Dubliners (6:25). Oliver Gogarty, a regular competitor when asked once as he emerged at the finishing line how he had performed, made witty

6:24   The bus-rank at Aston Quay
       and a Guinness barge on the
       Liffey
       (By courtesy Bord Failte, D5/52)

6:25 *The Liffey Swim* by
Jack B. Yeats
(By courtesy National Library
of Ireland, No. 941)

reference to the Liffey's pollution, by answering that he had not so much been swimming, as 'going through the motions.' In the race programme for 1925, the Beckett family's interest in swimming is evident; one of the judges, Jim Beckett, was an uncle of Samuel Beckett[29](6:26). This uncle was well-known in Dublin for his swimming achievements -

Dockrell, Tagert, Beckett, where
Are the men I worshipped there?
Some still rub the pink flesh dry
some have laid their towels by.[30]

O'Connell Bridge

Next to the Metal Bridge is O'Connell Bridge, named in honour of the 'Great Liberator', Daniel O'Connell, whose statue by the sculptor John Henry Foley[31] stands at its northern end, where the city's main thoroughfare, O'Connell Street begins (6:27) -

> doch I assure thee
> lying on O'Connell Bridge
> goggling at the tulips of the evening
> the green tulips
> shining round the corner like an anthrax
> shining on Guinness's barges

(Enueg II, pp. 13-14)

On Aston Quay, 'the quay where the bus rank is', the Ballast office[32] with its clock overlooking O'Connell Bridge and the Liffey once graced the quayside (6:28) -

> to the scribe sitting aloof he'd announce midnight no two in the morning three in the morning Ballast Office brief movements of the lower face no sound it's my words cause them it's they cause my words it's one or the other I'll fall asleep within humanity again just barely

(How It Is, p. 50)

6:26   Programme of the Annual
        Liffey Race, 1925
        (By courtesy The Civic Museum)

6:27   O'Connell Bridge with the
        Grand Central Cinema
        (By courtesy National Library of
        Ireland, Valentine, NS5243)

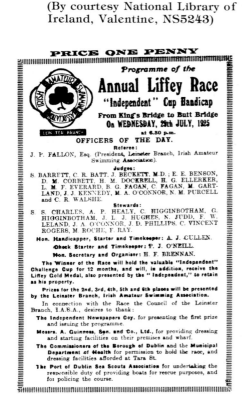

Close to O'Connell Bridge, the Grand Central Cinema once stood.[33] Belacqua, in *Dream of Fair to Middling Women,* plans a retreat to this cinema after a sortie to a public house at Chapelizod -

> There he would have one or two and then he would tram back and go to the pictures, he would slip into the womb of the Grand Central burning on the waterside, and then he would crawl back home across the cobbles and his heart is a stone.
>
> *(Dream of Fair to Middling Women, p. 25)*

Butt Bridge

Continuing towards the sea, the Liffey next passes under Butt Bridge[34] (6:29) -

> And I remind myself also that since I last went through my possessions much water has passed beneath Butt Bridge, in both directions.
>
> *(Malone Dies, p. 251)*

In the poem, *Serena III*, the south quays and Butt Bridge are important to the poem's theme of love and separation[35] -

> or on Butt Bridge blush for shame
> the mixed declension of those mammae
> cock up thy moon thine and thine only
> up up up to the star of evening
>
> *(Serena III, p. 25)*

The Liffey Basin

The Liffey quayside at Butt Bridge is overlooked by the handsome Custom House, designed by James Gandon.[36] Closer to the river's mouth there is the North Wall from where the British and Irish steamers used to depart for Liverpool[37] (6:30) -

> 'Well,' said Wylie, 'the better the day ... It is always pleasant to leave this country, but never more so than by the Saturday B. and I., with the ladies and gentlemen of the theatre enjoying the high-seas licence and a full night on the water.'
>
> *(Murphy, pp. 90-91)*

The North Wall achieves literary prominence in Beckett's drama *That Time,* in which it features as the 'wharf' for the B and I 'ferry' on which 'Voice A', an old man returns to Dublin after many years absence to revisit 'Foley's Folly', the ruin near Foxrock,[38] in which he played as a child -

> A: straight off the ferry and up with the nightbag to the high street neither right nor left not a curse for the old scenes the old names straight up the rise from the wharf to the high street and there not a wire to be seen only the old rails all

6:28 The Ballast Office Clock
(By courtesy *The Irish Times*)

6:29 Butt Bridge
(By courtesy D. Davison)

rust when was that was your mother ah for God's sake all gone long ago that time you went back that last time to look was the ruin still there where you hid as a child someone's folly

(That Time, pp. 228-229)

'Voice A' finds the trams of his childhood gone. The rails remain, the wires have disappeared.[39] A number eight tram from the 'high street', O'Connell Street, would have brought him within reasonable walking distance of his destination. He contemplates instead taking the number eleven bus, but this would only take him to the suburb of Clonskeagh leaving him with a five mile walk to Foley's Folly.[40] Perhaps because of his age 'Voice A' abandons this course and walks through the city from O'Connell Street to Harcourt Street Railway Station intending to catch the 'Slow and Easy' of his childhood to Foxrock, from where he would have had only a few minutes walk to Foley's Folly. But the Harcourt Street line is closed[41] -

A: that time you went back to look was the ruin still there where you hid as a child that last time straight off the ferry and up the rise to the high street to catch the eleven neither right nor left only one thought in your head not a curse for the old scenes the old names just head down press on up the rise to the top and there stood waiting with the nightbag till the truth began to dawn

6:30   The North Wall from where the British and Irish Steam Packet ships departed. (By courtesy National Library of Ireland, Lawrence, Royal 11589)

A: no getting out to it that way so what next no question of asking not another word to the living as long as you lived so foot it up in the end to the station bowed half double get out to it that way all closed down and boarded up Doric terminus of the Great Southern and Eastern all closed down and the colonnade crumbling away so what next

(That Time, p. 231)

Unable to reach his destination in the now unfamiliar world of his childhood which possesses neither the railway nor trams he used as a child, he can only revisit Foley's Folly through memory. He cannot fulfill his compulsion to verify its actual existence, the sole object of his journey. There is nothing for him to do but depart, resolving never to return -

A: back down to the wharf with the nightbag and the old green greatcoat your father left you trailing the ground and the white hair pouring out down from under the hat till that time came on down neither right nor left not a curse for the old scenes the old names not a thought in your head only get back on board and away to hell out of it and never come back or was that another time all that another time was there ever any other time but that time away to hell out of it all and never come back

(That Time, pp. 234-235)

6:31 The Gasometer on
      Sir John Rogerson's Quay
      (Photograph by D. Davison)

6:32 The Church of the Immaculate
Heart of Mary on City Quay
(Photograph by D. Davison)

The docks at the mouth of the Liffey throbbed with life in the 'thirties and 'forties; the ships, the dockers and stevedores, and the old ferry that used to ply its passengers from one quay to another gave the quays and dockland a personality that is no longer to be found. In the fast-moving poem, *Serena III*, many places on the south quays at the Liffey's mouth feature. The gasometer[42] that so dominates many views of the city is built on a site, the boundaries of which are Sir John Rogerson's Quay, Cardiff Lane, Forrest Street, and Misery Hill so named because it once led to a lazaretto[43](6:31). Now grey in colour the gasometer was once painted a deep red[44] -

> swoon upon the arch-gasometer
> on Misery Hill brand-new carnation
> swoon upon the little purple
> house of prayer
> something heart of Mary
> the Bull and Pool Beg that will never meet
> not in this world.

(Serena III, p. 25)

The 'something heart of Mary' is a reference to the Church of the Immaculate Heart of Mary on City Quay (6:32). The River Liffey ends at Dublin bay where its entrance is guarded by two lighthouses, one on the northern Bull wall, and the other on the south wall known as the Poolbeg[45](6:33). The name derives from the Irish for *little pool*, a reference to one of the two pools in the harbour of Dublin where ships could find deep water, the other larger pool being at Clontarf.

In the poem, *Serena III,* we are brought eventually to our point of departure on the River Circle at the origin of the Grand Canal in Ringsend[46] -

> whereas dart away through the cavorting scapes
> bucket o'er Victoria Bridge that's the idea
> slow down slink down the Ringsend Road

(Serena III, p. 25)

6:33   The Poolbeg Lighthouse
       (By courtesy National Library of
       Ireland, Lawrence, Imperial 36)

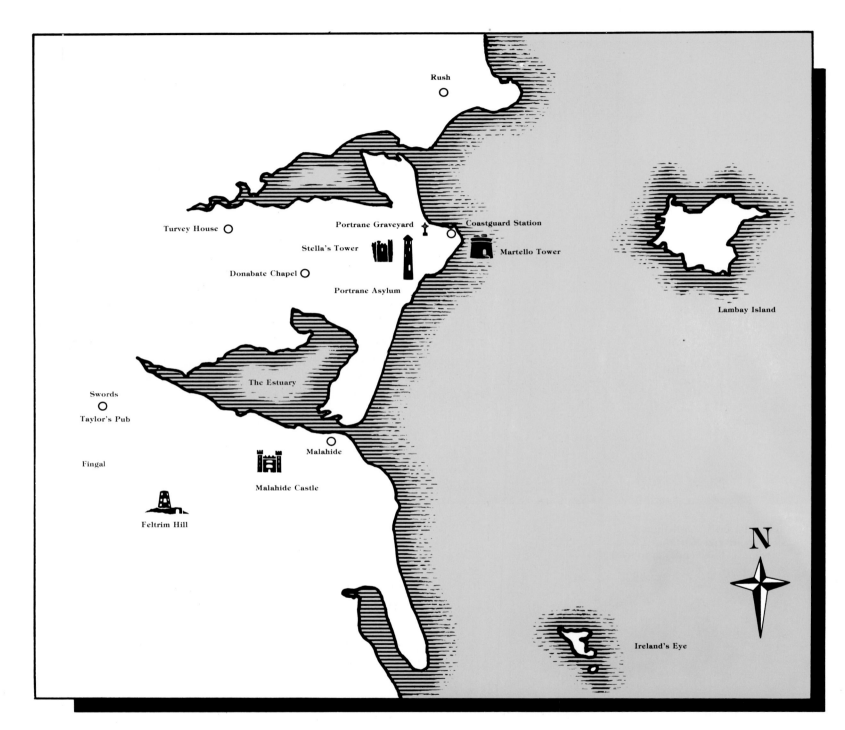

7.1 The coast of Fingal, Malahide and Portrane.

Chapter Seven

DUBLIN'S LUNATIC ASYLUMS

The disadvantaged in society are special to Beckett. His respect and affection for the poor and deformed we have already seen; now we turn to the mentally deranged. Beckett treats the insane with humour, sympathy, and admiration. In madness, the insane sometimes achieve the perfect escape from a chaotic society; no mean feat, in Beckett's view. Moreover, absorbed in their worlds, the insane are protected from the contamination of society and retain an integrity not to be found in the sane. Medical institutes feature prominently in the Beckett *oeuvre*,[1] as indeed does illness. Beckett's familiarity with medical terminology, and his skilful use of it in his writing can only have been achieved by a detailed study of the subject. Asylum's for the treatment of the insane are sanctuaries, where the dualities that compose the Beckettian personality are permitted expression and dialogue free of the interference that would necessarily stifle their existence in so-called normal society. This duality of personality in Beckett's characters is often explained as a manifestation of a schizoid or frankly schizophrenic personality,[2] and indeed there are occasions when it may be such. But Beckett's elaborate and complex character creations should not be disposed of too readily by the application of a neat diagnostic label. The conflict of personality in the Beckettian character is more often a consequence of the irrational, and at times, irreconcilable constraints imposed upon the individual by the dictates of society, which to some are incomprehensible, to many confusing, and to others so unacceptable that the emotional conflict consequent upon a profound attempt at rationalisation, leads to what society deems to be aberrant behaviour.

Beckett has selected two of Dublin's institutes for the treatment of the insane for special attention in his writing: Portrane Lunatic Asylum (now named St. Ita's Hospital) on the north shores of Dublin, and the House of St. John of God (now known simply as St. John of God Hospital) in Stillorgan. In *Murphy*, Beckett creates his own lunatic asylum, the Magdalen Mental Mercyseat, or MMM as it was known.[3] Indeed the

Page 226

Magdalen Mental Mercyseat, in which Murphy spent so many enjoyable days tending to its unfortunate, but, in so many ways, liberated inmates, possessed in its administration a novel system for denoting the accomplishment of a ward round which depended for its origins on Ireland -

> Murphy completed his round, an Irish virgin. (Finished on time a round was called a virgin; ahead of time, an Irish virgin.)
>
> *(Murphy, p. 165)*

Beckett is not the first Irish writer to take an interest in the mental health of Dublin's citizens. Jonathan Swift,[4] who bequeathed monies to found Dublin's first hospital for the insane (St. Patrick's Hospital, often known as 'Swift's Hospital'[5]) was more aware than most of the national malady -

> He gave the little Wealth he had,
> To build a House for Fools and Mad:
> And shew'd by one satiric Touch,
> No Nation wanted it so much:
> That kingdom he hath left his Debtor,
> I wish it soon may have a Better.[6]

The Portrane Lunatic Asylum

In the story 'Fingal' in *More Pricks than Kicks*, Belacqua sets out with his girl of the moment, Winnie, on a day's outing to the countryside and seashore of Fingal and Malahide (7:1) -

> The last girl he went with, before a memorable fit of laughing incapacitated him from gallantry for some time, was pretty, hot and witty, in that order. So one fine Spring morning he brought her out into the country, to the Hill of Feltrim in the country. They turned east off the road from Dublin to Malahide short of the Castle woods and soon it came into view, not much more than a burrow, the ruin of a mill on the top, choked lairs of furze and brambles passim on its gentle slopes. It was a landmark for miles around on account of the high ruin. The Hill of the Wolves.
>
> *(More Pricks than Kicks, p. 25)*

7:2 The Hill of Wolves at Feltrim (By courtesy National Library of Ireland, Lawrence, 7917)

Feltrim is a village in the district of Fingal, the name of which probably derives from a Danish settlement in the ninth century when the place was known as Fine-Gall.[7] The word Feltrim denotes the wild aspect of the area, ridge or hill of wolves.[8] The Hill of Feltrim, with its windmill (7:2), was also known as the 'Hill of Hospitality' after a family, renowned for that virtue, who lived at its base. The windmill on Feltrim, a famous landmark at the time of the lovers' visit, was demolished by vandals in 1973.[9] The Hill has ancient historical associations,[10] and a past rich in religious tradition.[11]

From the summit of the Hill of Wolves there is an excellent view of the Dublin countryside. The Dublin mountains in the distance attract Winnie, but not Belacqua whose attention is drawn towards the asylum where the story will eventually unfold -

> 'The Dublin mountains' she said 'don't they look lovely, so dreamy.'
> Now Belacqua was looking intently in the opposite direction, across the estuary ...
>
> She began to admire this and that, the ridge of Lambay Island, rising out of the brown woods of the Castle, Ireland's Eye like a shark, and the ridiculous little hills far away to the north, what were they?
> 'The Naul' said Belacqua. 'Is it possible you didn't know the Naul?'
>
> *(More Pricks than Kicks, p. 25)*

Lambay Island (7:3) is about three miles sail from the coast. Oval in shape, some two miles long and a mile and a quarter broad, its 1371 acres are a sanctuary for birds, seal and deer.[12] The 'brown woods of the Castle', are those of Malahide Castle (7:4), the residence of the Lord Talbot de Malahide until his death in 1973, when much of its valuable contents were sold. Determined action by a number of interested groups

7:3 Lambay Island
     (Photograph by D. Davison)

saved the castle and grounds which now serve as a gallery and tourist attraction. The woods of the demesne contain many representatives of a forest nobility: splendid old oaks, elms, ashes, horse-chestnuts and sycamores.[13]

Ireland's Eye is an interesting island of some 53 acres lying off Howth. (7:5) It was known to Ptolemy, who called it 'Adri deserta', and Pliny apparently gave it the name 'Andros'. The ruins of a small ancient chapel, founded by St. Nessan in the sixth century, are to be found on its south side.[14]

'The Naul' is renowned for its mill and stream, and the picturesque glen of the Naul with its cliffs, vegetation and caves which once were the refuge of bandits; the more infamous of these was *Shaun Kittock*, a perversion of the Irish meaning 'left-handed Jack', who long eluded capture for a number of daring depredations, but was eventually taken along with 'an Amazonian female, the intrepid companion of all his exploits, (and) both paid the debt due to the injured laws of the country.'[15]

7:4 Malahide Castle
(Photograph by D. Davison)

7:5 Ireland's Eye from Howth.
A Hill of Howth tram is in
the foreground
(By courtesy National Library of
Ireland, Lawrence, VR2075)

Belacqua and Winnie, from their lofty perch, admired the creeks of the
coast of Fingal. Suddenly Belacqua sighted the asylum -

'Look' he pointed.
She looked, blinking for the focus.
'The big red building' he said 'across the water, with the towers'...

'No' she said, 'it looks like a bread factory to me.'
'The Portrane Lunatic Asylum' he said.

(More Pricks than Kicks, p. 27-28)

From Fingal, Belacqua and Winnie walked to Malahide and onwards
along the shores of the beautiful estuary with its myriads of swans,
known in Norman times as *Lac de Cygnes*[16](7:6) -

They followed the estuary all the way round, admiring
the theories of swans and the coots ....

(More Pricks than Kicks, p. 28)

At the far shore of the estuary, the lovers took the coast walk rather than
the road towards Portrane, so avoiding the Catholic chapel in Donabate
(7:7) -

... over the dunes and past the Martello tower, so that they came on Portrane from
the south and the sea instead of like a vehicle by the railway bridge and the horrible
red chapel of Donabate.

(More Pricks than Kicks, p. 28)

7:6 Malahide estuary and swans
(Photograph by D. Davison)

7:7 The chapel at Donabate
(Photograph by D. Davison)

7:8   The Martello Tower on
Portrane Strand
(Photograph by D. Davison)

7:9   Portrane Lunatic Asylum
(Photograph by D. Davison)

7:10 The Round Tower with the
clock and laundry towers of the
asylum in the background
(Photograph by D. Davison)

7:11 George Petrie by Charles Grey
(By courtesy The Royal College
of Surgeons in Ireland)

The coast-line of Dublin is studded with Martello Towers built to repel the threatened Napoleonic invasion.[17] The Portrane tower is an inferior example (7:8) of the usually fine architectural features of these structures. Soon the pair reach Portrane Lunatic Asylum with its characteristic towers (7:9) -

> The place was as full of towers as Dun Laoghaire of steeples: two Martello, the red ones of the asylum, a watertower and the round.
>
> *(More Pricks than Kicks, p. 28)*

Portrane Lunatic Asylum was built on the lands of the Evans demesne between 1896 and 1901.[18] The Evans family, of Welsh extraction, first settled in Portrane in the early eighteenth century where a manor house was erected and later incorporated in the hospital.[19]

Belacqua and Winnie headed for the round tower seeking direction from a worker in a field -

> He said that their way lay straight ahead, yes, over the wall, and then the tower was on top of the field, or else they could go back till they came to the road and go along it till they came to the Banks and follow up the Banks.
>
> *(More Pricks than Kicks p. 29)*

The phallic symbolism of these towers has been a source of wonderment to the native and scholar alike (7:10). On close inspection, however, Belacqua was not impressed -

> The tower began well; that was the funeral meats. But from the door up it was all relief and no honour; that was the marriage tables.
>
> *(More Pricks than Kicks, p. 30)*

Belacqua had earlier sought some historical details from the workman, whose knowledge, though a little hazy, was firmly rooted in fact -

> Belacqua asked was the tower an old one, as though it required a Dr Petrie to see that it was not. The man said it had been built for relief in the year of the Famine, so he had heard, by a Mrs Somebody whose name he misremembered in honour of her husband.
>
> *(More Pricks than Kicks, p. 29)*

George Petrie (7:11), archaeologist, musician and artist was an authority on Ireland's round towers. A sensitive savant he travelled the country collecting its folk music, painting and researching its archaeology.[20]

From the tower Belacqua and Winnie admired the countryside and Lambay Island. They watched the patients being escorted through the

Page 233

asylum (7:12), and listened to children playing and crying in the workmen's cottages -

> Below in the playground on their right some of the milder patients were kicking a football. Others were lounging about, alone and in knots, taking their ease in the sun. The head of one appeared over the wall, the hands on the wall, the cheek on the hands.
>
> *(More Pricks than Kicks, p. 31)*

Winnie suddenly sighted some ruins in a distant field -

> 'The lovely ruins' said Winnie 'there on the left, covered with ivy'. Of a church, and two small fields further on, a square bawnless tower.
>
> *(More Pricks than Kicks, p. 30)*

Belacqua had also noticed these ruins to which he had been immediately attracted. After all, he had said of Portrane: 'Abstract the asylum and there was little left ... but ruins'.[21] Belacqua, 'who could on no account resist a bicycle,'[22] had earlier spotted the alluring sparkle of a workman's pedal-bike in the grass. Conveniently, an old flame of Winnie's turns up, Dr. Sholto, medical officer to the asylum. Having rid himself of all encumbrances, the most troublesome of which were Winnie and Sholto,

7:12 The playing fields at
 Portrane Asylum
 (Photograph by D. Davison)

7:13 The village of Rush
 (By courtesy National Library of
 Ireland, Eason, 1944)

Belacqua headed for the ruined tower, free as a bird on his stolen steed -

> It was a fine light machine, with red tyres and wooden rims. He ran down the margin to the road and it bounded alongside under his hand. He mounted and they flew down the hill and round the corner till they came at length to the stile that led into the field where the church was. The machine was a treat to ride, on his right hand the sea was foaming among the rocks, the sands ahead were another yellow again, beyond them in the distance the cottages of Rush were bright white, Belacqua's sadness fell from him like a shift.
>
> *(More Pricks than Kicks, p. 33)*

Rush (7:13) is a small fishing village, once celebrated for its curing of ling.[23] Belacqua eventually reached the field containing two ruins, the church (7:14), and further on, the tower (7:15).[24] It was the latter that he sought -

> He carried the bicycle into the field and laid it down on the grass. He hastened on foot, without so much as a glance at the church, across the fields, over a wall and a ditch, and stood before the poor wooden door of the tower. The locked appearance of this did not deter him. He gave it a kick, it swung open and he went in.
>
> *(More Pricks than Kicks, p. 33)*

While Belacqua was (in the words of his rival for Winnie's affection) 'sandpapering a tomb',[25] Sholto and Winnie were waiting at the gates of the asylum (7:16) at the appointed hour to meet him. Here Winnie struck up conversation with a local man from whom she sought the history of the ruins -

> 'That's the church' he said, pointing to the near one, it had just absorbed Sholto, 'and that' pointing to the far one, ''s the tower.'
> 'Yes' said Winnie 'but what tower, what was it?'
> 'The best I know' he said 'is some Lady Something had it.'
> This was news indeed.
> 'Then before that again' it all came back to him with a rush 'you might have heard tell of Dane Swift, he kep a' – he checked the word and then let it come regardless – 'he kep a motte in it.'
> 'A moth?' exclaimed Winnie.
> 'A motte' he said 'of the name of Stella.'
>
> *(More Pricks than Kicks, p. 34)*

The colloquial mention of 'Dane Swift's motte' is a reference to the legend that Jonathan Swift, Dean of St. Patrick's Cathedral in Dublin, incarcerated his mistress, Esther Johnson, better known as Stella, in this tower at Portrane.[26]

Waiting at the asylum gates news reaches Winnie and Sholto that

7:14   Portrane graveyard
(Photograph by D. Davison)

7:15 Stella's Tower at Portrane
(Photograph by D. Davison)

Belacqua had been sighted on a bicycle. On receipt of this information, Sholto called confidently for his motor -

> 'Whoever it is' said Sholto, master of the situation, 'we'll pass him before he gets to the main road.'
> But Sholto had underestimated the speed of his man, who was safe in Taylor's public-house in Swords, drinking and laughing in a way that Mr Taylor did not like, before they were well on their way.
>
> (More Pricks than Kicks, p. 36)

Swords is an ancient settlement boasting an early round tower on which 'triumphant Christianity has planted a cross', a belfry tower and church,[27] as well as Taylor's public house[28] (7:17). Swords also features in the poem, *Sanies I*, much of which retraces the Fingal walk of Belacqua and Winnie, but the narrator is alone and on a bicycle -

> all the livelong way this day of sweet showers from
>   Portrane on the seashore
> Donabate sad swans of Turvey Swords
>
> (Sanies I, p. 17)

7:16   The gates and gate-lodge to Portrane Asylum (By courtesy Kathleen McGrory. From *Yeats, Joyce and Beckett. New Light on Three Modern Irish Writers*. p. 145.)

7:17   Taylor's Public House in Swords village (Photograph by E. O'Brien)

7:18 Turvey House, Swords
(By courtesy Irish Architectural
Archive No. B 3/7/14)

The designation 'Turvey Swords'[29] is to an old mansion at the village of Turvey, which was demolished some years ago and to the swans that populate the waters of the area (7:18).

The House of Saint John of God

Leaving the Portrane Lunatic Asylum, we must now transfer our attention to another hospital for the mentally ill on the other side of the city, and also to another work, *Malone Dies*. However, before entering the House of Saint John of God, we are introduced to the institute by way of some hilarious dialogue in the General Post Office in *Murphy*. It will be recalled that Neary, late of Cork, while attempting, in a moment of profound depression, to beat his brains against the buttocks of the hero Cuchulain's statue in the G.P.O., was rescued from the menacing attention of a civic guard by Wylie, who immediately pleaded insanity for his friend -

> Wylie turned back, tapped his forehead and said, as one sane man to another: 'John o' God's. Hundred per cent harmless ...'
>
> 'Stillorgan,' said Wylie. 'Not Dundrum.'
>
> *(Murphy, p. 33)*

Page 240

Front view
House of St John of God

7:19   The House of St. John of God,
Stillorgan
(By courtesy the Hospital)

Wylie, by denoting the geographical location of the House of St. John of God at Stillorgan[30](7:19), as distinct from that of the Central Lunatic Asylum at Dundrum, indicated to the guard that Neary was a docile rather than a criminal lunatic.

In *Malone Dies*, the central figure, Macmann, finds himself in an asylum -

> At first he did not know it was one, being plunged within it, but he was told so as soon as he was in a condition to receive news. They said in substance, You are now in the House of Saint John of God, with the number one hundred and sixty-six. Fear nothing, you are among friends. Friends!
>
> *(Malone Dies, p. 257)*

With time Macmann found that many features of the place were not unfavourable; the gate lodge he found particularly charming (7:20) -

> But let us cast a glance at the main entrance, wide enough to admit two large vehicles abreast and flanked by two charming lodges covered with Virginia creeper and occupied by large deserving families, to judge by the swarms of little brats playing nearby, pursuing one another with cries of joy, rage and grief.
>
> *(Malone Dies, p. 280)*

Macmann did, of course, attempt to ascertain his rights -

> When asked for example to state whether Saint John of Gods was a private institution or run by the State, a hospice for the aged and infirm or a madhouse, if once in one might entertain the hope of one day getting out and, in the affirmative, by means of what steps, Lemuel remained for a long time plunged in thought, sometimes for as long as ten minutes or a quarter of an hour, motionless or if you prefer scratching his head or armpit, as if such questions had never crossed his mind, or possibly thinking about something quite different.
>
> *(Malone Dies, pp. 267-268)*

The grounds of the asylum were a source of pleasure to Macmann, and did indeed bear the official title of 'Pleasure grounds' (7:21) -

> It was a genuine English park, though far from England, extravagantly unformal, luxuriant to the point of wildness, the trees at war with one another, and the bushes, and the wild flowers and weeds, all ravening for earth and light.
>
> *(Malone Dies, p. 277)*

The beauty of the grounds, and in particular, the view of the surrounding countryside from the summit, had particular appeal -

> The entire top was occupied by the domain of Saint John and there the wind blew almost without ceasing, causing the stoutest trees to bend and groan, breaking the boughs, tossing the bushes, lashing the ferns to fury, flattening the grass and whirling leaves and flowers far away, I hope I have not forgotten anything. Good. A high wall encompassed it about, without however shutting off the view, unless

7:20 The gate-lodge of the House of
St. John of God
(By courtesy the Hospital)

7:21 The 'pleasure grounds' of the
House of St. John of God
(By courtesy the Hospital)

you happened to be in its lee. How was this possible? Why thanks to the rising ground to be sure, culminating in a summit called the Rock, because of the rock that was on it. From here a fine view was to be obtained of the plain, the sea, the mountains, the smoke of the town and the buildings of the institution, bulking large in spite of their remoteness and all astir with little dots or flecks forever appearing and disappearing, in reality the keepers coming and going, perhaps mingled with I was going to say with the prisoners! For seen from this distance the striped cloak had no stripes, nor indeed any great resemblance to a cloak at all. So that one could only say, when the first shock of surprise was past, Those are men and women, you know, people, without being able to specify further. A stream at long intervals bestrid – but to hell with all this fucking scenery. Where could it have risen anyway, tell me that. Underground perhaps. In a word a little Paradise for those who like their nature sloven.

(Malone Dies, p. 278-279)

Similarities though there are between the real St. John of God's in Stillorgan and the institute in *Malone Dies*, there are also differences.[31] One dissimilarity is in the administration of Beckett's 'Johnny Goddams' which appears to be lay, whereas that of St. John of God's Hospital is clerical. Beckett might have been stretching credibility had he cast Lemuel in clerical garb!

7:22 The day-room of the House of
St. John of God
(By courtesy the Hospital)

The institute featuring in 'The End', may also be modelled on St. John of God's and its chapel (7:22) -

> May I stay here just a little longer, I said, till the rain is over? You may wait in the cloister, he said, the rain will go on all day. You may wait in the cloister till six o'clock, you will hear the bell.
>
> *(The End, p. 53)*

Dublin may claim the distinction of starting the voluntary hospital movement in the early eighteenth century when Ireland was part of the United Kingdom of Great Britain and Ireland,[31] and many of the city's hospitals still depend on the voluntary charitable support of the community. John of God's was no exception, and a notice on the asylum board announcing the altruism of a local well-to-do, Lady Pedal, is prologue to the climax in *Malone Dies* -

> One morning Lemuel, putting in the prescribed appearance in the great hall before setting out on his rounds, found pinned on the board a notice concerning him. Group Lemuel, excursion to the islands, weather permitting, with Lady Pedal, leaving one p.m.
>
> *(Malone Dies, p. 281)*

Lady Pedal and her entourage are shown little in the way of gratitude by their charge in the macabre climax on Dalkey Island which has been considered in Chapter 3.

8:1   A Dublin public house
(Photograph by N. Johnson)

Page 246

Chapter Eight

DUBLIN: City of Character and Characters

A study of the relevance of Dublin to Beckett's art is incomplete without attending to the influence of the personality of the city and its people on his writing. This is most evident in the intimacy of dialogue which is so much a feature of the Beckett *oeuvre*. Some might call this the 'Irishness' of Beckett's dialect, which put another way, merely means that Beckett is, in fact, utilising the remarkably expressive power of the Dublin idiom with its subtle perversion of language to give to repartee not only rhythm, but also an emphasis that is absent from conventional speech. Conversation may or may not have been developed into an art in Dublin; what is certain, and was especially so in the first half of the century, is that Dubliners love to talk, anywhere, in the streets, the pub, the church, and a good listener need never be bored. The best of conversation can be heard in the Dublin pub, the inner temple as it were of confabulation, at the shrine of which the Dubliner worships with a singular passion.

The Dublin Pub

The city prides itself on an array of public houses providing for the most eccentric of inebriates. It would be a perverse drinker indeed who failed to find an establishment to suit his requirements in comfort, company and drink. The connoisseur of stout was particularly selective in his choice of public house in those not so distant days when the care of the barrel and pipes, and the pulling of the sacred pint was an art in which not all bartenders, or curates, as they were known in Dublin, were accomplished. A number of well-known Dublin pubs are mentioned by name in Becketts writings; these include - Kennedy's on Westland Row, 'McLoughlin's' on College Street, The Oval Bar on Middle Abbey Street, Mooney's on Lower Abbey Street, Taylor's of Swords, and The Yellow House in Rathfarnham.[1] Mention is also made of Wynn's Hotel in Lower Abbey Street, and the Grosvenor Hotel on Westland Row.

However, it is the character and ambience of the Dublin pub as a generic entity that emanates from Beckett's writing, rather than any specific establishment (8:1), Kennedy's being perhaps an exception, in that it fulfilled most of the conditions dear to Beckett -

> Whither next? To what licensed premises? To where the porter was well up, first; and the solitary shawly like a cloud of latter rain in a waste of poets and politicians, second; and he neither knew nor was known, third. A lowly house dear to shawlies where the porter was up and he could keep himself to himself on a high stool with a high round and feign to be immersed in the Moscow notes of the Twilight Herald. These were very piquant.
>
> *(More Pricks than Kicks, p. 54)*

The 'Twilight Herald' was an evening paper which exists to this day, and to which reference has been made earlier.[2] A pub depends for atmosphere on its staff and clientele. Belacqua had strong views on the company he wished to have around him when imbibing. The drinking cab drivers of the city, known otherwise as jarveys, poets and politicians were to be avoided at all costs.[3] He preferred to drink alone among the plain people of the city, the shawlies and joxers on the dole. The art, or science if you prefer, of drinking Dublin style is captured exquisitely in a passage from *More Pricks than Kicks* that illustrates the beauty and power of Beckett's prose (8:2) -

> Sitting in this crapulent den, drinking his drink, he gradually ceased to see its furnishings with pleasure, the bottles, representing centuries of loving research, the stools, the counter, the powerful screws, the shining phalanx of the pulls of the beer-engines, all cunningly devised and elaborated to further the relations between purveyor and consumer in this domain. The bottles drawn and emptied in a twinkling, the casks responding to the slightest pressure on their joysticks, the weary proletarians at rest on arse and elbow, the cash-register that never complains, the graceful curates flying from customer to customer, all this made up a spectacle in which Belacqua was used to take delight and chose to see a pleasant instance of machinery decently subservient to appetite. A great major symphony of supply and demand, effect and cause, fulcrate on the middle C of the counter and waxing, as it proceeded, in the charming harmonies of blasphemy and broken glass and all the aliquots of fatique and ebriety. So that he would say that the only place where he could come to anchor and be happy was a low public-house and that all the wearisome tactics of gress and dud Beethoven would be done away with if only he could spend his life in such a place.
>
> *(More Pricks than Kicks, p. 44-45)*

8:2 Interior of a public house: Lynch's, 43 Aungier Street. Proprietor Phil Lynch hand on pump, surveys his domain (By courtesy G.A. Duncan, Folder II, Sleeve 13)

Despite a look of incongruity and delapidation, the design and decor of the Dublin pub adhered to functional necessities, one such being the provision of an adequate supply of sawdust to absorb life's effluvia -

> You intimidate us, said Mercier, good for you.
> We put a bold front on it, said Camier, though actually shitting with terror. Quick some sawdust, my good fellow.
>
> *(Mercier and Camier, p. 83)*

8:3 Advertisments for alcholic
beverages

A number of well known drinks are mentioned in Beckett's works:
Guinness's stout of course,[4] Jameson's fifteen year old whiskey,[5] and
the champagne, Golden Guinea.[6] Beckett's personal preference, however,
seems to have been for Beamish stout[7](8:3), rather than for Guinness.

A pun on the words porter (a crude stout deriving its name probably from the fact that it was popular with porters), and stout gives especial delight to Murphy -

'Why did the barmaid champagne?' he said. 'Do you give it up?'
'Yes' said Celia.
'Because the stout porter bitter,' said Murphy

(Murphy, p. 97)

And the pun is developed further in *Watt* by incorporating the British beer or 'bitter' and the name 'Power', denoting a well known Irish whiskey-

And Louit, going down the stairs, met the bitter stout porter Power coming up.
(Watt, p. 196)

Alcohol is not the only beverage in Beckett's work to which the Irish are attracted, though it must be admitted that it does have a dominant place. The quaint cup of tea is not forgotten,[8] and the national dish, 'Irish Stew',[9] also receives mention.

The Dublin Idiom

Few writers have captured as effectively in prose the idiom of the Dubliner as Beckett.[10] Drinking in solitude in the city's pubs, he watched, listened and absorbed the musical cadence of dialogue, and later blended this with mannerism and personality in the creation of character in his writings. In the crapulent den of the story 'Ding Dong' there is a charming intermezzo from a beggar women. Her speech was that of a woman of the people, but of a gentlewoman of the people.[11] She is selling the impossible, a wonderful concept, and her voice and language leave Belacqua dazed -

'Seats in heaven' she said in a white voice 'tuppence apiece, four fer a tanner.'
'No' said Belacqua. It was the first syllable to come to his lips. It had not been his intention to deny her.
'The best of seats' she said 'again I'm sold out. Tuppence apiece the best of seats, four fer a tanner'...
'Have you got them on you?' he mumbled.
'Heaven goes round' she said, whirling her arm, 'and round and round and round and round.'
'Yes' said Belacqua 'round and round.'
'Rowan' she said, dropping the d's and getting more of a spin into the slogan, 'rowan an' rowan an' rowan.'

(More Pricks than Kicks, p. 47-48)

Beckett's appreciation of the Dublin idiom is shown to perfection in the beautiful reply to Belacqua's enquiry as to the cost of the celestial seats: 'For yer frien' she said 'yer da, yer ma an' yer motte, four fer a tanner.'[12]Belacqua succumbs to her charm and purchases two seats for fourpence (4d.), or to the beggar-woman 'Four dee', for which she takes the tanner dismissing his protest with an 'Arragowan'.[13]

The Dublin idiom is used often by Beckett, sometimes almost imperceptibly and always with subtlety. In fact, the use of the Dublin or Irish idiom, gives to many of Beckett's 'placeless' writings an unmistakable Irish identity; for example, when Clov declares himself to be 'A smithereen' in *Endgame*.[14] In *Murphy*, Ticklepenny throws out: 'Well, that beats the band'[15] to signify amazement. In *Watt*, much of the grammatical emphasis is Irish -

> God bless your honour, said the old man.
> Amen, said Arthur. Good day.
> I remember you when you was a boy, said the old man.
> I was a boy meself.
> Then we was boys together, said Arthur.
> You was a fine lovely boy, said the old man, and I was another.
> Look at us now, said Arthur.
> You was always wetting your trousers, said the old man.
> I wets them still, said Arthur.
>
> *(Watt, p. 253)*

And again in *Watt*, Mr. Nolan asks: 'Is that the gob?' to which Mr. Gorman replies: 'Have you got a firm holt on her?'.[16] Of course, the Lynch family in *Watt*, can be nothing but Irish with Christian names such as, Mat, Sean, Bridie, Pat, Larry, Con and Art.[17] In *Molloy* a common expression of concern is voiced, when Moran asks his son: 'What ails you?'[18]

More Pricks than Kicks is a Dublin book and its language is that of the city. The lobster purchased by Beckett is so fresh that it is 'Lepping fresh, sir.'[19] Winnie uses a mildly perjorative term to put Belacqua in his place: 'Don't be an eejit' she said, 'if it's straight on it's over the wall.'[20]

Beckett has remarked that "there is a temptation to treat every concept like 'a bass dropt neck fust in till a bung crate', and make a really tidy job of it."[21] There is indeed a temptation with *Waiting for Godot* to attempt to identify, not only the setting of the drama, but to go further and bestow its characters with a national identity. None the less, there are, as we have seen qualities in the Dublin landscape particularly suited to *Godot*, and there are also mannerisms of speech that give to the dialogue of the play a flavour that is unmistakably Irish.[22] The classic use of the double-mister is Joycean: 'Eh, mister! Your fly is open, mister!'[23] -

ESTRAGON: Mister ... excuse me, Mister ...
POZZO: You're being spoken to, pig! Reply! *(To Estragon.)*
Try him again.
ESTRAGON: Excuse me, Mister, the bones, you won't be wanting the bones?
Lucky looks long at Estragon.
POZZO: *(in raptures.)* Mister! *(Lucky bows his head.)*
(Waiting for Godot, p. 27)

In Lucky's tirade the name of an Irish game 'Camogie', played by women is thrown out.[24] Pozzo's possible origins are of interest; he may well have been one of the absentee landlords so common among the Anglo-Irish in nineteenth century Ireland. At least, Beckett would seem to be hinting at this in *Texts for Nothing* -

Why did Pozzo leave home, he had a castle and retainers. Insidious question, to remind me I'm in the dock.
(Texts for Nothing, p. 85)

Pozzo smoked a briar, obtained from Dublin's finest pipe-shop, Kapp and Peterson's of O'Connell Street [25](8:4) -

POZZO: I've lost my Kapp and Peterson!
ESTRAGON: *(convulsed with merriment.)* He'll be the death of me!
(Waiting for Godot, p. 35)

8:4 Kapp and Petersons, Tobacconists, O'Connell Street (By courtesy Royal Irish Automobile Club)

The words 'ballocksed' and 'amuck', as used in *Godot*, could be straight from a Dublin street conversation -

<blockquote>

VLADIMIR: That Lucky might get going all of a sudden. Then we'd be ballocksed.

ESTRAGON: Lucky?

VLADIMIR: He's the one who went for you yesterday.

ESTRAGON: I tell you there was ten of them.

VLADIMIR: No, before that, the one that kicked you.

ESTRAGON: Is he there?

VLADIMIR: As large as life *(Gesture towards Lucky.)* For the moment he is inert. But he might run amuck any minute.

(Waiting for Godot, p. 79)

</blockquote>

The exaggerated perversion of well-known French sayings is a favourite verbal past-time in Dublin, and Estragon is no stranger to the practice -

<blockquote>

ESTRAGON: Oh tray bong, tray tray tray bong.

POZZO: *(fervently.)* Bless you, gentlemen, bless you!

   (Pause.) I have such need of encouragement!

   (Pause.) I weakened a little towards the end, you didn't notice?

VLADIMIR: Oh perhaps just a teeny weeny little bit.

(Waiting for Godot, p. 38)

</blockquote>

It is of interest to observe that Beckett employs this idiomatic characteristic, either because he could not resist the temptation, or found it useful for emphasis, in his translation of Robert Pinget's *La Manivelle*[26]-

<blockquote>

GORMAN: The first car I remember I saw it here, here on the corner, a Pic-Pic she was.

CREAM: Not a Pic-Pic, Gorman, not a Pic-Pic, a Dee Dyan Button.

(The Old Tune, p. 178)

</blockquote>

Beckett goes even further and introduces the word 'ruinated', which is classic Moore Street dialogue: 'My dear Gorman do you know what it is I'm going to tell you, all this speed do you know what it is has the whole place ruinated, no living with it anymore, the whole place ruinated, even the weather.'[27] In *All That Fall*, there is another example of deliberate perversion of pronounciation: 'Ah yes, I am distray, very distray, even on week days.'[28]

The Gaelic language gains entry to the Beckett canon only in the form of a bridal toast on which occasion Walter Draffin wishes the happy pair, 'Slainte', or good health among other blessings -

<blockquote>

'To Hymen's gracious mussy and protection we commit them now, henceforth and for evermore. Slainte.'

(More Pricks than Kicks, p. 157)

</blockquote>

The near extinction of the Irish language, Gaelic, is alluded to in *All That Fall* when Dan exclaims: 'Do you know, Maddy, sometimes one would think you were struggling with a dead language', to which Mrs. Rooney replies: 'Well, you know, it will be dead in time, just like our own poor dear Gaelic, there is that to be said.'[29]

The word 'jizz', popular in Dublin slang, denotes liveliness or a spritely air. It is used to good effect in *Happy Days*: 'Come on, dear, put a bit of jizz into it ....,'[30] and again in a review of *Windfalls* by Sean O'Casey, when Beckett remarks that: 'The short stores have more jizz...'[31]

Policemen

Three groups of person are particularly repugnant to Belacqua - aesthetes and poets, jarveys, and above all, policemen (8:5). This aversion to the upholders of law in the Republic, where they are known as the Garda Siochána (guardians of the peace), is evident in many of Beckett's works; the first encounter on Lincoln Place is one of the more amusing -

> 'Wipe them boots' said the Guard.
> Belacqua was only too happy, it was the least he could do. Contriving two loose swabs of the Twilight Herald he stooped and cleaned the boots and trouser-ends to the best of his ability. A magnificent and enormous pair of boots emerged. He rose, clutching the fouled swabs, and looked up timidly at the Guard, who seemed rather at a loss as how best to press home his advantage.
> *(More Pricks than Kicks, p. 76)*

8:5 A large Dublin policeman
(By courtesy D. Davison)

A similar encounter with the law is set in the General Post Office when Neary is apprehended by a Civic Guard while attempting to beat his head against the buttocks of Cuchulain's statue. On this occasion we meet a city member of the constabulary speaking in the vernacular -

> 'Howlt on there, youze,' said the C.G....
> 'Come back in here owwathat,' said the C.G....
> 'Take my advice, mister ——' He stopped. To devise words of advice was going to tax his ability to the utmost. When would he learn not to plunge into the labyrinths of an opinion when he had not the slightest idea of how he was to emerge? And before a hostile audience! His embarrassment was if possible increased by the expression of strained attention on Wylie's face, clamped there by the promise of advice.
> *(Murphy, p. 33-34)*

In *Watt*, however, the policeman for once (and once only) gains the upper hand intellectually -

> I see no indecency, said the policeman.
> We arrive too late, said Mr. Hackett. What a shame.
> Do you take me for a fool? said the policeman.

> Mr. Hackett recoiled a step, forced back his head until he thought his throatskin would burst, and saw at last, afar, bent angrily upon him, the red violent face. Officer, he cried, as God is my witness, he had his hand upon it.
> God is a witness that cannot be sworn.
>
> *(Watt, p. 6)*

The police, as the instrument by which the ruling caste of society imposes on that society its perceived concept of normality, are incompatible with the Beckettian character, who, grotesque and deformed, can only survive by adapting to his peculiarities as best he can. Moreover, his behaviour, so often eccentric, is the antithesis of the conformity of conduct that the civic guards of Ireland endeavour to impose upon the country's inhabitants -

> Your papers! he cried. Ah my papers. Now the only papers I carry with me are bits of newspaper, to wipe myself, you understand, when I have a stool. Oh I don't say I wipe myself every time I have a stool, no, but I like to be in a position to do so, if I have to. Nothing strange about that, it seems to me. In a panic I took this paper from my pocket and thrust it under his nose. The weather was fine. We took the little side streets, quiet, sunlit, I springing along between my crutches, he pushing my bicycle, with the tips of his white-gloved fingers.
>
> *(Molloy, p. 21)*

Most of Beckett's characters are docile, harmless and law-abiding, even if somewhat resentful of the restrictions imposed upon them. Mercier and Camier, however, are exceptions in possessing a malevolent streak to their personalities in dealing with policemen[32] -

> Mercier picked up the truncheon and dealt the muffled skull one moderate and attentive blow, just one. Like partly shelled hard-boiled egg, was his impression.
>
> *(Mercier and Camier, p. 93)*

The Clergy and Religion

The importance of religion to the Irish at a time when ninety per cent of the nation attended mass regularly, is not now so readily appreciated. Beckett's characters are drawn from all shades of Irish life, and it is hardly surprising that the Catholic religion often attracts his attention. With penetrating insight he treats the practice of Catholicism at times with an almost affectionate humour, yet again with cruel satire, but the hypocrisy of religion in general and the intrusion of the church's hierarchy (8:6) into secular affairs draws his fiercest contumely: 'What is one to think of the Irish oath sworn by the natives with the right hand on the relics of the saints and the left on the virile member?'[33] In the acrostic, *Home Olga*, Catholic Ireland is presented with caustic brevity: 'And Jesus and Jesuits juggernauted in the haemorrhoidal isle.'[34] In the early satire, *Che Sciagura*, written in 1929, Beckett alludes to the 'uncompromising attitude advocated by the Catholic Truth Society,'[35] and introduces the philosopher Bruno, whose theory of contraries so often recurs in his writings[36] -

> 'Though unfamiliar with the publications of that body, I understand that the bulk of their pronouncements is of a purely negative character.'
> 'Maximal negation is minimal affirmation'
>
> *(Che Sciagura, p. 42)*

The priest is the corner-stone of the Catholic religion and Beckett has drawn lasting portraits of two, the intellectual Jesuit and the working parish-priest -

> 'Would you' he begged, putting his greatcoat on, 'would you, my dear good fellow, have the kindness to bear in mind that I am not a Parish Priest.'
> 'I won't forget' said the P.B. 'that you don't scavenge. Your love is too great for the slops.'
> 'Egg-sactly' said the S.J. 'But they are excellent men. A shade on the assiduous side, a shade too anxious to strike a rate. Otherwise ...' He rose. 'Observe' he said, 'I desire to get down. I pull this cord and the bus stops and lets me down.'
> The P.B. observed.
> 'In just such a Gehenna of links' said this remarkable man, with one foot on the pavement, 'I forged my vocation.'
>
> *(More Pricks than Kicks, p. 63)*

8:6   The Catholic hierarchy gather for the Eucharistic Congress, Dublin 1932: The Papal Legate, His Eminence Cardinal Lauri with His Grace the Archbishop of Dublin, the Most Rev. Dr. Byrne (From *Congress Photographs. Thirty-first International Eucharistic Congress, Dublin 1932.* Hely's Ltd. Dublin. Plate 1)

In *Molloy*, Moran, anxious to receive holy communion before setting out on his quest for Molloy,[37] finds his conscience troubled because he has broken the statutory twelve-hour fast by imbibing alcohol -

> Would I be granted the body of Christ after a pint of Wallenstein? And if I said nothing? Have you come fasting, my son? He would not ask. But God would know, sooner or later. Perhaps he would pardon me. But would the eucharist produce the same effect taken on top of beer, however light? I could always try. What was the teaching of the Church on the matter? What if I were about to commit sacrilege?
>
> *(Molloy, p. 97)*

He decides, nonetheless, to receive communion in spite of the lager, and to make matters worse he sucks peppermint on his way to the church, where he is obliged to seek special audience with the parish priest, Mass being long over -

> The Father is sleeping, said the servant. I can wait, I said. Is it urgent? she said. Yes and no, I said. She showed me into the sitting-room, bare and bleak, dreadful. Father Ambrose came in, rubbing his eyes. I disturb you, Father, I said. He clicked his tongue against the roof of his mouth protestingly.
>
> *(Molloy, p. 100)*

In making his case to Father Ambrose, Moran permits his creator, Beckett, to toss in a blasphemous analogy for this most sacred of Catholic sacraments[38]-

> I came to ask you a favour, I said. Granted, he said. We observed each other. It's this, I said, Sunday for me without the Body and Blood is like — . He raised his hand. Above all no profane comparisons, he said. Perhaps he was thinking of the kiss without a moustache or beef without mustard.
>
> *(Molloy, p. 100)*

The ringing of the angelus, an Irish Catholic custom announced to the entire nation at the hours of twelve-noon and 6 p.m. by church bell, radio and now television, did not pass unnoticed by Beckett[39] -

> But talking of the craving for a fellow let me observe that having waked between eleven o'clock and midday (I heard the angelus, recalling the incarnation, shortly after) I resolved to go and see my mother.
>
> *(Molloy, p. 16)*

Catholic doctrine and theology are fair game for intellectual amusement, as with Mr. Spiro, the editor of the monthly Catholic magazine *Crux*. The theological concept of Limbo (now deleted from Catholic doctrine), where the souls of unbaptised children passed eternity in blissful childsong, but were denied the presence of God, arises in *Texts for Nothing* [40] -

That's where the council will be tomorrow, prayers will be offered for my soul, as for that of one dead, as for that of an infant dead in its dead mother, that it may not go to Limbo, sweet thing theology.

(Texts for Nothing, p. 87)

Sex and religion often dominated conversation in Beckett's Dublin, as indeed they still do today -

Camier sat near the door at a small red table with a thick glass top. On his left hand strangers were belittling equal strangers, while to his right the talk, in undertones, was of the interest taken by Jesuits in mundane matters. In this or some cognate connexion an article was cited, recently appeared in some ecclesiastical rag, on the subject of artificial insemination, the conclusion of which appeared to be that sin arose whenever the sperm was of non-marital origin. On this angelic sex issue was joined, several voices taking part.
Change the subject, said Camier, or I'll report you to the archbishop. You're putting thoughts in my head.

(Mercier and Camier, p. 79)

The Protestant sense of christian duty is a feature of Dublin life to which Beckett makes reference in *All That Fall* when Miss Fitt responds resignedly to Mrs. Rooney's demand for assistance with: 'Well, I suppose it is the Protestant thing to do.'[41]

A number of churches feature in Beckett's writing: Tullow Parish Church; the Church of the Immaculate Heart of Mary; the Catholic Church at Donabate; the Church of St. John the Evangelist, and in *Dream of Fair to Middling Women* the centre of Catholic worship for the diocese of Dublin, the Pro-Cathedral in Marlborough Street (8:7), situated in an area of Dublin not always occupied by the pure and virtuous, receives mention -

Four skeivers and a good dig with a blade and there you have a Pro-Cathedral. And the pros and cons.

(Dream of Fair to Middling Women, p. 69)

8:7   The Pro-Cathedral, Marlborough Street (By courtesy Bord Fáilte, D4/47)

Censorship in Ireland

Amusing though it may be to observe and comment on religious practice and theology, the dictates of the Catholic Church in Ireland and its influence on the state were another matter. The censorship laws on literature were harsh and indiscriminate, a work of literature often being judged on its reputation, or on the basis of a cursory glance by a member of the Censorship Board. Beckett was well aware of the restrictions imposed on writers: 'Celia said that if he did not find work at once she would have to go back to hers. Murphy knew what that meant. No more music. This phrase is chosen with care, lest the filthy censors should lack an occasion to commit their filthy synecdoche.'[42] This precaution seems to have been effective. *Murphy* was not banned, but prohibition orders were issued in Ireland against *Watt* in 1954, *Molloy* in 1956 and *More Pricks than Kicks* in 1934.[43] The latter was given the registered number 465, a fact noted by Beckett in an essay, *Censorship in the Saorstat*, written in 1935, in which he takes a bitter swipe at the nation's readers: 'We now feed our pigs on sugarbeet pulp. It is all the same to them.'[44] In this essay Beckett has little mercy on the philistine guardians of morality in the so-called Free State, while at the same time he has great fun. The 1929 Censorship of Publications Act, brought in by the then Minister for Justice, on which he lavishes opprobrium, provided for the prohibition of the sale and distribution of unwholesome literature.

Definitions were, as ever, a problem for the semi-literate: "A plea for distinction between indecency obiter and ex professo did not detain a caucus that has bigger and better things to split than hairs, the pubic not excepted. 'It is the author's expressed purpose, it is the effect which his thought will have as expressed in the particular words into which he has *flung* (eyetalics mine) his thought that the censor has to consider'. (Minister for Justice)"[45] The reduction of the Censorship Board's membership from the proposed juristic dozen to five by Deputy Professor Tierney is seen by Beckett as a grave disservice to the nations writers 'as the jury convention would have ensured the sale of at least a dozen copies in this country, assuming, as in reverence bound, that the censors would have gone to bed simultaneously and independently with the text, and not passed a single copy of the work from hand to hand, nor engaged a fit and proper person to read it to them in assembly.'[46]

Ridiculous though the Bill was, debate on the topic descended to an astounding level of stupidity with the remarkable statement from Deputy J. J. Byrne: 'It is not necessary for any sensible individual to read the whole of a book before coming to the conclusion whether the book is good, bad or indifferent.'[47] Byrne earns immortality for this service to literature in the poem 'To Nelly' in *Watt* [48] -

To thee, sweet Nell, when shadows fall
Jug-jug! Jug-jug!
I here in thrall
My wanton thoughts do turn.
Walks she out yet with Bryne?
Moves Hyde his hand amid her skirts
As erst? I ask, and Echo answers: Certes.

(Watt, p. 9)

Catholic teaching in Ireland has had a profound effect on sexual mores in the country, not least in prohibiting the use of contraceptives. The embargo on the importation of contraceptives into the Republic prompted Beckett to write his first piece of satire in 1929. The title, *Che Sciagura*, is taken from Voltaire's *Candide*, 'Che sciagura d'essere senza coglioni,' meaning 'What a misfortune to be without balls,' and the pseudonym D.E.S.C. with which the piece is signed, is from the first letters of the last four words of the title.[49] The vicissitudes of contraceptives and their bearers entering the Republic are depicted in *Watt*; Beckett, again presumably not wishing unduly to raise the hackles of the nation's censor, disguises (rather thinly) the dreaded product as *Bando* an aphrodisiac -

> For the State, taking as usual the law into its own hands, and duly indifferent to the sufferings of thousands of men, and tens of thousands of women, all over the country, has seen fit to place an embargo on this admirable article, from which joy could stream, at a moderate cost, into homes, and other places of rendezvous, now desolate. It cannot enter our ports, nor cross our northern frontier, if not in the form of a casual, hazardous and surreptitious dribble, I mean piecemeal in ladies' underclothing, for example, or gentlemen's golfbags, or the hollow missal of a broad-minded priest, where on discovery it is immediately seized, and confiscated, by some gross customs official half crazed with seminal intoxication and sold, at ten and even fifteen times its advertised value, to exhausted commercial travellers on their way home after an unprofitable circuit.
>
> *(Watt, p. 168-169)*

Whatever the sadness of the nation's shortcomings may have been in the 'thirties and 'forties, the tragedy is that Ireland in the 'eighties has changed but little. It took a high-court action to enshrine the individual's right to use contraception, and a referendum to change the ridiculous law that placed the distribution of contraceptives in the hands of the medical profession. In the course of acrimonious hustling for the public conscience the sanctimonious ejaculations of some members of the Catholic majority offended many co-religionists, to say nothing of adherents to other creeds. The acquiescence of government to dictates of the Catholic hierarchy on national mores and culture drew from Beckett his most damning statement on Gaelic censorship: 'Sterilisation of the mind and apotheosis of the litter suit well together. Paradise peopled with virgins and the earth with decorticated multiparas.'[50]

Dublin Transport

Transportation in Dublin in the 'twenties and 'thirties consisted of the train, the bus or tram, rarely a cab, and, most often, the bicycle. For very special occasions an automobile was hired.

The Dublin Cab

The horse-drawn cab exists today in Dublin only as a tourist attraction, but, in the 'thirties these were the taxis of the city. The jarvey, (8:8) like the dreaded policeman, was present on every street in the background, occasionally coming forward to capture the limelight. Belacqua, as we have seen, was influenced in his choice of a pub by the clientele; he did not relish the company of jarveys. However, in *The Expelled* and *Malone Dies*, the jarvey and his horse receive Beckett's full attention and sympathy[51] -

> So I stopped a third time, of my own free will, and entered a cab. Those I had just seen pass, crammed with people hotly arguing, must have made a strong impression on me. It's a big black box, racking and swaying on its springs, the windows are small, you curl up in a corner, it smells musty.
>
> *(The Expelled, p. 27)*

In *The Expelled*, the cabby secures a permanent place in the Beckett canon when he forsakes a funeral engagement -

> In spite of the closed windows, the creaking of the cab and the traffic noises, I heard him singing, all alone aloft on his seat. He had preferred me to a funeral, this was a fact which would endure forever. He sang, *She is far from the land where her young hero*, those are the only words I remember.
>
> *(The Expelled, p. 30)*

Not only had this cabby forsaken the dead, he went further and offered the hospitality of his home to his passenger, who later slept in the stable beneath his lodging (8:9) -

> I found the cab in the dark, opened the door, the rats poured out, I climbed in ... Several times during the night I felt the horse looking at me through the window and the breath of its nostrils.
>
> *(The Expelled, p. 32)*

8:8 Horse-drawn cabs at a rank on O'Connell Street. The Rotunda Hospital and Round Rooms (now a cinema) are in the background (By courtesy National Library of Ireland, Eason 1681)

8:9 A horse and stables at the rere of city houses (Photograph by N. Johnson)

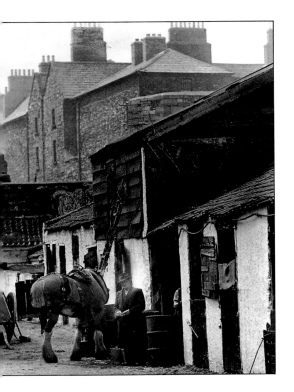

The motion of the horse-drawn cab, now a lost pleasure of the past, imparted to Malone that sensation of freedom so ardently sought but so fleetingly realised[52] -

> But the passenger, having named the place he wants to go and knowing himself as helpless to act on the course of events as the dark box that encloses him, abandons himself to the pleasant feeling of being freed from all responsibility, or he ponders on what lies before him, or on what lies behind him, saying, Twill not be ever thus ...
>
> *(Malone Dies, p. 231)*

In motion the despicable jarvey becomes a figure of some majesty -

> Then with his huge exasperated hands he tears at the reins or, half rising and leaning out over his horse, brings them down with a crack all along its back. And he launches his equipage blindly through the dark thronging streets, his mouth full of curses.
>
> *(Malone Dies, p. 231)*

His decrepit horse also achieves a fleeting dignity in full flight[53] -

> But once in motion it is transformed, momentarily, perhaps because of the memories that motion revives, for the mere fact of running and pulling cannot give it much satisfaction, under such conditions.
>
> *(Malone Dies, p. 231)*

The Bicycle

Beckett has stated that it would give him great pleasure to write four thousand words on his dear bicycle.[54] He has done at least that. The affection shown by Beckett for this once essential means of propulsion is such that it merits special mention in this chronicle. Another Dubliner, Brian O'Nolan, alias Flann O'Brien and Myles na Gopaleen, has also paid handsome tribute to the Dublin velocipede, which he believed to be half-man anyway by virtue of the passage of 'mollycules' from backside to saddle 'pari passu and vice versa'.[55] Few have honoured the machine in verse. Beckett, in poetry, captures the freedom and rhythm of the cyclist in full flight[56] -

> all the livelong way this day of sweet showers from
> Portrane on the seashore
> Donabate sad swans of Turvey Swords
> pounding along in three ratios like a sonata
> like a Ritter with pommelled scrotum atra cura on the step
> Botticelli from the fork down pestling the transmission
> tires bleeding voiding zeep the highway
> all heaven in the sphincter
> *the* sphincter
>
> müüüüüüüde now
> potwalloping now through the promenaders
> this trusty all-steel this super-real
> bound for home like a good boy ...

Then the slower motion of the free-wheeling rider -

> tired now hair ebbing gums ebbing ebbing home

And onwards again with a resurgence of energy and motion -

> clipped like a pederast as to one trouser-end
> sucking in my bloated lantern behind a Wild Woodbine
> cinched to death in a filthy slicker
> flinging the proud Swift forward breasting the swell of
> Stürmers
>
> *(Sanies I, pp. 17-18)*

The 'Wild Woodbine' is a reference to the popular cigarette of that name, and the 'proud Swift' was a well-known bicycle of the period.[57]

The rhythmic freedom of the cyclist is also conveyed in Beckett's prose. In the 'Fingal' chapter in *More Pricks than Kicks*, Belacqua's elation on a stolen bicycle is such, that his 'sadness fell from him like a shift'.[58]

8:10 A baker's van and horse
(Photograph by N. Johnson)

In the early *Dream of Fair to Middling Women*, two fundamental components of Dublin transport are brought together in a passage that again evokes the freedom of bicycle flight, when machine and rider overtake the horse and van from Findlater's, one of the city's well-known victuallers[59](8:10) -

> Behold Belacqua an overfed child pedalling, faster and faster, his mouth ajar and his nostrils dilated, down a frieze of hawthorn after Findlater's van, faster and faster till he cruises alongside of the hoss, the black fat wet rump of the hoss.
>
> *(Dream of Fair to Middling Women, p. 1)*

Even Beckett's cripples, crutches fastened to the cross-bar, experience the exhilaration of flying down-hill on a bicycle, and what's more with two aboard[60] -

> I trembled for my testicles which swung a little low. Faster! I cried. He bore down on the pedals. I bounded up to my place. The bicycle swayed, righted itself, gained speed. Bravo! I cried, beside myself with joy. Hurrah! cried my son. How I loathe that exclamation! I can hardly set it down. He was as pleased as I, I do believe. His heart was beating under my hand and yet my hand was far from his heart. Happily it was downhill. Happily I had mended my hat, or the wind would have blown it away. Happily the weather was fine and I no longer alone. Happily, happily.
>
> *(Molloy, pp. 157-158)*

The Dubliner's desire to convey two, or indeed more passengers (8:11), aboard a velocipede should have guaranteed the success of the tandem in the city, but it was only occasionally sighted.[61]

In pre-war Dublin when only the very privileged had motor cars, the bicycle was the commonest mode of transport. Even the local parson came and went on a Raleigh 'rustless all steel'[62](8:12) -

> He pedalled away like a weaver's shuttle (but not before she had convenanted to be glad) to administer the Eucharist, of which he always carried an abundance in a satchel on the bracket of his bike, to a moneyed wether up the road whose tale was nearly told.
>
> *(More Pricks than Kicks, p. 193)*

A bicycle is no more than the sum of its parts, and Beckett gives painstaking consideration to the mechanical constituents of the machine (8:13). In *Molloy*, Moran despatches his son, Jacques, to purchase a bicycle, for which he gives him the handsome sum of five pounds for a second-hand model, with the strictest instructions as to the composition of the machine.[63] Apart from frame and wheels, it must possess certain other modalities which, to the experienced cyclist, are of the utmost

8:11　A double-tandem on O'Connell Bridge (Photography by G.A. Duncan, No. A11/E1).

"*Rigid, Rapid and Reliable.*"

Ride a
RALEIGH
THE ALL·STEEL BICYCLE

Only £1 down and 12 monthly payments, or cash from £6 7s. 6d.
Send for "The Book of the Raleigh" free.
THE RALEIGH CYCLE COMPANY, LTD.,
5 LEINSTER ST., DUBLIN.　104 ANN ST., BELFAST.
AGENTS THROUGHOUT IRELAND.
Specify Sturmey-Archer 3-speed gear and Dunlop tyres on your Raleigh.

8:12　Advertisment for a Raleigh Rustless All-Steel Bicycle (From the *Irish Cyclist and Motor Cyclist*. June 9, 1926. p. 25)

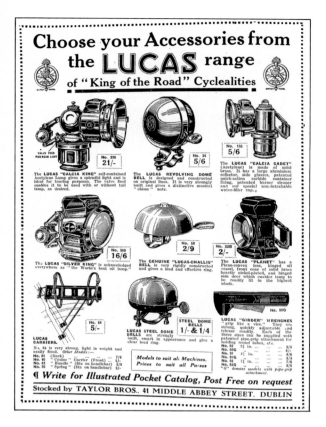

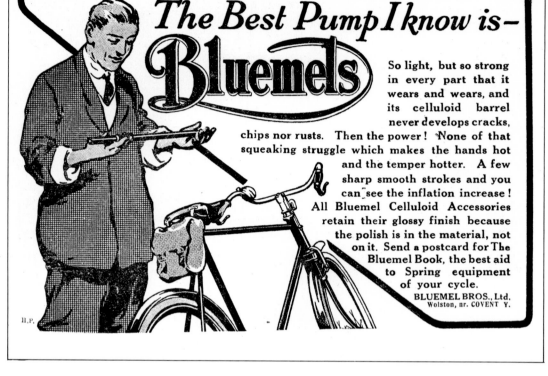

8:13 Advertisment for Bicycle Components (From the *Irish Cyclist and Motor Cyclist.* June 30, 1926.)

8:14 Advertisment for a bicycle pump (From the *Irish Cyclist and Motor Cyclist.* March 17, 1926. p. 21)

importance. A good carrier was essential if the bicycle was to convey both Moran and his son. A lamp, though not essential, might come in useful.[64] Even bicycle clips attract Beckett's attention, for there are those that go round[65], and those that leave the trouser ends sticking out.[66] The bicycle pump (8:14) is to the cyclist, as wind to a becalmed sailor. The pump, like the carrier, was one of the outstanding features of Jacques' purchase, fortunately, as it was soon needed -

> The dirty little twister was letting the air escape between the valve and the connection which he had purposely not screwed tight. Hold the bicycle, I said, and give me the pump. The tyre was soon hard. I looked at my son. He began to protest. I soon put a stop to that. Five minutes later I felt the tyre. It was as hard as ever. I cursed him.
>
> (Molloy, p. 156)

Hugh Kenner in an intriguing essay, 'The Cartesian Centaur',[67] blends the Cartesian concept of corporal perfection with the Beckettian portrayal of legless man rooted in his own immobility, yet capable of

Page 268

exhilarating propulsion on wheels, 'a man riding a bicycle, *mens sana in corpore disposito.'* The metamorphosis of man and machine, so implicit in much of Beckett's (and O'Brien's) writing, gives to the decay or destruction of the bicyle, a significance rich in symbolism. Mercier and Camier return to their beloved bicycle to find that little remains apart from the pump -

> Of it there remains, said Mercier, securely chained to the railing, as much as may reasonably remain, after a week's incessant rain, of a bicycle relieved of both wheels, the saddle, the bell and the carrier. And the tail light, he added, I nearly forgot. He struck his forehead a blow. What an addle-pate to be sure! he said. And the pump of course, said Camier.
> Believe it or not, said Mercier, it's all one to me, our pump has been spared.
> *(Mercier and Camier. p. 85)*

The disintegration of their bicycle heralds the dissolution of their relationship. As Hugh Kenner puts it: 'from the dismemberment of their bicycle we may date the disintegration of Mercier and Camier's original lock-step unity. In the final third of this novel they gradually become nodding acquaintances, like the two wheels which were once sustained by a single frame but are now free to pursue independent careers.'[68]

In *All that Fall*, the agony of a puncture, especially of a rear wheel with gear hub, is conveyed briefly but with remarkable mechanical precision by Mr. Tyler -

> Nothing, Mrs Rooney, nothing, I was merely cursing, under my breath, God and man, under my breath, and the wet Saturday afternoon of my conception. My back tyre has gone down again. I pumped it hard as iron before I set out. And now I am on the rim.... Now if it were the front I should not so much mind. But the back. The back! The chain! The oil! The grease! The hub! The brakes! The gear! No! It is too much!
> *(All that Fall, p. 15)*

The frustration and despair of the unfortunate cyclist are shared by the listener, even if he has never ridden a punctured bicycle, as Tyler bounces away on on his wounded mount.[69]

But of all the components that constitute the bicycle, it is the bell that most appeals to Beckett -

> And similarly I might have told him to be careful about the bell, to unscrew the little cap and examine it well inside, so as to make sure it was a good bell and in good working order, before concluding the transaction, and to ring it to hear the ring it made.
> *(Molloy, p. 145)*

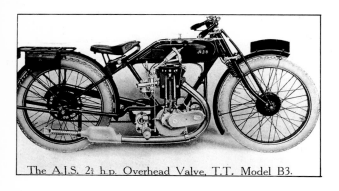

The A.J.S. 2¼ h.p. Overhead Valve, T.T. Model B3.

8:15 A.J.S. Motor Cycle
(By courtesy The National Motor
Museum at Beaulieu)

Beckett even uses the sounds of the bicycle, its bell, wheels and brakes, to convey the village atmosphere in the radio-play, *All That Fall* -

Dragging feet. Sound of bicycle bell. It is old MR TYLER coming up behind her on his bicycle, on his way to the station. Squeak of brakes.

(All That Fall, p. 14)

However, for Molloy an improvement on the bell was the horn, the sound of which gave him exquisite pleasure[70] -

Dear bicycle, I shall not call you bike, you were green, like so many of your generation. I don't know why. It is a pleasure to meet it again. To describe it at length would be a pleasure. It had a little red horn instead of the bell fashionable in your days. To blow this horn was for me a real pleasure, almost a vice. I will go further and declare that if I were obliged to record, in a roll of honour, those activities which in the course of my interminable existence have given me only a mild pain in the balls, the blowing of a rubber horn – toot! – would figure among the first.

(Molloy, p. 16)

Beckett, a keen cyclist,[71] did not confine himself to the bicycle and in March 1925 while an undergraduate at Trinity,[72] we find him aboard a motorcycle in the Dublin University novices' trial in which he rode a 2¾h.p. A.J.S. (8:15) through the Wicklow and Dublin mountains.

The apotheosis of solitude: Dublin's personalities.

In keeping with the principle on which this book is based, I will deal only with the personae of Dublin who receive mention in Beckett's prose and criticism. With his many Dublin friends, acquaintances and enemies, if such there be, I have no business. Indeed, we should not see it as surprising that Beckett, throughout his life, has only been associated closely with a handful of loyal friends -

For the artist, who does not deal in surfaces, the rejection of friendship is not only reasonable, but a necessity. Because the only possible spiritual development is in the sense of depth. The artistic tendency is not expansive, but a contraction. And art is the apotheosis of solitude.

(Proust, p. 64)

Most, but not all of the personalities featuring by name in Beckett's literature are, understandably, writers. Direct references are few, which is hardly surprising, if indeed Beckett held poets and aesthetes in the same low regard as did Belacqua who classed them with the despicable jarvey.[73] Moreover, Beckett may perhaps have found the 'Irishness' of home literature somewhat oppressive -

> 'I hate Omar' she said 'and your fake penumbru. Haven't we had enough of that in this festering country. Haven't we had enough Deirdreeing of Hobson's weirds and Kawthleens in the gloaming hissing up petticoats of sorrarrhoea? Haven't we had enough withered pontiffs of chiarinoscurissimo? 'The Mist' she sneered 'an it roolin' home UP the glen and the mist agin an'it rollin' home DOWN the glen? Up, down, hans arown ... Merde. Give me noon. Give me Racine'
>
> (Dream of Fair and Middling Women, p. 176)

The Poets of Ireland

Though Beckett may have shrunk from the company of poets, he did read the poetry emanating from his native city, and in a critical essay, 'Recent Irish Poetry',[74] published under the pseudonym Andrew Belis, in 1934, he expressed uncompromisingly his views on the poetry of established poet such as Yeats, and of those, as yet, relatively unknown poets, among whom were Denis Devlin and Brian Coffey. In this essay Beckett divided the Irish poetic force into two groups, the more numerous antiquarians, and the others who had been likened by W.B. Yeats to " 'the fish that lie gasping on the shore', suggesting that they might at least learn to expire with an air."[75] The antiquarians, Beckett maintained, delivered 'with the altitudinous complacency of the Victorian Gael the Ossianic goods.'[76] The older antiquarians listed by Beckett were W.B. Yeats, Padraic Colum, James Stephens, Pamela Travers, Monk Gibbon, George Russell, Austin Clarke, F.R. Higgins, and among the younger poets in this category, he included Brian O'Higgins, J.H. Pollock and Miss Large. James Stephens[77] was dismissed as a 'beauty expert'; F.R. Higgins[78], though an antiquarian, wrote poetry which in common with Ledwidge's verse had the stuff of good modern poetry, 'a good smell of dung', and Monk Gibbon[79] was 'the poet of the children'. But it was at the older 'antiquarians', that the young Beckett (he was 27 years old at the time of writing 'Recent Irish Poetry'), directed the thrust of his criticism.

William Butler Yeats[80] does not fare well in 'Recent Irish Poetry'. Beckett's criticism of Yeat's may be seen more as that of a voice protesting against the confinement of poetry within the accepted conventions and traditions. It is the voice of the avant garde railing against the establishment which is, as is often the case, the cry of youth

against age, age which portrays the complacency of success rather than the wisdom of experience -

> The device common to the poets of the Revival and after, in the use of which even beyond the jewels of language they are at one, is that of flight from self-awareness, and as such might perhaps be described as a convenience. At the centre there is no theme. Why not? Because the centre is simply not that kind of girl, and no more about it. And without a theme there can be no poem, as witness the exclamation of Mr Yeats's 'fanatic heart': 'What, be a singer born and lack a theme!' ('The Winding Stair'). But the circumference is an iridescence of themes – Oisin, Cuchulain, Maeve, Tir-nanog, the Táin Bo Cuailgne, Yoga, the Crone of Beare – segment after segment of cut-and-dried sanctity and loveliness.[81]
>
> *(Recent Irish Poetry, p. 71)*

At a later and more mellow stage of life, Beckett looks to the beauty of Yeats's poetry, and pays homage to the majesty of *The Tower* by quoting from it, and taking from it the title for '... but the clouds ...'[82]

> .... but the clouds of the sky ... when the horizon fades ... or a bird's sleepy cry ... among the deepening shades ...
>
> *(...but the clouds ... p. 262)*

In the early prose works, Beckett called on Yeats's remarkable features, not devoid of effeminacy, to convey an impression of the beauty of one of Belacqua's paramours -

> Indeed she was better than lovely, with its suggestion of the Nobel Yeats, with her jet of hair and her pale set face, the whipcord knee and the hard bust sweating a little inside the black jersey.
>
> *(More Pricks than Kicks, p. 114)*

Yeats was awarded the Nobel Prize for literature in 1923, (8:16) an honour to be bestowed on Beckett in 1969.

Austin Clarke, Dublin poet, dramatist and novelist,[83] fares little better as one of the older antiquarians in the essay 'Recent Irish Poetry.' Thomas MacGreevy, (of whom more later), occupied a position intermediate between the antiquarians and the newer generation of 'poor fish', among whom were included Blanaid Salkeld, Erik Dodds, Francis Macnamara, Percy Usher, Francis Stuart, R.N.D. Wilson, Leslie Yodaiken, Sean O'Casey, Lyle Donaghey, Geoffrey Taylor, and, of particular interest, Denis Devlin and Brian Coffey.[84] Blanaid Salkeld's poetry was possessed of much that was 'personal and moving, when not rendered blue in the face by the sonnet form.'[85] Beckett hoped to see Arland Ussher's (8:17) *Man Poem* safely between boards, before the author improved it 'out of existence'.[86] Lyle Donaghy[87] was another of the 'poor fish' writing promising poetry, and Geoffrey Taylor had 'performed a very diverting ballet away from the pundits.'[88] But of the new generation of Irish poets, Denis Devlin and Brian Coffey were 'without question the most interesting.'[89]

Denis Devlin[90](8:18), poet and diplomat, was born in Scotland, educated in Ireland, and had a distinguished career in the Irish foreign service in Italy, New York and London.

> Phrases twisted through other
> Reasons reasons disproofs
> Phrases lying low
> Proving invalid that reason
> With which I prove its truth
> Identity obscured
> Life the reflections of
> One mirror in another
> Reasons reasons disproofs.

Of this verse Beckett wrote -

> It is no disparagement of Mr Devlin to observe that this is still too much by the grace of Eluard.[91] What matters is that it does not proceed from the *Gosoons Wunderhorn* of that Irish Romantic Arnim-Brentano combination, Sir Samuel Ferguson and Standish O'Grady, and that it admits – stupendous innovation – the existence of the author.
>
> *(Recent Irish Poetry, p. 76)*

8:16 *William Butler Yeats, Poet, (1865-1939)* by J.B. Yeats (A detail by courtesy National Gallery of Ireland, No. 872)

8:17 Arland Ussher. 'Portrait d'un joune homme assis' by Augustus John (By courtesy The National Swedish Arts Museum. No. NM 2766)

8:18 On the Military Road, Featherbed Pass, August 1931. Left to right: Mervyn Wall, Denis Devlin, Paddy Crean (later to become Head Chaplain in the Irish Army) all aged 23 years (By courtesy Mr. M. Wall)

Reviewing Devlin's volume *Intercessions*, in 1938, Beckett wrote: 'Mr Denis Devlin is a mind aware of its luminaries.'[92]

> Night my pure identity that breathe
> One in all breaths, absorber of all breaths
> Night that gestate in symbol-troubled women,
> Dumb breeders of being
> Wombed in your cathedrals let us watch
> Till the forgotten matutinal colours flame
> Various the rosewindows through ...

Beckett expressed strong feelings on these lines from *Communication from the Eiffel Tower* -

> If I knew of any recent writing to compare with this I should not do so.
> If only the 8 in the last line had been left on its side. So: ∞
>
> *(Review Intercessions, p. 93)*

Beckett's high regard for Devlin and Brian Coffey,[93] and their importance to the modern Irish poetic revival, was by virtue of their submission to 'the influences of those poets least concerned with evading the bankrupt relationship referred to at the opening of this essay – Corbiére, Rimbaud, Laforgue, the *surréalistes* and Mr Eliot, perhaps also to those of Mr Pound – with results that constitute already the nucleus of a living poetic in Ireland.'[94]

Playwrights and novelists

Beckett seemed more at home in the company of novelists and playwrights than among poets. His friendship with Joyce, and his affection for Synge have been previously mentioned. A few other novelists gain entry by name to Beckett's writing, but their presence is not, of course, an indication of either his regard, or lack of esteem, for their achievements.

The influence of James Joyce on the literature of Samuel Beckett is considerable, but easily overstated.[95] Beckett has dissociated himself from Joyce, not only in terms of merit, but more importantly in technique: 'The more Joyce knew the more he could. He's tending toward omniscience and omnipotence as an artist. I'm working with impotence, ignorance.'[96] His tribute to Joyce for the centenary of Joyce's birth is evidence of his esteem for his fellow countryman[97] -

> I welcome the occasion to bow once again, before I go, deep down, before his heroic work, heroic being.
>
> Samuel Beckett. Paris. 29.9.80

Beckett's first published work appeared in 1929. It was a critical essay on Joyce's *Work in Progress* entitled, 'Dante ... Bruno . Vico .. Joyce'[98] which appeared in *Our Exagmination Round his Factification for Incamination of Work in Progress*, published by Sylvia Beach's Shakespeare and Company in Paris. Among the contributors was another Irishman and close friend of Beckett, Thomas McGreevy. Of *Finnegans Wake*, Beckett wrote -

> Here form *is* content, content *is* form. You complain that this stuff is not written in English. It is not written at all. It is not to be read – or rather it is not only to be read. It is to be looked at and listened to. His writing is not *about* something; *it is that something itself.*
>
> *(Dante ... Bruno . Vico .. Joyce, p. 27)*

Beckett had no sympathy for a non-comprehending public -

> And if you don't understand it, Ladies and Gentlemen, it is because you are too decadent to receive it.
>
> *(Dante ... Bruno . Vico .. Joyce, p. 26)*

In 1932, Beckett wrote the acrostic *Home Olga* to James Joyce. The phrase 'Home Olga' was a private joke shared by a circle of friends in Paris in the early 1930's. Its origins were in Ireland, where one evening at a party, a bored husband had arisen abruptly from the assembled company, and with the expeletive 'Home Olga' had swept his wife from the party, without so much as a word of farewell to the hostess. At subsequent gatherings the phrase signalled departure and later rendezvous at a pre-selected cafe. The poem pays tribute in an obscure manner to Joyce's exile from home, his disillusionment with the Irish Catholic church and Irish sexual mores, *Finnegans Wake*, and an adieu to virginity in Joyce's *Chamber Music*; there is also acknowledgement of Joyce's love of Jewish humour in the phrase, 'the tip of a friendly yiddophile', which refers to a joke then popular in Dublin: 'Take a tip from me – as the Jew said to the Rabbi – '[99]

> *J* might be made sit up for a jade of hope (and exile, don't you know)
> *A*nd Jesus and Jesuits juggernauted in the haemorrhoidal isle,
> *M*odo et forma anal maiden, giggling to death in stomacho.
> *E* for the erythrite of love and silence and the sweet noo style,
> *S*woops and loops of love and silence in the eye of the sun and view of the mew,
> *J*uvante Jah and a Jain or two and the tip of a friendly yiddophile.
> *O* for an opal of faith and cunning winking adieu, adieu, adieu.
> *Y*esterday shall be tomorow, riddle me that my rapparee.
> *C*he sarà sarà chr fu, there's more than Homer know how to spew,
> *E*xempli gratia: ecce himself and the pickthank agnus
>   – e.o.o.e.
>
> *(Home Olga, p. 8)*

Joyce (8:19), for his part was more aware than most of his young friends potential, and he paid tribute to Beckett in *Finnegans Wake* [100] -

> Sam know miles bettern me how to work the miracle. And I see by his diarrhio he's dropping the stammer out of his silenced bladder since I bonded him off more as a friend and as a brother to try and grow a muff and canonise his dead feet down on the river airy by thinking himself into the fourth dimension and place the ocean between his and ours, the churchyard in the cloister of the depths, after he was capped out of beurlads scoel for the sin against the past participle and earned the factitation of codding chaplan and being as homely gauche as swift B.A.A. Who gets twickly fullgets twice as allemanden huskers. But the whacker his word the weaker our ears for auracles who parles parses orileys. Illstarred punster, lipstering cowknucks. 'Twas the quadra sent him and Trinity too. And he can cantab as chipper as any oxon ever I mood with, a tiptoe singer! He'll prisckly soon hand tune your Erin's ear for you ...

George Bernard Shaw,[101] Dublin born dramatist and man of letters, did not rate very highly with Beckett, if we are to judge by the two references to him in his writing. The first is in the unpublished *Dream of Fair to Middling Women*, when Belacqua, in intellectual turmoil, in front of Dahlberg's Last Supper exclaims[102] -

> Who are your patrons? Greeks? Kings? Lovers? Gladly for Apollo a warrior's bust, the ravishing Campaspe. Yah! Wid me on dee table. You can keep your George Bernard Pygmalion. And your prostated elephanticatics. The man of my peace. Did you never hear tell how Big George cubed a nude in a corslet and a mirror and a sleeping cistern?

(Dream of Fair to Middling Women, p. 70)

8:19 Guests at the 'Déjuner Ulysse', at the Hotel Leopold in Les Vaux-de-Cernay near Versailles on June 27, 1929, to commemorate the publication of *Ulysses* in French, and the twenty-fifth anniversary of Bloomsday on 16 June. Seated at the table are (from left to right) Phillippe Soupault, Nora Joyce, and Leon-Paul Fargue. Standing behind Dujardin is Thomas MacGreevy. Beckett, though invited to the luncheon, is not in the photograph
(By courtesy Reading University Library)

A. J. Leventhal writing of Beckett's alleged reticence and shyness warned:[103] 'Yet I can indicate a text shorn of reticence and critical with gusto and a pithiness that suggests that the writer is made of the stuff that will not compromise and not be afraid to say so. Invited to endorse a tribute to Bernard Shaw on the centenary of his birth by Dublin's Gaiety Theatre, he (Beckett) replied -

> You ask me for a tribute to G.B.S., in French, for your souvenir programme.
> This is too tall an order for me.
> I wouldn't write in French for King street.[104]
> I wouldn't suggest that G.B.S. is not a great play-wright,
> whatever that is when it's at home.
> What I would do is give the whole unupsettable apple-cart for a sup of the Hawk's Well,[105] or the Saints',[106] or a whiff of Juno,[107] to go no further.
> Sorry.

J.M. Synge, [108](8:20) the Dublin playwright, whose *Playboy of the Western World* is a classic of the Irish theatre, was a source of consolation to Belacqua in moments of torment: 'He thought of Synge and recovered his spirits'.[109] Mention has already been made of Beckett's choice of the Elpis Nursing Home, where Synge died, for Belacqua's demise in *More Pricks than Kicks*. Beckett appreciated in Synge's writing what he called the 'rupture of the lines of communication', which permitted the breakdown of the object in poetry[110] -

> Those who are not aware of the rupture, or in whom the velleity of becoming so was suppressed as a nuisance at its inception, will continue to purvey those articles which, in Ireland at least, had ceased to be valid even before the literary advisers to J.M. Synge found themselves prematurely obliged to look elsewhere for a creative hack.

> *(Recent Irish Poetry, p. 70)*

The Dublin-born playwright, Sean O'Casey,[111] receives favourable comment from Beckett in a review of *Windfalls*.[112] Beckett identified O'Casey's mastery of knockabout as the essence of his success, indeed of all theatrical achievement -

> Mr. O'Casey is a master of knockabout in this very serious and honourable sense – that he discerns the principle of disintegration in even the most complacent solidities, and activates it to their explosion. This is the energy of his theatre, the triumph of the principle of knockabout in situation, in all its elements and on all its planes, from the furniture to the higher centres. If 'Juno and the Paycock', as seems likely, is his best work so far, it is because it communicates most fully this dramatic dehiscence, mind and world come asunder in irreparable dissociation – 'chassis' (the credit of having readapted Aguecheek and Belch in Joxer and the Captain being incidental to the larger credit of having dramatised

the slump in the human solid). This impulse of material to escape and be consummate in its own knockabout is admirably expressed in the two 'sketches' that conclude this volume, and especially in 'The End of the Beginning', where the entire set comes to pieces and the chief character, in a final spasm of dislocation, leaves the scene by the chimney.

(The Essential and the Incidental, pp. 82-83)

The Dublin poet and painter, George Russell,[113] better known by his pseudonym AE, was read by the most unlikely of people in Beckett's fiction; first, there is the landlady Miss Carridge in *Murphy* -

> She waited till she heard the old boy's door close, neither loudly nor softly, and then went back to her book: *The Candle of Vision,* [114] by George Russell (A.E.).
>
> *(Murphy, p. 108)*

In *Watt,* Mr. Case, the signal man at Foxrock Station, who 'had a very superior taste in books',[115] is also to be found reading Russell, on this occasion, *Homeward Songs by the Way* -

> To while away the time, and at the same time improve his mind, Mr. Case was reading a book: *Songs by the Way,* [116] by George Russell (A.E.).
>
> *(Watt, p. 227)*

It is, perhaps, surprising that Dublin theatre does not emerge more forcibly in Samuel Beckett's writing. However, a Dublin actor, Jack MacGowran (8:23) adopted the persona of Beckettian malefolk with such effect that Beckett regarded him as one of the finest interpreters of his work. MacGowran saw Beckett more as 'a philosopher of hope than despair', and as an actor he felt duty bound to make visible to as great an audience as possible Beckett's 'complex comic vision ... all too often dismissed as despairing.' MacGowran valued his unique relationship with Beckett: 'It's a wonderful marriage (that of writer and actor) to this degree – that one is born in a generation as an actor where a living writer of the calibre of Beckett can work hand in hand with that actor and so bring out the best in both. It rarely happens. And I feel lucky and fortunate to have been born of his generation and to have lived with him, and to have known him so long and deeply'.[117]

8:20 *John Millington Synge* by Jack B. Yeats (By courtesy Anne Yeats. This is taken from the sketch book 'Swinford and London', July, 1905)

In 1959, Beckett wrote the radio-play *Embers* for MacGowran, and at about the same time he began, and later abandoned a mime play, written for and dedicated in title to J.M. MacGowran: *J.M. Mime.*[118] Beckett collaborated with MacGowran in 1962 in a programme for the Dublin Theatre Festival entitled: *End of Day: An entertainment from the work of Samuel Beckett.*[119] Three years later Beckett supervised MacGowran's

Page 280

performance of *A Television Exploration of the World of Samuel Beckett* for BBC television.[120] Beckett's first television play, *Eh Joe*, was written for MacGowran and performed in 1965.[121] Apart from these unique collaborations between Beckett and MacGowran, MacGowran performed in most of Beckett's drama to which he brought an expression and intonation that demonstrated clearly the pervading influence of Dublin in the Beckett *oeuvre*.

After MacGowran's death in 1973, *All Strange Away* by Samuel Beckett, was published in a limited edition illustrated by Edward Gorey, the proceeds from which went to Jack MacGowran's widow.[122]

From writers to painters

Beckett's appreciation of art has been discussed in the chapter on the National Gallery of Ireland. The relationship of art to literature in Beckett's writing is a symbiotic one, whereby each form elevates the other. Thomas MacGreevy was the bridge over which Beckett crossed freely from the world of Dublin poets, novelists and playwrights to that of painting where the remarkable artist Jack Yeats was to become for Beckett, the embodiment of the genius and integrity that constitutes the creative artist.

Thomas MacGreevy (8:22) was born in Tarbert in County Kerry in 1893.[123] Wounded in the first World War, he spent his convalescence in France studying that country's artistic culture. For seven years he was *Lecteur* at the *École Normale Supérieure*, during which time he published much literary criticism and a volume of poems, one of the most popular being 'Aodh Ruadh Ó Domhnaill' in which he recounts his search for the grave of Red Hugh O'Donnell in Spain [124]-

> And all Valladolid knew
> And out to Simancas all knew
> Where they buried Red Hugh.

In 1950 MacGreevy was appointed Director of the National Gallery of Ireland, and henceforth he devoted himself to establishing for the Gallery and its national collection, a place of rank among the famous galleries of Europe with which he was so familiar.

To this end he published a number of catalogues and critical works on artists, among whom were Jack Yeats and Nicholas Poussin.[125] He died in Dublin in 1967.

8:21 Jack MacGowran with Samuel Beckett (By courtesy Reading University Library)

8:22 *Thomas MacGreevy* by Sean O'Sullivan (By courtesy National Gallery of Ireland, No. 7971)

With the exceptions of Devlin and Coffey, Beckett identified more closely with the poetic vision of MacGreevy than with other contemporary Irish poets of repute. Beckett placed MacGreevy in an independent niche intermediate between the older generation of antiquarian poets, of whom Yeats was the archetype, and the newer poets who no longer regarded 'the stuff of song as incorruptible, uninjurable and unchangeable ...'[126] MacGreevy's poems, or as Beckett preferred to call them, elucidations, 'the vision without the dip', were regarded by him as 'probably the most important contribution to post-War Irish poetry.'[127] Statements such as this coming from Beckett, should be given careful consideration, to say nothing of Mr. MacGreevy's poetry. But Beckett goes further[128] -

> To the mind that has raised itself to the grace of humility 'founded' – to quote from Mr McGreevy's *T.S. Eliot* – 'not on misanthropy but on hope', prayer is no more (no less) than an act of recognition. A nod, even a wink. The flag dipped in Ave, not hauled down in Miserere. This is the adult mode of prayer syntonic to Mr McGreevy, the unfailing salute to *his* significant from which the fire is struck and the poem kindled, and kindled to a radiance without counterpart in the work of contemporary poets writing in English, who tend to eschew as understatement anything and everything between brilliance and murk. The equable radiance of -
>
> > But a moment, now, I suppose,
> > For a moment I may suppose,
> > Gleaming blue,
> > Silver blue,
> > Gold,
> > Rose,
> > And the light of the world.
> > *(Gloria de Carlos V)*[129]
>
> and of -
>
> > The end of love
> > Love's ultimate good
> > Is the end of love ... and
> > Light ...
> > *(Seventh Gift of the Holy Ghost)*[130]
>
> (Humanistic Quietism, pp. 68-69)

Dublin's sky, especially at dusk, and the impact of colour and the commonplace aspects of the city are evident throughout Beckett's writing. It is none too surprising then to find him in affectionate empathy with his friend's personal cry of anguish in his poetic vision of Dublin from a lurching horse cab[131] -

> The brightness of brightness,
> Towering in the sky
> Over Dublin
>
> *(Crón Tráth na nDéithe)*

MacGreevy's talent as a poet may, in Beckett's view, be attributed to the fact that "he knows how to wait for the thing to happen, how not to beg the fact of this 'bitch of a world' – inarticulate earth and inscrutable heaven."[132]

> I labour in a barren place,
> Alone, self-conscious, frightened, blundering;
> Far away, stars wheeling in space,
> About my feet, earth voices whispering.
>
> *(Nocturne)* [133]

Small wonder that Beckett and MacGreevy should be at one, with others, in declaring -

> Poetry builds a nexus between the 'I' and the 'you' by leading the emotions of the sunken, telluric depths upward toward the illumination of a collective reality and a totalistic universe.
>
> *(Manifesto. Poetry is Vertical)* [134]

The scholars need to get on with the important business of taking MacGreevy's poetry seriously, not merely because of his association with Beckett, but because it is worthy of elevation in its own right.

MacGreevy as art critic was not without interest to Beckett. Some aspects of MacGreevy's influence in art have been discussed in the section on the National Gallery of Ireland in Chapter 5. Beckett acknowledged MacGreevy's appreciation of the Gallery's acquisitions in his early writings,[135] and he also thought highly of his art critisism.[136]

Of MacGreevy's art criticism, the work that most interested Beckett was his mongraph on Yeats, *Jack B. Yeats. An Appreciation and an Interpretation,* [137] the first published critical appraisal of his friend's art. There are some interesting threads in this work that draw together the artistic personalities of MacGreevy, Beckett and Yeats: 'For me then, Jack Yeats uses his mastery to depict and express the Ireland that matters. Ireland, it will be said, is small. Does it matter? Does anything in Ireland matter? The answer is that every place in which there are human beings matters.'[138] What, in a sense, is more Beckettian in ambition than MacGreey's assessment of Yeats's treatment of his subject? 'But like every genuine artist, Jack Yeats knows that the humanities are far more important than the brocades or the rags in which they are clothed. He also knows, as, for instance, Jacopo Bassano and Velazquez had known before him, that paint can make rags as humanly beautiful if not as socially elegant as the brocades. And thus he has been able to express the humanities in terms of an underdog, conquered people.'[139]

MacGreevy was puzzled by what at first seemed an odd comment by Beckett on Jack Yeat's painting: "A few months ago,' he wrote, 'Samuel Beckett wrote me that he had been looking at some recent works by Jack Yeats. 'He grows Watteauer and Watteauer' he commented. I was startled by the comparison, for, superficially, nothing could be more different than the work of the two artists, Watteau's figures being in the first instance all linear draughtsmanship of the most exquisitely pencilled quality, whereas with Jack Yeats's figures the drawing is a matter of swift and summary, though extraordinarly telling, brushwork."[140] MacGreevy went on to explain this odd artistic comparison in a way that would have done justice to Bruno's theory of contraries: "Juan Ramon Jiminez used to tell a story of a Spanish tramp who said to a grandee, 'You are above the law and I am below the law so we are equals'. In Ireland the whole people were below the law so something of the same kind might be said in comparing Watteau's figures and Jack Yeats's."[141]

Yeats's choice of background for his drama is similar to that used by Beckett: "The foreground might be a field, a stretch of bogland or seashore, a village street or even a city street, but in Ireland the city street often provides glimpses of the mountains and it was against that mountain background, so suggestive of unchanging, extra-human, transcendent things, and, by implication, of the precariousness of all human achievement, that he painted the people of Ireland, men, women and children, at work and play, farmers, labourers, car-drivers, jockeys, ballad-singers, tramps, women, old and young, barefooted boys in rakish-looking caps – 'men with the eyes of people do be looking at the sea,' as I once heard it expressed, girls with the eyes of those who belong to people do be looking at the sea."[142] Moreover, MacGreevy's account of the Yeatsian subject can be applied almost verbatim to the Beckettian character: 'The artist (Yeats) had always treated strollers, tinkers, gypsies and tramps of every kind, seriously, with respect. They were symbolical of the whole human odyssey. The world, after all, is no more than a temporary camping place, to which men come, and from which they go, like travelling tinkers.'[143]

In describing the human depth to a Yeats painting, MacGreevy saw in the overwhelming pastoral beauty of the west of Ireland a power capable of turning 'one's perception into something very like prayer.'[144] A similar sentiment is expressed in Beckett's evocation of a spring evening in *More Pricks than Kicks*, when descriptive words seeming no longer adequate, he captures the majesty of the moment in a beautiful line of prayer - 'It was one of those Spring evenings when it is a matter of some difficulty to keep God out of one's meditations.'[145] The perfection of a work of art, as the most sublime manifestation of man's creative capability, is in effect, a prayer of praise to the creation of mankind. Was it not MacGreevy's poetry, and his artistic perception and appreciation of beauty and nature, which drew the comment from Beckett that: 'All poetry, as discriminated from the various paradigms of prosody, is prayer'?[146]

Reviewing MacGreevy's book on Yeats for *The Irish Times*, Beckett found it both strange and commendable that 'the first major reaction to art of genius' should come from a compatriot of the artist.[147] In this review Beckett defines competent art criticism, and in doing so pays further tribute to MacGreevy: 'There is at least this to be said for mind, that it can dispel mind. And at least this for art-criticism, that it can lift from the eyes, before *rigor vitae* sets in, some of the weight of congenital prejudice. Mr MacGreevy's little book does this with a competence that will not surprise those who have read his essay on Mr Eliot, or his admirable translation of Valery's *Introduction à la Méthode de Léonard de Vinci*, nor those who follow, in the *Record*, his articles on writers and artists little known, as yet, in the Republic.'[148]

MacGreevy and Beckett both saw in Jack Yeats, not only a consummate painter, but more importantly, an artist whose dedication to his art demanded entraordinary integrity. Yeats's refusal to compromise his art may have had a significant influence on Beckett's own artistic development. 'Beauty is truth and a just balance', Yeats said, 'but not a compromise, the artist compromises when he refuses to paint what he himself has seen, but paints what he thinks some one else would like him to have seen.'[149]

Page 286

Jack Yeats (8:23) defies categorisation.[150] Perhaps the term 'savant' fits most snugly on his artistic persona, except that it is misused so frequently that the wrong impression is conveyed. Yeats now has an established reputation as a painter, and perhaps even in Ireland, the educated classes are aware of his genius in this regard, though he is more likely to be remembered as the brother of 'W B' by those whose knowledge of the poet begins and ends with the island of his dream that was dished up to them daily in childhood. What should be known about Jack Yeats, and will be acknowledged hopefully some day, is that he was an artist towering above others, not only in his *genre*, but outside of it as well. Jack Yeats was not reticent in expressing his opinion of his art to his brother: "You say my painting is now 'great'. Great is a word that may mean so many different things. But I know I am the first living painter in the world. And the second is so far away that I am only able to make him out faintly. I have no modesty. I have the immodesty of the spear head."[151] Here was the artist of renaissance Ireland, a genius with brush and palette, who was accomplished in poetry, ingenious if not brilliant in prose, and sublime in the integrity of his vision of art. Of the advantages in belonging to a talented family, (and there is no denying the genius of the Yeats' family[152]), undoubtedly the most valuable is the genetic code that directs the rose to bloom, but a serious drawback, (well illustrated in the sublimation of recognition of Jack Yeats) is that appreciation is allocated to the clan, rather than to the individuals that comprise it, as though the quantum available was genealogically determined. John Pilling, in his study of Jack Yeats the writer concludes with a comment worth heeding: 'We have known for a long time that he painted fine pictures; surely it is time to acknowledge that he wrote fine literature as well.'[153]

Jack Yeats's literary output is considerable and includes at least seven books of prose, a number of which, for example *The Amaranthers*, are experimental in structure and style, three published plays, five books for children and for the miniature stage, a number of published and unpublished poems, and a variety of short stories and articles on many subjects.[154]

Beckett reviewed *The Amaranthers* when it was published in 1936: 'The chartered recountants take the thing to pieces and put it together again.

8:23 *Jack Yeats* in his studio
(By courtesy Anne Yeats)

They enjoy it. The artist takes it to pieces and makes a new thing, new things. He must. Mr Jack Yeats is an artist. *The Amaranthers* is art, not horology. Ariosto to Miss - *absit nomen'*. [155] Attractive though Yeats's writing may be (and it certainly justifies more intense exploration than it has been given to date) it is his art that appeals most strongly to Beckett-

He is with the great of our time, Kandinsky and Klee, Ballmer and Bram van Velde, Rouault and Braque, because he brings light, as only the great dare to bring light, to the issueless predicament of existence, reduces the dark where there might have been, mathematically at least, a door. The being in the street, when it happens in the room, the being in the room when it happens in the street, the turning to gaze from land to sea, from sea to land, the backs to one another and the eyes abandoning, the man alone trudging in sand, the man alone thinking (thinking!) in his box – these are characteristic notations having reference, I imagine, to processes less simple, and less delicious, than those to which the plastic *vis* is commonly reduced, and to a world where Tir-na-nOgue makes no more sense than Bachelor's Walk, nor Helen than the apple-woman, nor asses than men, nor Abel's blood than Useful's, nor morning than night, nor the inward than the outward search.

(MacGreevy on Yeats, p. 97)

That Yeats happens to be a painter is neither here nor there in Beckett's opinion of him as an artist. [156] The essence of Yeats the artist, is his dedication to the achievement of the attainable in art (unattainable for most), and his denial of self in that pursuit. Once the artist arrives at the stage of development of being aware of the breakdown of the object, he may then state "the space that intervenes between him and the world of objects; he may state it as no-man's-land, Hellespont or vacuum, according as he happens to be feeling resentful, nostalgic or merely depressed. A picture by Mr Jack Yeats, Mr Eliot's 'Waste Land', are notable statements of this kind." He may go further: 'He may even record his findings, if he is a man of great personal courage.' [157] It is this quality of courage attained at such cost, as Beckett himself well knows, that caused him to 'merely bow in wonder', in admiration at Yeats's determination to free himself of all restraining bonds: 'The artist who stakes his being is from nowhere, has no kith.' [158]

From Art to Philosophy, Divinity and Science

Beckett, a writer much concerned with the philosophy of life, was well acquainted with the philosophical writings of Descartes, Geulinex, Bruno, and Vico among others. [159] Irish philosophical deliberations were also of interest to him. Arnold and Gerard Boot,[160] two doctors, the former of whom practised in Dublin in the mid-sixteenth century, and both of whom made bold enough to refute Aristotelian philosophy, have earned thereby a place in the Beckett canon -

What's that?
An egg?
By the brothers Boot it stinks fresh.
Give it to Gillot.

(Whoroscope, p. 1)[161]

Beckett was familiar with the philosophical writings of the Bishop of Cloyne, George Berkeley,[162] who had studied and taught at Trinity College some two hundred years before Beckett (8:24). Berkeley first receives mention in *Dream of Fair to Middling Women*,[163] when the narrator urges his readers to distinguish between the object and its representation by

8:24 *George Berkeley, Philosopher, (1685 – 1737), with his Wife and Friends* by John Smibert
This is a smaller version of *The Bermuda Group* painted during Berkeley's American residence which features: standing: John Smibert (the artist), John Moffat, John James, George Berkeley; seated: Richard Dalton, Miss Handsock, Mrs. Anne Berkeley, Henry Berkeley. (By courtesy National Gallery of Ireland, No. 465)

heeding the Berkeleian dictum that existence is perceiving or being perceived[164] -

> if we could only learn to school ourselves to nurture that divine and fragile Funkelein of curiosity struck from the desire to bind for ever in imperishible relation the object and its representation, the stimulus to the molecular agitation that it sets up, percipi to pecipere ...
>
> *(Dream of Fair to Middling Women, p. 142)*

Beckett's screenplay, *Film*, attempts a visual interpretation of Berkeley's *esse est percipi* (to be is to be perceived), in which the camera high-lights the dependence of existence on perception[165] -

> *Esse est percipi*
> All extraneous perception suppressed, animal, human, divine, self-perception maintains in being.
> Search of non-being in flight from extraneous perception breaking down in inescapability of self-perception.
>
> *(Film, p. 31)*

In *Murphy*, the Bishop of Cloyne gains entry on no less than three occasions. First, in relation to his philosophy of immaterialism[166] -

> 'I don't wonder at Berkeley,' said Neary. 'He had no alternative. A defence mechanism. Immaterialise or bust. The sleep of sheer terror. Compare the opossum'.
>
> *(Murphy. p. 43)*

Berkeley's advocacy of tar-water in later life does not find acceptance in the Murphy mind[167] -

> This did not involve Murphy in the idealist tar. There was the mental fact and there was the physical fact, equally real if not equally pleasant.
>
> *(Murphy. p. 76)*

Murphy's game of chess with Mr. Endon provides an ideal opportunity to introduce the Berkeleian *esse est percipi* -

> Then this also faded and Murphy began to see nothing, that colourness which is such a rare postnatal treat, being the absence (to abuse a nice distinction) not of *percipere* but of *percipi*. His other senses also found themselves at peace, an unexpected pleasure.
>
> *(Murphy, p. 168)*

In *Waiting for Godot*, Lucky in his tirade refutes Berkeley's idealism[168] -

> ... in a word the dead loss per caput since the death of Bishop Berkeley being to the tune of one inch four ounce per caput approximately by and large more or less to the nearest decimal good measure round figures stark naked in the

8:25   *Dean Jonathan Swift* by
Charles Jervas
(By courtesy National Gallery of
Ireland, No. 177)

8:26   *Lawrence Sterne, Author,*
(1713-1768) by Robert West
(after Reynolds)
(By courtesy National Gallery of
Ireland, No. 130)

8:27   *Robert James Graves* by
Charles Grey
(By courtesy National Library of
Ireland, No. 3786)

stockinged feet in Connemara in a word for reasons unknown no matter what matter the facts are there ...

(Waiting for Godot, p. 44)

Another Dublin divine to whom Beckett was attracted was Jonathan Swift. The similarities in outlook, humour and literary style between Swift (8:25) and Beckett have been the subject of much comment.[169] Direct references to the witty Dean of St. Patrick's Cathedral in Dublin have previously been noted. There are, in addition, allusions to *Gullivers Travels* in *Murphy*.[170]

Another popular eighteenth century Irish writer to receive brief mention in Beckett's drama, (but whose influence on Beckett's writing may have been significant) is Lawrence Sterne, (8:26) author of the comic novel, *Tristam Shandy*, and a grandson of Richard Sterne, Archbishop of York[171]-

> A: Are you familiar with the works of Sterne, Miss?
> S: Alas no, sir.
> A: I may be quite wrong, but I seem to remember, there somewhere, a tear an angel comes to watch as it falls. Yes, I seem to remember ... admittedly he was grandchild to an archbishop. *(Half rueful, half complacent.)* Ah these old spectres from the days of book reviewing, they lie in wait for one at every turn.
> *(Rough for Radio II, pp. 119-120)*

Moving from philosophy to medicine we find a Dublin physician of eponymous repute receiving mention in *Murphy*. Robert James Graves (8:27) was physician to the Meath Hospital in Dublin. With William Stokes, he introduced bedside clinical teaching in place of the didactic system operating in the early nineteenth century, whereby a student could qualify without ever examining a patient. Graves, Stokes, and Dominic Corrigan were the leaders of a medical renaissance which achieved international acclaim as the 'Dublin School'.[172] In his famous *Lectures*, published in 1843, Graves described the disease of the thyroid known as exopthalmic goitre, by which he is remembered eponymously. Beckett coupled his eponym with that of Bright[173] in *Murphy*. -

> He suffered much with his feet, and his neck was not altogether free of pain. This filled him with satisfaction. It confirmed the diagram and reduced by just so much the danger of Bright's disease, Grave's disease, strangury and fits.
> *(Murphy, p. 55)*

That we should include with men of science and learning, the disreputable *Billy in the Bowl*, may seem an incongruity.[174] Suffice it to say that is not because he will not fit anywhere else, which is true, but rather because he fits snugly beside the Dublin men of science as an object of their handiwork, for we may presume that Billy fell foul of the surgeon's lancet in those dim Georgian days, even though the profession is exonerated by the assertion that this otherwise fine specimen of manhood was simply delivered into the world sans legs, feet and even tootsies -

> But before executing his portrait, full length on his surviving leg, let me note that my next vice-exister will be a billy in the bowl, that's final, with his bowl on his head and his arse in the dust, plump down on thousand-breasted Tellus, it'll be softer for him.
>
> *(The Unnamable, p. 317)*

That 'billy in the bowl' was a common enough phenomenon is evident from Hogarth's engraving 'Industry and Idleness' (8:28), but it is likely that Beckett had in mind Dublin's Billy, a character of some standing despite his shortcomings. Billy survived the many threats to existence imposed on him by his deformity, as well as the vicissitudes of time, for he lives on in the folklore of Dublin. Legless, he propelled himself through the city of Dublin in a wooden bowl shod with iron. Despite his deformity he had a striking appearance – 'fine dark eyes, aquiline nose, well formed mouth, dark curling locks, with a body and arms of Herculean power.'[175] An attempt at robbery landed him in Green Street Gaol under sentence of hard labour for life, where he became 'one of the lions of the day' and received many callers.

Billy's mastery of his disability could not but fascinate Beckett, for whom man's ability to cope with the immobility imposed by deformity has been a recurring theme. In *Rough for Theatre I* there is a blind 'Billy' with only one leg, who is dependent on the alms bowl for survival.[176] Sam Lynch, in *Watt*, confined to a wheelchair like Billy has phenomenal libidinous inclinations -

> Some said it was her cousin Sam, whose amorous disposition was notorious, not only among members of his immediate family, but throughout the neighbourhood, and who made no secret of his having committed adultery locally on a large scale, moving from place to place in his self-propelling invalid's chair, with widow women, with married women and with single women ...
>
> *(Watt, p. 104)*

In *Endgame* the consequences of immobility are depicted with ruthless humour. Deformed man on his bicycle is central to *Molloy*. In *Malone Dies*, the narrator, no longer capable of compromised motion even on a bicycle, contemplates none the less the feasibility of mobility even in his extreme situation -

> I wonder If I could not contrive, wielding my stick like a punt-pole, to move my bed. It may well be on castors, many beds are. Incredible I should never have thought of this, all the time I have been here. I might even succeed in steering it, it is so narrow, through the door, and even down the stairs, if there is a stairs that goes down. To be off and away.
>
> *(Malone Dies, p. 254-255)*

The inevitable decay of flesh is skilfully chronicled by Beckett in his depiction of man's loss of mobility: man on a bicycle, man in a wheelchair, man on castors, man mobile in a bowl like Billy, or man in a bowl, fixed immobile but cerebrating, like Mahood in *The Unnamable*.[177]

8:28 *Billy in the Bowl*
(Detail from *Industry and Idleness* by William Hogarth)

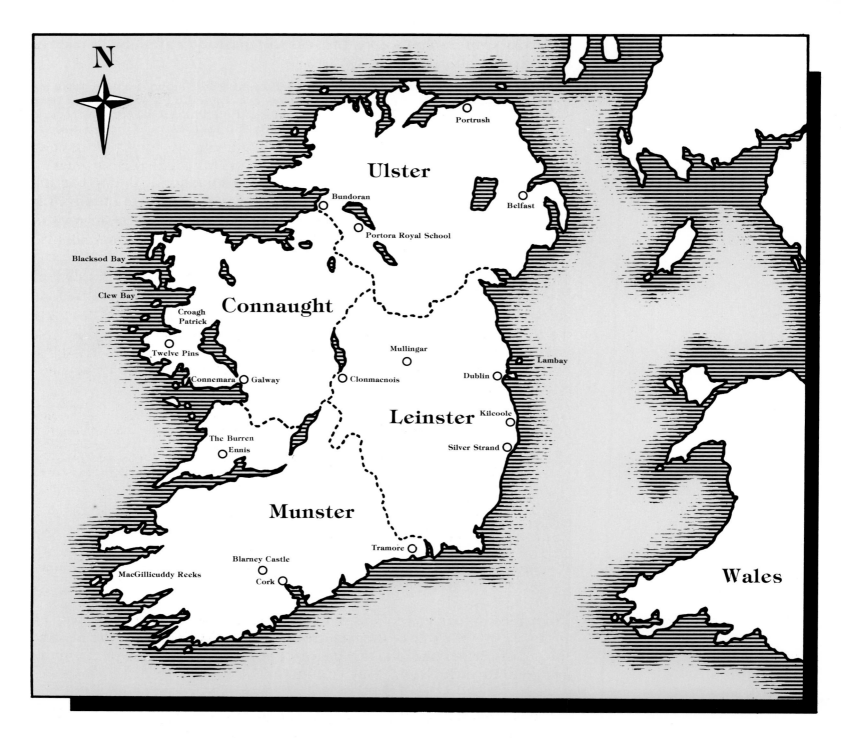

9:1 Ireland. Beyond the Pale

Page 294

Chapter Nine

BEYOND THE PALE

Beckett is a Dubliner. Where he makes mention of Irish places and people, most relate to the capital city, or its neighbouring counties of Wicklow and Meath. Occasionally, however, he reaches to more distant parts of Ireland, beyond the Pale (9:1), that area, so named in the Middle Ages to denote the lands of Dublin and its adjoining counties over which the forces of the crown ruled supreme, but beyond which English authority was titular, rather than absolute.[1]

County Cork

Neary, the savant from Cork,[2] hails from the second city of the land, a definition based on size and population, rather than the opinion of its citizens who hold that their premier status in many facets of Irish life entitles them to a position second to none. Certainly, if Neary's uncanny abilities are representative, Corkmen are unique -

> Murphy had lately studied under a man in Cork called Neary. This man, at that time, could stop his heart more or less whenever he liked and keep it stopped, within reasonable limits, for as long as he liked. This rare faculty, acquired after years of application somewhere north of the Nerbudda, he exercised frugally, reserving it for situations irksome beyond endurance, as when he wanted a drink and could not get one, or fell among Gaels and could not escape, or felt the pangs of hopeless sexual inclination.
>
> *(Murphy, p. 6)*

Neary lived on Grand Parade in Cork City (9:2) -

> 'My grove on Grand Parade,' said Neary, 'is wiped as a man wipeth a plate, wiping it and turning it upside down.'
>
> *(Murphy, p. 36)*

From here Neary conducted his affair with Miss Counihan as best he could. Cast in the role of the beautiful Kathleen Ní Houlihan, (the heroine image of Erin), she chose, as was appropriate, a graveyard for an assignation with Neary (9:3) -

> Finally she gave him a forenoon appointment at the grave of Father Prout (F.S. Mahony) in Shandon Churchyard, the one place in Cork she knew of where fresh air, privacy and immunity from assault were reconciled.[3]
>
> *(Murphy, p. 38)*

9:2 Grand Parade, Cork
(By courtesy National Library of
Ireland, Valentine, 92)

Francis Sylvester Mahony (9:4), known to his intimates as Frank Mahony, was born at Cork in 1804.[4] With ambitions towards the priesthood, Mahony became a seminarian to the Fathers of the Society of Jesus in Paris and later in Rome. It was not long before the Jesuits detected in their protegé a talent for scholarship, more artistic, than spiritual: 'In temperament he was known to be habitually disputatious, occasionally choleric, and, under anything like direct opposition, whether in trivial or important matters, persistently self-opinionated.'[5] Despite the Jesuits' efforts to convince Mahony that, whatever his calling, it came not from God, he persisted in his pursuit of orders and was ordained at Lucca. Not long after he recognised the wisdom of the Jesuits in barring him from their holy ranks, and he gradually abandoned the clerical life for one literary and Bohemian. He contributed regularly to newspapers and periodicals, sometimes under the *nom de plume* of the Benedictine monk, *Don Jeremy Savonarola*, but his literary talents were given full rein with the foundation of *Fraser's Magazine* in 1830. As the Reverend Father Andrew Prout, Parish Priest of Watergrasshill, Sylvester Mahony of Cork, poured out monthly, over two years, the now famous *Reliques*, in which

9:3 Shandon Church Steeple; Father
Prout's tomb lies in the graveyard
behind the church
(By courtesy Bord Fáilte, C21/52)

9:4 Father Prout:
The Rev. Francis Mahony
(An engraving from a photograph
by M. Weyler: frontispiece to *The
Works of Father Prout* ed. by
Charles Kent. George Routledge
and Sons. London and New York,
1881)

he unleashed his satirical humour and indulged his classical erudition.[6] He introduced himself to the literary world as the kidnapped foundling of Jonathan Swift and Stella, cruelly abandoned on the bleak summit of Watergrasshill, naked but for a trinket containing a lock of his mother's hair, and a 'gifted motto of my gifted father's composition, three simple words, but beautiful in their simplicity - PROUT STELLA REFULGES'. Taken to the Cork Foundling Hospital, the future author of the *Reliques* "was at once christened 'Prout', from the adverb that begins the sentence, and which being the shortest word of the three, it pleased the chaplain to make his future patronymic."[7] The heir to Swift's genius eventually escaped from the Foundling Hospital in a milk churn, an event he later attempted to immortalise in 'The Lament for Stella', which ends with the memorably banal lines -

> And may folks find that this young fellow
> Does credit to his mother *Stella*.[8]

Mahony spent his life travelling through Europe contributing regularly to periodicals and newspapers. Settling eventually in Paris, he led the life of an eccentric recluse and died at No. 19, rue des Moulins on May 18th, 1866.[9] His remains were brought for internment to his birthplace 'on the banks of the river Lee, under the shadow of the spire and within sound of those Bells of Shandon he had sung of so lovingly and harmoniously in his best-remembered lyrical masterpiece'[10] -

> With deep affection
> And recollection
> I often think of
>   Those Shandon bells,
> Whose sounds so wild would,
> In the days of childhood,
> Fling round my cradle
>   Their magic spells.
> On this I ponder
> Where e'er I wander
> And thus grow fonder,
>   Sweet Cork, of thee;
> With thy bells of Shandon,
> That sound so grand on
> The pleasant waters
>   Of the river Lee.

Neary's protestations of love in Shandon Churchyard did little to endear him to Miss Counihan, but his love for her knew no bounds, nor did her's for Murphy. She decided to secure Neary's assistance, which she did on the Mall, one of Cork's main thoroughfares -

> He did not see her again for nearly four months, when she knocked into him skilfully in the Mall. She looked ill (she was ill). It was August and still she had no news of Murphy.
>
> *(Murphy, p. 40)*

Neary, who resided within earshot of Prout's Shandon bells, fled his home in hopeless pursuit of Miss Counihan's affections when she departed for Dublin in pursuit of Murphy. Severing his connection with Cork he threw the keys of his home into the River Lee (9:5) -

> The next morning Neary closed the Gymnasium, put a padlock on the Grove, sunk both keys in the Lee and boarded the first train for Dublin, accompanied by his *âme damnée* and man-of-all-work, Cooper.
>
> *(Murphy, p. 41)*

Blarney, a village in County Cork, is situated on the bank of the beautiful Shournagh river. It boasts a fifteenth century castle overlooking a glorious eighteenth century demesne, *The Groves of Blarney* (9:6). Below the battlements of the Castle is the famous Blarney stone, which if kissed (an intricate, if unhygienic, process) will bestow upon the kisser the gift of almost perpetual chatter[11] -

> 'Have you a Mr. Murphy staying here?' said Wylie.
> 'We have come all the way from Cork,' said Neary, 'we have torn ourselves away from the groves of Blarney, for the sole purpose of cajoling him in private.'
>
> *(Murphy, p. 154)*

The place names of Ringaskiddy, Ballinclashet, and Passage West in County Cork have not only phonetic appeal for Beckett, but also permit a pun[12] -

> Of such was Neary's love for Miss Dwyer, who loved a Flight-Lieutenant Elliman, who loved a Miss Farren of Ringaskiddy, who loved a Father Fitt of Ballinclashet, who in all sincerity was bound to acknowledge a certain vocation for a Mrs. West of Passage, who loved Neary.
>
> *(Murphy, p. 7)*

One of Beckett's more poignant pieces of prose is centered on Cobh, a port formerly called Queenstown, situated some fourteen miles east of Cork. The Cork ship *Sirius*, first steamer to cross the Atlantic, sailed from Cobh on April 1st, 1838, and the harbour is still the principal Irish port of call for transatlantic liners. Cobh is also the cathedral town of the Catholic diocese of Cloyne, and St. Colman's Cathedral dominates the harbour.[13] Beckett alludes to the port's scenic characteristics as well

9:5 The River Lee overlooked by St. FinBarre's Cathedral (By courtesy Bord Fáilte, C18/53)

Page 299

9:6   The Groves of Blarney and
      Blarney Castle
      (By courtesy Bord Fáilte,
      No. CO20/46)

9:7 A tender departing Cobh with passengers for a steamer (Photograph by G.A. Duncan, No. P755)

as to the emotions, sincere and maudlin, of the emigrants being brought from the quay to the liner (9:7) -

Next dusk shall gather round him seated in the tug. It rocks itself upon the evening water livid under the bright decks. The whistler has come out with the emigrants and their friends, they have climbed aboard, with a slow frail music he feeds their lament, they cry down from the rail and their silence weaves an awning over the tug, the tug is grappled to the high bulwark by their cries and their silence and the tendrils of the whistling. Beyond Cobh across the harbour fireflies are moving in Hy-Brasil's low hills, the priests are abroad there with bludgeons. The captain of the tug stands by his wheel on his little bridge, his head is thrown back, he is abusing the young German mate in charge of the unlading, he is not afraid. The saloon band vomits Dear Little Shamrocks, it pukes the crassamenta of its brasses down on top of the tug, we are all boys together, we belch therefore the chorus, the liana of silence and whistling is sundered, we are set adrift. Next to Belacqua the slut bawn is now weeping, she is weeping and waving a fairly clean portion of Bourbon bloomer. That is very meet, proper and, given her present condition, her bounden duty. Before Xmas she shall be in Green St, she shall be in Railway St. under the new government. She was born well, she lived well and she died well, Colleen Cresswell in Clerkenwell and Bridewell.
(Dream of Fair to Middling Women, p. 125)

The slut's future is uncompromisingly depicted: from the Dublin Kips in Railway Street she will inevitably find herself before the magistrates of Green Street Courthouse, on her way to the Bridewell prison for her misdemeanors.

9:8   The Macgillicuddy Reeks
      overlooking the Upper Lake,
      Killarney
      (By courtesy National Library of
      Ireland, Valentine, 4234)

County Kerry

Killarney[14](9:8) is the beauty spot of Ireland most beloved by the tourist, and considered by many, including most probably Beckett, to be over-rated -

> But the eye, let's leave him his eye too, it's to see with, this great wild black and white eye, moist, it's to weep with, it's to practise with, before he goes to Killarney.
> *(The Unnamable, p. 362)*

The name of Miss Macgillycuddy in the play *Radio 1*[15] derives from the Macgillicuddy's Reeks, a mountain range in County Kerry.

County Clare

We have already met Mr. Ernest Louit, a scholar of Trinity College (Chapter 4). It was to county Clare that Louit took himself to pursue his researches for his dissertation, *The Mathematical Intuitions of the Visicelts.*[16] But this scholarly thesis regrettably met a sad fate in the gentlemen's cloakroom of Ennis railway station (9:9), where it disappeared.[17] Louit had not, however, returned empty-handed; he brought with him a primitive mathematical genius, Mr. Thomas

9:9　Ennis Railway Station
The train on the right is on the West Clare narrow guage line famed in song by Percy French
(By courtesy Nancy Cosgrove)

9:10   The Burren, Co. Clare
(Photograph by D. Davison)

Nackybal, native of Burren. The district, known as the Burren (9:10) occupies the northern part of the County of Clare with Galway Bay to its north, and the Atlantic coast to the west. It is a magical landscape of carboniferous limestone permeated by underground rivers, glacial erratics, caves, clints, grykes, and turloughs.[18] The contrast of sea, sky and limestone gives the Burren a beauty that is unique, to which nature, with lavish generosity, has added a fauna that softens and colours the greyness of the landscape.

County Galway

To the north of Clare, lies the county of Galway in the province of Connaught -

> Hard to think of her as a girl. Wonderful woman though. Connaught, I fancy.
> *(Krapp's Last Tape, p. 58)*

It is to the ancient city of Galway[19] that Belacqua carried his bride, Thelma, on their honeymoon (9:11) -

> For Thelma's thoughts, truant to the complicated manoeuvres required of a snow-white bride, had flown on the usual wings to Galway, Gate of Connaught and

dream of stone, and more precisely to the Church of Saint Nicolas whither Belacqua projected, if it were not closed when they arrived, to repair without delay and kneel, with her on his right hand at last for a pleasant change, and invoke in pursuance of a vow long-standing, the spirits of Crusoe and Columbus, who had knelt there before him.

(More Pricks than Kicks, p. 135)

St. Nicolas is the patron saint of sailors and captives, and Christopher Columbus is reputed to have prayed in the collegiate Church of St. Nicholas of Myra in Galway (founded in 1320) before sailing west in the *Santa Maria*. It may not be unreasonable to assume that Alexander Selkirk also set sail from Galway to legendary shipwreck.[20] The Great Southern Hotel (9:12), a fashionable hostelry, on the city's main square, was chosen for the consummation of Belacqua's nuptials, after which the happy bride would be able to watch the sun set on Galway Bay.[21]

Connemara[22] is a western region of Galway, renowned for its colourful landscape of mountain, lake and Atlantic shore line. Characteristic stone

9:11   Church of St. Nicholas of Myra, Galway (By courtesy National Library of Ireland, Lawrence, 784)

9:12   The Great Southern Hotel, Galway (By courtesy National Library of Ireland, Lawrence, 937)

walls demarcate the bleak fields of the region (9:13) which is mentioned by Lucky in his outburst in *Waiting for Godot*[23] -

> ... the tears the stones so blue so calm alas alas on on the skull the skull the skull the skull in Connemara in spite of the tennis the labours abandoned left unfinished graver still abode of stones in a word I resume alas alas abandoned unfinished the skull the skull in Connemara in spite of the tennis the skull alas the stones Cunard *(mêleé, final vociferations)* tennis ... the stones ... so calm ... Cunard ... unfinished ...
>
> *(Waiting for Godot, pp. 44-45)*

County Mayo

County Mayo is north of Galway. The Atlantic ocean gives Mayo a beauty that has much in common with its southern neighbours, Galway, Clare and Kerry, and yet, each of these coastal counties has an unique individuality. The counties of Mayo, Galway and Kerry provide the threatening atmosphere for one of Beckett's most beautiful and poignant poems, *Serena II*. His pregnant Kerry Blue bitch, dreaming of the western shores of her homeland, symbolises the cycle of life[24] -

> this clonic earth
>
> see-saw she is blurred in sleep
> she is fat half dead the rest is free-wheeling
> part the black shag the pelt
> is ashen woad
> snarl and howl in the wood wake all the birds
> hound the harlots out of the ferns
> this damfool twilight threshing in the brake
> bleating to be bloodied
> this crapulent hush
> tear its heart out
>
> in her dreams she trembles again
> way back in the dark old days panting
> in the claws of the Pins in the stress of her hour
> the bag writhes she thinks she is dying
> the light fails it is time to lie down
> Clew Bay vat of xanthic flowers
> Croagh Patrick waned Hindu to spite a pilgrim
> she is ready she has lain down above all the islands of glory
> straining now this Sabbath evening of garlands
> with a yo-heave-ho of able-bodied swans
> out from the doomed land their reefs of tresses
> in a hag she drops her young
> the whales in Blacksod Bay are dancing
> the asphodels come running the flags after
> she thinks she is dying she is ashamed ...
>
> *(Serena II, pp. 23-24)*

9:13   The stone-walls of Connemara
(Photograph by G.A. Duncan,
No. P677)

The 'claws of the Pins' is a reference to the mountain range in County Galway, known by its peaks as The Twelve Pins or Bens (9:14). Clew Bay is a deep inlet on Mayo's coast line with Achill Island on its north western limit (9:15). Croagh Patrick[25](9:16), a mountain reputedly visited by Ireland's patron saint, Patrick, is popular for its penitential pilgrimage held on Garland Sunday each year. Blacksod Bay,[26] to the north of Achill, is a ragged bay visited at times by whales (9:17).

County Donegal

The popular seaside resort, Bundoran (9:18), on the coast of the County Donegal, is useful to Beckett in a verse lampooning a publisher named Doran, who among others, had rejected *Murphy* [27] -

> Oh Doubleday Doran
> Less Oxy than moron
> You've a mind like a whore on
> The way to Bundoran.

9:14   The Twelve Bens
       (By courtesy National Library of
       Ireland, Lawrence, 923)

9:15   Clew Bay from near Mulrany,
       Co. Mayo
       (By courtesy Bord Fáilte, M5/61)

The rejection of *Murphy* by some forty publishers prompted a despairing, but unique, proposal from Beckett for his future publications[28] -

> My next work shall be on rice paper wound about a spool, with a perforated line every six inches and on sale in Boots. The length of each chapter will be carefully calculated to suit with the average free motion. And with every copy a free sample of some laxative to promote sales. The Beckett Bowel Books, Jesus in farto. Issued in imperishable tissue. Thistle-down endpapers. All edges disinfected. 1000 wipes of clean fun. Also in Braille for anal pruritics. All Sturm and no Drang.

County Antrim

Another sea-side resort, Portrush in County Antrim, Northern Ireland, is mentioned in *More Pricks than Kicks* (9:19) -

> It seemed inconceivable that she should have been so blinded to his real nature as to let her love, born in a spasm more than a year ago in the Portrush Palais de Danse, increase steadily from day to day till now it amounted to something like a morbid passion.

(More Pricks than Kicks, p. 116)

9:16   Croagh Patrick, Co. Mayo
       (By courtesy National Library of
       Ireland, Lawrence, Imperial 1263)

9:17 Blacksod Bay, Co. Mayo
(By courtesy Bord Fáilte, M22/54)

9:18 Bundoran, Co. Donegal
(By courtesy National Library
of Ireland, Lawrence, 4941)

9:19 Portrush, Co. Antrim
(By courtesy National Library
of Ireland, Lawrence, 972)

Carrickarede Island, off Ballintoy in County Antrim,[29] is a rock separated from the mainland by a deep chasm of water; it is mentioned by Beckett in an obscure riddle -

'I propose at once the elemental limits.'
'Abstract the Antrim road, Carrickarede Island, and the B. & I. boat threading the eye of the Liffey on Saturday night.'

(Che Sciagura, p. 42)

The British and Irish Packet, the boat service between Dublin and Liverpool, has already been considered in Chapter 6. The Antrim Road[30] in Belfast features again in *The Possessed*, an allusive dramatic parody, written by Beckett in 1931[31] -

I am from the North,
from Bellyballaggio
where they never take their hurry
minxing marriage in their flaxmasks
omygriefing and luvvyluvvyluvving and wudiftheycudling
from the fourth or fifth floor of their hemistitched hearts
right and left of the Antrim Road
That's why I like him
Ulster my Hulster!
Daswylyim!

(The Possessed, pp. 99-100)

County Offaly

The midland counties of Laois and Offaly[32] are mentioned in *More Pricks than Kicks*, to impart to the reader an estimate of the stupidity of a belligerent policeman. In *Murphy*, the imagery of ancient burial rites is portrayed by reference to Clonmacnois (9:20) in County Offaly -

> They covered the tray and carried it out to the refrigerators. Neary saw Clonmachnois on the slab, the castle of the O'Melaghlins, meadow, eskers, thatch on white, something red, the wide bright water, Connaught.
>
> *(Murphy p. 182)*

Clonmacnois is renowned in ecclesiastical history for 'the number and opulence of its religious establishments, its schools for instruction in the liberal arts, and the veneration in which it was held as a place of sepulture for the royal families of Ireland.'[33] Its schools were attended by the children of the neighbouring princes, and so derives the name *Cluain-Mac-Nois*, meaning the 'Retreat of the Sons of the Noble.' The first abbey was founded at Clonmacnois by St. Keiran in 548, and in later centuries a castle, nunnery and cathedral were erected. The latter was erected by the O'Melaghlins, princes of Meath. The ecclesiastical ruins are very extensive comprising numerous small churches surrounding the cathedral, two round towers, the episcopal palace, and the cemetery, which was a favourite place of sepulture with the neighbouring chieftains, many of whom are buried there. Many ancient inscriptions in Irish, Hebrew and Latin, have been discovered among the ruins. The 'wide bright water' is a reference to Ireland's longest river, the Shannon, on the banks of which Clonmacnois is situated close to the bog of Allen.

9:20   Clonmacnois, Co. Offaly
(By courtesy National Library of
Ireland, Lawrence, Cabinet 6939)

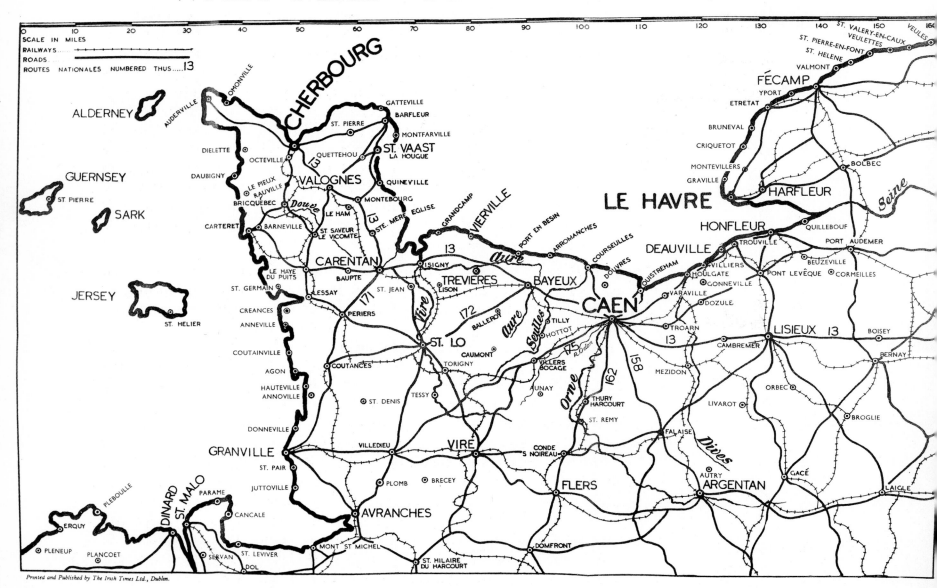

The Irish Times
WAR MAP OF NORMANDY

Printed and Published by The Irish Times Ltd., Dublin.

Chapter Ten

SAINT-LÔ:'Humanity in Ruins'

It may seem strange, even inappropriate, that a book on Beckett's homeland should end with a chapter on a devastated town in Normandy. Yet, remarkable though the association between Dublin and Saint-Lô may be, it has a special significance in that it symbolises Beckett's departure from Ireland and the severance of old ties and friendships. Saint-Lô was to have an effect so profound, that Beckett expressed his anguish in two moving poems and in an unpublished broadcast for Radio Éireann. Ireland, neutral during the war, made a gesture in Saint-Lô (10:1) that in itself was of historical significance; but, to Beckett, the relevance was deeper. It was not merely that the homeland he had left was assisting in a small way the country he had now adopted, but among those Irishmen foremost in the operation were some of his closest friends.

Samuel Beckett's long association with France began in June 1926, when as a undergraduate at Trinity College, he went on a cycling holiday to the Lôire Valley.[1] Returning to Trinity, he became a close friend of Alfred Péron, who had been appointed an exchange *lecteur* from the École Normale Supérieure.[2] After graduation from Trinity, Beckett in turn went to Paris as *lecteur* to the École in October 1928. Here he met his predecessor, Thomas MacGreevy, who introduced him to James Joyce and an intimate group of writers and intellectuals. With his friend Péron, Beckett translated part of *Finnegans Wake* into French.[3] In 1930 Beckett returned to Trinity College as lecturer in modern languages, but a year later, after receiving his Master of Arts degree, he resigned his academic post. After a brief stay in Germany he returned to Paris where he remained until 1932. This was followed by five unsettled years in Dublin, London and Germany, after which he returned to Paris.[4] With the outbreak of the second world war, Beckett joined his friend Alfred Péron in the French resistance cells, *Gloria* SMH (for His Majesty's Service spelled backwards) and Etoile.[5] In 1942 he escaped from Nazi-occupied Paris and travelled to Roussillon, where he again became involved with

10:1 The Irish Times War Map
of Normandy
(By courtesy of Miss J. Gaffney)

the local resistance movement, the *maquis*.[6] At the end of the war, he returned to Dublin, and re-established his friendship with Alan Thompson, now a physician on the staff of the Richmond Hospital (10:2). Thompson, at the time, was a member of a small team of Irish Red Cross workers engaged in organising a relief hospital for the bombed town of Saint-Lô. Beckett readily accepted an invitation from his friend to join the team as interpreter.

The Irish Red Cross's involvement with Saint-Lô began after the allied invasion of France in 1945, when the Irish Red Cross offered assistance to the French Red Cross,[7] and representatives from Ireland visited the war-devastated areas. They selected the town of Saint-Lô on the main Cherbourg-Paris line (10:3) as being in urgent need of assistance.[8] This town of some 13,000 people, had served as an important operational centre for the German Army (10:3-10:6). On a June afternoon in 1944, without warning, the allied forces blitzed the town. So devastating was the attack that hardly a building was left standing, and thousands of citizens were killed.[9] A year later bodies were still being removed from the debris and 3,000 people were living among the ruins (10:7-10:9). The city's only hospital had been destroyed in the blitz. A local correspondent likened Saint-Lô to 'an upturned dustbin' where life began again, almost incredibly, after the holocaust: 'Life started again in spite

10:2 Dr. Alan Thompson (right) with Prof. Leonard Abrahamson (left) and Dr. Gerard T. O'Brien, physicians, in a Richmond Hospital Staff Photograph, 1933 (By courtesy St. Laurence's Hospital)

10:3-6   Saint-Lô before the blitz
(By courtesy Miss M. Crowley)

10:3-6   Saint-Lô before the blitz
(By courtesy Miss M. Crowley)

10:7-9   The ruins of Saint-Lô
(By courtesy Miss M. Crowley
and Miss J. Gaffney)

of the deadening atmosphere, in spite of the dust, the impassable streets, the darkness, the lack of water and of hygiene, the lack of everything; in spite of the winter with its succession of ills, in spite of the cold which never leaves you, the lack of heating and of shelter in this windy area; in spite of the mud which is everywhere, impregnating those few clothes you have left. Life took up again, but it was exhausting, because the battle against the ruins became also a battle against sickness and death, but to be ill in Saint-Lô was unimaginable, though sadly inevitable for many. There was no longer a hospital, and the overworked doctors who returned had no place to work and perhaps save lives ... In reply to the Health Ministry and the Red Cross, Ireland made the kind gesture of adopting Saint-Lô and brought all that was necessary and more.'[10]

The Irish Red Cross offered a hospital unit of 100 beds, and as no building was available for conversion, it was planned to erect wooden huts on the outskirts of the bombed town. The Irish Red Cross undertook to equip, staff and maintain the hospital for as long as would be necessary. The transportation of supplies for such a hospital from Dublin to France was a considerable undertaking, as was the recruitment of medical and nursing staff, the success of which owed much to the hospital's matron, Miss Mary Crowley.[11] In August 1945, an advance party consisting of Colonel Thomas J. McKinney, Director of the Unit, Dr. Alan Thompson, physician, and 'Mr. S.B. Beckett, Quartermaster-Interpreter,' left Dublin for Saint-Lô.[12] As well as accepting the post of interpreter, Beckett had also agreed to act as storekeeper to the hospital.[13] Later in the month the *Menapia* set sail for Cherbourg, the nearest port to Saint-Lô, with 174 tons of equipment, six ambulances, a utility wagon, and a lorry aboard. (10:10) There were special facilities for 'the transport in cold storage of supplies of blood serum and penicillen'.[14] On Monday, 27th August, 1945, another contingent consisting of Mr. Freddie McKee, assistant surgeon, Dr. Arthur Darley, assistant physician, Dr. Jim Gaffney, pathologist, Mr. Killick, technician, and Mr. Dunne, assistant storekeeper, departed from Dun Laoghaire on the *SS Cambria* (10:11) for London, from where they sailed to Dieppe on *T.S.S. Isle of Guernsey*.

The Irish Red Cross had established headquarters at the Hôtel des Arcades in Dieppe, where Beckett met the hospital staff arriving from Dublin and drove them through Rouen to Saint-Lô.[15] Dr. Gaffney[16] has described his first impressions of war-torn Normandy: 'Coming into Dieppe we got our first view of wholesale destruction ... We walked down the gangway and were met by Col. McKinney (10:12) and Sam Beckett

10:10 The Irish Red Cross
ambulances awaiting loading at
Dublin docks: a group of nurses
stand in the background
13 August 1945.
(By courtesy Mr. M. Thompson)

10:11 Mr. Freddie McKee,
Dr. Arthur Darley and
Dr. Jim Gaffney chatting with
Lt. Col. Martin Fallon, R.A.M.C.
(By courtesy Miss J. Gaffney)

(storekeeper). They had the big Ford V8 Utility wagon with them, and after going through Customs we got in. We weren't hungry as we had had an excellent four-course lunch on board and later tea; but nevertheless Sam brought us 3 huge bags of pears, grapes and plums.

It was novel being driven on the right-hand side of the road and Sam believes in getting the 150 miles done as quickly as possible. Five miles out of a village like Croagh called St. Aubin sur Seine and luckily, just at a garage, a queer noise was heard from the engine and we had to have it looked over by a young mechanic. Sam Beckett is official interpreter as well as storekeeper and although a Dublin man has lived for 10 years in France, so the language is no trouble.'[17] After a night's rest in a nearby village the party travelled onwards by train, leaving Beckett and his assistant Dunne, to follow-on with the restored wagon. Gaffney has left the following account on his first impression of Saint-Lô: '... It took us about three quarters of an hour to find the hospital. This wasn't surprising, as one street of ruins looks very much like another ... Many of the streets can only be traversed on foot by stepping from one pile of bricks to another, or from one rusted girder on to the end of a buried

10:12   Colonel Thomas J. McKinney
        in a Red Cross ambulance
        (By courtesy Miss J. Gaffney)

10:13   Dr. J.C. Gaffney (left)
        standing among the ruins of
        Saint-Lô with Mr.M. McNamara,
        secretary, Irish Red Cross Society
        (By courtesy Miss J. Gaffney)

bedstead. Many cellars still lie under the debris and demolition work goes on slowly but surely (10:13). Digging the other day, they found the body of one of the local bakers and two of his assistants; and as we arrived we heard the distant explosions of two mines ... Of the pre-war population of about 12,000 many cleared out altogether, and they have accounted for about 1,500 bodies, while about 700 remain unaccounted for ... The Mental Hospital also is a shell, many of the inmates being killed. In the local jail (which is large) about 29 prisoners were burned to death - locked in, they couldn't get permission in time to release them. The locals say the Americans dropped H.E. incendiary and phosphorous bombs on the town; biggest attack was about June 6, 1944, but it was later bombarded by heavy artillery in September. For about six weeks the town kept changing hands between the Germans and the Americans. There are still about 5,000 people in it, but you would wonder where or how they live; mostly in boarded up cellars, on mattresses. Yet, with all their sufferings, they are tackling the problem of reconstruction, cheerfully.'[18]

The eight members of the advance team lived together in one of ten huts erected by the French (10:14). There was electricity but no running water

10:14   The Early Huts at Saint-Lô
         (By courtesy Mr. M. Thompson)

10:15   Members of the Hospital
         Staff standing in front of the
         storekeeper's lorry, from left
         to right: Dr. A.W. Darley,
         a French Military guard,
         Mr. S.B. Beckett, Surgeon
         F.F. McKee, Dr. J.C. Gaffney,
         Mr. M.B. Killick, Colonel
         T.J. McKinney, and Mr. T. Dunne.
         The men in the lorry are German
         prisoners-of-war
         (*Irish Times* photograph,
         28 September 1945,
         by courtesy Miss J. Gaffney)

or sanitation. Beckett, Thompson and Dunne superintended the stacking and sorting of 250 tonnes of supplies, which were brought from Cherbourg by rail and lorry. The store was situated in the lofts over the stables of a stud-farm a half mile from the hospital. They were assisted by German prisoners of war.[19] There was little to do when the day's work was complete, other than read, write, and play darts, chess, draughts or bridge. The Colonel advocated a policy of mingling with the local people, and provided expenses for forays into Saint-Lô to concerts, race-meetings and the occasional dance.[20] Hot running water was available at an American base 30 miles away where the luxury of an occasional shower was availed of. The padre of this camp, a Father Bardick, from Connecticut, who appreciated the comforts of life, took the Irish group to 'a magnificent chateau where the Rev. Mother welcomed us and gave a seven-course dinner to the whole eleven of us; got around the piano afterwards and sang for further orders till about one a.m. They want us to come again to have a real look around and we promised to do so. Dr. Thompson and Beckett said they hadn't thought that convents were such nice places'.[21]

Beckett appears to have fulfilled the role of driver, as well as that of storekeeper and interpreter. He drove regularly to Dieppe[22] and Cherbourg (10:15) to collect supplies and meet personnel, and also to Paris, often accompanied by Gaffney: 'Sam Beckett was driving him (Col. McKinney) to Paris on Friday and I had to get my still, so off we went. Sam and I took turns driving a small ambulance and the roads are very good indeed except where there are potholes etc. from tank tracks and small explosions. Driving here is easy and quite safe, I should say, as traffic is practically nil, any cars that are on the road are about 10-12 years old and they do about 25 miles per hour. We kept to about 35-40 m.p.h. and the day was lovely.'[23] In Paris, Beckett usually went to his flat, but he did not neglect his Irish friends who were unfamiliar with the sights of the capital, as Jim Gaffney recorded: 'Saturday morning we did some of my business till lunch time and also Sam took me into Notre Dame which was magnificent. Sam has an assistant storekeeper here named Tommy Dunne, a very decent little Dublin chap. Sam is a T.C.D. graduate, interested in writing and in letters generally; he has lived in Paris the last 6 years or 7. He is a most valuable asset to the unit - terribly conscientious about his work and enthusiastic about the future of the hospital, likes a game of bridge and in every way a most likeable chap, aged abut 38-40, no religious persuasion; I should say a free thinker - but he pounced on a little rosary beads which was on a stall in Notre Dame to bring back as a little present to Tommy D. It was very thoughtful of him.'[24]

The advance party worked tirelessly to prepare the hospital for the reception of patients. Among the first to receive treatment at the new hospital was an eleven-year-old boy who lost three fingers when a hand-grenade with which he was playing detonated.[25] Other advances were also achieved. The first lavatory was installed in October and had the unusual effect of making some of the team homesick. The housekeeper of the Hospital, Madame Pilorgat brought all visitors to the hospital to view the new apparatus, which she described glowingly as 'magnifique'.[26] By Christmas 1945 the full Irish staff, consisting of ten doctors, each a specialist, 31 state-registered nurses, most of whom had specialist training, a pharmacist, pathologist, and administrative staff, had arrived (10:16).[27] By March 1946, 80 in-patients were receiving treatment, and over 120 patients attended the out-patient department.[28]

10:16   Members of staff in the grounds
of the Irish Hospital in Saint-Lô
(By courtesy Miss M. Crowley)

VILLE DE SAINT-LO

Dimanche 7 Avril 1946

INAUGURATION
de l'Hôpital Irlandais

Sous la Présidence :
de Monsieur le Sous-Secrétaire d'Etat à la Population,
de Monsieur le Ministre d'Irlande,
des Représentants des Ministères
de la Reconstruction et de l'Urbanisme, des Affaires Etrangères
de Monsieur le Président de la Croix-Rouge Française,
de Monsieur le Président de la Croix-Rouge Irlandaise,
de Monsieur le Préfet de la Manche,
de Monsieur le Maire de Saint-Lô.

avec le concours de la Musique des Equipages de la Flotte

sous la direction de l'Enseigne de Vaisseau GUILBERT

A 12 h. 15 — Salle des Fêtes du Collège Municipal

Réception des Autorités

A 14 h. 15 — Collège Municipal

DEPART DU CORTEGE

A 14 h. 30 — Place des Beaux-Regards

MANIFESTATION DE RECONNAISSANCE
de la population St-Loise envers ses bienfaiteurs Irlandais

DISCOURS OFFICIELS

A l'issue de la Manifestation :

INAUGURATION DE L'HOPITAL

A 17 h. — Place des Beaux-Regards

GRAND CONCERT PUBLIC

par la Musique des Equipages de la Flotte

Première Musique Militaire de France (80 Exécutants)

A 22 h. — Salle Municipale des Fêtes

GRAND BAL DE NUIT

Le Maire invite la population à assister en foule à cette manifestation et à pavoiser en l'honneur de ses Hôtes

Le Président du Comité des Fêtes,   Le Maire,
L. SAINTHUILLE.   G. LAVALLEY.

NOTA. — La souscription des discours sera ouverte place des Beaux-Regards.

LECLERC, Imprimeur, Saint-Lô

10:17   The poster for the
Inauguration Ceremony of the
Irish Hospital in Saint-Lô
(By courtesy Miss M. Crowley)

Finally, all was ready for the inaugural ceremony which took place on Sunday, 7th April, 1946. A Dublin contingent consisting of Mr. Maguire (Chairman of the Irish Red Cross) and his wife, Dr. Shanley, Mrs. Frank Fahy, Dr. Alan Thompson, and Colonel Thomas McKinney arrived the day before the inauguration. The Irish Ambassador, Mr. Murphy and his wife, the Secretary, Mr. McDonald, and Miss Maura McEntee reporting for the *Irish Press*, arrived from Paris.[29] On Sunday, the Inauguration Ceremony began at 9.30 a.m. with mass celebrated by the hospital chaplain (10:17), Fr. Brendan Hynds, and attended by the officers of the municipality, the delegates from Dublin, the hospital staff and the public. After a banquet luncheon attended by 140 guests, the Gendarmery with the Band of the French Fleet led a parade to martial music through the ruined streets lined by the enthusiastic citizens of Saint-Lô waving paper Irish tricolours. At the War Memorial in what was once the beautiful Cathedral Square of Saint-Lô (10:18), a wreath was solemnly placed on the grave of the Unknown Soldier and was followed by 'a very fine, if subdued rendering of the Soldier's Song, and then a beautiful playing of the Marseillaise'.[30] After speeches and music (10:19) the assemblage returned to the Hospital where 'the Band played a short fanfare while the green, white and orange was slowly run up a huge flagstaff (10:20) in a high position in the grounds - half way up our Anthem was played, followed by the Marseillaise, arms presented by the gendarmes and a movie camera turning.'[31] The remainder of the festive day was given over to an inspection of the hospital (10:21), with the provision of liberal hospitality,[32] an open-air concert, a Ball in the town, and a smaller dance in the recreation hut of the hospital which ended in the small hours of the morning.[33]

The completed hospital consisted of 25 wooden huts (10:22), with the kitchen, theatres, x-ray department, treatment centres, and wards concentrated in 16 one-storey huts radiating from a main connecting corridor. The out-patients department, casualty, laboratory, staff quarters, and two tubercular wards of 20 beds, the offices, stores and chapel occupied the remaining huts (10:23). The grounds were tastefully laid out with flowers, shrubs and vegetable gardens. According to Miss Crowley, 'the general appearance was homely, bright and cheerful, and besides the constant stream of patients, their relatives and friends, no stranger, I think, ever passed without calling and all received the

10:18　Saint-Lô Square
before the bombing
(By courtesy Miss M. Crowley)

10:19　Delegates and officials at the
Inauguration Ceremony in
Saint-Lô square
(By courtesy
Mr. and Mrs. P. Carey)

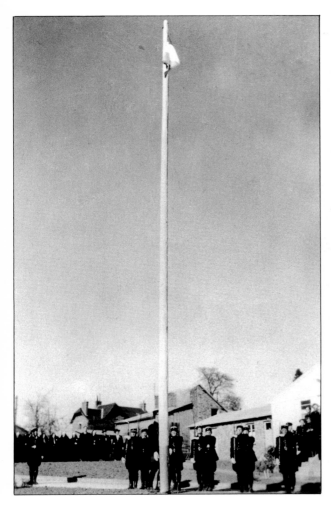

10:20   The Irish tricolour on its
        high flagstaff
        (By courtesy Miss M. Crowley)

10:21 Dr. Alan Thompson with
      a group of visitors
      in the hospital
      (By courtesy
      Mr. and Mrs. P. Carey)

10:22   The *Hôpital de la Croix
        Rouge Irlandaise de Saint-Lô*
        from the main entrance
        (By courtesy Miss M. Crowley)

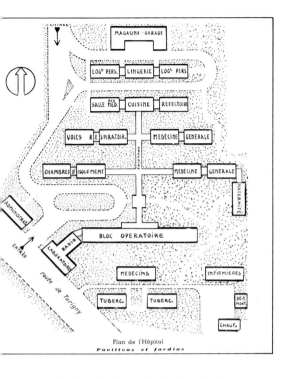

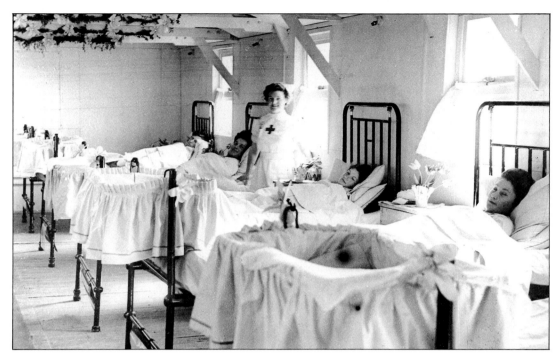

10:23 A plan of the hospital
(From: Lelievre, Raymond.
'L'Hôpital Irlandais de Saint-Lô.'
Terre Normande 1946.
No. 3. p. 14. By courtesy
Mr. and Mrs. P. Carey)

10:24 The Maternity Ward with
Sister Nan O'Leary
(By courtesy Miss M. Crowley)

hospitality of the house.'[34] The hospital had an active maternity unit where the 'comfortable lying-in beds, with the swing cots attached, and mobile back rests added greatly to the comfort of the mothers and attracted much interest' (10:24). The surgical unit with 26 beds, had a modern well-equipped theatre with its wall covered in aluminium plate and its floors with cork lino (10:25). With frequent casualties from exploding mines the theatre was kept busy. The medical unit was in demand for the treatment of diseases of malnutrition. There was a bright and cheerful paediatric section with 10 cots and two small side wards. The patients in the tuberculosis wards were all male, most of whom had contracted the disease in concentration camps.[35] The hospital ambulance service with its seven ambulances operating throughout the Normandy area, was much in demand. "The wards filled up very quickly and with the gracious welcome afforded by the Irish, the queues for consultation grew daily, and one found there people worthy of admission to the court of miracles. The Irish welcomed everyone, so much so that a good woman, imagining herself ill despite the assurances of her doctor who steadfastly refused to send her to the hospital, declared: 'If that is all

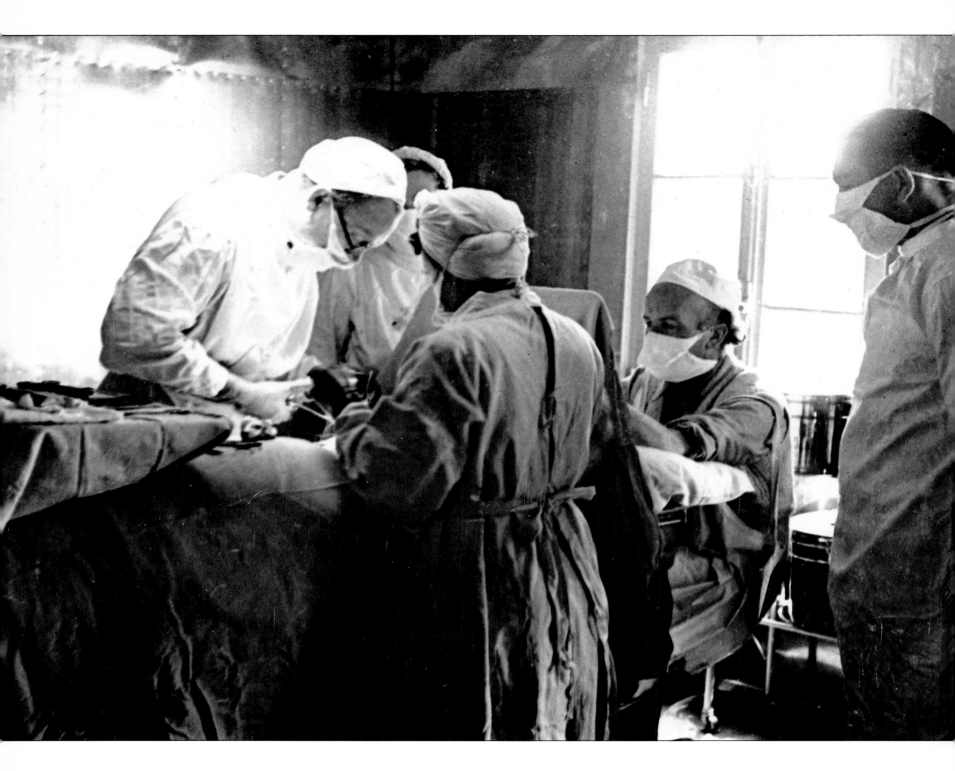

10:25 An operation in progress in the operating theatre. Mr. Freddie McKee is the surgeon, the anaesthetist is Dr. T. Boland; Sister B. O'Rahelly is facing the camera, and Sister M. Doherty has her back to the camera. The hospital chaplain Father Hynds is looking on. (By courtesy Mr and Mrs P. Carey)

10:26 Thirteen German prisoners-of-war 'on loan from the French Government for domestic help.' (By courtesy Miss M. Crowley)

10:27 The entrance gates to the Irish Hospital at Saint-Lô (By courtesy Mr. and Mrs. P. Carey)

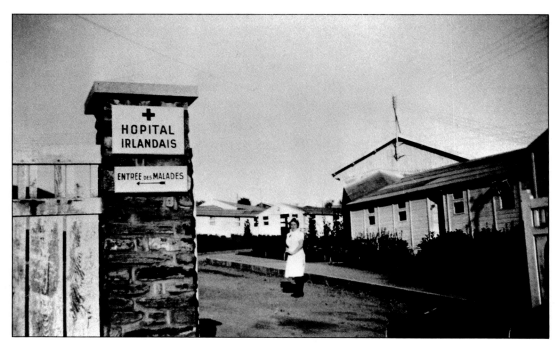

you can do, I will call the Irish and I tell you they will come and collect me in their ambulance if call I them, and they will do all that I ask of them.' What more beautiful tribute can be made?"[36]

General labour for the hospital was hard to come by, and the French authorities provided thirteen German prisoners of war who were brought in each morning under armed guard and taken away in like fashion each evening (10:26). Miss Crowley found them 'well disciplined, always cheerful and willing to learn and the service they rendered played no small part in the success of the hospital.'[37] On 10th June 1946, Samuel Beckett, the storekeeper of Saint-Lô wrote an account of the Irish Hospital for broadcasting to the Irish people on Radio Éireann.[38] It is published here in full incorporating all the manuscript changes in Beckett's hand -

On what a year ago was a grass slope, lying in the angle that the Vire and Bayeux roads make as they unite at the entrance of the town, opposite what remains of the second most important stud-farm in France, a general hospital now stands. It is the Hospital of the Irish Red Cross in Saint-Lô, or, as the Laudiniens themselves say, the Irish Hospital (10:27). The buildings consist of some 25 prefabricated wooden huts. They are superior, generally speaking, to those so scantily available for the wealthier, the better-connected, the astuter or the more flagrantly deserving of the bombed-out. Their finish, as well without as within, is the best that priority can command. They are lined with glass-wool and panelled in isorel, a strange substance of which only very limited supplies are available. There is real glass in the windows. The consequent atmosphere is that of brightness and airiness so comforting to sick people, and to weary staffs. The floors, where the exigencies of hygiene are greatest, are covered with linoleum. There was not enough linoleum left in France to do more than this. The walls and ceiling of the operating theatre are sheeted in aluminium of aeronautic origin, a decorative and practical solution of an old problem and a pleasant variation on the sword and ploughshare metamorphosis (10:28). A system of covered ways connects the kitchen with refectories and wards. The supply of electric current, for purposes both of heat and of power, leaves nothing to be desired. The hospital is centrally heated throughout, by means of coke. The medical, scientific, nursing and secretarial staffs are Irish, the instruments and furniture (including of course beds and bedding), the drugs and food, are supplied by the Society. I think I am right in saying that the number of in-patients (mixed) is in the neighbourhood of 90.[39] As for the others, it is a regular thing, according to recent reports, for as many as 200 to be seen in the out-patients department in a day. Among such ambulant cases a large number are suffering from scabies and other diseases of the skin, the result no doubt of malnutrition or an ill-advised diet. Accident cases are frequent. Masonry falls when least expected, children play with detonators and demining continues.[40] The laboratory, magnificently equipped, bids well to become the official laboratory for the department, if not of an even wider area (10:29). Considerable work has already been done in the analysis of local waters.

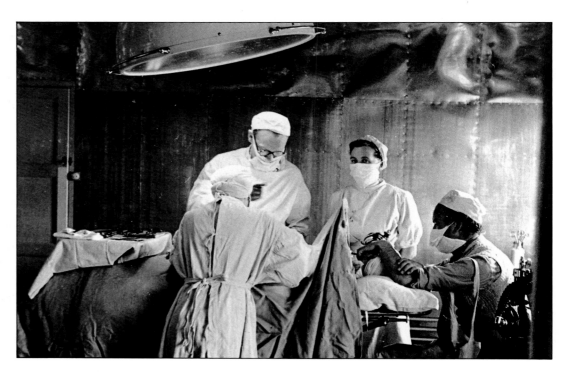

10:28 The operating theatre:
Mr. F. McKee is operating
with Dr. T. Boland giving the
anaesthetic. Sister B. O'Rahelly
is facing the camera, and Sister
M. Doherty has her back to
the camera
(By courtesy
Mr. and Mrs. P. Carey)

10:29 Dr. James Gaffney in his
laboratory
(From 'L'Hôpital Irlandais de
Saint-Lô.' *Terre Normande*
1946. No. 3. p. 15. By courtesy
Mr. and Mrs. P. Carey)

These few facts, chosen not quite at random, are no doubt familiar already to those at all interested in the subject, and perhaps even to those of you listening to me now. They may not appear the most immediately instructive. That the operating-theatre should be sheeted with an expensive metal, or the floor of the labour-room covered with linoleum, can hardly be expected to interest those accustomed to such conditions as the *sine qua non* of reputable obstetrical and surgical statistics. These are the sensible people who would rather have news of the Norman's semi-circular canals or resistance to sulphur than of his attitude to the Irish bringing gifts, who would prefer the history of our difficulties with an unfamiliar pharmacopia and system of mensuration to the story of our dealings with the rare and famous ways of spirit that are the French ways. And yet the whole enterprise turned from the beginning on the establishing of a relation in the light of which the therapeutic relation faded to the merest of pretexts. What was important was not our having penicillin when they had none, nor the unregarding munificence of the French Ministry of Reconstruction (as it was then called), but the occasional glimpse obtained, by us in them and, who knows, by them in us (for they are an imaginative people), of that smile at the human condition as little to be extinguished by bombs as to be broadened by the elixirs of Burroughes and Welcome, the smile deriding, among other things, the having and not having, the giving and the taking, sickness and health.

It would not be seemly, in a retiring and indeed retired store-keeper (10:30), to describe the obstacles encountered in this connexion, and the forms, often grotesque, devised for them by the combined energies of the home and visiting temperaments. It must be supposed that they were not insurmountable, since they have long ceased to be of much account. When I reflect now on the recurrent

Page 335

10:30 The 'retiring storekeeper' of
the Irish Hospital at Saint-Lô;
Samuel Beckett wearing the
uniform of the Irish Red Cross
(By courtesy Miss J. Gaffney)

Page 336

problems of what, with all proper modesty, might be called the heroic period, on one in particular so arduous and elusive that it literally ceased to be formulable, I suspect that our pains were those inherent in the simple and necessary and yet so unattainable proposition that their way of being we, was not our way and that our way of being they, was not their way. It is only fair to say that many of us had never been abroad before.

Saint-Lô was bombed out of existence in one night. German prisoners of war, and casual labourers attracted by the relative food-plenty, but soon discouraged by housing conditions, continued, two years after the liberation, to clear away the debris, literally by hand. Their spirit has yet to learn the blessings of Gallup and their flesh the benefits of the bulldozer. One may thus be excused if one questions the opinion generally received, that ten years will be sufficient for the total reconstruction of Saint-Lô. But no matter what period of time must still be endured, before the town begins to resemble the pleasant and prosperous administrative and agriculatural centre that it was, the hospital of wooden huts in its gardens between the Vire and Bayeux roads will continue to discharge its function, and its cured. 'Provisional' is not the term it was, in this universe become provisional. It will continue to discharge its function long after the Irish are gone and their names forgotten. But I think that to the end of its hospital days it will be called the Irish Hospital, and after that the huts, when they have been turned into dwellings, the Irish huts. I mention this possibility, in the hope that it will give general satisfaction. And having done so I may perhaps venture to mention another, more remote but perhaps of greater import in certain quarters, I mean the possibility that some of those who were in Saint-Lô will come home realising that they got at least as good as they gave, that they got indeed what they could hardly give, a vision and sense of a time-honoured conception of humanity in ruins, and perhaps even an inkling of the terms in which our condition is to be thought again. These will have been in France.[41]

This broadcast is of interest in that it gives not only an account of the Irish Hospital, but describes also the emotional consequences of the experience, or, at least, what the emotional consequences were for one of Beckett's sensitivity. Beckett expresses emotion most deeply in poetry and two profound poems emanate from his experiences and a friendship in Saint-Lô.[42] The first, entitled simply *Saint-Lô*, was published in the *Irish Times* on June 24th, 1946. It is a complex statement on the survival of humanity in the depth of ruin and despair and is generally regarded as one of his finest poems.[43] The river Vire winding its way through the ruined city links the past (10:31), the destruction of the present, and the inevitable rebirth witnessed by Beckett, with the future havoc which all-forgetting humanity will just as inevitably inflict upon itself again[44] -

Vire will wind in other shadows
unborn through the bright ways tremble
and the old mind ghost-forsaken
sink into its havoc

(Saint-Lô, p. 32)

10:31   The River Vire
        (By courtesy Miss M. Crowley)

10:32   Arthur Darley (second from
        left) at Saint-Lô. Also in this
        photograph from left to right
        are: Mr. F. McKee,
        Dr. J. Gaffney, Mr. T. Dunne, and
        an ambulance orderly
        (By courtesy Mr. M. Thompson)

Arthur Darley (10:32) contracted tuberculosis either at Saint-Lô, or shortly before his departure from Ireland to serve with the Red Cross.[45] Son of a skilled musician, he was an accomplished violinist, and entertained the staff in the evenings in the hospital. He was in charge of the tuberculosis hut at Saint-Lô, where he was most popular with the patients. Fluent in French, gentle in manner, and selfless in his dedication to the sick of Saint-Lô, he began his out-patients clinic (for which patients began queuing before dawn) at 9 a.m. and continued through the day to 6 p.m. Appreciation was shown by gifts of Calvados of which Darley had an immense stock. This he indulged in occasionally himself, always placing his violin in the safe-keeping of Miss Crowley, before an evening in the town.[46] His death distressed Beckett deeply and he wrote the poem *Mort de A.D.*, between 1947 and 1949, in tribute to his friend. In this poem, which Beckett has never translated from the original French,[47] he expresses his anguish and depression at his friend's suffering, the futility of existence destined to pain before annihilation, and the spiritual hunger of Darley, eased only by his frantic reading of the 'lives of the saints'[48] -

> et là être là encore là
> pressé contre ma vieille planche vérolée du noir
> des jours et nuits broyés aveuglément
> à être là à ne pas fuir et fuir et être là
> courbé vers l'aveu du temps mourant
> d'avoir été ce qu'il fut fait ce qu'il fit
> de moi de mon ami mort hier l'oeil luisant
> les dents longues haletant dans sa barbe dévorant
> la vie des saints une vie par jour de vie
> revivant dans la nuit ses noirs péchés
> mort hier pendant que je vivais
> et être là buvant plus haut que l'orage
> la coulpe du temps irrémissible
> agrippé au vieux bois témoin des départs
> témoin des retours

(Mort de A.D., p. 56)

Beckett's last task at Saint-Lô was to obtain rat poison from Paris to enable the matron, Mary Crowley, (10:33) to rid the maternity and children's wards of infestation.[49] His resignation was effective from January 1946, but he continued to give whatever help he could to the hospital from Paris.

10:33 Matron Mary Crowley in
       her office at Saint-Lô
       (By courtesy Miss M. Crowley)

Page 340

And what of this remarkable institute, the *Hôpital Irlandais de Saint-Lô*? On December 31st, 1946 it was handed over to the French Red Cross as a fully functioning hospital, which has been subsequently rebuilt and is now a major hospital in Saint-Lô.[50] The citizens of Saint-Lô demonstrated their appreciation to the Irish staff on their departure, when it is recorded that 'the entire population of St. Lô, headed by the Mayor, and crowds from other parts of Normandy, marched to the Hospital with banners bearing words of appreciation, presented floral tributes to and warmly acclaimed the departing staff.'[51] There were many tributes: "Ireland and her Red Cross (which was only founded in 1939)

10:34   The certificate accompanying
        the Silver Medal of Recognition
        by France, awarded to
        Dr. Alan Thompson
        (By courtesy Mr. M. Thompson)

10:35   Alan Thompson, wearing his
        Fellows gown, with Eamonn
        De Valera, President of Ireland
        to his right, and Bethel Solomons
        President of the Royal College of
        Physicians of Ireland, 1946-48
        (An *Irish Times* photograph; by
        courtesy the Royal College of
        Physicians of Ireland)

are well deserving of the gratitude of the Normands, who were the first to receive the beneficence of this organisation. The Irish Hospital not only welcomed the sick, it also received the curious like me, and it was while toasting the whiskey, 'the Calva', of Ireland, that I made acquaintance with these admirable people whom we adopted and received so gratefully within our walls - our walls which exist no more."[52]

The French Government expressed its gratitude to the Irish staff of the *Hôpital De La Croix Rouge Irlandaise* with the award of the *Medaille de la Reconnaissance Francaise*[53](10:34). Dr. Alan Thompson returned to his post of Senior Physician on the staff of the Richmond (later St. Laurence's) Hospital in Dublin. He was appointed Professor of Medicine to the Royal College of Surgeons in Ireland in 1962. His distinguished position in Dublin medicine (10:35) was acknowledged by his profession when he was elected to the office of President of the Royal College of Physicians of Ireland in 1966, and in 1967 when the College celebrated its tercentenary. Thompson remained in close contact with Beckett until his death on 23 March 1974.[54]

Samuel Beckett bade his friends and Ireland farewell in Saint-Lô. He returned only occasionally to Dublin thereafter to visit his family (10:36). He took with him to France those memories of his homeland that would inspire and colour his writing, and he turned to the language of his adopted country, which gave to his writing an added power of expression -

> The uniform, horizontal writing, flowing without accidence, of the man with a style, never gives you the margarita. But the writing of, say, Racine or Malherbe, perpendicular, diamanté, is pitted, is it not, and sprigged with sparkles; the flints and pebbles are there, no end of humble tags and commonplaces. They have no style, they write without style, do they not, they give you the phrase, the sparkle, the precious margaret. Perhaps only the French can do it. Perhaps only the French language can give you the thing you want.[55]
>
> *(Dream of Fair to Middling Women, p. 42)*

Perhaps indeed only the French could do it. Beckett brought with him to France the inspirational forces that derived from his formative years in Ireland. The French language provided him with a means of expression, a power to express that which he is compelled to express. It is that expression which has so greatly enriched our understanding of existence.

10:36   Samuel and Frank Beckett photographed at the lily pond, Shottery,[56] Killiney in 1954 (By courtesy Caroline Murphy)

Envoi

who may tell the tale
of the old man?
weigh absence in a scale?
mete want with a span?
the sum assess
of the world's woes?
nothingness
in words enclose.

(Tailpiece, *Watt*, p. 274)

Notes and References

Referenced works are denoted in the text by superior numerals. Full details of works quoted in the text are given when first referred to in each chapter; where the work is referred to again in the same chapter it is indicated in an abbreviated form. Full publication details of Beckett's writings may be found in the Bibliography; only the title and page number is given in the Notes and References.

INTRODUCTION

1. For this phrase I am indebted to: Leventhal, A.J. 'The Beckett Hero'. In *Samuel Beckett. A Collection of Critical Essays.* ed. Martin Esslin. Prentice-Hall. New Jersey. 1965. p. 48. S.E. Gontarski's recent monograph *(The Intent of Undoing in Samuel Beckett's Dramatic Texts.* Indiana University Press. Bloomington. 1985.) only came into my possession after the main text of *The Beckett Country* had gone to press. He too has commented on Beckett's struggle 'to write himself out of the text' (p. xiv), and he demonstrates the value of careful study of the early dramatic manuscripts in the compilation of 'textual biographies': "The construction of textual biographies allow us to focus on points of similarity not apparent in the completed work. Beckett's characters (and evidently Beckett himself) are haunted by persistent images, memories, and nightmares; it is the situation quintessentially dramatised by the voices and ghosts of another 'cluster' of plays, the almost fantastic teleplays: *Eh Joe, Ghost Trio,* and *'... but the clouds ...'*. We find, for example, renderings some fifty years apart of the trauma of learning to swim, in 'For Future Reference' (1930) and *Company* (1980). And the image of a girl in a punt, which so haunted the sixty-nine-year-old Krapp in 1958, also assailed Belacqua in the unpublished *Dream of Fair to Middling Women* in 1932. For Beckett, Proust's involuntary memory is often raised to the level of active assailant." (p. xviii).

2. *Watt.* p. 249.

3. The autobiographical trends in Beckett's writing have been noted by many, among whom are: Pilling, John. "Review article: 'Company' by Samuel Beckett." *Journal of Beckett Studies.* John Calder, London. 1982. no. 7. pp. 128-131; Brater, Enoch. 'The Company Beckett Keeps: The Shape of Memory and One Fablist's Decay of Living.' in: *Samuel Beckett. Humanistic Perspectives.* eds: Morris Beja, S.E. Gontarski, Pierre Astier. Ohio State University Press. 1983. pp. 166-167; Esslin, Martin. 'Samuel Beckett's Poems.' in: *Beckett at 60. A Festschrift.* Caldar and Boyers. London. pp. 59-60; Leventhal, 'The Beckett Hero.' p. 48.

4. For a discussion of the similarities and differences between Beckett and Proust see: Pilling, John. 'Beckett's Proust' *Journal of Beckett Studies.* John Calder. London. 1976. no. 1. pp. 8-29; Zurbrugg, Nicholas. "Beckett, Proust, and 'Dream of Fair to Middling Women'" *Journal of Beckett Studies.* John Calder. London. 1985. no. 9 pp.

43-64; Esslin, Martin. *Mediations. Essays on Brecht, Beckett, and the Media.* Eyre Methuen. London. p. 94; Oberg, Arthur K. 'Krapp's Last Tape and the Proustian Vision' in: *Samuel Beckett, Krapp's Last Tape. A Theatre Workbook.* ed. James Knowlson. Brutus Books London. 1980. pp. 151-157; Lamont, Rosette C. 'Krapp: Anti-Proust. *Krapp's Last Tape. A Theatre Notebook.* pp. 158-173.

5. Proust, Marcel. *Remembrance of Things Past.* Volume XII. 'Time Regained'. Chatto and Windus. London. 1972. p. 279.

6. Kennedy, Sighle. 'Spirals of Need: Irish Prototypes in Samuel Beckett's Fiction'. in: *Yeats, Joyce and Beckett. New Light on Three Modern Irish Writers.* eds. Kathleen McGrory and John Unterecker. Bucknell University Press, Lewisberg, and Associated University Presses, London. 1976. p. 166.

7. Esslin, Martin. *Mediations.* p. 111. McMillan also stresses the importance of typographical knowledge in interpreting Beckett's poetry: 'But even when we have adjusted our aesthetic expectations, there remains the practical problem of a detailed knowledge of place necessary to understanding. At one level at least the trajectory is a real one situated in geographical locations not necessarily familiar to Beckett's readers.' (McMillan, Dougald III. *'Echo's Bones:* Starting points for Beckett.' in: *Samuel Beckett. The Art of Rhetoric.* eds. Morot-Sir, Edouard., Harper, Howard., McMillan, Dougald III. North Carolina Studies in the Romance Languages and Literature. Chapel Hill. 1976. pp. 165-187).

8. Leventhal. A.J. 'The Thirties.' *Beckett at Sixty.* p. 11.

9. For a discussion on Beckett's Anglo-Irish origins see: Mays, J.C.C. 'Young Beckett's Irish Roots.' *Irish University Review.* 1984. vol. 14, no. 1. pp. 18-33; Mercier, Vivian. *Beckett/Beckett.* Oxford University press. Oxford. New York. Toronto. Melbourne. 1977. pp. 20-45.

10. 'Human Wishes.' *Disjecta. Miscellaneous Writings and a Dramatic Fragment by Samuel Beckett.* ed. Ruby Cohn. John Calder. London. 1983. p. 162.

11. Montgomery, Niall. 'No Symbols Where None Intended', *New World Writing.* 1954. no. 5. p. 326.

12. *The Calmative, Collected Shorter Prose.* pp. 35-36.

13. *Leventhal. A.J. 'Nobel Prizewinner'. The Irish Times.* Mon. Nov. 3. 1969. The reference to Anouilh is: Anouilh, Jean. *Arts-Spectacles,* no. 400, February 27-March 5, 1953, p. 1.

14. Cockerham, Harry. 'Bilingual playwright.' in: *Beckett the shape changer. A symposium edited by Katharine Worth.* Routledge and Kegan Paul. London and Boston. 1975. p. 143.

15. Mercier. *Beckett/Beckett.* p. 154. Mercier considers it 'unlikely that there will ever be a holy place of pilgrimage like Yeats's tower or Joyce's tower in any posthumous Beckett cult'. (*Beckett/Beckett,* p. 45), and Mays expresses similar sentiments in that he considers it unlikely that sources of memory and allusion in Beckett's writing will ever 'provide an excuse for pilgrimages to Foxrock or Three Rock Mountain.' ('Young Beckett's Irish Roots.' p. 33).

16. Kennedy. 'Spirals of Need'. p. 154.

17. "'An Imaginative Work' A Review of *The Amaranthers* by Jack B. Yeats". *Disjecta.* pp. 89-90.

18. *The Expelled. Collected Shorter Prose.* p. 33. For a discussion of recurring themes in Beckett's writings see: Levy, Eric P. " '*Company*': the mirror of Beckettian mimesis." *Journal of Beckett Studies.* John Calder. London. 1982. no. 8. p. 103.

19. Gontarski has also been impressed by the abundance of realistic detail to be found in the earlier drafts of Beckett's writing: 'Often the early drafts of Beckett's work are more realistic, the action more traditionally motivated, the world more familiar and recognizable, the work as a whole more conventional than the final.' (*Intent of Undoing*, pp. 3-4).

20. For example Mays mentions allusions to 'the Vale of Shanganagh', 'Decco's Cave' and 'Sallygap', which I have been unable to identify with certainty. (Mays, 'Young Beckett's Irish Roots'. p. 22).

21. *Watt.* p. 249. Similar sentiments are expressed in *The Unnamable* p. 329 -

    "The island, I'm on the island, I've never left the island, God help me. I was under the impression I spent my life in spirals round the earth. Wrong, it's on the island I wind my endless ways. The island, that's all the earth I know. I don't know it either, never having had the stomach to look at it. When I come to the coast I turn back inland. and my curse is not helicoidal, I got that wrong too, but a succession of irregular loops, not sharp and short as in the waltz, now of a parabolic sweep that embraces entire boglands, now between the two, somewhere or other, and invariably unpredictable in direction, that is to say determined by the panic of the moment."

22. *The End. Collected Shorter Prose.* p. 70.

23. Beckett, Samuel. Personal communication to the author. 16.5.85.

CHAPTER 1: EARLY INFLUENCES:
Home, Foxrock and Environs

1. Bair, Deirdre, *Samuel Beckett. A biography.* Picador. Pan Books. London. 1980. p. 13. I encountered so many errors and inaccuracies, together with important conclusions based on doubtful sources, that I have avoided referring to Ms Bair's biography, except on a few occasions where I believe the information to be relevant and the source to be reliable. For a critical review of the scholarly aspects of this biography see: Leventhal, A.J. *The Herald Tribune.* June 29, 1978, and Esslin, M. 'The Unnamable Pursued by the Unspeakable.' *Mediations. Essays on Brecht, Beckett, and the Media.* Eyre Methuen. London. 1980. pp. 155-167.

2. Other references to birth may be found in: *First Love. Collected Shorter Prose.* p. 1; *Murphy,* p. 52; *Company,* pp. 15-16; pp. 19-20. In *The Unnamable* and *How It Is*, Beckett brings a terrifying realism to pre-natal existence: 'Surely no one has ever dared to speak out of the womb as Beckett does ...' Leventhal, A.J. 'The Beckett Hero.' in *Samuel Beckett. A Collection of Critical Essays.* ed. by Martin Esslin. Prentice-Hall. New Jersey. 1965. p. 42. Whether or not Beckett *can* actually recall the moments before or after birth is *not* important; what matters is the ability to imagine it in a way that conveys the experience to the reader. (Esslin, Martin. 'Introduction'. *Collection of Critical Essays.* pp. 9-10). Beckett claims to have a painfully real memory of life before birth: 'I have a clear memory of my own fetal existence. It was an existence where no voice, no possible movement could free me from the agony and darkness I was subjected to'. (Interview with John Gruen, *Vogue* (London), February 1970, quoted by Worth, Katherine. *The Irish Drama of Europe from Yeats to Beckett.* The Athlone Press of the University of London, 1978. p. 243). Beckett's womb creations are considered by: Rabinovitz, Rubin, *The Development of Samuel Beckett's Fiction.* University of Illinois Press. Urbana and Chicago. 1984, p. 168, and by Esslin, Martin. *Mediations.* pp. 86 and 95. Beckett's fascination with the embryonic posture may also be noted in the indolent hero of *More Pricks than Kicks*, Belacqua Shuah, who adopts the foetal posture of Dante's Florentine lute maker as depicted in the Botticelli drawing. (Knowlson, James, *Samuel Beckett: an exhibition.* Turrett Books, London. 1971. pp. 40-41.) This posture is evident again in *Molloy*, p. 11. References to birth and the accomplishments of the accoucher Dr. Haddon may be found in the early draft of *Footfalls* (Knowlson, James and Pilling, John. *Frescoes of the Skull. The Later Prose and Drama of Samuel Beckett.* Grove Press. New York. 1980. p. 236), and *Company.* p. 16. In *Watt* (pp. 10-13), there is the hilarious account of birth by 'the lady' in the opening scene of the novel, which parodies 'The Night before Larry was Stretched', and in which Beckett considers, but does not develop, the feelings of the foetus when the umbilical cord is severed. Murphy is ever conscious of the amniotic environment from which he was so cruelly evicted, so much so that he goes hatless for fear of evoking memories of the caul. (*Murphy, p. 53).*

3. We may note a repetitive theme in *Waiting for Godot,* p. 52.

    'Christ! What's Christ got to do with it?
    You're not going to compare yourself to Christ!'

    The Christ analogy with self is taken even further in *Watt* (p. 157).The biblical and religious associations in Beckett's writing have been studied by a number of scholars: Rabinovitz, Rubin. " 'Molloy' and the archetypal traveller." *Journal of Beckett Studies.* John Calder. London. Autumn 1979. no. 5. pp. 25-44; Cohn, Ruby. *Samuel Beckett: the comic gamut.* Rutgers University Press. New Brunswick, New Jersey, 1962.

p. 26; Mayoux, Jean-Jacques. 'Samuel Beckett and Universal Parody.' in *Collection of Critical Essays*. ed. Esslin. pp. 77-91; Pilling, John. *Samuel Beckett*. Routledge and Kegan Paul, London, Henley and Boston, 1976. p. 117; Zeifman, Hersh. 'Religious Imagery in the Plays of Samuel Beckett.' in: *Samuel Beckett, a collection of criticism edited by Ruby Cohn*. McGraw-Hill Book Company. New York. 1975. pp. 85-94; Morrison, Kristin, 'Neglected Biblical Allusions in Beckett's Plays: Mother Pegg Once More.' in: *Samuel Beckett. Humanistic Perspectives*. eds. Morris Beja, S.E. Gontarski, Pierre Astier. Ohio State University Press. 1983. pp. 91-98.

4. I am indebted to Mr. and Mrs. Noel Hughes who permitted me to visit and photograph *Cooldrinagh* on many occasions.

5. *The Irish Builder*. Supplement. Feb 26. 1903. facing p. 1604.

6. The advertisement for the sale of 'Cooldrinagh', quoted by Vivian Mercier, summarises many of the property's features with a somewhat complacent air: 'COOLDRINAGH', BRIGHTON ROAD, FOXROCK, CO. DUBLIN. This is a charming Tudor style family residence well set back from the road on the corner of Kerrymount Avenue and standing amid totally secluded mature gardens laid out in lawns, tennis court and croquet lawn. This property was designed by Frederick Hicks, architect, and was completed to an extremely high standard of finish. The main rooms face south and west and have spacious proportions and the entire property is in excellent condition. Churches and schools are conveniently situated and there are excellent shops situated in Foxrock Village which is five minutes walk from the property. 'Cooldrinagh' is approached by a sweeping gravelled driveway'. (Mercier, Vivian. *Beckett/Beckett*. Oxford University Press. Oxford. New York. Toronto. Melbourne. 1977. pp. 20-21). The name *Cooldrinagh* derives from the Gaelic and means 'back of the blackthorn hedge' or copse. *Cooldrinagh* was the name of May Beckett's father's mill near Leixlip. Apparently this venture was a financial failure that brought great hardship to the Jones' family as a result of which May Beckett had to commence nursing in the Adelaide Hospital in Dublin at an early age. (Information to the author from Samuel Beckett).

7. Further references to the larch occur in: *A Piece of Monologue, Collected Shorter Plays*, p. 26; *Molloy*, p. 37; *Watt*, pp. 45-46; *Texts for Nothing, Collected Shorter Prose*. p. 73, *Sanies I. Collected Poems*. p. 17. The lemon-verbena that flowered at the foot of the red-tiled porch of *Cooldrinagh* was another evocatory sensation for Beckett. This plant continues to flower every summer in spite of its considerable age: 'Lemon-scented Verbena: *Aloysia* or *Verbena Triphylla*, a deciduous shrub (naturally a small tree), reaching in the southern parts of the British Isles 10 to 15 feet or more in height; young shoots angular. Leaves mostly in threes, very fragrant, lance-shaped... Flowers numerous, small, pale purple, produced in August in slender, terminal, stalked, downy panicles, 3 to 5 in. high. Native of Chile; introduced in 1784. Near London this well-known shrub needs the protection of a wall, and is often grown in cold conservatories for the pleasant lemon-like scent of the leaves.' (Bean, W.J. *Trees and Shrubs Hardy in the British Isles*. 8th. ed. vol 1. John Murray. London. 1976. p. 284).

8. References to the summer house in *Cooldrinagh* may also be found in 'Heard in the Dark', *Journal of Beckett Studies*, John Calder. London. no. 5, Autumn 1979, pp. 7-8, and *As the Story was Told, Collected Shorter Prose*, p. 211. Beckett has acknowledged with sincere affection the remarkable influence of his father on his development, yet it is the apparently more dominant maternal presence that attracts analysis: 'Where are his (Beckett's) deepest roots: in Dante, Descartes, Dublin? Shakespeare, Paris, Swift, Joyce? His relationship with his mother,

with his own unconcious?' (*Samuel Beckett. The Critical Heritage* eds. Graver, Lawrence, and Federman, Raymond. Routledge and Kegan Paul. London, Henly and Boston, 1979. p. 38).

9. Sir Horace Plunkett, lived at Kilteragh, a mansion he had built on Westminster Road in Foxrock. His house was burned down in the 'troubles' and Sir Horace departed Ireland for good, a disillusioned man; see: Clare, Liam. *Arson at Kilteragh*. Foxrock Local History Club publication. (National Library of Ireland, call no. P9. IR 94133). Miss Rosemary Darley remembers frequent raids in Foxrock area for the theft of guns and money. Plunkett was reputed to have owned the first motor car in Ireland, a fact subsequently proved incorrect. However, he did drive a De Dion Bouton, and a photograph of Sir Horace driving this car along Merrion Square is featured in: *Seventy Years Young. Memories of Elizabeth, Countess of Fingall told to Pamela Hinkson*. London, Collins, 1938, Second edition, p. 227. For an interesting but perhaps excessively interpretive analysis of the De Dion Bouton in *Company*, see: Brater, Enoch. 'The *Company* Beckett Keeps: The Shape of Memory and One Fablist's Decay of Lying.' in: *Humanistic Perspectives*. p. 163. For a discussion of the De Dion Bouton in Robert Pinget's play *La Manivelle*, see pages 9 and 254 of *The Beckett Country*. Beckett cannot recall if his father actually owned a De Dion Bouton; he certainly had a large automobile. (Information to the author from Samuel Beckett).

10. Mention of the 'Tale of Breem' or Breen, may be found also in *Texts for Nothing, Collected Shorter Prose*, p. 74, and the *Calmative, Collected Shorter Prose*, p. 49. John de Courcy Ireland kindly undertook the task of searching local maritime historical records for the 'Tale of Breem' without success.

11. For discussion of *The Gloaming*, (Reading University Library, MS 1396/4/6) see: Knowlson and Pilling. *Frescoes of the Skull*. pp. 288-231

12. Glenavy, Lady Beatrice, *Today we will only gossip*. Constable. London. 1964. p. 48.

13. Harvey, Lawrence, *Samuel Beckett. Poet and Critic*. Princeton University Press, New Jersey, 1970, p. 71. The reference to 'the fairy tales of Meath', is to the county of Meath to the north of Dublin, which is rich in folklore, antiquities and history of famous battles. The great cairn of Knowth and and the Newgrange tumulus are among the most famous prehistoric monuments in the whole of Europe. For a good general account of the area see: Killanin, Lord and Duignan, Michael. *Shell Guide to Ireland*. The Ebury Press. 1962. pp. 420-423.

14. For another example of Beckett's affection for the donkey see: *Dream of Fair to Middling Women*, p. 114. The confrontation of quadruped and narrator recurs in *The Expelled, Collected Shorter Prose*. p. 32, and in *The End, Collected Shorter Prose*, p. 54. For more detailed accounts of animals in Beckett's writing see: Pilling, *Samuel Beckett*. pp. 62-63; and Connor, Stevan, 'Beckett's animals.' *Journal of Beckett Studies*. John Calder. London. Autumn 1982. no. 8. pp. 29-44.

15. *Endgame*, p. 30.

16. For a more detailed analysis of the role of Beckett's mother in *How It Is* and *Footfalls* see: Knowlson and Pilling. *Frescoes*. pp. 65-67, and p. 227. It is not possible to say how much Beckett's drama was influenced by his mother's illness, Parkinson's Disease, but many Beckettian characters certainly manifest the Parkinsonian features of gait and mobility; see also: Esslin, Martin. 'Voices, Patterns, Voices. Samuel Beckett's later plays.' in *Gambit International Theatre Review*. 1976. vol. 7. no. 28. p. 95. Beckett's reference to the shaving mirror

at New Place - 'my mother did her hair in it, with twitching hands' (*Texts for Nothing, Collected Shorter Prose*, p. 91) is to his mother's illness, Parkinson's Disease.

17. May Beckett sold *Cooldrinagh* on Kerrymount Avenue in 1941 and purchased a smaller house with a splendid view of the Dublin mountains, named *New Place* in a quiet cul-de-sac, Tory Lane off Brighton Road, less than five minutes walk from *Cooldrinagh*. It is unlikely that Beckett had any say in the naming of *New Place,* though the choice of the same name as was attached to one of the finest houses in Stratford, the home of the dramatist William Shakespeare, now seems somewhat prophetic. I am indebted to Mr. and Mrs. G.C. Stapleton, the present owners for permitting me to visit and photograph *New Place*, now named *Amesbury.* Beckett began writing *Molloy* in *New Place*: 'I realised that I knew nothing. I sat down in my mother's little house in Ireland and began to write *Molloy.*' (Mercier, *Beckett/Beckett.* 1979. p. 161).

18. That Beckett's childhood was a happy one is confirmed by Beckett himself in an interview with the American critic Tom Driver, who asked Beckett if his plays dealt with those facets of human experience which religion must also deal with: 'Yes, for they deal with distress. Some people object to this in my writing. At a party an English intellectual – so-called – asked me why I write always about distress. As if it were perverse to do so! He wanted to know if my father had beaten me or my mother had run away from home to give me an unhappy childhood. I told him no, *that I had a very happy childhood.* Then he thought me more perverse than ever. I left the party as soon as possible and got into a taxi. On the glass partition between me and the driver were three signs: one asked help for the blind, another help for orphans, and the third relief for the war refugees. One does not have to look for distress. It is screaming at you even in the taxis of London.' (Quoted from Reid, Alec. *All I can manage, more than I could: An approach to the plays of Samuel Beckett.* The Dolmen Press. Dublin. 1968. p. 15).

19. Mrs. Sheila Brazil (née Walsh) of Foxrock has been of exceptional help to me in identifying locations in Foxrock and the personalities of Beckett's childhood days. Mrs. Brazil succeeded her mother as post-mistress to the village in 1925 and remembers such details as the telephone number of *Cooldrinagh* when the Becketts first lived there - Foxrock 87. I am indebted to Mrs. Brazil for the information on the Elsner sisters, whose school was on Leopardstown Road. Both sisters taught music and it may not be unreasonable to attribute at least some of Beckett's appreciation of music to the Elsner sisters.

20. From Beatrice Glenavy's memoirs we learn that the father of the Elsner sisters was a musician, from whom her father took cello lessons. Herr Elsner had apparently come from Germany to Ireland where he settled, and his 'family did much in later years for music in his adopted land.' Lady Glenavy gives an interesting reminiscence of a music lesson with Herr Elsner's daughters: 'On Saturday mornings I went to a private school at the end of our road run by Herr Elsner's daughter Ida for languages and piano lessons. I was no linguist but I worked hard at the piano. There was certainly nothing dull or ordinary about Ida Elsner's method of teaching. During my piano lesson she used to do the house-work, leaving the door open so that she could hear if I struck a wrong note. She would yell down from an upstairs room, 'B Flat!', or whatever it should have been, to correct me. One day when Ida was out, a sister of Miss Elsner's who was also a teacher of music took my lesson. I went through my scales and exercises and then my Grieg pieces. She sat in absolute silence. When I had finished she said, 'Ach, Ida will make something out of you.' (Glenavy. *Today we will only gossip.*)

p. 18; p. 25). It is tempting to make comparison between this account of a music lesson by Ida Elsner, and that of the Italian music teacher in *Embers* (p. 29-30).
There is little information available on the Elsner family, but *Thom's Official Directory* provides at least an outline of the families presence in the city. First mention of the Elsners is in 1868, when William F. Elsner, professor of music, is listed as having a studio at 17 Lower Pembroke Street. His wife, Pauline, also a Professor of Music had a studio in their home 'Taunus', on Leopardstown Road. (*Thom's Official Directory*, 1873. p. 1749). Thirty years later in 1904, the daughter, Miss. W. Pauline is to be found as a pianoforte teacher at 21 Ely Place, and Miss Ida, was a teacher of music and languages at 'Taunus' (*Thom's Directory,* 1904. p. 1864), at which location she is still in practice in 1958, but there is no longer any reference to Ida (*Thom's Directory,* 1958, p. 1725).

21. I am indebted to Mrs. Brazil for identifying the moustached postman as John Thompson, and for obtaining his photograph which is reproduced with the permission of his daughter Mary Thompson. He was, according to Miss Rosemary Darley, a delightful character full of humour and conversation.

22. Among many valuable contributions, Mrs. Brazil's identification of the whistling consumptive postman in *Watt,* as Bill Shannon, was among the more important. That she was able to supply me with a photograph was all the more remarkable. His identity has been confirmed by Beckett. The third postman to the area was Mr. Dignam who had only one eye. Mrs. Brazil recalls the care that the postmen gave to their appearance, and she remembers the brass buttons of their uniforms being cleaned with powder prior to an inspection.

23. Bill Shannon features also under the alias 'Severn' in *Watt,* pp. 65-66.

24. According to Dr. Desmond de Courcy Wheeler, who purchased *Cooldrinagh* shortly after May Beckett sold the house, there was a larch-tree in *Cooldrinagh* which turned green one week before the others in spring, and brown ahead of the rest in autumn.

25. According to Mrs. Brazil the milk-boy to *Cooldrinagh* would have come either from the dairy of a Mr. Tully, who lived in the cottages in Foxrock village, or from the dairy on the late Sir Horace Plunkett's farm on Westminster Road, which was run by a Mr. Ogilvy. She considers the former more likely. The milk-boy from Tully's field where he had three or four cows, was renowned for his generosity ('his usual liberality.' *Watt.* p. 148) in always leaving a 'tilly' for the cat.

26. Bibby, the childhood nanny, is mentioned in *Happy Days,* p. 44, and in *Texts for Nothing. Collected Shorter Prose,* p. 79. Mrs. Brazil recalls a housekeeper to the Beckett household named 'Ludo' a sobriquet that derived from her frequent ejaculations - 'I must rush home (to *Cooldrinagh*) to play Ludo.'

27. There is another poignant reference to a beggar-woman of childhood in *Texts for Nothing, Collected Shorter Prose.* p. 75. For an interesting discourse on the role of the deprived hero in Beckett's literature see: Fletcher, John. *The Novels of Samuel Beckett.* Chatto and Windus. London. 1964. pp. 225-226. These women of the roads, once so much a part of the Irish landscape had a profound effect on Beckett. Writing on the sources for *Not I,* Gontarski quotes Beckett: 'I knew that woman in Ireland ... I knew who she was – not 'she' specifically, one single woman, but there were so many of those old crones, stumbling down the lanes, in the ditches, beside the hedgegrows. Ireland is full of them. And I heard 'her' saying what I wrote in *Not I.* I actually heard it.' (Gontarski, S.E. *The Intent of Undoing in Samuel Beckett's Dramatic Texts.* Indiana University Press. Bloomington. 1985. p. 132).

28. Information from Mrs. S. Brazil.

29. William Wellington Bentley purchased vast tracts of land in Foxrock in the 1860s. He advertised the area as 'renowned for the salubrity of the air.' Here he built the Tourist's Hotel, establishing the Foxrock Club in it. He persuaded the Post Office to open a branch, and the railway company to open a station beside his hotel, and he himself built the station house. He also had the Protestant Church of Tully erected on Brighton Road. With these facilities and ample land he hoped to develop a garden city and select holiday resort within easy reach of the city dwellers. His plans, however, ended in financial disaster; the hotel fell into disuse and was known by the inhabitants as Bentley's folly. (O'Donovan, John. 'How the man who developed Foxrock got his fingers burned.', *Evening Press.* 1979. Wed. May 2nd. p. 10.)

Mrs. Sheila Brazil recalls that Foxrock village in Beckett's childhood consisted of a small cottage shop, McEvoy's that 'sold everything', Tracey's garage, the station, and the Hotel which fell into disuse in the late nineteenth century and was converted into tenements. (The Foxrock Tourist Hotel is listed as vacant in *Thom's Directory*, 1873. p. 1693.) Miss Rosemary Darley remembers the unsurfaced roads of Foxrock with hens and other animals wandering aimlessly (and safely) about. When the occasional car passed it threw up a cloud of dust. The rural sounds in *All That Fall* were very real to Beckett - cartwheels, bicycle brakes, motor-vans with thunderous rattles, squawk of hen, the moo of cattle, the baa of sheep, the bark of dogs, the cackle of hens, the chirp of birds, a 'pretty little woolly lamb' (p. 34), and in *Watt* the goat 'dragging its pale and chain' on the road leading to the station (p. 245) adds a realistic acoustic dimension to pastoral tranquility.

30. Simms, George O. *Tullow's Story. A portrait of a county Dublin parish.* Published privately, Dublin, 1984. p. 74.

31. For an interesting account of the development of the small village of Cornelscourt see: Farrell, Ted. *The Story of Cornelscourt.* Foxrock Local History Club. 1985. no. 14.

32. 'Connolly. W., grocer, tea, wine and provision merchant' on Bray Rd., Foxrock. *(Thom's Directory)*, 1922. p. 1791. Mrs. Brazil recalls that the Beckett family dealt with Connolly's, receiving their groceries daily from Mr. Connolly's van. The establishment consisted of a bar with armchairs in front of an open fire for the 'regular' customers, and a grocer's store occupying the major portion of the premises. Today the site is occupied by a public house, *The Magic Carpet.*

33. *All That Fall. Collected Shorter Plays*, p. 15.

34. Beckett asked me (in 1984) to provide him with the derivation of the name Ballyogan for translation into French. I assumed the derivation to be from Bally Eoghan, which in English would be the equivalent of Johnstown, but the derivation is thought to be from the 'Town of St. Mochainn or Mocheim' a saint who died in AD 584. (O'Reilly, Patrick. 'The Christian Sepulchral Leacs and free-standing crosses of the Dublin half-barony of Rathdown.' *Journal of the Royal Society of Antiquaries of Ireland.* 1901: vol. 31. pp. 135-258.)

Beckett's fascination with the derivation of Irish placenames is apparent in the amusing passage on the 'Molloy Country':

'This market-town, or village, was, I hasten to say, called Bally, and represented, with its dependent lands, a surface area of five or six square miles at the most. In modern countries this is what I think is called a commune, or a canton, I forget, but there exists with us no abstract and generic term for such territorial subdivisions. And to express them we have another system, of singular beauty and simplicity, which consists in saying Bally (since we are talking of Bally) when you mean Bally and Ballyba when you mean Bally plus its domains and Ballybaba when you mean the domains exclusive of Bally itself. I myself for example lived and come to think of it still live, in Turdy, hub of Turdyba. And in the evening, when I went for a stroll, in the country outside Turdy, to get a breath of fresh air, it was the fresh air of Turdybaba that I got, and no other.'

(Molloy, p. 134)

Ballyba itself may have origins in Ballybetagh, a townland close to Kilternan. The word has its origins in early Anglo-Norman times when the 'betaghs' (Irish *biotach* = food provider) who occupied one of the lower rungs of the feudal ladder were believed to have held land in common. Other possible derivations are from Ballaly, from the Norse Olaf or Ambhaib, meaning the place of Olaf, or from Ballyman. (Turner, Kathleen. *If you seek monuments. A guide to the Antiquities of the Barony of Rathdown.* Rathmichael Historical Society. 1983. 11.22.23.)

35. Elrington Ball. F. *History of the County of Dublin.* Part 1. Alex Thom & Co. Dublin. 1902. p. 98.

36. The history of the cairns and dolmens or cromlechs of the foothills and mountains of Dublin is as fascinating to the archaeologist, as to the folklorist and philosopher. The first settlers came to Ireland about 6000 BC but it was not until about 2,500 BC that man left a lasting memorial to his presence, the portal dolmen, of which there are some 150 in Ireland, mostly on the eastern coast. Conforming to a standard construction of two upright stones of approximately similar height, supporting a tablestone often of massive proportions, these granite structures form an entrance to a chamber constructed of stones which was sealed with a further granite slab. How a primitive people moved and positioned these massive stones remains a mystery. The entire structure was probably covered with a cairn of earth, of which nothing remains today. These burial tombs were usually situated on low ground facing west close to a stream. The larger rock chambers were intended to hold several bodies, perhaps members of a distinguished family, or chiefs fallen in conflict. Excavated urns suggest that internment was sometimes after cremation; see: Turner, *If you seek monuments 2,* and O'Neill, Henry. 'The Rock Monuments of the County of Dublin'. *Journal of the Royal Society of Antiquaries of Ireland.* 1872. vol. 2 pp. 40-46.

Megalithic dolmens of which the best example is that in Glen Druid close to Barrington's Tower, are also found on the Dublin mountains and foothills at Glensouthwell, Kilternan, Larch Hill and Mount Venus. Other burial monuments on the Dublin mountains include gallery graves at Ballyedmonduff, Kilmashogue, and Loughanstown. For a good general account of the archaeology of the Dublin region see: Elrington Ball. F. 'History and Archaeology. The Environs of Dublin.' in: *Handbook to the City of Dublin and the Surrounding District.* eds. G.A.J. Cole and R. Lloyd Praeger. University Press. Dublin 1908. pp. 223-239. For a glossary see: *Irish Antiquities. General Guide.* The Stationary Office. Dublin, n.d.

37. Beckett has stated his own religious outlook quite clearly: 'I have no religious feeling. Once I had a religious emotion. It was at my first Communion. No more. My mother was deeply religious. So was my brother. He knelt down at his bed as long as he could kneel. My father had none. The family was Protestant, but for me it was only irksome and I let it go. My brother and mother got no value from their religion when they died. At the moment of crisis it had no more depth than an old school-tie. Irish Catholicism is not attractive, but it is deeper.

When you pass a church on an Irish bus, all the hands flurry in the sign of the cross. One day the dogs of Ireland will do that too and perhaps also the pigs.' (Driver, T.F. 'Beckett by the Madelaine.' *Columbia University Forum.* Summer 1961, vol. 4, no. 3, pp. 21-5).

38. For a history of the church and parish see: Simms. *Tullow's Story.* For a drawing of the 're-construction of Carrickmines Church, Co. Dublin', see: *The Irish Builder.* Supplement, July 16, 1904. facing p. 444).

39. O'Reilly, 'The Christian sepulchral leacs.'

40. O'Reilly, 'The Christian sepulchral leacs.' The church bearing the name St. Brigid was reputedly founded by the saint, a fact that is given further credence by the carving of a female figure with a crozier on the Latin cross close to the graveyard (St. Brigid held the unique distinction among women of having been consecrated). Other ecclesiastical links with the diocese of Kildare lend support to the association with St. Brigid.(Turner, *If you seek monuments,* 50) A claim, however, has also been made for a later saint commemorated in the Martyrology of Donegal as 'Brigit, daughter of Leinin' who resided at Killiney in the latter-half of the sixth century.

41. Turner, *If you seek monuments.* 50.

42. O'Reilly. 'The Christian sepulchral leacs.'

43. I first located Foley's Folly as an old farm house built in the late nineteenth century by one named Taylor on the Two Rock mountain, with a sweeping view of Dublin Bay, and known as 'Taylor's Folly'. However, Beckett, redirected me to Barrington's Tower, a tower built by John Barrington in 1818. I am grateful to Professor S. Doyle, the present owner of Barrington's Tower, for permission to visit the tower, now incorporated as part of the main house, and for permission to publish the photograph of the Tower, as it was in Beckett's youth. In the first manuscript of *That Time* (Reading University Library, MS No. 1477/1) the name 'Barrington's Tower', though erased, is clearly visible; this later became 'Maguire's' and finally 'Foley's Folly'. I am indebted to Professor James Knowlson for this information.

44. Shepherd, W.E. *The Dublin and South Eastern Railway.* David and Charles. London and Vancouver. 1974. pp 171-184. See also: Baker. M.H.C. *Irish Railways since 1916.* Ian Allen. London. 1972. and Doyle, Oliver, and Hirsch, Stephen. *Railways in Ireland 1834-1984.* Signal Press. Dublin 1983.

45. Craig, Maurice. *Dublin 1660-1860.* The Cresset Press London. 1952. pp. 298-302.

46. The station master was Thomas Farrell whose son Reggie kindly provided me with the photograph of his father, and an award certificate of which his father received many. Thomas Farrell was the third member of the family to hold the position of station-master at Foxrock. His grandfather had been station-master when the station was opened in the 1850's, and his father had been station-master before him. Thomas Farrell was appointed station-master in 1928. Among the members of his staff were Mr. Doyle, the foreman, Jim McEvoy, the signal man known as 'Himself', who cared for the station shrubbery and was often seen shining the levers in his cabin, Jack Doyle, another signal man, and two boy-porters, Michael Egan, and a younger brother of Jack Doyle. David Davison remembers a regular passenger on the line boasting proudly that the station masters of Foxrock 'cleaned the rail tracks with emery paper.' Another passenger, Gladys McConnell, recalls that delays were inevitable in spring time when the passengers and staff alighted *en-masse* to enjoy the spectacle of the hares jumping on the racecourse.

47. *Watt*, p. 229.

48. Beckett probably named the station Boghill because of the proximity of a bogfield known locally as 'the bog' lying between the chemist's shop and Hainault Road. I am indebted to Mrs. Brazil for this information. There is a hamlet in north County Dublin named Ballyboghill, close to The Naul, and to the site of one of the most famous nunneries of the English Pale, *Grace Dieu*, which was dismantled to provide materials for the building of Turvey House. (Killanin and Duignan, *Shell Guide.* p. 80.)

49. *All That Fall, Collected Shorter Plays,* p. 12.

50. *All That Fall, Collected Shorter Plays,* p. 12.

51. *Watt*, pp. 235-235.

52. 'Coming from the Country. No. 5. Harcourt Street Railway Station.' *Evening Telegraph.* Fri. June 13, 1924.

53. Mrs. Brazil has identified 'Cack-faced Miller' as Ivan Miller a member of the family of Miller & Co. Wine merchants in Thomas Street, regarded in his youth, she recalls, as one of the 'bucks who was up to all sorts of pranks'.

54. Beckett may have had the respected French Catholic paper, *La Croix,* in mind when he created Mr. Spiro's periodical *Crux.*

55. 'Coming from the Country', 1924. Mrs. Brazil remembers the newspaper stall being the focal point of Harcourt Street Station. From here papers were delivered to the first-class carriages.

56. 'Coming from the Country,' 1924.

57. 'Coming from the Country,' 1924.

58. 'Coming from the Country,' 1924.

59. The name Leopardstown derives from Baile-na-Lobhar, or Leperstown, so named from the founding of a leper colony in the region, in the fourteenth century. (Ring, Geoff. 'Irish Racecourses. No. 2'. *Irish Field.* March 22. 1952). The racecourse was founded in 1888 on lands owned by the monks of the Order of St. Bernard, and its colourful history has been outlined in a series of articles by Victor Zorian, in the *Sunday Chronicle,* June 1955.

60. Lake, Carlton. *No Symbols where none intended. A Catalogue of Books, Manuscripts, and Other Material Relating to Samuel Beckett in the Collections of the Humanities Research Center.* The University of Texas at Austin, 1984. p. 93.

61. *All That Fall. Collected Shorter Plays,* p. 12.

62. Mrs. Brazil has identified Mr. Slocum as Mr. Frederick Clarke, who lived in Leopardstown. Fred Clarke, by profession a veterinary surgeon, was an accomplished amateur rider with some 100 wins to his credit and he also trained horses for many years at Leopardstown racecourse, where Vincent O'Brien began his successful training career as assistant to Fred Clarke. I am indebted to Mr. Clarke's widow Mrs. Carmel Clarke for placing press cuttings and photographs at my disposal.

63. The full programme, the music played by the Band of the 1st Battalion Rifle Brigade, biographical essays on each of the pilots and a chronology of flying achievements since the first flight in 1890 is to be found in: 'Aero Club of Ireland. Inaugural Aviation Meeting at Leopardstown. August 29th and 30th 1910.' *Official Programme.* ed. J.C. Percy. 80 pp. illustrated. (In the Civic Museum, South William Street, Dublin.)

64. *The Irish Times.* 30 August 1910. p. 7. The Aviation meeting at Leopardstown attracted thousands of people to the area and the event was given extensive coverage in the newspapers; *The Irish Times* carried reports for three days: Mon. August 29. 1910. p. 7; Tues. August 30. 1910. pp. 7. 9; Wed. August 31. 1910. p. 4. A comprehensive account of the meeting 'Those magnificent men in their Flying Machines', was delivered by Liam Clare to the Foxrock Local History Club, on 22nd September 1981, and is published in a pamphlet available in the National Library of Ireland (Call no. IR 94133 P9). A shorter account may be found in the *Irish Aviator,* 1984, No. 7. pp. 8-11. There is no mention in the reports of a 'loop-the-loop', but a child's imagination must not be faulted for embellishing a little on what must have been a spectacular occasion: 'There was one most alluring effect during Drexel's first flight. As he dipped his tail towards Ballycoras in his concluding circuit a rainbow shot its lovely colours through the skies. Rainbows do not daunt flying men, so through the glorious spectrum he sped and alighted like a bird on the green sward whence he had started'. (*The Irish Times.* August 30. 1910. p. 7) See also: Byrne, Liam. *History of Aviation in Ireland.* Blackwater. Dublin 1980. p. 35.

The racecourse continued to attract visitors from the sky. In 1912 an aeronautic race from Leopardstown to Belfast was abandoned due to the weather. *(Irish Life.* September 6, 1912). In 1943 a British Beaufighter crashed on the course, and the crew of three who were unhurt were interred at the Curragh military prison from which they later escaped. In 1944 an American Dakota crash-landed safely on the course, and in 1955 the first helicopter to grace the Irish skies gave a display to race-goers at Leopardstown.

65. *Freeman's Journal,* August 29th, 1910.

66. Beckett's fascination with the relative distance of an object from the observer was shared by Marcel Proust. Albertine's observation on an aeroplane - 'high up in the sky, so high' - provokes Proust to deliberate on the reality of the distance of an object from an observer: 'Perhaps at a time when distances by land had not yet been habitually shortened by speed as they are to-day, the whistle of a passing train a mile off was endowed with the beauty which now and for some time to come will stir our emotions as the hum of an aeroplane five thousand feet up, with the thought that the distances traversed in this vertical journey are the same as those on the ground, and that in this other direction, where the measurements appeared to us different because it had seemed impossible to make the attempt, an aeroplane at five thousand feet is no further away than a tram a mile off, is indeed nearer, the identical trajectory occurring in a purer medium, with no separation of the traveller from his starting point, just as on the sea or across the plains, in calm weather, the wake of a ship that is already far away on the breath of a single zephyr will furrow the ocean of water or of grain'. (Proust, Marcel. *Remembrance of Things Past.* Vol. X. *The Captive.* Part Two, Trans. C.K. Scott Moncrieff. Chatto and Windus. London 1972. pp. 273-4.)

67. Tyler was a market-gardener who lived on a small farm opposite Kerrymount Avenue on Cornelscourt Hill Road. Samuel Beckett has told me how he used to go to Tyler's market garden to purchase a few peach apples before retreating to Barrington's Tower with his book. Tyler had something wrong with his eyes, Beckett remembers, though he cannot recall for sure if he had only one eye. Miss Rosemary Darley remembers that he had 'bulging eyes'. Tyler the market-gardener should not be confused with Tyler, the retired bill-broker in *All That Fall,* whom he resembles in name only.

The 'hill of extraordinary steepness' was Cornelscourt Hill Road on which Beckett was walking with his mother, returning from Connolly's in Cornelscourt. (Personal communication from Samuel Beckett.)

68. The name Croker is found, not only in *More Pricks than Kicks, Company,* and *Not I,* but there is a 'Mrs. Aphasia Budd-Croker, button designer in residence, Commercial Road East,' as well as 'the late Mrs. Darcy-Croker' in *Theatre II, Collected Shorter Plays,* p. 80, and the name Croak occurs in *Words and Music, Collected Shorter Plays,* p. 127.

69. Richard Croker was born in Clonakilty in Co. Cork in 1841, whence his parents fled the ravages of the Great Famine arriving penniless in New York in 1848. Croker worked his way up to become the 'Boss' of Tammany Hall, an organisation started by M'Loughlin, an engineer who was a boss or superintendent in the Navy Yard in Brooklyn. The appellation was passed on to his successors. 'Boss' Croker, who took a lucrative interest in horse racing, became a millionaire during his term of office. When the anti-racing party in New York State made life difficult for the racing fraternity, he left America for England to continue horse-training. However, the Jockey Club had reservations about some of his followers and he was refused permission to train on Newmarket Heath. Croker then came to Ireland where he bought *Glencairn.* The stables and gallops adjoining the mansion were ideal for training his horses. Here he lived quietly where a contemporary visitor found him to be 'not fond of society, and entertains but little, but he is hospitality itself to his visitors of all degree. He is fond of music, he is fond of art, and when he speaks of either, discloses a critical judgement ... Mr. Croker smokes, thinks, and acts. He is almost an abstainer.' (MacS, J.G. 'A Leader of Men and a Leader in sport. Mr. Richard Croker. A Sketch.' *Ireland.* June 1907. 466-9). This estimate of Mr. Croker's aestheticism is at variance with the popular account of the furnishing of his library for which he is said to have ordered two thousand copies of Hall and Knight's *Algebra* to achieve a uniform effect of deep maroon. In Ireland the racing establishment treated him no better than in England, and though he owned more horses than anyone in the country, ran more and won more races, he was refused admittance to the Turf Club. As one racing authority put it: 'But as the Club is constituted at present, Mr. Croker had as much chance of being translated up to heaven alive as he had of securing selection to the Club'. Undeterred by all this he raced very successfully, 'in the most lordly fashion, and was soon head of the winning owners in Ireland. He not only refused to sell his own winners, but he insisted on buying the best horses that ran against his.' (MacCabe, F.F. 'A Memorable Year in Irish Racing.' in Richardson, Charles. *Racing at Homme and Abroad.* The London and Counties Press Association Ltd London. 1927.

Croker's family can be traced back to Sir John Croker of Lineham, Devon, Cup and Standard Bearer to King Edward IV. in the fifteenth century. (Burke's Irish Family Records. London. Burke's Peerage Ltd. 1976. p. 296). For a biography of Richard Croker see: Lewis A.M. *Boss Croker of New York City and Glencairn.* New York, 1901 and for an entry on *Glencairn* see: Cosgrave, E. McDowel. *Dublin and County Dublin.* London. 1908.

I am grateful to Mr. Patrick Cronin, Mr. Liam Clare and Mr. Richard Mooney of the National Library of Ireland for directing me to the above sources.

70. *Glencairn* belonged to Judge Murphy who sold it to Boss Croker in 1904. It was 'extensively remodeled by him, so that it became a mixture of Baronial and American Colonial, with a veranda of granite columns running round it and an Irish battlement tower.' Bence Jones, M.

Burke's Guide to Country Houses. Vol. 1. Ireland. Burke's Peerage Ltd. London, 1978 p.136. For an account of the quest for a suitable residence for the British Ambassador see: McKittrick, David. 'Desperate search ended in 'nightmarish' house.' *Irish Times.* Jan 4, 1984.

71.   Williams, Hyland. *The Irish Derby.* J.A. Allen & Co. London and New York. 1980. p. 117-123. See also: Wellcome, John. *Irish Horseracing. An Illustrated History.* Gill and MacMillan. London 1982. pp. 119-125.

72.   McCabe. 'A Memorable Year.' Mrs. Walsh, the mother of Mrs. Brazil, who was postmistress in Foxrock, transmitted the good news to *Glencairn* by morse code.

73.   I am grateful to Hugh O'Brien for this information.

74.   It is of interest to note Beckett's confusion over Croker's horses. In *More Pricks than Kicks,* he mistakes *Pretty Polly* for Croker's Derby-winning Orby, but according to Fletcher, Beckett was of the opinion that Croker's horse was named Joss. (Fletcher Beryl S, and Fletcher John, *A Student's Guide to the Plays of Samuel Beckett.* Faber and Faber. London and Boston. 2nd ed. 1985. p. 217), which brings us back to the 'large coloured print of the horse Joss, standing in profile in a field,' which hung in the waiting room of Foxrock Station. If, as seems likely, Beckett mistakenly named Croker's horse Joss, it might not be unreasonable to assume that a cheaply reproduced colour print of the Derby hero once hung in the Foxrock waiting-room.

75.   Williams. *The Irish Derby.* p. 119.

76.   I visited Kilgobbin cemetery, a peaceful graveyard, on three occasions, but, after a meticulous search, I was unable to locate the Boss's new resting place. On my last visit, an aged man smoking a pipe came up to me as I was cleaning the earth from yet another grave slab and asked for whom I searched. He led me to another part of the cemetery and pointing to a finely sculpted granite cross, said – 'You'se will find the Boss on top of his motte, as he would have liked, over there.' The ornately carved cross marks the burial place of Stella Bowman of Glencairn (1868-1914). On the ground at the base of the cross a granite slab overgrown almost entirely with grass reads: 'Richard Webster Croker. Born Nov 23rd 1841, At Clonakilty County Cork Ireland. Died at Glencairn April 29th 1922. R.I.P.' It is recorded that the Boss's shade resented being moved from its chosen resting place in *Glencairn,* and there have been frequent sightings of 'his burly, bearded, frock-coated figure floating through the house and grounds'. Such spiritual peregrinations were not without prediction. When the Boss was in his prime in New York a rumour quickly went the rounds one day that he had died, and a friend, amazed at finding him alive and well, eating crab in a fashionable restaurant, informed him that his demise had just been widely reported - 'Is that so?' said the 'Boss', ordering the next dish from the waiter 'And where did they say I had gone to?' (MacS. J.G. 'A Leader of Men'.)

77.   *Not I, Collected Shorter Plays,* p. 216.

78.   For an analysis of Mouth's tale see: Kelly, Katherine. 'The Orphic Mouth in 'Not I'. *Journal of Beckett Studies.* John Calder. London. Autumn 1980. no. 6. pp. 73-80.

79.   I am grateful to Sir Alan Goodison, British Ambassador to Ireland and to his wife, and members of the staff at *Glencairn* for permitting me to visit the house and grounds on more than one occasion.

80.   It seems likely that *Glencairn* may have been an influence in the creation of Mr. Knott's establishment, but Beckett has corrected my mistaken theory that *Glencairn* was in fact Mr. Knott's house, when he had *Cooldrinagh* in mind. Rubin Rabinovitz maintains that Beckett's desire to 'universalise the action' purposely makes identification of Knott's house difficult. ('The Deterioration of Outside Reality in Samuel Beckett's Fiction', in *Yeats, Joyce and Beckett. New Light on Three Modern Irish Writers.* eds. Kathleen McGrory and John Unterecker. Bucknell University Press, Lewisburg; Associated University Presses, London. 1976. p. 168).

81.   For a detailed analysis of this poem see: Harvey, *Poet and Critic.* pp. 92-93.

CHAPTER 2: THE DUBLIN MOUNTAINS

1.   D'Alton, John. *The History of County Dublin.* Hodges and Smith, Dublin. 1838. Reprinted Tower Books, Cork. 1976. For a general history of Dublin city and county, see pp. 1-26.

2.   Turner, Kathleen. *If you seek monuments. A guide to the antiquities of the Barony of Rathdown.* Rathmichael Historical Society. 3.

3.   Personal communication to the author from S. Beckett.

4.   Beckett wrote to me on 16.5.'85 - 'The old haunts were never more present. With closed eyes I walk those back roads.'

5.   Joyce, Weston St. John. *The Neighbourhood of Dublin. Its Topography, Antiquities and Historical Associations.* M.H. Gill and Son Ltd. Dublin and Waterford. 1912. pp. 128-142.

6.   Later in *Murphy* (p. 191) the sky again reminds Celia of Ireland.

7.   '...but the clouds...' from 'The Tower'. *Collected Poems of W.B. Yeats.* Macmillan & Co. London. 1963. pp. 218-225. Considered by Beckett to be one of W.B. Yeats's greatest lines (Personal communication.)

8.   *Malone Dies,* p. 118.

9.   *More Pricks than Kicks,* pp. 98-99.

10.   References to the burning mountain gorse are also to be found in: *Malone Dies,* p. 119; *Enueg I, Collected Poems,* p. 11.

11.   *Malone Dies,* p. 117.

12.   Mercier has pointed out that some of the geographical details present in the original French of *Mercier and Camier* are altered or are omitted in the translation. An example is the Old Military Road, built by the British across the Dublin and Wicklow mountains to facilitate the army

in combating the rebels who retreated to the lonely mountain peaks. (Mercier, Vivian. *Beckett/Beckett*. Oxford University Press. Oxford. New York. Toronto. Melbourne. 1977. p. 42.)

13. The derivation of the name 'Prince Williams Seat' is obscure, but it may be related to the nearby plantation of pines and larches close to which a monument was erected by the Marquess of Downshire to commemorate the plantation of 500 Irish acres in 1831 'for a future supply of useful timber for the Estate and improvement of the County and the Benefit of the Labouring Classes.' The plantation was called 'the Coronation Plantation, in honour of his Most Gracious Majesty, King William IV.' (Joyce. *Neighbourhood of Dublin*. pp. 379-380). Unfortunately T.P. Le Fanu does not elaborate on the derivation of the name in his paper 'The Royal Forest of Glencree'. (*The Journal of the Royal Society of Antiquaries of Ireland*. 1893. vol 3. 5th. Series. pp. 268-280.)

14. The romantic poet, George Darley (1795-1846), whose verse was held in high regard by Beckett's close friend, Con Leventhal (Leventhal, A.J. *George Darley (1795-1846). A Memorial Discourse.* Dublin University Press Ltd. 1950), was of the opinion that a single fern on the Three Rock Mountain was worth a whole English forest:
   ... the loved shapes that on his fancy grow -
   Mountains high-capt with floating clouds or snow,
   The cottage glistening through its woodbine screen
   He finds it gone but never will forego.
   Retrospection (George Darley)

15. Joyce. *Neighbourhood of Dublin*. pp. 134-135. 'These burial mounds of piled stones are not unusual in districts where stone is found in quantity; they are the stone-district parallels of the earthen tumuli. Like them they are of different sizes but are usually circular in plan and often of considerable height. Some certainly contain passages and chambers formed of large stones; others are are no more than piles of stone covering a cremation or are even cenotaphs. There are mounds which appear to be tumuli but may actually be cairns covered with grass. A kerb of large stones encircling the cairn, or more or less visible within its circumference, is sometimes to be observed. Its stones may be set upright or laid lengthways.' (*Irish Antiquities. General Guide.* The Stationary Office. Dublin. n.d. p. 12.)

16. The word Tibradden may derive from 'Tigi Bretan', the place of the Briton or Welshmen. (Turner. *If you seek moments.* 25), though Joyce considers the name to derive from the name of a chieftain - Bradden - buried on its summit. According to Joyce a rude carving of a cross and a human face once stood beside the ancient cairn on Tibradden. When the cairn was opened towards the end of the nineteenth century an urn was found in it, and is preserved in the National Museum. (Joyce. *Neighbourhood of Dublin*. p 135). See also: Moriarty, Christopher. 'Tibradden Mountain.' *The Irish Times*, 31 March 1984.

17. Harvey, Lawrence. *Samuel Beckett, Poet and Critic.* Princeton University Press. New Jersey. 1970. p. 310.

18. Craig, Maurice. *Dublin 1660-1860.* The Cresset Press. London. 1952. pp. 154-155. The stones and other relics of a large cairn that once stood on the site of the Hell Fire Club were used for the erection of this structure, which, whatever use it may have been put to, was doomed because of the sacrilegious conduct of the builder. Indeed, the roof was blown off in a mighty storm by the agency of the devil, it was popularly believed. However, with its roof firmly replaced the Hell Fire Ruin has withstood the ravages of both time and the devil. (Joyce. *Neighbourhood of Dublin,* pp. 123-124).

19. Joyce. *Neighbourhood of Dublin*. p. 373-376.

20. Joyce. *Neighbourhood of Dublin*. p. 377-378.

21. There is an interesting reference to turf being stolen off the bog in *Dream of Fair to Middling Women* (p. 46) 'His mother had bought from two little boys who stole turf off the bog, whose parents incited them to steal turf off the bog. On two counts, subsequently, by the Civic Guards, those plush bosthoons, they were indicted: breach of turbary and cruelty to the ass. They hawked it round from door to door in an ass and cart and his Mother wrote to say she had bought half a load.' There are two more oblique references to turf in *Murphy*, (p. 91, and p. 135).

22. For a vivid, if somewhat partisan account of the period see: O'Malley, Ernie. *The Singing Flame.* Anvil Books Ltd. Dublin. 1978.

23. Noel Lemass was the brother of a future Taoiseach (Prime Minister) of Ireland, Sean Lemass. Macardle, Dorothy. *The Irish Republic. A documented chronicle of the Anglo-Irish conflict and the partitioning of Ireland, with a detailed account of the period 1916-1923.* Corgi Books. London, 1968. p. 786.

24. The Lemass memorial is not the first political monument to receive mention in Beckett's work: 'In the centre, roughly, towered huge a shining copper beech, planted several centuries earlier, according to the sign rudely nailed to the bole, by a Field Marshal of France peacefully named Saint-Ruth. Hardly had he done so, in the words of the inscription, when he was struck dead by a cannon-ball, faithful to the last to the same hopeless cause, on a battle-field having little in common, from the point of view of landscape, with those on which he had won his spurs, first as brigadier, then as lieutenant, if that is the order in which spurs are won, on the battlefield.' (*Mercier and Camier,* p. 10). Field Marshall Saint-Ruth was the Marquis de St. Ruth, Commander of the French forces sent by Louis XIV to support Sarsfield. St. Ruth died at the Battle of Aughrim Hill, near Ballinasloe on July 12th 1691. Beckett's monument to St. Ruth must be fictional as there is certainly no such memorial in Dublin. Patrick Sarsfield, whom the hapless St. Ruth came to assist, was the general of the Irish forces; he negotiated the Treaty of Limerick with the Williamite forces in 1691: 'Inspired by the example of the great Sarsfield he had risked his life without success in defence of a territory which in itself must have left him cold and considered as a symbol cannot have greatly heated him.' (*Mercier and Camier,* p. 13). For details of the Battle of Aughrim Hill see: Beckett, J.C. *The Making of Modern Ireland 1603-1923.* Faber and Faber. London. 1971. pp. 146-149. For a brief biographical note on Patrick Sarsfield see: Boylan, Henry. *A Dictionary of Irish Biography.* Gill and MacMillan. Dublin. 1978. pp. 320-321.

25. O'Hegarty, P.S. With a chapter by Daniel Corkery. *A Short Memoir of Terence MacSwiney.* The Talbot Press Ltd. Dublin and T. Fisher Unwin Ltd. London. 1922.

26. O'Hegarty. *Terence MacSwiney.* p. 83.

27. Beckett's political comments, though few, are generally of a satirical nature. In *Dream of Fair to Middling Women* (p. 141) he supports the ejection of the Garrison forces from the headquarters of British rule, Dublin Castle, but his enthusiasm for this event is somewhat weakened by this assessment of the alternative power: 'The point it seems almost worth our while trying to make is not that the passing of the Castle as it was in the days of the Garrison is to be depreciated. Not at all. We hope we know our place better than that. We uncover our ancient Irish wedgehead in deference to that happy ejection. Nor are we in the least prone to suggest that the kennel is a less utopian community than the pen or coop or shoal or convent or any other form of national or stylicised pullulation.'

At Portora Royal School Beckett would have been introduced to both Unionist and Nationalist political aspirations. The school's Roll of Honour (in the charge of W.N. Tetley, Esq.) recorded the pupils of the school who gave their lives in the First World War, (*Portora*. 1918. XIII. no. 1. pp. 18-26). The school magazine also recorded the deaths of those closer to home: 'We deeply deplore the tragic death of another old Portora boy, Captain A.C. Lendrum, M.C., who, while discharging his duty as R.M. in the Co. Clare was foully murdered by Sinn Féin assassins.' (*Portora*. 1920. XV. no. 1. p. 2).

28. Lake, Carlton. *No Symbols where none intended. A Catalogue of Books, Manuscripts, and Other Material Relating to Samuel Beckett in the Collections of the Humanities Research Center.* The University of Texas at Austin. 1984. p. 36.

29. Leventhal, A.J. 'The Beckett Hero' in: *Samuel Beckett. A Collection of Critical Essays.* ed. Martin Esslin. Prentice Hall. New Jersey. 1965. p. 49.

30. Leventhal. 'The Beckett Hero'. p. 49. The same point is made by: Reid, Alec. *All I can manage, more than I could: An approach to the plays of Samuel Beckett.* The Dolmen Press. Dublin. 1968. p. 31.

31. Similarities between Mercier and Camier and Vladimir and Estragon are discussed in: Cohn, Ruby. *Back to Beckett.* Princeton University Press. New Jersey. 1973. p. 66; Fletcher, John. *The Novels of Samuel Beckett.* Chatto and Windus. London. 1964. pp. 113-118. For a discussion on the influence of Beckett's wartime experiences, and a case for the setting of *Godot* in Roussillon see: Gontarski, S.E. *The Intent of Undoing in Samuel Beckett's Dramatic Texts.* Indiana University Press. 1985. pp. 35-36. The case for a Franco-Irish setting is made by Mercier, *Beckett/Beckett.* p. 53.

32. Synge, John M. *In Wicklow, West Kerry, and Connemara.* With drawings by Jack B. Yeats. Maunsel and Co. Ltd., Dublin. 1911. pp. 58-9. Beckett holds Synge's writings in high esteem, and he is attracted by Synge's sensitive personality; see: Knowlson, James. 'Beckett and John Millington Synge' in: Knowlson, James, and Pilling, John. *Frescoes of the Skull.* Grove Press. New York. 1980. pp. 259-274.

33. The Wicklow mountains receive deprecatory comment elsewhere in *More Pricks than Kicks.* (p. 26).

34. The city and plains are of no interest to the lovers in 'Love and Lethe', *More Pricks than Kicks.* (p. 100).

35. This reference is from *Serena II, Collected Poems,* p. 24. Other references to the piers may be found in: *Mercier and Camier,* pp. 97-98 - 'tiny arms in the glassy sea outflung'; in *Mercier and Camier,* p. 98 - 'Even the piers of the harbour can be distinguished on very clear days'; in *Watt,* pp. 45-46, the wildness of the 'sea breaking over the pier' is part of 'the whole bloody business' of life's cycle; in *More Pricks than Kicks;* p. 100 - 'the long arms of the harbour like an entreaty in the blue sea.'

CHAPTER 3: THE SEA

1. For an account of the coastal resorts on the southern aspects of Dublin Bay see: D'Alton, John. *The History of County Dublin:* Hodges and Smith. Dublin 1838. Reprinted by Tower Books, Cork 1976. pp. 425-457, and Ball, Francis Elrington. *A History of the County Dublin: The people, parishes and antiquities from the earliest time to the close of the eighteenth century.* Part I. Alex Thom. Dublin 1902. pp. 1-81.

2. For a brief history of *The Bailey* see: Ryan, John. *Remembering How We Stood. Bohemian Dublin in the Mid-Century.* Gill and Macmillan. Dublin. 1975. pp. 20-31, and O'Connor, Ulick, *The Story of a Famous Tavern. The Bailey Dublin.* The Three Candles. Dublin. 1968.

3. *More Pricks than Kicks,* p. 96.

4. A Morgan 8 h.p. three-wheeler could be purchased new in 1926 for £95 for the standard model, £115 for the de-luxe, £130 for the Aero, and £116 for the Family model, with Tax at £4. (Advertisement. *The Irish Cyclist and Motor Cyclist,* June 23. 1926.)

5. Belacqua was not the only Dubliner to encounter difficulty in crossing the Ringsend Basin. This bridge had been a source of contention to Dubliners ever since the old draw-bridge, the *Brunswick Bascule,* as it was known, was opened in 1796 with full nautical pomp. ('The Brunswick Bascule. Formerly known as the Ringsend Draw Bridge'. *The Irish Builder.* Nov. 15. 1879. p. 350.) When this was swept away in the flood of 1802, it was replaced by a structure even more difficult to traverse: 'To the poor carmen of Irishtown and Sandymount it is a source of continual outlay, in repairing their wheels and to the numerous passengers, who travel on their cars a constant cause of apprehension in consequence of the horses being obliged to be driven on the metals of the bridge and thereby endangering their falling.' (Newspaper cutting dated, 14 December 1864, in The Walsh Manuscripts. *Pearse Street.* National Library of Ireland). It was this structure that halted Belacqua, who would, no doubt, be relieved to learn that it has since been replaced by a functional, if architecturally vacuous, structure named, *McMahon Bridge,* which was erected in 1962.

6. The coastal townships of Irishtown and Ringsend have an interesting and ancient history. Ball, Francis Elrington. *An Historical Sketch of the Pembroke Township.* Alex Thom & Co. Dublin. 1907. pp. 38-45.

7. Kevin O'Higgins, the first Minister for Justice, introduced a law requiring publicans to shut down in the middle of the day from 2.30 p.m. to 3.30 p.m. This quickly became known as 'The Holy Hour', a reference to a popular Dublin religious devotion. O'Connor. *The Bailey,* p. 27.

8. For an analysis of this poem see: Harvey, Lawrence. *Samuel Beckett. Poet and Critic.* Princeton University Press. New Jersey. 1970. pp. 151-153; Fletcher, John. 'The Private Pain and the Whey of Words: A Survey of Beckett's Verse.' in: *Samuel Beckett. A Collection of Critical Essays.* ed. Martin Esslin. Prentice Hall. New Jersey. 1965. pp. 23-32.

9. A swamp is mentioned also in *Molloy,* pp. 75-76 and in *Dream of Fair to Middling Women* there are references to 'Marshy Dublin', (p. 99), and to Dublin's 'yellow marsh fever,' (p. 150).

10. 'Hide yourself in the Rock' in addition to its topographical reference to Blackrock, may also be a biblical reference to Peter the Rock of

the Church of Christ. (James Knowlson, personal communication). For a history of Blackrock see: MacCoil, Liam. *The Book of Blackrock.* Carraig Books Ltd., Blackrock. 2nd Ed. 1981.

11. *Serena II, Collected Poems,* p. 24. The steeples of Dun Laoghaire are also referred to in *More Pricks than Kicks,* p. 28.

12. For an account of the construction of the granite piers that enclose Dun Laoghaire harbour see: Pearson, Peter. *Dun Laoghaire. Kingstown.* O'Brien Press. Dublin. 1981. pp. 13-39, and *A Pictorial and Descriptive Guide to Dublin and its Environs.* Ward, Lock and Co. Ltd. London. 1936-37. pp. 136-137, from which the following details have been taken. The harbour with its two massive granite piers guards an entrance 850 feet wide, encompassing an area of 250 acres of water, varying in depth from 15 to 27 feet. The East Pier is 3,500 feet and the West Pier 4,950 feet in length. The construction of the harbour began in 1817, the first stone being laid by the Earl of Whitworth, then Lord Lieutenant of Ireland. The work was finally completed 42 years later in 1859 at a cost of a million pounds. Four years after its construction King George IV embarked for England from the port of Dunleary, and the town's name was changed to Kingstown. Later the original name was changed to the Gaelic form, Dun Laoghaire.

13. The Carlyle pier was a jetty built as a berth for the mailboat. Other references to the Carlyle pier occur in *Dream of Fair to Middling Women,* pages 4, 5, 6 and 10.

14. The mail-boats of the London, Midland and Scottish Railways, twin-screw steamers powered by 9,000 horse power engines capable of speeds of 24 knots, could cross the 64 miles route from Dun Laoghaire to Holyhead in 2½ hours, the entire journey from London being accomplished in under ten hours at a cost in 1936 of 128s, Ist Class, or 76s. 6d. 3rd Class. *A Pictorial and Descriptive Guide* pp. 9-11. Not only did the service carry the Irish Mail, it also brought thousands of emigrants to England.

15. The town of Dun Laoghaire was a delightful example of Victorian architecture, in which there was harmony in the scale and texture of the buildings and many ornaments that gave it its unique character. Marine activities endowed Dun Laoghaire with its personality; apart from the comings and goings of the mail-boat, there were no less than three gracious yacht clubs as well as the sea-baths. Sadly much of its architectural integrity has been upset by modern development, though it still retains considerable charm. Belacqua had a selection of stanchions to choose from. On the East Pier giant granite stanchions make convenient seats, and there are smaller granite ones linked by chains on the road overlooking the Carlyle pier, but it seems that Belacqua settled for one of the wooden stanchions on the jetty itself.

16. Lake, Carlton. *No Symbols where none intended. A Catalogue of Books, Manuscripts, and Other Material Relating to Samuel Beckett in the Collections of the Humanities Research Center.* The University of Texas at Austin. 1984. pp. 49-50. For a discussion of the significance of this event see also: Knowlson, James, and Pilling, John. *Frescoes of the Skull. The Later Prose and Drama of Samuel Beckett.* Grove Press. New York. 1979. p. 88.

17. In discussions for the preparation of the film documentary, *Samuel Beckett. Silence to Silence,* by Radio Telefis Eireann, Beckett confided to Sean O'Mórdha 'a little apologetically' that what occurred on the pier that fateful night was 'a revelation.'

18. *Krapp's Last Tape, Collected Shorter Plays,* p. 60.

19. Lake, *No Symbols.* pp. 49-50.

20. Pearson. *Dun Laoghaire.* pp. 37-39. p. 155. The anemometer was designed by Professor Robinson of Trinity College, Dublin, and when built in 1852 was one of the first in the world. The lighthouse at the sea-end of the East Pier 'flings its brilliant beam of light across the bay' every thirty seconds. In clear weather it is visible at sea for a distance of 25 miles. Nearly opposite on the extreme promontory of Howth Head is the Baily Lighthouse, and far out at sea the Kish Lightship, 'in the vicinity of which the mail-boat *Leinster* was sunk by a German submarine in 1917 with an appalling loss of life.' (*A Pictorial and Descriptive Guide* p. 136.)

21. It is interesting to compare the two versions of this turning-point in Beckett's life: 'Spiritually a year of profound gloom and indigence until that memorable night in March, at the end of the jetty, in the howling wind, never to be forgotten, when suddenly I saw the whole thing. The vision at last. This I fancy is what I have chiefly to record this evening, against the day when my work will be done and perhaps no place left in my memory, warm or cold, for the miracle that ... (*hesitates* ...) for the fire that set it alight. What I suddenly saw then was this, that the belief I had been going on all my life, namely - (KRAPP *switches off impatiently, winds tape forward, switches on again*) - great granite rocks the foam flying up in the light of the lighthouse and the wind-guage spinning like a propeller, clear to me at last that the dark I have always struggled to keep under is in reality my most - (KRAPP *curses, switches off, winds tape forward, switches on again*) - unshatterable association until my dissolution of storm and night with the light of the understanding and the fire.' (*Krapp's Last Tape, Collected Shorter Plays,* p. 60.)

22. Beckett does not refer often to his writings, or the influences that motivate his work. However, there have been a few occasions when he has alluded, however fleetingly, to his work. The earliest reference by Beckett to his own writing is to the unpublished *Dream of Fair to Middling Women*: 'The powers of evocation of this Italianate Irishman were simply immense, and if his Dream of Fair to Middling Women, held up in the limae labor stage for the past ten or fifteen years, ever reaches the public, and Walter says it is bound to, we ought all to be sure to get it and have a look at it anyway.' (*More Pricks than Kicks,* p. 153). In fact, Beckett's *Dream of Fair to Middling Women* has not yet reached the public; the unpublished manuscript is in Dartmouth College. The reasons for this delay have been provided earlier by Beckett: 'Walter's book was a long time in coming out because he refused to regard it as anything more than a mere dump for whatever he could not get off his chest in the ordinary way.' (*More Pricks than Kicks,* p. 143). In the novel *Mercier and Camier* (p. 111), Beckett hints at future fame: 'I am not widely known, said Watt, true, but I shall be, one day. Not universally perhaps, my notoriety is not likely ever to penetrate to the denizens of Dublin's fair city, or of Cuq-Toulza.' In the same work (p. 111), Beckett refers to Murphy's fate, a reference as much to the sad failure of this work as to its central character: 'I knew a poor man named Murphy, said Mercier, who had a look of you, only less battered of course. But he died ten years ago, in rather mysterious circumstances. They never found the body, can you imagine.'

23. The first mention of the 'Forty Foot Hole' is in the unpublished play *Eleutheria.* (Pilling, John. "Review article: 'Company' by Samuel Beckett." *Journal of Beckett Studies.* John Calder. London. Spring 1982. no. 7. p. 127.)

24. Harvey, *Poet and Critic,* p. 298.

25. Wall, Mervyn. *Forty Foot Gentlemen Only.* Allen Figgis. Dublin. 1962. p. 30 The general bathers and those responsible for managing the Sandycove Bathers' Association, the organisation which provides and maintains the bathing facilities, have not always been of a literary mien as is evident from the unpunctuated notice 'Forty Foot Gentlemen Only', and a memorandum to members in 1880 which ran: 'At this meeting the *late* Mr. E.V. Ponsonby was appointed Honorary Secretary, *a post he still holds.*' (Wall. *Forty Foot Gentlemen.* p. 14.)

26. Joyce chose the granite turret of the Martello tower overlooking the Forty Foot for the opening of *Ulysses:*
'Stately, plump Buck Mulligan came from the stairhead, bearing a bowl of lather on which a mirror and a razor lay crossed. A yellow dressing-gown, ungirdled, was sustained gently behind him by the mild morning air. He held the bowl aloft and intoned:
- *Introibo ad altare Dei.*'
(Joyce, James. *Ulysses.* The Bodley Head. London. 1964. p. 1.)

27. For an account of Coliemore and Dalkey Island see: Gaskin, James J. *Varieties of Irish History from Ancient and Modern Sources and Original Documents.* W.B. Kelly. Dublin. 1869. pp. 349-350.

28. The name Dalkey means 'thorny island' from the Irish *dealig,* a thorn and *inish,* an island. It is first mentioned as *Declinise* in 1179. (Turner, Kathleen. *If you seek monuments. A guide to the antiquities of the Barony of Rathdown.* Rathmichael Historical Society. 1983. 27.)

29. Gaskin. *Varieties.* p. 55.

30. Murray, James. 'The Kingdom of Dalkey. A Sea Surrounded Park.' *Ireland.* August 1907. pp. 591-594. See also: D'Alton. *County Dublin.* pp. 444-447, and Ball, *History of the County of Dublin,* Part I. pp. 71-84.

31. Enoch, Victor J. *The Martello Towers of Ireland.* Eason & Son, Ltd. Dublin. 1974.

32. Wakeman, W.F. 'Primitive Churches in County Dublin'. *Journal of the Royal Society of Antiquaries of Ireland.* 1890-1891. 5th. Series. vol. 21. pp. 697-702.

33. Walsh, John E. *Rakes and Ruffians. The Underworld of Georgian Dublin.* Four Courts Press. Dublin. 1979. p. 111.

34. In *Cascando, (Collected Shorter Plays,* pp. 138-143,) there are similarities of landscape with *Malone Dies,* and again in *How It Is,* (p. 94-95) and *The End, (Collected Shorter Prose,* pp. 68-70); The receding landscape would appear to be that of Dublin Bay.

35. Gaskin. *Varieties.* p. 155.

36. *Molloy,* p. 45. and pp. 69-74. The pebbles on Killiney strand, carried from the northern regions with Ice Age glaciers, were put to good use in the eighteenth century as Dr. Rutty recorded: 'Our shores, particularly from Shanganagh to Bray, abound with pebbles of all colours and often beautifully variegated ... they bear the polish and serve to make the tops of snuff boxes, seals, heads of canes, sleeve-buttons and handles of knives. etc'. (Turner. *If you seek monuments* 1.)

37. *Molloy,* p. 26.

38. Somerville-Large, Peter. *Irish Eccentrics. A Selection.* Hamish Hamilton. London. 1975. p. 10. For a comparison of Murphy with Endymion, another of Dublin's famous self-named eccentrics see: Kennedy, Sighle. *Murphy's Bed. A Study of real sources and sur-real associations in Samuel Beckett's first novel.* Bucknell University Press. Lewisburg. 1971. pp. 226-228.

39. If we accept Beatrice Glenavy's identification of Ada in *Embers* as Cissie Beckett, then the location of this play is Raheny, close to Howth, where she lived by the sea. (Glenavy, Lady Beatrice, *Today we will only gossip.* Constable. London. 1964. pp. 178-179).
Seaside caves also feature in *Cascando, (Collected Shorter Plays,* p. 138); *Malone Dies,* p. 226; *The End, (Collected Shorter Prose,* p. 59); *Molloy,* p. 68.

40. The sea is the setting for death in *Malone Dies* , (p. 289); *The End, (Collected Shorter Prose,* pp. 68-70); *How It Is,* (pp. 94-85); *Cascando, (Collected Shorter Plays,* pp. 140-144); *Embers, (Collected Shorter Plays,* p. 91 et seq) and *Eh Joe,* (pp. 19-21.)

41. For an analysis of *Embers* see: Lawley, Paul. " 'Embers'; an interpretation." *Journal of Beckett Studies.* John Calder. London. Autumn 1980. no. 6. pp. 9-36.

42. *Embers. Collected Shorter Plays,* p. 93.

43. *Embers. Collected Shorter Plays,* p. 93.

44. The last tram-line in Ireland was the broad guage Hill of Howth route, which was closed in 1961. It was a most pleasant run of five and a half miles in open-top double-deck cars beginning at Howth, proceeding up the Hill of Howth with magnificent views across Dublin Bay, and then descending down the opposite side of the Hill to arrive in Sutton some thirty minutes later. For a history of this interesting line see: Flewitt, J.C. *The Hill of Howth Tramway.* Transport Research Associates. 1968, and Baker, Michael C. *Irish Railways since 1916.* Ian Allan. London. 1972. p. 169.

45. *Embers. Collected Shorter Plays,* p. 103.

46. This tragedy may be set in Beckett's brother's house *Shottery,* in Killiney. The beach can be reached from the house by walking down a long garden, at the end of which there is a wooden wicket, leading to a piece of common land that brings one to a viaduct carrying the railway line, after passing under which the stony beach of Killiney, surrounded by hills behind, is reached. Turning left, that is north, a short walk along the shingle brings one to the rocky cove of Whiterock. Other references to the sea which cannot be located precisely are found in *That Time, (Collected Shorter Plays,* pp. 232-233); *For to End Yet Again, (Collected Shorter Prose,* p. 179); *Company,* (pp. 75-76); *Endgame,* (p. 25.)

47. Harvey, *Poet and Critic* p. 226.

48. The reference to an old woman in a graveyard in *Ill seen Ill said* (p. 29) may also have its origins in the cemetery at Redford. It may even be, as suggested by Fletcher and Fletcher, (Fletcher, Beryl, and Fletcher, John. *A Student's Guide to the Plays of Samuel Beckett.* Faber and Faber. London. Boston. 2nd ed. 1985. p. 242) that the speaker in *A Piece of Monologue* 'is preoccupied with autobiographical reminiscences,' and that it is Beckett's mother's burial at Redford Cemetery that inspires: 'Grey light. Rain pelting. Umbrellas round a grave. Seen from above. Streaming black canopies. Black ditch beneath. Rain bubbling in the black mud. Empty for the moment. That place beneath. Which ... he all but said which loved one?' (*A Piece of Monologue, Collected Shorter Plays,* p. 268).

49. For a discussion on cemeteries in Beckett's writing see: Rabinovitz, Rubin. *The Development of Samuel Beckett's Fiction.* University of Illinois Press. Urbana and Chicago. 1984. p. 40.

50. Beckett did not approve of slovenly ritual, such as making the sign of the cross carelessly at funerals; see: *The Expelled, (Collected Shorter*

Prose, pp. 26-27); and in *Mercier and Camier,* (p. 34) the use of a six-cylinder hearse during the period of war-time petrol rationing is not approved.

51. Gontarski, S.E. *The Intent of Undoing in Samuel Beckett's Dramatic Texts.* Indiana University Press, Bloomington. 1985. pp. 131-149.

52. Beckett has dropped the final vowel from Kilcoole. The word Kilcoole derives from the gaelic Ceill Chomgaill. (Killanin, Lord, and Duignan, Michael V. *Shell Guide to Ireland.* The Ebury Press. London 1962. p. 187.)

53. The 'Kilcool' manuscript. Trinity college, Dublin MS no. 4664. Gontarski has studied the forty-three pages of this dramatic monologue which Beckett worked on in 1963. The manuscript is a series of attempts at composition, and in Gontarski's view 'might as well be considered a series of different plays'. The importance of the manuscript rests not alone on its dependence on childhood reality in Ireland, but the fact that it draws to some extent from both *Happy Days* and *Play* which preceded it and that it evolves eventually into *Not I* and later *That Time,* thus providing a unique insight into Beckett's creative technique. (Gontarski. *Intent of Undoing.* p. 141.) Gontarski's analysis of the relevance of the 'Kilcool' manuscript to *Not I* is as follows: "The origin of at least the play's central conflict grew out of the artistic struggle to give shape to some recollections, potentially autobiographical, set first in Kilcool, then near the Leopardstown Race Course (Croker's Acres) near Beckett's birthplace in Foxrock. Beckett's first attempts were to record and try to develop memories of Ireland, but until he undid that material and the self from which it emerged (and this indeed is the subject of *Not I,* as the title simply and straightforwardly proclaims), Beckett's creative efforts were unsuccessful. Once he defined his subject and orchestrated the narrative fragments not along a temporal line, as he did in 'Kilcool', but musically, relying not on causality but on repetition and variation of his fourteen thematic categories, the creative process proved fruitful. Beckett's creative struggle with both 'Kilcool' and *Not I* offers a serious challenge to the critical assertions that this play clearly aligns Beckett with surrealist methods of composition, that 'the play shares with the film *(Un chien andalou)* a principle of organisation', or that the plot is incoherent, either to imitate the chaos of life or to parody surrealist composition." (Gontarski. *Intent of Undoing.* p. 148-149.)

54. Information to the author from Samuel Beckett.

55. Kilcoole beach achieved a certain notoriety in 1914 when Sir Thomas Myles, a Dublin surgeon, and James Creed Meredith landed 600 rifles for the Irish Volunteers. (Killanin and Duignan. *Shell Guide.* p. 187.)

56. Gontarski. *Intent of Undoing.* p. 136.

57. *Happy Days,* p. 31. In *Molloy,* (p. 57) love is associated, not with a manicure as in *Dream,* but with a pedicure.

58. The name Jack's Hole probably derives from a dangerous part of the sea. Many areas around the coast of Ireland have similar names which usually indicate a dangerous bathing area.

CHAPTER 4: EDUCATION

1. The school is entered in *Thom's Official Directory,* 1922. p. 1912 as 'Elsner, Miss Ida, teacher of modern languages and music', *Taunus.* Leopardstown Road.

   There is a reference in *Come and Go, (Collected Shorter Plays,* p. 194), to Miss Wade's School for girls, where many daughters' of neighbouring Foxrock families would have attended. It is entered in *Thom's Directory,* 1922. (p. 1842) merely as: 'Misses, girl's boarding and day school', situated at Morehampton House, No. 78, Morehampton Road, but in *Thom's Directory* for 1904 (p. 1680) the school is listed: 'Wade the Misses G and E. Select school for young ladies'.

2. The school is entered in *Thom's Official Directory,* 1922. (p. 1576) as: 'Le Peton, Alfred, professor of French', 3-4 Earlsfort Place.

3. For a brief history of Portora see: Quane, Michael. *Portora Royal School* (1618-1968). Cumann Seanchais Chlochair, Monaghan. 1968.

4. *Portora,* the schoolboys' magazine is a most valuable source, if for no other reason, than it is the only source extant which comments on events and pupils at the school. Regrettably, there is virtually no reference in it to academic achievement, though two related activities, debating and association with the library are commented on from time to time; the predominant interest of the magazine, however, is with sporting activities. The progress of the pupils in their sporting endeavours is commented on, from time to time, by the teachers who coached in the various sports. Apart from reports on sporting events, there are contributions in verse and prose from the pupils, which unfortunately for historical research, but no doubt in the best interest of the young contributors, were either unsigned or appeared over a pseudonym. The *Portora* was brought out annually until 1918, after which it was published each term (*Portora.* 1918. no. 1. vol. XIII. p. 1). Unfortunately some issues are missing for the period 1918-1923; these are for the terms Hilary 1918, Michaelmas and Trinity 1919, and Michaelmas 1921.

5. *Portora.* 1919. vol. XIII. no. 2. p. 20.

6. *Portora.* 1920. vol. XV. no. 1. p. 11.

7. The dominance of sporting activities over academic achievement in the schoolboy magazine may be, in fact, a reflection on the school ethos. A report by inspectors of the Intermediate Education Board in 1910 observed that the headmaster, Mr. A.C. McDonnell, was an enthusiast for rugby football, and that the school gave most of its attention to 'games and athletic pursuits.' The inspectors also found 'in each form a sediment of idlers who have no intention of working.' (Quane. *Portora.* p. 52). Vivian Mercier, who left Portora in 1936, confirms the preoccupation of the school with sport, a feature not uncommon in many of Ireland's major schools up to recent times. 'The one tradition that the boys themselves take much stock in is the Rugby football tradition, which is a good seventy years old now. There are few enthusiasts for cricket, and a few fanatics for rowing - a sport that

breeds fanatics - but for two out of three terms in the year we played nothing but Rugger and often talked little else too ...' (Mercier, Vivian, 'The Old School Tie'. *The Bell*. vol. XI. no. 6. March 1946. pp. 1081-90).

8. *Portora*. 1920. vol. XV. no. 1. p.1.

9. *Portora*. 1920. vol. XIV. no. 3. p. 3.

10. *Portora*. 1920. vol. XIV. no. 2. p. 18.

11. It is of interest to note some of the comments made by Samuel Beckett's coaches in *Portora*: in rugby, 'he played some brilliant games. Is quick to seize an opening and gathers the ball very cleanly.' (1923, vol. XVII. no. 2. p. 11); in cricket, 'he can bat well at times but has an awkward habit of walking across the wicket to all balls' (1920, vol. XIV. no. 3. p. 16); 'He has some really stylish strokes, but he ought to put more force into them. Is inclined to step across his wicket too much in playing long hops. His bowling is not up to expectation from last year's form, his length being erratic. An excellent field who tries hard.' (1921. vol. XV. no. 3. p. 13.); by 1922 he had developed into 'an attractive batsman', and 'a very good medium-pace bowler with a sharp break-back' as well as being 'a brilliant field who brings off one-hand catches in fine style.' (1922. vol. XVI. no. 3. p. 15). For the record, the following bowling and batting averages for 1922, which placed him first in the school in bowling, and third in batting, are noted. (1922. vol. XVI. no. 3. p. 16):

    Batting: Innings 9; total runs 132; highest score 34; times out 0; average 14.69.
    Bowling: Overs 15.5; maidens 13; runs 80; wickets 17; average 4.71.

    In boxing Samuel Beckett excelled as a light heavy-weight whose success was attributed to 'good speed and footwork, and using both hands to good effect.' (1922. vol. XVI. no. 3. p. 8). As far as I can ascertain, he was never beaten! Beckett was also involved with the library to which he contributed (unspecified) books. (1922. vol. XVII. no. 1. p. 11). He was elected to the committee of the Portora Royal School Literary and Scientific Society in 1921, and in a debate on 'Woman's Emancipation', he and another, "succeeded in proving themselves capable 'ladies' men", but in spite of their 'violent and eloquent speeches' they were defeated by a majority of ten votes. (Report in the Beckett File at Portora, taken from the *Portora*, Michaelmas 1921, one of the missing issues).

12. *Portora*. 1922. vol. XVI. no. 3. p. 2.

13. *Portora*. 1923. vol. XVIII. no. 1. p. 2.

14. The *Portora* magazine for Michaelmas, 1925 (vol. XIX. no. 3. p. 1) paid tribute to Mr. W.N. Tetley, Treasurer of the Old Portora Union, from 1891 to 1925, by publishing a photograph of Tetley, and an account of his loyal service to the school: 'The outstanding event of last term was the departure of Mr. W.N. Tetley after nearly 35 years of loyal service. Acting on doctor's orders he left us last July, taking with him the affection of many, and the deep respect of all. It is probably no exaggeration to say that no master ever gave more excellent service to the School than Mr. Tetley. After the tragic death of Mr. Burgess in 1917 Mr. Tetley acted as Headmaster for a term, and carried out the duties well, as he did everything. He has given to all who came in contact with him here a fine example of fidelity to high ideals and of unswerving devotion to duty. He maintains his interest in the School, and by consenting to remain Hon. Treasurer of our Union he keeps unbroken his connection with Portora. A fine scholar, and in earlier days an excellent cricketer and oarsman, his tastes and interests cover a wide field. He has earned, indeed, in one by-path of science a considerable name. Mr. Tetley is staying at present at Llandudno, but hopes by next March to come to live in Belfast. All Portorans, past and present, will join in the wish that he may have many years of happy life in retirement.

    We, Masters and Boys, presented Mr. Tetley when leaving with a fine telescope suitably inscribed, and the Old Portora Union has just sent him a valuable presentation.'

    Beckett's other teachers at Portora included Miss Evelyn Tennant and later Miss Harper for French, Mr. Breuil for English, Mr. Seale the Headmaster for Latin, and Mr. A.T.M. Murfet for Classics (Knowlson, James. *Samuel Beckett: an exhibition*. Turret Books. London. 1971. p. 21). Mr. Murfet 'prophesied a distinguished literary career for him!' (Kennedy, Sighle. *Murphy's Bed. A Study of real sources and sur-real associations in Samuel Beckett's first novel*. Bucknell University Press. Lewisburg. 1971. pp. 42-43).

15. The final version of the poem *For Future Reference* (as published in: Harvey, Lawrence. *Samuel Beckett. Poet and Critic*. Princeton University Press, New Jersey, 1970. pp. 299-301) has been revised by Beckett, and differs considerably from the original version published in *Transition*. June 1930. vol. 19-20. pp. 342-343.

16. The choice of the name Mahood is of interest. One of the pupils at Portora was named E.P. Mahood; he left the school in 1921. As has already been noted by Vivian Mercier. (Mercier, Vivian. 'Ireland/The World: Beckett's Irishness' in: *Yeats, Joyce, and Beckett. New Light on Three Modern Irish Writers*. eds. Kathleen McGrory and John Unterecker. Bucknell University Press. Lewisburg, and Associated University Presses, London. 1976. p. 152), the names of two pupils at Portora, that of E.D. Camier, who left in 1926 and his own name, V.H.S. Mercier (Mercier left in 1936), probably provided Beckett with the names (but not the characters) for *Mercier and Camier*. Another instance of an unusual name of an old Portora boy being applied by Beckett to one of his fictional characters is that of Surgeon Bor in 'A Case in A Thousand. A Short Story.' (*The Bookman*. 1934: vol. 86. pp. 241-242). The pupil G.T. Bor joined Frank Beckett in the Hallow E'en concert in 1920 'to get the ball rolling with a fine cheery duet and gained just applause.' (*Portora*. 1920. vol. XV. no. 1. p. 11).

    For an analysis of the nomenclative metamorphosis of Mahood in *The Unnamable* see: Cohn, Ruby. *Samuel Beckett: the comic gamut*. Rutgers University Press. New Jersey. 1962. p. 122. For Beckett's fascination with the letter M for many of his heroes see: Leventhal, A.J. 'The Beckett Hero'. In *Samuel Beckett. A Collection of Critical Essays*. ed. Martin Esslin. Prentice Hall. New Jersey. 1965. p. 48. For a discussion on the occurrence of Beckettian names in *Thom's Official Directory* see: Fletcher, John. *The Novels of Samuel Beckett*. Chatto and Windus. London. 1964. pp. 125-126.

17. Mercier. 'The Old School Tie'.

18. The beauty of the Lakes of Portora impressed Jonathan Swift who visited Charles Grattan during his mastership there in the early eighteenth century. (Quane. *Portora*, p. 11) -

    My horses foundered on Fermanagh ways,
    Ways of well-polished and well pointed stone,
    Where every step endangers every bone.

But that the world might think I played the fool,
I'd change with Charlie Grattan for his school.
What fine cascades, what vistas might I make,
Fix'd in the centre of the Iernian lake.

Other poetical associations may be noted here: The Rev. Robert Burrowes, appointed headmaster in 1798, was the author of the well-known ballad *De Night before Larry was Stretched* (Quane, *Portora*, p. 15), and the Scotsman, Henry Francis Lyte, who attended Portora composed the hymn *Abide with me* in 1813 (Quane, *Portora*, p. 60).

Another famous pupil, once infamous enough to have his name removed from the prize boards, was Oscar Wilde, whose portrait now hangs in the school.

19. *Portora*. 1920. vol. XIV. no. 3. p. 12.

20. *Portora*. 1920. vol. XIV. no. 3. p. 12.

The Spartan discipline at Portora was not confined to swimming. A report written about the time of Beckett's entry to school reads: 'At Portora it was a point of honour to take a cold bath every morning, and thirty boys scrambled over two baths. When we came in from football we washed ourselves meticulously from head to foot in a scant lavatory. The Irish schoolboy faced the battle of life unhampered by any acquired need of personal comfort.' (Quane. *Portora*. p. 51). Indeed, the theme of self-reliance is evident in Portora's 1985 brochure, which also emphasises the school's ecumenical outlook: "Pupils are taught and encouraged to use these natural resources, (its geographical setting of lakeland, moor and mountain) through many outdoor pursuits, to develop the qualities of self-reliance so important in the development of a young person's character.

Portora's motto is 'Omnes Honorate': 'Honour All Men'. The school seeks to impress on every pupil the everlasting solidity of this ancient motto: so important if our pupils are to enter the world of work as serving and useful members of society. Portora is also conscious of its fine tradition as an Irish Public school with the tradition of service that that has always implied. Moreover, while in no way compromising its religious and political origins, Portora is conscious that its pupils be aware of the validity of the differing traditions within Irish society, and to this end works in close cooperation on various projects with neighbouring schools in County Fermanagh, and also is 'twinned' with the Jesuit College of Clongowes Wood, at Naas, in Co. Kildare."
(By courtesy the Headmaster, Portora.)

21. *Portora*. 1920. vol. XIV. no. 3. p. 13.

22. *Portora*. 1921. vol. XX. no. 3. p. 17.

The Junior Long Race, 420 yds, was won in a time of 13m 14½ secs. The Junior Sprint Race, was won in a time of 1m 13¾ secs.

23. *Portora*. 1923. vol. XVII. no. 3. p. 19.

24. I am indebted to Mr. George C. Andrews for this verse and the details surrounding its origins.

25. Bair, Deirdre. *Samuel Beckett. A Biography*. Picador, Pan Books. 1980. pp. 544-545.

26. 'Some home truths about the ancients.' Signed BAT. (*Portora*. 1922. vol. XVII. no. 1. p. 7.)

27. *Portora*. 1922. vol. XVII. no. 1. pp.7-8.

28. Beckett File. Portora. This memoir was requested when Beckett was awarded the Nobel Prize.

29. For a history of Trinity College see: Bailey, Kenneth C. *A History of Trinity College Dublin 1892-1945*. The University Press and Hodges Figgis & Co. Ltd. Dublin 1947.

30. The same quotation may be found in 'Sedendo et Quiescendo'. *Transition: An International Workshop for Orphic Creation*. ed. Eugene Jolas. Sevire Press. Holland. March. 1932. vol. 21. pp. 13-20.

31. For a brief background to the sectarian influences on Dublin's universities see: Dowling, P.J. *A History of Irish Education. A Study in conflicting loyalties*. The Mercier Press. Cork. 1971. pp. 159-175.

32. For an account of Beckett's achievements at Trinity see: Mercier, Vivian *Beckett/Beckett*. Oxford University Press. Oxford, New York, Toronto, Melbourne. 1979. p. 33 and Knowlson, *an exhibition*. p. 22. In 1926 Beckett played cricket for the Trinity first eleven, winning his 'pink', an athletic award equivalent to an Oxford or Cambridge 'blue'. Beckett played for the Dublin University Cricket Club first XI in 1925 and 1926. His performance is described as follows: 'A solid rather than spectacular bat who frequently opened the innings, he had a very respectable career, scoring 313 runs in his first season (average 18.4), with a top score of 61. In 1926 his average dropped to 11.5 (115 runs), but he also took 15 wickets. He played in the matches against Northamptonshire in both years, and in 1926 he opened both the batting and bowling at the County Ground, Northampton. It was not a good match for him. His bowling was put to the sword by a strong County batting side, and he finished with 0 for 47 (although he did take two catches off Tom Dixon's bowling). Powell, the Northamptonshire fast bowler, bowled him for 4 in the first innings, and a young leg-spinner called S. Adams claimed Beckett's wicket with the first ball in first-class cricket in the second.' (Milne, M.H.A., Perry, N.P., Halliday, M. *A History of the Dublin University Cricket Club*. eds. M.R. Beamish, and E.H. Murray. Dublin University Cricket Club, 1982. p. 93).
In 1927 Beckett obtained first of First Class in Modern Literature.

33. A further satirical comment on Junior Fellows may be found in *Murphy*, p. 43.

34. The horse Hans was capable of performing remarkable mathematical calculations but only in the presence of his owner from whom the horse sensed the correct answers. (Pfungst, Otto. *Clever Hans; the Horse of Mr. von Osten*. Holt. New York. 1911. Republished: Holt, Rinehart and Winston. New York. 1965.)

35. Rabinovitz, Rubin. *The Development of Beckett's Fiction*. University of Illinois Press. Urbana and Chicago. 1984. p. 164, p. 172. Mention is also made of a reference to a 'Madden Prizeman' in the unpublished *Echo's Bones*. Samuel Molyneux Madden, second son of Samuel Madden, (1686-1765) a divine, miscellaneous writer and philanthropist, bequeathed a fund to Trinity college, to be distributed in premiums at fellowship examinations, the first of which was bestowed in 1798. (*Dictionary of National Biography*. (Compact Edition). Oxford University Press. London. 1975. p. 1294.)

36. *Watt*, p. 248.

CHAPTER 5: THE CITY

1. Belacqua takes his name from Dante's late repentant in the *Purgatorio*:

   > Thither drew we on; and there were persons,
   > lounging in the shade behind the rock, even
   > as a man settles him to rest for laziness.
   > And one of them, who seemed to me weary, was
   > sitting and clasping his knees, holding his
   > face low down between them.
   >
   > (Dante. *Purgatorio*. Canto IV, lines 136-141).

   Belacqua was a Florentine maker of musical instruments, and was notorious for his sloth. (*The Purgatorio of Dante Alighieri*: The Temple Classics. J.M. Dent & Sons. London. 1964. p. 47).
   The title of Beckett's first novel, *More Pricks than Kicks* is taken from the words of Jesus to Saul in *Acts* 9:5. 'I am Jesus whom thou persecutist; it is hard for thee to kick against the pricks'. Beckett always chooses his title with care, for example: *Dream of Fair to Middling Women* draws from Tennyson's 'A Dream of Fair Women' and Chaucer's *Legend of Good Women*. (Mercier, Vivian. *Beckett/Beckett*. Oxford University Press. Oxford. New York. Toronto. Melbourne. 1979. p. 188.) The name *Watt* is usually interpreted as indicating Watt as a questioner, one who asks 'what?' but there are many alternative explanations. (Rabinovitz, Rubin. *The Development of Samuel Beckett's Fiction*. University of Illinois Press. Urbana and Chicago. 1984. p. 136; p. 147). One such alternative explanation for Watt's name is that it is taken from the nickname of Tyler the market-gardener on Cornelscourt Hill Road, who was known as 'Watt' Tyler. (Information to the author from Samuel Beckett). See also Note 117 below. The three women in *Come and Go* are based on Eliot's 'In the room the women come and go/Talking of Michelangelo.' (Kenner, Hugh. *A Reader's Guide to Samuel Beckett*. Thames and Hudson. London. 1973. p. 174.)

2. For a historical note on Greene's Bookshop and Clare Street see: Liddy, Pat. *Dublin Today*. Irish Times Publication. 1984. p. 106.

3. The name would seem to derive from the open space, or green that once existed in front of Trinity College in the sixteenth century, but the University soon attracted development, as did the Parliament Buildings, now the Bank of Ireland, built almost contemporaneously with the College, and College Green soon became a green in name only. (*Handbook to the City of Dublin and the Surrounding District*. The University Press. Dublin. 1908. p. 288.)

4. In the seventeenth century the city of Dublin expanded rapidly beyond the confines of the city walls which had previously contained it. The city rulers, with more foresight than their successors can ever be credited with, established two extensive amenity areas, the Phoenix Park and St. Stephen's Green. Though the latter was not developed for sometime, fashionable Dubliners paraded themselves on the Beaux walk on its northern aspect in the early eighteenth century. It owes its present splendour as a public park to the munificence of Lord Ardilaun, who, in 1880, carried out, at a cost of £20,000, the scenic transformation which converted it from an ordinary city square into one of the handsomest of city parks. Its perimeter is flanked by Dublin's finest Georgian houses, many of which have been pulled down, but among today's notable buildings are Iveagh House, Clanwilliam House, Newman House, University Church, the Royal College of Surgeons, the Shelbourne Hotel and a number of gentlemen's clubs dating, in custom as well as location, from the Georgian era: *Handbook to the City of Dublin*. p. 288-290.

5. Green Street Courthouse, situated behind the four courts, was designed by Richard Johnston, the architect of the Gate Theatre, in 1792. (Guinness, Desmond. *Georgian Dublin*. B.T. Batsford Ltd. London. 1979. p. 57.) It is still in use today, and its theatrical associations are not confined only to its origins; Roger McHugh wrote a historical play based on a famous trial of a journeyman-carpenter, for murder of the Head Constable of the Royal Irish Constabulary, which was staged in the Abbey Theatre. (McHugh, Roger. *Trial at Green Street Courthouse. A Historical Play in Ten Scenes*. Browne and Nolan, Ltd. Dublin. n.d.) Green Street Courthouse is also mentioned in *Dream of Fair to Middling Women*, p. 125.

6. The firm of Beckett and Medcalf was founded in 1910. *Thom's Official Directory*, 1910. (p. 1516) carries the following entry: 6 Clare Street. 'Beckett and Medcalf, quantity surveyors. Beckett, Wm. F., F.S.I. Cooldrinagh, Foxrock. Medcalf, Wm., F.S.I. 1 Knapton Tce., Kingstown.' The premises has changed little over the years and the door still boasts the original brass name plate. The firm formerly occupied the hall and first floors, but the business is now conducted by Mr. Ian MacMillen on the top floor, where Beckett lived and wrote. Mr. Thomas O'Dowd has offices in the adjoining backroom. I am indebted to Mr. MacMillen for valuable information and for permitting me to photograph his office and the garret. Mr. O'Dowd kindly provided me with photographs of rooms in the house.

7. *More Pricks than Kicks*, written in the early 'thirties and published in 1934, is set in Dublin of the late 'twenties. The murderer Henry McCabe, a central figure in the story 'Dante and the Lobster' was executed on December 9th, 1926. *Murphy*, first published in 1938, is set a decade later than *More Pricks than Kicks* in or around the autumn of 1935. It was on September 19th, that Neary attempted to bash his head against Cuchulain's buttocks in the General Post Office (p. 33). That the year was 1935 is also evident from a later clue - 'The lucky number did not coincide with a Sunday for a full year to come, not until Sunday, October 4th, 1936, could the maximum chance of success attend any new venture of Murphy's.'(p. 55).An astronomical dating of events is also possible and is given scholarly consideration by: Kennedy, Sighle. *Murphy's Bed. A Study of real sources and surreal associations in Samuel Beckett's first novel*. Bucknell University Press. Lewisburg. 1971. See also: Kenner, Hugh. *A Reader's Guide to Samuel Beckett*. Thames and Hudson. London. 1973. p. 57; Rabinovitz, Rubin. *The Development of Samuel Beckett's Fiction*. University of Illinois Press. Urbana and Chicago. 1984. p. 107, p. 123; It should be also possible to date approximately the events in Murphy from the age of Celia, one of the heroines of the novel *Murphy*, though her age is stated by the author to be unimportant (p. 11). 'When her parents, Mr. and Mrs. Quentin Kelly died, which they did clinging warmly to their respective partners in the ill-fated Morro Castle, Celia, being an only child, went on the street' (p. 12). As the sinking of the *Morro Castle* occurred on September 8th, 1934, this date cannot therefore be taken as an indication of Celia's true age. The sinking of the *Morro Castle* by fire, permitting Beckett the sarcasm of the Kellys' 'clinging warmly to their respective partners', was a major maritime disaster which claimed 125 lives before the ship ran aground on a New Jersey holiday beach. I am grateful to Dr. John de Courcy Ireland, Research Officer, The Maritime Institute of Ireland, Haigh Terrace, Dun Laoghaire, Co. Dublin, for this information. Two other maritime disasters feature in *All That Fall*, (p. 24): 'Wasn't it that they sung on the *Lusitania*? ... Or was it the *Titanic*?' 1,200 people died in the sinking of the *Lusitania*

off the coast of Ireland in 1915, 1,513 drowned in the *Titanic* in 1912. (Fletcher, Beryl S., and Fletcher, John. *A Student's Guide to the Plays of Samuel Beckett.* Faber and Faber, London. Boston. 2nd ed. 1985. p. 83. See also: de Courcy Ireland, John. *Ireland and the Irish in Maritime History.* Glendale Press. Dublin. 1986.)

8. The garret in Clare Street has been used for many years as a storeroom for papers, documents and other assorted items among which are a bath, paper press, gas-fire, a greatcoat and an assortment of shoes. The skylight provides just enough light to capture to perfection the atmosphere of Murphy's garret in the Mercyseat.

9. The arrest and subsequent trial of Henry McCabe were reported in great detail in all the daily newspapers over a period of eight months. I have been unable to find a newspaper photograph of McCabe, and certainly the *Evening Herald* does not have a photograph of him on the eve or day of the execution. A further mention of McCabe's visage occurs on p. 11 (*More Pricks than Kicks*): 'Now the long barrel-loaf came out of its biscuit-tin and had its end evened off on the face of McCabe.' The following reports appeared in *The Irish Times*: March 31, 1926 First reports of fire at *La Mancha* which occurred on March 30th; April 1, 1926. Photograph of ruin of *La Mancha*; April 24. 1926. Depositions taken at Swords; Nov. 9, 1926. Trial of gardener opens; Nov. 10, 1926. Report of trial; Nov. 11, 1926. Report of trial; Nov. 12, 1926. Pathologist gives evidence; Nov. 13, 1926. Closing reports of trial; Nov. 15, 1926. 'Death sentence on McCabe. End of a remarkable case.'; Dec. 12, 1926. 'Execution of McCabe - carried out without a hitch by Pierpoint, assisted by Robinson.'

10. For a full account and discussion of the trial see: Deale, Kenneth E.L. 'The Malahide Murder Mystery.' *Beyond any reasonable doubt? A book of murder trials.* Gill and MacMillan, Dublin. 1971. pp. 93-121.

In the graveyard at Malahide the statue of the Virgin Mary stands on the victims' grave -

Of your charity pray for the souls of
Margaret McDonnell, late of Ballygar,
Co. Galway, who died at La Mancha, Malahide,
19th January 1914,
her sisters
Annie McDonnell
Alice McDonnell
her brothers
Joseph McDonnell
Peter McDonnell
And their faithful servants
James Clarke
Mary McGowan
who died at La Mancha, Malahide, on or
about 31st March 1926.
RIP

Mother of Sorrows intercede for them.

11. *The Irish Times.* Dec 12. 1926.

12. Other references to McCabe in *More Pricks than Kicks* may be found on pages 20 and 80.

13. Oliver probably had had sight of the early edition of the *Evening Herald*, (Wed. December 8th, 1926) the front page headline of which declared –

'*NO REPRIEVE* McCabe to be Executed To-morrow'

'Henry McCabe, who was sentenced to death in connection with the murders at La Mancha, Malahide, will be executed in Mountjoy Prison to-morrow. The Executive Council, having decided not to make any recommendation to the Governor-General for the exercise of the prerogative of mercy, no reprieve will be granted. Arrangements are being completed in Mountjoy for the execution.'

14. Beckett has used the fictitious name Ellis for the hangman, who was in fact, Pierpoint, assisted by Robinson. (*The Irish Times,* Dec 12, 1926.)

15. For an account of the trial and an analysis of Beckett's reaction to it see: Kroll, Jeri L. 'The surd as inadmissible evidence: the case of Attorney-general -v- Henry McCabe.' *Journal of Beckett Studies.* John Calder. London. Summer 1977, no. 2. pp. 47-58.

16. Signorina Ottolenghi has been identified as Bianca Esposito, an important influence, as she taught Beckett Italian as well as perhaps introducing him to Dante: Little, Roger. 'Beckett's Mentor, Rudmose-Brown: Sketch for a Portrait.' *Irish University Review.* 1984. vol. 14. no. 1. p. 40. See also: Mercier. *Beckett/Beckett.* p. 34.

17. The first piped-gas lamp appeared in Dublin in 1825, and this form of lighting was used up to 1957. 'All gaslights in Dublin were lit and extinguished manually by lamplighters. The lamplighter wore a blue serge uniform, with Dublin's coat of arms on his cap. He carried a pole, which he thrust up through the bottom of the lantern, turning the little tap and lighting the gas jet. At one time 25 lamplighters lit the city's 3,750 gas lamps.' O'Connell, Derry, *The Antique Pavement. An illustrated guide to Dublin's street furniture.* An Taisce. The National Trust for Ireland. 1975. pp. 23-25.

18. Two references to Dublin's lamplighters may be found in *Dream of Fair to Middling Women:* 'it was the hour of the nimble lamplighters flying through the suburbs on bicycles' (p. 139); 'when the posts came abroad on the lamplighters' spoors' (p. 155).

19. Knowlson, James and Pilling, John. *Frescoes of the Skull. The Later Prose and Drama of Samuel Beckett.* Grove Press. New York. 1980. pp. 196-197. *Not I* did suggest 'a modernist's John the Baptist' independently it would seem of Beckett's statement of the association with Caravaggio's masterpiece: Brater, Enoch "Fragment and Beckett's form in 'That Time' and 'Footfalls.' " *Journal of Beckett Studies.* John Calder, London. 1979. no. 2 p. 73.

20. It is of interest to note that the artist Avigdor Arikha, a close friend of Beckett, is of the opinion that literary critics too often ignore the influences of the visual arts on Beckett's work. (Gontarski, S.E. *The Intent of Undoing in Samuel Beckett's Dramatic Texts.* Indiana University Press. Bloomington. 1985. p. 132.) This view is confirmed by the few rather fragmentary studies dealing with this important aspect of Beckett's art. For discussion on art in Beckett's literature see: McMillan, Dougald. 'Samuel Beckett and the Visual Arts: The Embarrassment of Allegory' in: *Samuel Beckett,* ed. Ruby Cohn. McGraw Hill Book Company, 1975. pp. 121-135; for a less authorative account see: Copeland, Hannah Case. *Art and the Artist in the works of Samuel Beckett.* Mouton. The Hague and Paris. 1975; see also: Mercier, *Beckett/Beckett.* pp. 88-117; Rabinovitz, *Samuel Beckett's Fiction.* pp. 155-162.

21. The following works relating to Irish art and the National Gallery of Ireland have been consulted: Strickland, Walter George. *A Dictionary of Irish Artists.* Vol. I & II. Irish University Press. 1969; Crookshank, Anne and The Knight of Glin. *The Painters of Ireland c. 1660-1920.* Barrie and Jenkins. London. 1978; *Catalogue of Pictures and Other Works of Art in The National Gallery of Ireland and The National Portrait*

Gallery. Alex Thom. Dublin. 1920; *Catalogue of Oil Pictures in The General Collection. National Gallery of Ireland.* The Stationery Office. Dublin. 1932; *National Gallery of Ireland. Illustrated Catalogue of Paintings*. Gill and Macmillan. Dublin 1981; *National Gallery of Ireland. Illustrated Summary Catalogue of Drawings, Watercolours and Miniatures*. The National Gallery of Ireland. 1983; I wish to express my gratitude to Dr. Michael Wynne, Keeper of he Gallery, who advised me on the likely interpretation of the more obscure references to art in Beckett's works, and directed me to the appropriate paintings. I would also like to acknowledge the assistance I received from Mr. Homan Potterton, Director, of the National Gallery of Ireland, Mr. Michael Olahan, Ms Barbara Dawson, Ms Frances Gillespie, Ms Catherine de Courcy, Mr. James Geran, Head Attendant, and his staff. (The abbreviation NGI for the National Gallery of Ireland will be used in the attribution details of paintings that follow.)

22. For an interesting and scholarly account of the foundation and building of the National Gallery of Ireland see: de Courcy, Catherine. *The Foundation of The National Gallery of Ireland*. The National Gallery of Ireland, Dublin 1985. See also: *The Dublin Builder*, Feb, 1, 1864: 6, 17-18.

23. *Portrait of An Old Lady* by a Flemish painter, The Master of the Tired Eyes about 1540. Purchased by NGI in 1931. no 903.

24. *Pietà* by Pietro Perugino (1446-1523). Umbrian School. Purchased by NGI in 1931. no. 942. A footnote in Beckett's text reads: 'This figure, owing to the glittering vitrine behind which the canvas cowers can only be apprehended in sections. Patience, however, and a retentive memory have been known to elicit a total statement approximating to the intention of the painter.' (*More Pricks than Kicks*, p. 93) Dr. Michael Wynne has pointed out a small technical error in the above statement - the painting is on a panel and not canvas. There are other references to a Pietà, though which is not clear, in *Assumption*, and *Dream of Fair to Middling Women*, p. 62.

25. Ruby's countenance may also be studied in the *Pietà* in the Uffizi, Florence (n. 40a), but her features are shown to best advantage in *La Maddalena* in the Pitti, Florence (n. 67), in which the same model has been used by Perugino. For reproductions see: Castellaneta, Carlo. *L'opera Completa del Perugino*. Rizzoli Editore. Milano. 1969. plates xxiii and xxxvi.

26. Botticelli, Sandro. Florence (1445-1510). Two paintings in the National Gallery of Ireland were attributed to Botticelli in the 'twenties: *The Story of Lucretia* (no. 110. now attributed to the Master of Marradi), and *A Portrait of a Musician* (no. 470. now attributed to Fillipino Lippi).

27. *Sanies I. Collected Poems*, p. 17.

28. The reference to 'sweaty Big Tom' is to the Florentine painter Masaccio (1401-?1428), who was born Tommaso di Ser Giovanni di Mone and nicknamed 'Masaccio' (Hulking Tom). The painting that Beckett had in mind was the central panel of the *Madonna and Child* in the National Gallery, London. (Information to the author from Samuel Beckett). For details on Masaccio see: Murray, Peter and Linda. *A Dictionary of Art and Artists*. Penguin Books. 1968. pp. 256-257. The National Gallery of Ireland does not have a painting by Masaccio, and I originally attributed Beckett's reference to the 'gem of ravished Quattrocanto' to *The Virgin and Child* by Paolo Uccello (1397-1475). Florentine School. no. 603. Purchased by NGI in 1909.

29. These paintings in the National Gallery of Ireland, *The Battle of Anghiari* (no. 778) and *The Taking of Pisa* (no. 780) were attributed to Uccello by Thomas McGreevy when he was Director of the Gallery. (McGreevy, Thomas. *Catalogue of Pictures of the Italian Schools*. The Stationary Office, Dublin. 1956. p. 6.) McGreevy wrote: 'I have replaced the Uccello label on Nos. 778 and 780 because (a) they are important Uccellesque panels, (b) they were traditionally by Uccello, (c) the reasoned arguments between Schubring, against, and Roger Fry, for, though more diffidently, the attribution, seemed to me to be inconclusive, thus leaving the traditional attribution more or less where it was, and (d) I myself found the Uccello monogram on the trappings of one of the horses in No. 780. Langton Douglas's catalogue entry, rejecting the attribution, unsupported by either reasoning or documentation, does not seem to me to merit serious attention.' Both paintings are now attributed to the 'Florentine School.' (*Catalogue of Oil Paintings*, p. 53).

30. *Ecce Homo* by Tiziano Vecellio Titian (c. 1480-1576). Venetian School, no. 75. Purchased by NGI in 1885. 'Exhibited at Burlington House in 1883 as by Titian, the painting was published by Richter two years later as the work of the great Venetian master. In the same year it entered the collection where it retained its status in all the published catalogues, (1890, 1898, 1904) up to 1914. In the edition published that year, Walter Armstrong, the Director, changed the attribution to Matteo Cerezo, a seventeenth century Spanish artist and cited an iconographic source in Andrea Solario's painting of the same subject in the Poldi Pezzoli Museum. The Cerezo label was retained till 1955, when the then director, Thomas McGreevy, on the suggestion of Bernard Berenson, sent the picture to be examined and cleaned in London. St. John Gore, having viewed the restored canvas, (which brought to light the *pentimento* of the reed's original position), and after consulting with Professor Wilde and others, reattributed the picture to Titian and proposed a dating of c 1560... In 1956 McGreevy corrected the error of his illustrious predecessor and reaffirmed the traditional attribution to Titian ...' Keaveney, Raymond. 'Tiziano Vecellio, called Titian (Pieve de Cadore c. 1480/85 - 1576 Venice).' *Masterpieces from the National Gallery of Ireland. A Loan Exhibition at the National Gallery, London. 27 March - 27 May 1985*. The National Gallery of Ireland. Dublin 1985. pp. 7-8.

31. McMillan. 'Beckett and the Visual Arts.' p. 125.

32. Harvey, Lawrence E. *Samuel Beckett. Poet and Critic*. Princeton University Press. New Jersey. 1970. p. 111.

33. *A Bouquet of Flowers* by Jan van Huysum (1682-1749), Amsterdam School. Purchased by NGI in 1864. no. 50.

34. Esslin, Martin. *Mediations. Essays on Brecht, Beckett and the Media*. Eyre Methuen. London. 1980. p. 113.

35. Harvey. *Beckett. Poet and Critic*. p. 111, footnote.

36. *Rest on the Flight into Egypt* by Rembrandt van Ryn (1606-1669), Leyden and Amsterdam Schools. Purchased by NGI in 1883. no. 215. For further details on this interesting masterpiece see: *Masterpieces from the National Gallery of Ireland*. pp. 62-65.

37. *St. Luke Drawing the Virgin* after Rogier van der Weyden (1339/1440-1464). Flemish School. Purchased by NGI in 1866. no. 4.

One of the four evangelists, Luke was a disciple of St. Paul and is thought to be the author of the Acts of the Apostles. He was a physician by profession but medieval legend adds that he was also an unusually skilled painter and, according to John of Damascus, painted a picture of the Virgin which is in Rome. The Virgin favoured him by disclosing many things to him, in particular certain events in her life, such as the Annunciation and Christ's Nativity, for these things are known only from the gospel of St. Luke. (The Golden Legend, quoted by Bernen, Satia and Robert. *Myth and Religion in European Painting 1270-1700.* Constable. London. 1973. p. 171.) No known portrait of Matthew by St. Luke exists, but Copeland suggests that Beckett could have been influenced by a number of medieval paintings and illuminations in which an Evangelist is pictured at work with the Holy Spirit in the form of a dove at his ear, revealing to him the Holy Word. Paintings such as the Romanesque illumination of St. John the Evangelist from the *Gospel Book of Abbot Wedricus* (Janson, *History of Art*, colorplate 20, p. 236), Poussin's *Le Paysage avec Saint-Mathieu et l'Ange* (Anthony Blunt, Nicolas Poussin, 2 Bollingen Series 35.7. New York: Bollingen 1967, plate 150), or Carel Fabritius' *St. Matthew Writing His Gospel* (The New Yorker, 1 August 1970, p. 65) are suggested as likely examples. (Copeland, *Art and the Artist*, p. 60). More likely than any of the above is *the Inspiration of Saint Matthew* in the Contarelli Chapel, Church of San Luigi dei Francesi in Rome, 2nd version by Caravaggio. (See: Moir, Alfred. *Caravaggio*. The Library of Great Painters. Henry N. Abrams. New York. 1982. Colour plate No. 17. I am indebted to Dr. M. Wynne for this suggestion). However, of the many suggestions the one that seems to me most likely is that of James Knowlson (personal communication) who has concluded that the quotations from *Dream of Fair to Middling Women* (p. 123) and *Murphy* (p. 147) both refer to Rembrandt's painting of *Saint Matthew* in the Louvre. For a colourplate reproduction see: *St. Matthew and the Angel* (no. 407.) Paris, Musée du Louvre. Plate LIV in: *The Complete Paintings of Rembrandt*. Introduction by Gregory Martin. Note and catalogues by Paolo Lecaldano. Weidenfeld and Nicolson. London. 1973.

38. The NGI has a large collection of Sean O'Sullivan's portraits, but this one of Beckett is not among them. The NGI possesses only one portrait of Beckett, an indifferent pencil on paper portrait by Hilda Roberts. (no. 7884). Sean O'Sullivan (1906-1964) studied painting at the Central School of Art in London and at the Academie Julien in Paris before returning to Dublin, at the age of twenty-one when he was elected to the Royal Hibernian Academy, the youngest artist ever to be so honoured. (Boylan, Henry. *A Dictionary of Irish Biography*. Gill and Macmilian. Dublin. 1979. p. 288). He was a prolific portrait painter, and though much of his work was of a high quality, he often achieved only a bland likeness of his subjects.

39. *Watt*, p. 247.

40. James Arthur O'Connor (1792-1841), is best known for his landscape painting, but, like 'Art Conn O'Connery' he was as competent in painting figures as is evident in *The Poachers*. For biographical details see: Strickland. *Dictionary of Artists*. vol. 2. pp. 179-182. The NGI collection includes *The Poachers*, no. 18; *Moonlight*, no. 158; *A View of the Glen of the Dargle*, no. 163; *A Landscape*, no. 489; *A View of the Devil's Glen*, no. 825; *A Landscape*, no. 1114; *A Landscape: Homeward Bound*, no. 1182; *A Landscape*. no. 1241; *A Landscape*. no. 1242; *Ballinrobe House*. no. 4010. The latter five were purchased after 1940, and Beckett is unlikely to have been familiar with them. For a contemporary work on O'Connor see: Hutchinson. John. *James Arthur O'Connor*. The National Gallery of Ireland. 1985.

41. McMillan, 'Beckett and the Visual Arts.' p. 129.

42. *Antwerp from the City Walls*, Circle of Jan ('Velvet') Brueghel the Elder (1568-1625), Flemish School. Provenance unknown. no. 6869.

43. Brueghel the younger was influenced by his father and he may also have painted a *Christ in the House of Martha and Mary*. (*Masterpieces from The National Gallery of Ireland*. p. 56.)

44. *Christ in the House of Martha and Mary* by Peter Paul Ruebens (1577-1640) and Jan Brueghel the Younger (1601-1678). Bequeathed to NGI in 1901. no. 513. This painting was attributed to Peter Paul Ruebens and Jan 'Velvet' Brueghel (the Elder) in both the 1920 and 1932 catalogues of paintings in the National Gallery of Ireland. The 1932 attribution reads: 'In this picture (Christ in the House of Martha and Mary) the figures are by Rubens; the landscape by Jan commonly called Velvet, Brueghel; the birds, fruits, and similar accessories by Jan van Kessel.' (*Catalogue of Oil Pictures in the General Collection*. 1932. p. 110). The attribution to 'Velvet' Brueghel remains in the 1981 *Summary Catalogue of Paintings*; in 1985 the attribution was changed to 'Velvet' Brueghel's son, Jan Brueghel the Younger by Adrian Le Harivel. (*Masterpieces from the National Gallery of Ireland*. pp. 56-59).

45. Roderic O'Conor (1860-1940), like Beckett, left Ireland as a young man and spent most of his life in France, where he mixed with the famous artists of the post-impressionist period including Gauguin. Daring in his use of colour, his paintings portray excitement and vitality, and his work is now much sought after. For a biographical essay see: Campbell, Julian. *The Irish Impressionists. Irish Artists in France and Belgium, 1850-1914*. The National Gallery of Ireland. 1984. pp. 96-103; for a comprehensive catalogue see: Johnston, Roy. *Roderic O'Conor*. Barbican Art Gallery, City of London and the Ulster Museum, Belfast. 1985.

46. The paintings by Roderic O'Conor in the NGI are: *A Self Portrait*, no. 922; *La Ferme de Lezaver, Finistère*, no. 1642; *A Quiet Read*, no. 1806; *A Reclining Nude before a Mirror*, no. 4038; *A Landscape with Rocks*, no. 4057; *La Jeune Bretonne*, no. 4134; *Between the Cliffs, Aberystwyth*, no. 4324. It is of interest to note that the subject of the portrait in Erskine's room and Roderic O'Conor, as well as Watt himself, all had red hair.

47. Little is known about Conn O'Donnell who does not appear in Strickland's *Dictionary of Irish Artists*, or in Crookshank's *Painters of Ireland*.

48. McMillan, 'Beckett and the Visual Arts.' p. 130.

49. McMillan, 'Beckett and the Visual Arts.' p. 130.

50. *A Portrait of a Mandarin* by George Chinnery (1774-1852). Bequeathed to NGI in 1918. no. 785. Chinnery was born in London, and came to Ireland in 1797 to paint portraits. He was successful and married a Dublin woman. The union did not prove a harmonious one, and he soon departed Ireland for the East, where he remained for twenty years painting portraits of leading citizens and native princes in Madras, Calcutta, Canton and Macao where he died in 1852. (Strickland. *Dictionary of Irish Artists*. Vol. 1. pp. 170-177.) Works by Chinnery in the NGI collection include *A Portrait of a Mandarin*, no. 785; *Mrs. Conyngham*, no. 837; *Mrs. Eustace*, no. 999; *The Artist's Wife*, no. 1000; *A Chinese Scene*, no. 1006; *A Chinese Scene, Women making Tea*, no. 1007; *A Chinese Scene, Boats by Lake*, no. 1008.

51. John Slattery (fl. 1850-1858). See: Strickland. *Dictionary of Irish Artists*. vol. 2. pp. 358-359.

52. William Carleton (1794-1869), a novelist whose books include *Traits and Stories of the Irish Peasantry* (1830), *Tales of Ireland* (1834), *Fardorougha the Miser* (1839), *The Black Prophet* (1847), *Willy Reilly and his dear Colleen Bawn* (1855), and *Redmond Count O'Hanlon, the*

Irish Rapparee (1862). For a biography see: Kiely, Benedict. *Poor Scholar. A study of the works and days of William Carleton (1794-1869).* Sheed and Ward. London. 1947. Republished by The Talbot Press. Dublin. 1972.

53. For an account of the senior Mr. Knott's musical problems see: Lees, Heath " 'Watt': Music, Tuning and Tonality". *Journal of Beckett Studies.* John Calder. London. 1984. no. 9. pp. 22-23.

54. *A Fruit Piece, with Skull, Crucifix and Serpent* by Jan de Heem (1606-1683/4). Purchased by NGI in 1863. no. 11.

55. Beckett's visual creations in the theatre are as close as Beckett comes to painting. In the theatre he has been able to draw together the three arts he so greatly appreciates and of which he has considerable knowledge - literature, music and painting. For further discussion on this subject see: Brater, Enoch, "Fragment and Beckett's form in 'That Time' and 'Footfalls' ". *Journal of Beckett Studies.* John Calder. London. Summer 1977. no. 2. pp. 70-81; Hansford, James. "Imaginative Transactions in 'La Falaise' ". *Journal of Beckett Studies.* John Calder. London. 1985. no. 10. pp. 76-86; Esslin, *Mediations.* p. 152. Worth, Katherine. *The Irish Drama of Europe from Yeats to Beckett.* The Athlone Press of the University of London. 1978. pp. 245-249.

56. *Watt*, p. 128.

57. 'There is no difference, says Bruno between the smallest possible chord and the smallest possible arc, no difference between the infinite circle and the straight line. The maxima and minima of particular contraries are one and indifferent. Minimal heat equals minimal cold.' Beckett, Samuel. 'Dante ... Bruno . Vico ... Joyce.' in *Our Exagmination round his Factification for Incamination of Work in Progress.* Faber and Faber, London 1972, p. 6.

58. Copeland, *Art and the Artist*, p. 48, and McMillan, 'Beckett and the Visual Arts,' p. 128.

59. *Alcuni cerchi* by Vasily Kandinsky. Painted by Kandinsky in 1926, it was exhibited in *I Maestri del Guggenheim,* in Milan from 12 May to 26 July 1985 in the Gallery of Contemporary Art. Messer, Thomas M. *I Maestri del Guggenheim.* (Guggenheim E. Milano). Ratti. Como. 1985. pp. 24-25. For Beckett's comments on Kandinsky see: Mercier. *Beckett/Beckett.* p. 100.

60. *Watt*, p. 247.

61. Rabinovitz, *Samuel Beckett's Fiction.* p. 160.

62. The Master of Female Half-Lengths was a sixteenth century Flemish painter who enjoyed considerable success 'thanks to the zealously pursued speciality that gave him his makeshift name.' His subjects, usually young women have been described as 'sedate, with a touch of rougishness and complacency and what they are writing or reading, the musical tones they are emitting, are quite unlikely to be either indecent or titillating but rather harmless poesy with a bit of eroticism thrown in.' (Friedlander, Max J. *Early Netherlandish Painting.* English Edition. Vol. XII. Leyden. 1975. pp. 18-21.) See also: *Encyclopedia of the Arts.* ed. Herbert Read. Merideth Press. New York. 1966. p. 608.

63. Beer, Ann. " 'Watt', Knott and Beckett's bilingualism." *Journal of Beckett Studies.* John Calder. London. 1985. no. 10. pp. 37-75.

64. 'MacGreevy on Yeats.' *Disjecta.* p. 97.

65. MacGreevy, Thomas. *Jack B. Yeats. An Appreciation and an Interpretation.* Victor Waddington Publications. Dublin. 1945. pp. 14-15.

66. *A Lady and Two Gentlemen, (left and right: for 'La Conversation', c. 1715; centre: for 'La Mariée de Village', c. 1710, also ill. for 'Figures de Différents Caractères', 1725/28)* by Jean Antoine Watteau (1684-1721). Purchased by NGI in 1891. no. 2299.

67. For a biography of Jack Yeats see: Pyle, Hilary. *Jack B. Yeats. A biography.* Routledge and Kegan Paul. London. 1970; for biographical essays see: Beckett, Samuel; Caldwell, Martha; O'Doherty, Brian; O'Malley, Ernie; Oshima, Shotaro; Rose, Marilyn Gaddis; De Vere White, Terence. *Jack B. Yeats. A Centenary Gathering.* ed. with an introduction by Roger McHugh. Dolmen Press, Dublin 1971.

68. McMillan. 'Beckett and the Visual Arts.', p. 122.

69. For historical notes on these buildings see: Craig, Maurice. *Dublin 1660-1860.* The Cresset Press. London. 1952. p. 132 p. 302.

70. *Thom's Official Directory.* 1922. Nos. 17-21 Lower Mount Street, 'The Elpis Nursing Home, under the superintendence of Miss Margaret Huxley and Mrs. Francis Manning.' Originally I thought the place of Belacqua's demise to be Hume Street Nursing Home, but Beckett redirected me to the Elpis Nursing Home, which he had chosen because it was the scene of Synge's death described so poignantly by Moore. It is of interest to note that Synge is thought to have died of Hodgkin's disease a condition that often causes glandular swelling of the neck, and that Belacqua succumbed to anaesthesia while being operated on for a swelling of his neck.

71. *More Pricks than Kicks*, p. 186.

72. Moore, George. *Hail and Farewell. Vale.* William Heinemann. London. 1920. pp. 201-4.

73. 'Brady's' is not listed in *Thom's Directory* for 1922 or 1926, but 'Moore, John J., fish, poultry, ice, game and oyster merchant' may be found at no. 32 Dawson Street. (*Thom's Directory.* 1926. p. 1563.) The 'great poulterer's of D'Olier Street' was probably the establishment of Joseph Dunn, 'fish, poultry, game and ice merchant.' (*Thom's Directory.* 1922. p. 1567.) For a historical note on D'Olier Street see: Liddy, *Dublin,* pp. 160-161.

74. The Irish Automobile Club was founded in the Shelbourne Hotel in 1901. The Club provided a valuable ambulance service during the first World War and in 1919, George V honoured the Club with the designation *Royal* Irish Automoblie Club. I am grateful to the Secretary, Wilfred Fitzsimmons for this information. Historical records of the Club may be consulted in the Guinness/Segrave Library in the Club.

75. The 'Bon Bouche Restaurant' was situated at No. 51 Dawson Street (*Thom's Directory,* 1922. p. 1565) and also at No. 89, Grafton Street (*Thom's Directory,* 1922. p. 1609); 'Fuller's (Ltd.), American Confectioners' was at No. 84 Grafton Street (*Thom's Directory,* 1922. p. 1609). For a historical note on Grafton Street see: Liddy, *Dublin.* pp. 134-135.

76. B. Hyam, Men's and Boy's Outfitters, was situated at 33-34 Westmoreland Street. (*Thom's Directory,* 1926. p. 1745.)

77. For a discussion on the relevance of colour in Beckett's work see: Knowlson, James. *Light and Darkness in the Theatre of Samuel Beckett.* Turret Books. London. 1972; Pilling, John. *Samuel Beckett.* Routledge & Kegan Paul, London, Henley and Boston. 1976. pp. 56-57; Solomon, Philip H. "Purgatory unpurged: time, space, and language in 'Lessness' ". *Journal of Beckett Studies.* John Calder. London. 1980. no. 6. pp. 63-72.

78. The proprietor of the public house at no. 9 College Street was J. J. Burgess, Wine and Spirit Merchant, and the building was named Crampton House after Sir Philip Crampton's memorial which stood outside and was demolished by Dublin Corporation in the 'fifties. Beckett may have taken the name McLoughlin from a large legal firm M'Loughlin and Son, which occupied nos. 18 and 19 College Green. (*Thom's Directory.* 1922. pp. 1547 and 1550.) For a historical note on College Street, which changed but little until recently, see Liddy, *Dublin*, pp. 150-151.

79. O'Brien, Eoin. 'The Georgian Era, 1718-1835.' in: *A Portrait of Irish Medicine. An Illustrated History of Medicine in Ireland.* eds. E. O'Brien, A. Crookshank, G. Wolstenholme. Ward River Press. Dublin. 1984. pp. 99-101.

80. This story was related to me by the late Paul Murray, a contemporary of Jammy Clinch. Jammy (J.D.) Clinch, born 1901, played club rugby for Wanderers in 1919 the year he entered Trinity. He played his first colours match for Trinity in 1922, and his first cap for Ireland was in 1923 against Wales, after which he went on to play on thirty occasions for Ireland. While at Trinity he also participated in boxing and swimming and in 1921 he competed in the Liffey Swim for the Irish Independent Challenge Cup. Jammy's long career both on and off the rugby pitch was always colourful and anecdotes relating to him abound. He died in 1981. I am grateful to Jammy's daughter-in-law, Wendy Clinch, for these details and the photograph of Jammy at Trinity.

81. The location of Moore's statue was not lost on Joyce: 'He crossed under Tommy Moore's roguish finger. They did right to put him up over a urinal: meeting of the waters.' Joyce, James. *Ulysses.* The Bodley Head. London. 1964. p. 205.

For a biographical note on Thomas Moore, the author of *Irish Melodies,* see: Kilroy, James., in *Dictionary of Irish Literature.* ed. Robert Hogan. Gill and Macmillan. 1985. pp. 466-469.

82. Strickland. *Dictionary of Irish Artists.* vol. 2. pp. 122-125.

83. For an account of this building see: Craig, *Dublin.* pp. 283-284.

84. The beggar in the wheelchair beneath the arcade of the Bank of Ireland may be the model for B, the cripple in the wheelchair, in *Rough for Theatre I, Collected Shorter Plays,* pp. 65-73.

85. For a historical note on The Coombe see: Liddy, *Dublin,* pp. 86-87.

86. Bovril did not confine its advertising to College Street; its signs were everywhere, most especially on the trams. Messers Bovril & Co. were not without their competitors, foremost among their rivals being the firm of Oxo. These two purveyors of meat extract vied for attention on bill boards and trams, and even on the skyline. Though Bovril may have had pride of place opposite Trinity College, Oxo was not far away seeking the eye of the denizens of Merrion Square and Nassau Street with an electric sign above Senator Fanning's public house (now the Lincoln Inn) in Lincoln Place at the rear of Trinity. Niall Sheridan, a consummate raconteur has preserved a tragi-comic saga of the Oxo sign. One day the first O in Oxo failed to light, and an electrician named Joe, known not only for his professional prowess, but also well liked for his wit and geniality, was summoned to rectify the fault. But, having dallied a little too long in the convivial bar of Fanning's before ascending to his task, he slipped from the rooftop and was killed. That evening there was an air of gloom in Fanning's, where Brinsley MacNamara, Austin Clarke, Fred Higgins, and Seamus O'Sullivan were among the gathering. Oliver St. John Gogarty joined the company and the bartending senator, to mark the sad occasion, stood a free drink on the house. Raising his glass to the proprietor, Gogarty bowed and, adroitly misquoting Milton, intoned: 'They also stand who only serve and wait.' It was suggested that he should write an epitaph for the late electrician. The senator provided a pencil and a brown paper bag of the type designed to hold snugly a half-dozen Guinness, and Gogarty after some thought wrote -

'Here is my tribute to engineer Joe,
Who fell to his death through the O in OXO,
He's gone to a land which is far far better,
He went, as he came, through a hole in a letter.'

(O'Brien, Eoin. 'The Wit of Oliver Gogarty'. *British Medical Journal.* 1976: vol. 1. p. 828.)

For a historical note on Fox's Corner, see Liddy, *Dublin.* pp. 136-137.

87. A glance at the entries in *Thom's Directory* for 1927 shows the following assortment of businesses in the northern part of Pearse Street: Nicholl, Thomas J. & Son Ltd. Coal merchant; Tedcastle, M'Cormick & Co. Ltd. Coal merchant; Sharp and Emery, Monumental works; Cervi, Lawrence, ice-cream saloon; Carroll J.J. & Co. ship owners and coal merchant; Cervi, Guiseppe, fried fish shop; Sharp, Edmund, Sculptor; Palace Cinema, J. J. Jack Eppel. Manager; Andreucetti, A. Italian supper saloon; Harrison, Chas. W. & Sons. Sculptors and Modellers; Hibernian Dairies; Smyth, George & Son, Monumental Sculptors and all kinds of church work. Metal foundries, engineering works, architects, solicitors, drapers, tobacconists, film distributors, advertisers, printers, and magazine proprietors are all represented. For a history of Pearse Street, see also the *Walsh Manuscripts.* National Library of Ireland.

88. *Thom's Directory.* 1904. (p. 1435.) lists Pearse, James., ecclesiastical and architectural sculptor.

89. For a life of Padraic Pearse see: Edwards, Ruth Dudley. *Patrick Pearse: the triumph of failure.* Gollancz. London. 1977.

90. For a historical note on Tara Street Fire Station and the Fire Brigade see: Liddy, *Dublin*, pp. 152-153.

91. A number of inter-related references may be found in this short passage from *More Pricks than Kicks.* The 'Piazza della Signoria', once the political centre of Florence, owes its spectacular appearance to the Palazzo Vecchio and the Loggia dei Lanzi on two sides, and to an array of magnificent sculpture that includes the equestrian statue of Cosino the Younger and the Fountain of Neptune. 'The No 1 tram' which passed along Pearse Street in the 'twenties to the terminus at the Martello Tower at Sandymount may have suggested to Beckett an association between the Florentine fire-station and St. John as there is a Church of St. John almost beside the Martello Tower. (That this church is dedicated to St. John the Evangelist and not St. John the Baptist may not have been known to Beckett). The reference to the

'Feast of St. John' probably reflects Beckett's considerable interest in Dante whom he was studying at the time:

> O gather them to the foot of the dismal shrub
> I was of the city that changed its first patron for
> the Baptist, on which account he
>
> with his art will always make it sorrowful; and
> were it not that at the passage of the Arno
> there yet remains some semblance of him,
>
> those citizens, who afterwards rebuilt it on the
> ashes left by Attila, would have laboured in
> vain. I made a gibbet for myself of my own
> dwelling.
>
> (*The Inferno.* Canto XIII; lines 143-150; p. 143.)

These lines may be explained as follows: 'In Pagan times the patron of Florence was Mars, but when the Florentines were converted to Christianity they built a church in the place of the temple that had been raised in his honour, and dedicated it to St. John the Baptist. The statue of Mars was first stowed away in a tower near the Arno, into which river it fell when the city was destroyed by Attila (whom Dante, following a common error of the time, confounds with Totila). It was subsequently re-erected on the Ponte Vecchio, though in a mutilated state; but for this circumstance, so the superstition ran, the Florentines would never have succeeded in rebuilding the city. As it was, they attributed the unceasing strife within their walls to the offended dignity of the heathen God.' (*The Inferno of Dante Aligheiri.* The Temple Classics. J.M. Dent & Sons. London. E.P. Dutton & Co. New York. 1970. p. 145.)

The 'Cascine' is an eighteenth century park on the banks of the Arno that was laid out around the Grand Ducal dairy farms. It was once possible to walk down a narrow dark passageway by the side of the 'sinister Uffizi' Museum to the parapets on the bank of the river Arno. The Palazzo Vecchio, with its magnificent collection of paintings, sculpture and tapestries, is dominated by a lofty bell-tower, which was brought to Belacqua's mind by the watch-tower of the Tara Street fire-station. The Florentine religious reformer Girolamo Savonarola (1452-1498) in an outburst of fanatical zeal organised a bonfire of vanities and works of art on Pazza della Signoria in 1497, and within a year he was burned at the stake on the same spot, which is today marked by a bronze plaque.

9 2 . De Burca, Seamus. *The Queen's Royal Theatre. Dublin 1829-1969.* De Burca. Dublin. 1982.

9 3 . *More Pricks than Kicks*, p. 42.

9 4 . For a history of the Abbey see: Byrne, Dawson. *The Story of Ireland's National Theatre: The Abbey Theatre.* Dublin. The Talbot Press. Dublin. 1929; Kavanagh, Peter. *The Story of the Abbey Theatre.* The National Poetry Foundation. University of Maine at Orono. 1984.

Beckett may not have been unaware of the irony in Murphy's choice of location for the deposition of his remains. The old Abbey Theatre opened in 1904 on the premises that had once served as the Mechanic's Institute and City Morgue. For a discussion on 'the necessary house' see: Rabinovitz, *Samuel Beckett's Fiction.* p 123, and Kennedy, *Murphy's Bed*, pp. 267-268. For an account of the plays attended by Beckett see: Knowlson, James. *Samuel Beckett: an exhibition.* Turret Books. London. 1971. pp. 22-23.

9 5 . The Gate Theatre, now part of the Rotunda Buildings on Parnell Square, was founded by Michaél mac Liammóir and Hilton Edwards as The Dublin Gate Theatre Studios. It opened with *Peer Gynt* on 14 October, 1928, and has been an important influence on Irish Theatre ever since. For a historical essay on the Gate Theatre see: Pine, Richard. 'The Gate Theatre 1928-1978'. in: *All For Hecuba: an exhibition to mark the GOLDEN JUBILEE 1928-1978 of the Edwards-mac Liammóir partnership and of the Dublin Gate Theatre.* ed. Richard Pine. Dublin. 1978, and Liddy, *Dublin.* pp. 26-27.

9 6 . *More Pricks than Kicks*, p. 43. *Thom's Directory*, 1927, (p. 1488.) lists the sanitary engineers Messers. Dunwoody and Dobson at No. 32, and Messers. M'Manus, Hallet, and Best, plumbers and sanitary engineers at No. 6.

9 7 . Michael Coughlan, wine and spirit merchant occupied nos. 1-2 Lombard Street, and at the intersection of Townsend Street with Lombard Street, Annie Shine occupied no. 111 (later to come under the proprietorship of Richard Beamish); J. Crilly occupied no. 112 Townsend Street, each being grocers, wine and spirit merchants. (*Thom's Directory*, 1927.)

9 8 . The Grosvenor Hotel was situated at no. 5 Westland Row, under the proprietorship of the Metropole Hotels Co. Ireland. (*Thom's Directory.* 1922. p. 1793.) See also the *Walsh Manuscripts* in the National Library of Ireland.

9 9 . Joyce, *Ulysses*. pp. 89-90. p. 106.

1 0 0 . When I visited Kennedy's in 1983, Mrs. Kennedy kindly gave me details of the establishment's history and a billhead which read 'W. & M. KENNEDY, High-class Family Grocers and Italian Warehousemen, Teas, Choice Wines and Old Liquer Whiskies.' Mr. Kennedy, whose health was failing, adjusted the lights, and my notes record that 'Mr. Kennedy turned on the gloom'.

1 0 1 . For a historical note on the Public Library, Pearse Street see: *The Weekly Irish Times.* 10 April 1909.

1 0 2 . O'Dwyer, Frederick. *Lost Dublin.* Gill and Macmillan. Dublin. 1981. p. 69.

1 0 3 . Joyce, *Ulysses.* p. 682.

1 0 4 . May Oblong's fame lives on in a play written in her memory; *The End of Mrs. Oblong* had it's World Premiere in the Eagle Theatre, Glasthule in 1973, where it ran to over 200 performances. (Seamus de Burca. *The End of Mrs. Oblong.* P.H. Bourke. Dublin. 1975.) For an account of the 'Kips' and its Madams, see: O'Connor, Ulick. *The Times I've Seen: Oliver St. John Gogarty, A Biography.* Ivan Obolensky, Inc. New York. 1963. pp. 54-58.

1 0 5 . The Kips survived until the late 'twenties in spite of many determined attempts to eradicate the area and its occupants. In 1908, when Tyrone Street was demolished by the police, Gogarty composed the sonnet 'When the Clearance was Intended to the Kips', which later appeared with its title modified to 'When the Clearance was Intended to the City' in *Hyperthuleana*, a collection of poems published privately in 1916 by the Gaelic Press, Dublin. The poem is quoted in full in: O'Connor. *Gogarty.* pp. 145-146.

1 0 6 . Quoted in Lyons, J.B. *Oliver St. John Gogarty, The man of many talents.* Blackwater, Dublin. 1980. p. 38.

Dougald McMillan comments also on Becky Cooper's notoriety, labelling her as 'Dublin's most famous prostitute', whose skills and attraction excelled that of the foreign girls:

> Italy's girls are pretty
> and France's girls are willing
> But dearer far to me
> Is Becky's for a shilling.

(McMillan, Dougald. *'Echo's Bones:* Starting Points for Beckett.' *Samuel Beckett. The Art of Rhetoric.* eds. Morot-Sir, Edouard., Harper, Howard., McMillan, Dougald III. North Carolina Studies in the Romanic Languages and Literature. Chapel Hill. 1976. p. 178).

Beckett did not hold Gogarty's poetry in high regard as is evident from the absence of any critical appraisal of it in his essay on 'Recent Irish Poetry', nor is he impressed by Yeats' esteem for Gogarty's poetry, which many believed was a manifestation of friendship rather than critical analysis: "Mr W.B. Yeats, as he wove the best embroideries, so he is more alive than any of his contemporaries or scholars to the superannuation of these, and to the virtues of a verse that shall be nudist. 'There's more enterprise in going naked'. It eliminates swank - unless of course the song has something to swank about. His bequest in 'The Tower' of his pride and faith to the 'young upstanding men' has something almost second-best bed, as though he knew that they would be embarrassed to find an application for those dispositions. Yet when he speaks, in his preface to Senator Gogarty's 'Wild Apples,' of the 'sense of hardship borne and chosen out of pride' as the ultimate theme of the Irish writer, it is as though he were to derive in direct descent the very latest prize canary from that fabulous bird, the mesozoic pelican, addicted, though childless to self-eviscerations." (*Disjecta*, pp. 71-72). This essay was published in 1934 three years before Beckett appeared as chief witness for the prosecution in the libel action: Sinclair v. Gogarty. For an account of this trial see: O'Connor, *Gogarty*. pp. 319-332, and Leventhal, A.J. 'The Thirties' in *Beckett at Sixty. A Festschrift.* Calder and Boyars, London. 1967. pp. 8-9.

107. The rain in Ireland, of which there is plenty, though usually derided brings to the scenery of the land a freshness and charm that not many appreciate; Beckett was one who did: 'What would Ireland be, though without this rain of hers. Rain is part of her charm. The impression one enjoys before landscape in Ireland, even on the clearest of days, of seeing it through a veil of tears, the mitigation of contour, to quote Chas's felicitous expression, in the compresses of our national visibility to what source can this benefit be ascribed if not to our incontinent skies?' (*Dream of Fair to Middling Women*, p. 213).

108. *More Pricks than Kicks*, p. 77.
The relevance of the figure 8 in Beckett's philosophy is manifest in an unpublished manuscript 'The Way' in the Humanities Research Center in Austin. Beckett plots a journey 'Whose route circumscribes the figure 8.' This composition is, in Carlton Lake's opinion, 'the distillation of all the journeys made by all of Beckett's eternal wanderers.' (Lake, Carlton, *No Symbols where none intended. A Catalogue of Books, Manuscripts and Other Material Relating to Samuel Beckett in the Collections of the Humanities Research Center.* Humanities Research Center. The University of Texas at Austin. 1984. pp. 172-174.) It is of interest to note Beckett's use of the figure eight printed on its side in 'The Way', and also in his review of Denis Devlin's poems. (Beckett, Samuel. 'Denis Devlin'. *Transition. Tenth Anniversary,* 27 April-May. 1983. pp. 289-294. Republished *Disjecta*. p. 93.)

109. *Dream of Fair to Middling Women,* p. 135.

110. For historical details of this illustrious Dublin rugby club see: *Bective Rangers Football Club. Centenary Year 1981-1982.* Published Privately. Dublin 1982.

111. For a historical note on the O'Connell Monument see: Liddy, *Dublin,* pp. 36-37, and O'Connell Street, pp. 1-3.

112. The General Post Office was erected in 1818. 'It is a very imposing and magnificent building of granite, measuring 223 feet in front, 150 feet in depth, and fifty feet in height, and consists of three stories. It is built in the Ionic order, having in the centre a noble hexastyle portico of Portland stone, eighty feet from north to south, and extending over the flagway of the street; the pillars are fluted, and four feet and a half in diameter. Above the pediment are colossal statues of Hibernia, in the centre, with Mercury and Fidelity at each extreme ... The building was designed by Francis Johnston, commenced in 1815, and completed in 1817, at a cost of more than £50,000.' (*Dublin and its Environs: with A Map of the City.* James McGlashan, Dublin. 1846. pp. 37-38. See also Craig, *Dublin,* p. 285, and Liddy, *Dublin.* pp. 12-13.)

113. *The Fall of Cuchulain* is by Oliver Sheppard; see: Crookshank, Anne. *Irish Sculpture from 1600 to the present day.* The Department of Foreign Affairs. Dublin 1984. pp. 52-53.

114. The signatories of the Proclamation of the Republic, 24th April 1916, were: Thomas J. Clarke; Seán MacDiarmada; Thomas MacDonagh; P.H. Pearse; Eamonn Ceannt; James Connolly; Joseph Plunkett. MacLochlainn, Piaras F. *Last Words. Letters and statements of the leaders executed after the Rising at Easter 1916.* Kilmainham Jail Restoration Society. 1971.

115. Con Leventhal has written of an unusual request from Beckett. "B.'s hegira took him round various European countries with stays in London from which city an urgent postcard. Would I betake me to the Dublin Post Office and measure the height from the ground of Cuchulain's arse? This ancient hero, imagined by Yeats as standing beside those who fought in the G.P.O. in 1916, has a statue erected to him there 'to mark the place /By Oliver Sheppard done'. A crowd gathered round as I knelt with a tape measure to carry out my task and was lucky to get away without arrest." Leventhal, 'The Thirties'. *Beckett at Sixty.* p. 11.

116. The Dublin tramway system at its zenith had 19 routes running on 61 miles of track, which spread radially from the six-track layout at Nelson's Pillar. The system started with horse cars in 1872, but was electrified between 1897 and 1901. There was an average total of 330 tram-cars, the first of which was replaced by a bus in 1932. The last line to survive was that to Dalkey, the No.8, (also the longest line in Ireland) which was closed in 1949. The tram tracks remained (some remnants can still be seen) as nostalgic mementos of a bygone era for many years. For further details see: Finlay, Ian F. *The trams of Ireland in old picture postcards.* European Library. Zaltbommel/Netherlands. 1984, and Baker, Michael H.C. *Irish Railways since 1916.* Ian Allan. London. 1972. p. 148.

In *Watt* there is a reference to a tram from which Watt is deposited on Charlemont Street Bridge (p. 14).

117. Harvey, (*Beckett. Poet and Critic*, p. 242) suggests that Beckett may have been fascinated by Maurice Hare's limerick with its philosophical comment on predestination -

> 'There was a young man who said, 'Damn'!
> I suddenly see what I am,
> A creature that moves
> In predestined grooves,
> In fact not a bus but a tram!'

The name *Watt* may derive from *Wattman* (a French term for 'tram-driver', and in *Waiting for Godot* the names Puncher and Wattmann in Lucky's speech (p. 42) jokingly refer to a ticket-taker and a tram-driver. (Rabinovitz. *Samuel Beckett's Fiction*. p. 136, p. 147.) See also Note no. 1 above.

118. As this Dublin landmark has disappeared forever, it is of interest to record a contemporary account of its features: 'Nelson's Pillar was erected in 1808, at a cost of £6,856, raised by public subscription, to commemorate the achievements and victories of that illustrious admiral. It stands in Sackville-Street (now O'Connell Street), somewhat north of the General Post Office, and in a line between Earl and Henry Streets. It is a Doric pillar, elevated upon three steps. The pedestal is thirty feet in height, and twenty in diameter on the panels of which are inscribed the names and dates of Nelson's principal victories. The shaft of the column is fluted, and rises to the height of seventy-one feet eight inches, with a capital of seven feet, upon the abacus of which is iron palisading, enclosing a platform from which rises a podium or pedestal twelve feet six inches in height; on this stands the colossal statue of Nelson, thirteen feet high, leaning on the capstan of a ship. The column is hollow, and can be ascended to the platform by 168 steps; and a fine view of the city and bay will, if the day be clear, repay the trouble of the ascent, the charge for which is six pence.' From *Dublin and Its Environs*: p. 150. From another account (*Handbook to the City of Dublin*, p. 50) the extent of the view can be appreciated - 'a splendid panoramic view of the city, bounded by the Bay on the east, by the Carlingford and Mourne mountains to the north, and by the Dublin Hills and the Wicklow mountains on the south-west and south.'

119. Craig. *Dublin*. p. 287.

120. For a historical note see: Liddy, *Dublin*. pp. 48-49.

121. For a history of this institute which was destroyed completely in the fighting in 1916 and rebuilt in 1926 see: 'Oculus. Wynn's Hotel, Dublin.'

The Irish Builder and Engineer. 1927. vol. 69. p. 73. An interesting pamphlet outlining its somewhat turbulent history is available from the Hotel.

122. There is another reference to Nassau Street in *Dream of Fair to Middling Women*, p. 149. (quoted on p. 187).

123. North Great George's Street is not to be confused with South Great George's Street to which reference is made in *Dream of Fair to Middling Women*. (p. 132).

" 'Haffner's pork sausingers.' The Polar Bear narrowed down the field of research 'are prime, but their birds are dear. And if my family thinks' cocking the jaws 'that I am going to burst myself sweating up Georges Street' ..."

A well-known family butchers renowned for its home-made sausages - Haffner, F. & Sons, pork butchers and sausage makers was situated at no. 50 South Great George's Street. (*Thom's Directory*, 1922. p. 1601)

The address for 'the bboggs' at no. 55 North Great George's Street is fictitious, as there is no such number on the street. The street has some fine examples of Georgian Architecture and is now being restored by its residents.

124. *More Pricks than Kicks*. p. 147. Beckett may have taken the name *Tamar* from *Tomar's Wood* which is mentioned in accounts of the famous Battle of Clontarf in 1014. (Cosgrave, Dillon. *North Dublin: City and Environs*. Catholic Truth Society of Ireland. Dublin 1909. p. 117.) Alternative explanations worthy of consideration are that the name has Biblical origins (Kroll, Jeri. "Belacqua as artist and lover: 'What a Misfortune'," *Journal of Beckett Studies*, John Calder. London. 1978. no. 3. p. 24), or some connection through folklore with the name of the river Tamar in Cornwall, the name of which means 'Great Water'; 'Legend has it ... that the river was born as a result of a nymph, called Tamara, escaping into the real world and meeting two giants who lived on the granite wilderness of Dartmoor, in neighbouring Devon. The giants, Tavy and Tawrage, captured Tamara and were about to ravage her when her father arrived on the scene to help her. But Tamara had quickly picked up the ways of the wicked world and didn't want to be saved. So her father turned her into a beautiful river to which she gave her name ...' Mead, Robin. 'The Tamar'. *In Britain*, June 1985. p. 27.

125. For details on Charlemont House see: Craig. *Dublin*. p. 223-224. Charlemont House is now the home of the Hugh Lane Municipal Gallery of Modern Art.

CHAPTER 6: THE RIVER CIRCLE

1. Named after Joseph Huband, a director of the Grand Canal Company in 1791. (M'Cready, C.T. *Dublin Street Names Dated and Explained*. Carraig Books. Blackrock. 1982. pp. 14-16.) For a historical note see: Liddy, Pat. *Dublin Today*. Irish Times Publication. 1984. pp. 102-103.

2. This nursing home, named the Merrion Nursing Home, was at No. 21 Herbert Street in the charge of Miss E.G. Barrett. (*Thom's Official Directory*. 1958. p. 1094.)

3. Beckett told me that he spent three days, waiting up throughout the

nights, with his mother during her last illness. May Beckett is buried with her husband at Redford Cemetery in Greystones.

4. It may be noted here that Herbert Lane, running behind the Merrion Nursing Home was the site of the famous Pike Theatre where *Waiting for Godot*, directed by Alan Simpson, had its Irish premiere in 1955.

For a review of Irish productions of *Godot* see: Murray, Christopher. 'Beckett Productions in Ireland. A Survey.' *Irish University Review*. 1984. vol. 14. no. 1, pp. 103-125.

5. Baggot-Street Bridge, named after Robert Lord Bagod, c. 1280; the bridge was later named Macartney Bridge after a member of the Grand Canal Company, but the name did not pass into popular usage. Leeson-Street Bridge is named after Joseph Leeson, Earl of Milltown, 1763; the bridge was later named Eustace Bridge after a member of the Grand Canal Company, but again never passed into popular usage. (M'Cready. *Street Names*. p. 15.) For a historical note on the Grand Canal see: Liddy. *Dublin*. pp. 90-91, and Joyce, Weston St. John. *The Neighbourhood of Dublin. Its Topography, Antiquities and Historical Associations*. M.H. Gill and Son. Dublin and Waterford. 1912. pp. 437-448.

6. For an account of Patrick Kavanagh's life and the committee that erected the canal bank memorial see: Ryan, John. *Remembering How We Stood. Bohemian Dublin at the Mid-Century*. Gill and Macmillan. Dublin. 1975. pp. 91-126.

7. Charlemont Street bridge is named after James Caulfield (1728-99), first Earl of Charlemont, General of the Irish Volunteers, friend and patron of Henry Grattan. (M'Cready, *Street Names*. p. 15).

8. Portobello Bridge derives it's name from the area; it was later renamed La Touche Bridge after William Digges La Touche, a member of the Grand Canal Company, but the name is rarely used. (M'Cready, *Street Names*. p. 15).

9. The Portobello Nursing Home, formerly a Hotel and now an office building, has an illustrious medical history. The Portobello Nursing Home was founded in 1901 on which date it is first entered in *Thom's Directory*, (p. 1504): 'Home, Hospital. Portobello House. Miss S.E. Hampson, lady superintendant.' Sarah Hampson was one of the first 'Nightingale' nurses to come from London (St. Thomas's Hospital) to Dublin where she was appointed first nursing superintendant of the Rotunda Lying-in Hospital. For further details see: Wolstenholme, Gordon. 'The Victorian Era' in: *A Portrait of Irish Medicine: An Illustrated History of Medicine in Ireland*. eds. O'Brien, E., Crookshank, A., Wolstenholme, G. Ward River Press. Dublin. 1984. pp. 136-137.

Under the charge of Matron Tess O'Sullivan from the 'thirties to its closure in the 'sixties, many of Dublin's most famous citizens (among whom was Jack Yeats, often visited by Beckett) were treated. This nursing home is often erroneously stated to be the one in which May Beckett died. For a historical note on the Grand Canal Hotel, or La Touche House as it was once known, see: Liddy, *Dublin*. pp. 89-90.

Mercier, walking with Camier along the Grand Canal, points to a skin hospital which he describes as a 'grim pile' (*Mercier and Camier*, p.121). As Portobello Nursing Home was never a skin hospital, and as it is a fine building architecturally, Mercier cannot have been referring to it. St. Annes Skin Hospital on Northbrook Road might be just visible (with the help of a little imagination) from the canal bank, and if the institute seen by Mercier has any basis in reality, it must be it that Beckett had in mind.

10. For an analysis of this moving poem see: Harvey, Lawrence. *Samuel Beckett. Poet and Critic*. Princeton University Press. New Jersey. 1970. pp. 128-130; Fletcher, John. 'Beckett as Poet' in *Samuel Beckett. A collection of criticism edited by Ruby Cohn*. McGraw Hill. New York. 1975. pp. 42-43; Coe, Richard. 'Beckett's English' in *Samuel Beckett Humanistic Perspectives*. eds. Morris Beja, S.E. Gontarski, and Pierce Astier. Ohio State University Press. 1983. pp. 42-44.

11. Parnell bridge is named after Sir John Parnell, bart. (c. 1766.) (M'Cready, *Street Names*. p. 15).

12. See also *That Time, (Collected Shorter Plays.* p. 231.) The rails and timber symbolise the crucifixion. (Esslin, Martin. *Mediations. Essays on Brecht, Beckett and the Media*. Eyre Methuen. London. 1980. p. 112).

13. The Isolde Stores is not listed in *Thom's Official Directory* in 1922 or 1945; in fact the name Isolde does not appear in the 1922 Directory, but 'Isolde - gardens' is listed in 1945 (p. 1285). For a history of this ancient and interesting locality see: Ball, Francis Elrington. *A History of the County of Dublin*. Part 4. Alex Thom. & Co. Dublin. 1906. pp. 163-178, and D'Alton, John. *The History of County Dublin*. Tower Books. Cork. 1976. pp. 271-175.

14. *Dream of Fair to Middling Women*, p. 25.

15. A battle between Sir William Skeffington and Silken Thomas took place at Island Bridge in 1535, but it is unlikely that Beckett's reference to the bridge being 'consumed utterly by brimstone' refers to this event. The original bridge was swept away by floods in 1787 when it was replaced by the present structure, known for many years as Sarah Bridge, after Sarah, Countess of Westmoreland who laid the first stone. (Joyce. *Neighbourhood of Dublin*. pp. 344-345.)
It is appropriate, as we are in the vicinity of the Phoenix Park, to mention here that Dublin's Royal Zoological Gardens are situated in this great expanse of parkland. It is, perhaps, unusual that the zoo which features so vividly in the memories of many Dubliners is mentioned only once and briefly in Beckett's work in *The Expelled, (Collected Shorter Prose*. p. 29.)

16. The Lucan Spa Hotel is entered in *Thom's Directory*. 1906. (p. 1791.): 'Lucan Hydro and Spa Hotel Co. (Limited).' The 'Stillorgan Sunshine Home' mentioned in the same breath as the 'Lucan Spa Hotel' would have been well known to Beckett as it was situated next door to the kindergarten school of the Misses Elsner on Leopardstown Road. 'Children's Sunshine Home - matron Miss Pearson; treasurer, Miss Overend.' (*Thom's Directory*. 1945. p. 1418.) This institution is still in existence.

17. Formerly called the Royal Barracks this Georgian building was handed over to the National Army in 1922 and renamed in honour of Michael Collins. (Guinness, Desmond. *Georgian Dublin*. B.T. Batsford. Ltd., London. 1979. pp. 38-39).

18. Harvey, John. *Dublin. A Study in Environment*. Batsford Ltd. London and New York. 1949. p. 61. The Poddle, so named in a statute of 1463 and called Puddell in 1603, is an artificial water-course, partly fed by streams, but chiefly derived from the river Dodder. (M'Cready, *Street Names*. p. 83).

19. See also: *The End, Collected Shorter Prose*. p. 67.

20. For an account of the old city and its gates see: Fitzpatrick, Samuel A. Ossory. *Dublin. A Historical and Topographic Account of the City*. Methuen and Co. London. 1907. p. 51-53. For a detailed map showing the location of the city's rivers and ancient gates, see: Clarke, Howard B. *Dublin c. 840 to c. 1540: the Medieval Town in the Modern City*. Ordinance Survey. Dublin. 1978.

21. *The Calmative. Collected Shorter Prose*, p. 54 and p. 62.

22. *More Pricks than Kicks*, p. 190.

23. The Tolka river rises in County Meath, and some nineteen miles later reaches the sea near the mouth of the Liffey. (Cosgrave, Dillon. *North Dublin City and Environs*, Catholic Truth Society of Ireland. Dublin. 1909. p. 30.)

Page 369

24. The dramatic colours of the Liffey skies at sunset had also impressed Belacqua in *More Pricks than Kicks* (p. 41).

25. Good examples of drinking fountains for horses may be found on Stephen's Green, (this one bears the inscription: 'Presented by the Corporation and citizens of Dublin in memory of Lady Laura Grattan, 1880'), and St. Patrick's Close. (for a drawing of this monument see: Liddy. *Dublin*. p. 82, p. 122) Most, however, have disappeared.

26. See also for mention of Guinness barges: *Enueg I, Collected Poems*. p. 10.; *Dream of Fair to Middling Women*, p. 25. For a historical note on the famous Guinness Barges see: Liddy, *Dublin*. pp. 58-59.

27. Wellington Bridge is named in memory of the Duke of Wellington's victory at Waterloo in 1815. The metal bridge was erected in 1816 at a cost of £3,000 in lieu of a ferry and a toll was charged from which the name the Ha'penny Bridge derives. For a historical note see Liddy. *Dublin*. pp. 62-63.

28. The Bridge features again later in *Dream of Fair to Middling Women* (p. 139): 'Now Belacqua is on the bridge with Nemo, they are curved over the parapet, their bottoms are outlined and not in vain in the dusk descending. He lifts his head in due course to the doomed flowers, the livid tulips. Very poignant, yes, they lananate his little breast, they seldom fail to oblige. His hips are brought down and his head again, yes the gulls were there. They never miss an evening. They are grey shish in the spewing meatus of the sewer. Now it is time to go, it is yet time. They lapse down together and away along the night quays, they have oeded, (sic) they are being harried from the city. It is the placenta of the departed, the red rigor of post partum.' See also: *Enueg I*, and *Enueg II, Collected Poems*. p. 10 and p. 13, in which the above passage forms the basis for the poetic lines on the Liffey.

29. Jim Beckett, one of Ireland's most talented all-round sportsmen was born on 20 October, 1884 and died on 19 March, 1971 in the Adelaide Hospital. The following obituary notice summarises his achievements: "DEATH OF DR. JIM BECKETT NOTED SPORTSMAN. Dr. Jim Beckett, who has died in Dublin, was a superb sportsman, who in water polo had the unique distinction of representing Ireland 25 times between 1902 and 1925. Educated at Wesley College and Trinity College, Dublin, he graduated in medicine in 1911. On the outbreak of the first World War he went to France with the R.A.M.C. He will be long remembered in the Adelaide Hospital, Dublin, where he was anaesthetist for 25 years. Dr. Beckett played rugby for Old Wesley from 1903 to 1910, and represented Leinster on three occasions. As far back as 1910 and 1911 he was Captain of Dublin United Hospitals' team against London colleagues. Boxing held his interest and in 1910 and 1911 he was heavyweight champion of Dublin University. In swimming he held all the Irish championships at various times and the 100 yards six times between 1902 and 1919. It was in 1909 he made the Irish record of 61 seconds which remained unbroken for 27 years. He won the Dublin University Championship three times. In water polo he captained Ireland in the 1924 Olympic games in Paris. He was past president of the Irish Amateur Swimming Association and Leinster Rugby Referees' Association. Dr. Beckett had an abiding interest in music and for 23 years from 1924, he gave splendid service as hon. secretary of the Strollers in Dublin. Yesterday, at his funeral in Enniskerry, Co. Wicklow, the band of the Strollers sang a requiem in St. Patrick's Church. Bishop Hodges in an appreciation based on long friendship, said that 'Dr. Jim' had been a man of wonderful qualities for whom the trumpets must have sounded triumphantly. In the service he was joined by the Rev. Canon A.E. Stokes and the Rev. J.M.G. Carey.

The chief mourners were Mrs. Peggy Beckett (widow); Dr. Desmond Beckett (son); and Mrs. Margo Magan and Mrs. Olga Main (daughters). Sam Beckett, the Irish playwright, a nephew of the late Dr. Beckett, sent a telegram of sympathy from Paris, regretting inability to attend the funeral because of illness." (By courtesy Margo Magan; probable source *The Irish Times*.)

30. O'Connor, Ulick. *Sport is my Lifeline. Essays from The Sunday Times*. Pelham Books, London. 1984. p. 116. O'Connor in quoting the verse from memory has substituted Jim Beckett, with whose swimming prowess he was familiar, for Tallon. The original verse was written in tribute to Dockrell, Tallon and Tagert, Ireland's leading amateur swimmers in about 1909 by L.A.G. Strong in a poem, *The Forty-Foot. A Retrospect* -

> Well, that's ten years ago and more,
> And I am far from Kelly Shore,
> And Ring Rock: no one that I love
> Is left at all in Sandycove . . .
> Dockrell, Tallon, Tagert – where
> Are the men I worshipped there?
> Some still rub the pink flesh dry,
> Some have laid their towels by.
> Some go by the Round Tower still,
> Some are passed to Hy Brasil . . .

(Quoted from Wall, Mervyn. *Forty Foot Gentlemen Only*. Allen Figgis. Dublin 1962. pp. 24-25.)

31. For a description of the statue and a biographical essay of John Henry Foley who sculpted so much of Dublin's statuary see: Strickland, Walter George. *A Dictionary of Irish Artists*. Irish University Press. Shannon. 1969. Vol. 1. pp. 357-365.

32. The Ballast Office on the corner of Westmoreland Street and Aston's Quay, recently demolished and rebuilt to resemble, at least in its exterior appearance, the old Ballast Office (except that the famous clock for some inexplicable reason has been placed on the Quay side rather than as formerly on the Westmoreland Street facade), was established to improve navigation on the Liffey, and had the authority to compel ships to take ballast from the centre of the Liffey channel rather than from the banks which were being destroyed by the practice. (Broad, Ian. 'Dublin's South Side.' *The Irish Times*. March 6, 1975. p. 10.)

33. For a brief history of the building that housed the Grand Central Cinema and from where Percy Bysshe Shelley once addressed the citizens of Dublin, see: Liddy, *Dublin*. pp. 54-55.

34. Named after Sir Issac Butt, it was erected in 1879 as a centre pivoted swing bridge, and was replaced by the present concrete structure in 1932. (O'Dwyer, Frederick *Lost Dublin*. Gill and Macmillan, Dublin 1981. p. 62).

35. For an analysis of this poem see: Harvey. *Beckett. Poet and Critic*. pp. 96-98.

36. For a history of this impressive building see: McParland, Edward. *James Gandon. Vitruvius Hibernicus*. A. Zwemmer Ltd. London. 1985. pp. 45-72.

37. The reference to 'the ladies and gentlemen of the theatre' is possibly to the cast of a play returning to London after playing for a week or two at the Gaiety Theatre. (I am indebted to Matthew Murtagh for this suggestion). The B & I Boat also features in an obscure riddle in the

early dialogue *Che Sciagura*. (See Chapter 9). An early account of the B & I service reads: 'The British and Irish Steam Packet Co. maintains a splendid service of steamers between Liverpool and Dublin's North Wall. A steamer sails each week-night direct from Liverpool to Dublin and vice versa. This route is favoured by those who prefer a longer sea journey but perhaps a more attractive feature is the opportunity which passengers are offered of obtaining a full night's sleep on the journey across. Ordinary return fares from London to Dublin 1st Class, 115s, 3rd class Rail and Saloon, 82s, 3rd class, 65s.' (*Handbook to the City of Dublin and the Surrounding District*. The University Press. Dublin. 1908. pp. 12-13.)

38. 'Foley's Folly' is in reality Barrington's Tower in Foxrock. See also Chapter 1.

39. The trams serving the southside of Dublin were replaced in 1947 by buses. (Baker, Michael H.C. *Irish Railways since 1916*. Ian Allan. London. 1972. p. 183).

40. I was at a loss to explain why Voice A even considered the number eleven bus, as there are other more direct bus routes to Foxrock. However, Beckett told me that his father often travelled on the number eleven from his office (the number eleven would have passed up Dawson Street close to his offices in Clare Street), and then walk from Clonskeagh to Foxrock. Presumably, if the weather was bad he could have taken the 'Slow and Easy' train from close-by Dundrum Station to Foxrock. Voice A's opening statement suggests that he may previously have taken William Beckett's course to Foley's Folly:
'that time you went back that last time to look was the ruin still there where you hid as a child when was that (*Eyes close*.) grey day took the

eleven to the end of the line and on from there no no trams then all gone long ago that time you went back to look was the ruin still there where you hid as a child that last time not a tram left in the place only the old rails when was that' (*That Time*, p. 228)

41. The last train ran on the Dublin and South Eastern (Harcourt Street) line at 4.25 p.m. on December 31st, 1958. (Shepherd, W.E. *The Dublin and South Eastern Railway*. David and Charles. London and Vancouver. 1974. pp. 171-184.)

42. The gas works situated close to the Gasometer are mentioned briefly in *Dream of Fair to Middling Women*, (p. 32).

43. Broad, 'Dublin's South Side.'

44. Harvey. *Beckett, Poet and Critic*. pp. 96-98. For an alternative analysis of this poem see: McMillan, Dougald. '*Echo's Bones*: Starting Points for Beckett' in *Samuel Beckett. The Art of Rhetoric*. eds. Morot-Sir, Edouard., Harper, Howard., McMillan, Dougald III. North Carolina Studies in the Romanic Languages and Literature. 1976. p. 181.

45. For further details on these lighthouses see: Craig. *Dublin*. pp. 89-93. These lighthouses are probably the 'lights' referred to in *The Calmative*, (*Collected Shorter Prose*.p. 39.)

46. Another river, the Dodder, enters the sea at Ringsend and is crossed a short distance from its mouth by Ballsbridge, known to irreverent local wags as 'Testicle Viaduct'; it is mentioned once in *Dream of Fair to Middling Women*: 'Telephone for Surgeon Battey, Ballsbridge two and a bit. See how my sweat is yellow, see how it stains my pilch. My pus is laudable yellow sweet and faint.' (p. 73.)

CHAPTER 7: DUBLIN'S LUNATIC ASYLUMS

1. There are a number of references to Dublin hospitals in Beckett's writing: The Portobello Nursing Home (pp. 200-201); The Elpis Nursing Home (pp. 156-157); The Merrion Nursing Home (pp. 195-197); The Coombe Maternity Hospital (p. 163); Holles Street Hospital (The National Maternity Hospital) (p. 165). The association of The Royal Hospital at Kilmainham in Dublin, the Chelsea Royal Hospital, the Western Hospital in London, and of the Hôpital Necker in Paris to events in Beckett's literature are examined by: Coe, Richard N. 'Beckett's English' in *Samuel Beckett. Humanistic Perspectives*. eds. Morris Beja, S.E. Gontarski, Pierre Astier. Ohio State University Press. 1983. p. 47. Other Beckettian institutes which might be general hospitals, geriatric institutes or mental asylums are to be found in *How It Is* (p. 85), *The End* (*Collected Shorter Prose*. pp. 51-54), and the opening sequence of *Malone Dies*.

In *Watt*, there is an asylum of sorts, but it is not readily identifiable. If it has a basis in reality, the proximity of the institute to Mr. Knott's house suggests again St. John of God's asylum in nearby Stillorgan, but even this is not close enough as Mr. Knott's garden appears to almost adjoin that of the asylum. Moreover, 'Sam' wears a uniform which suggests that Beckett may have had close-by Leopardstown Hospital in mind. This institute cared for the old-age pensioners of the British Services until recently. It is entered in *Thom's Official Directory*, 1960. (p. 832.): 'Training Hospital for Wounded Soldiers.'

My father was visiting physician to this hospital, and he often took me with him on his rounds to instruct me in clinical medicine. My memory of this hospital is dominated by its air of tranquility. In spacious wooded grounds the inmates, dressed in blue serge uniforms wandered aimlessly and peacefully about smoking their pipes. (I think there was a weekly tobacco allowance). The hospital wards in which I palpated and auscultated the obliging inmates were in single story 'pavilions' connected by corridors. The matron and the resident doctor, who often hosted splendid soirées, resided in a fine mansion with beautiful views of the Dublin mountains, and adjoining Leopardstown racecourse and Croker's gallops. For a discussion of the asylum in *Watt* see: Cohn, Ruby. *Back to Beckett*. Princeton University Press. New Jersey. 1973. pp. 44-45, and Mercier, Vivian. *Beckett/Beckett*. Oxford University Press. Oxford. New York. Toronto. Melbourne. 1979. pp. 166-167.

2. Barnard, G.C. *Samuel Beckett. A New Approach. A Study of the Novels and Plays*. J.M. Dent & Sons. Ltd., London. 1971. p. 132.

3. The MMM probably has its origins in Bethlehem Royal Hospital in Kent where Beckett's close friend Dr. Geoffrey Thompson, a psychiatrist, was working in the thirties. Boyle, Kay. 'All Mankind Is Us' in: *Samuel Beckett; a collection of criticism edited by Ruby Cohn*. McGraw-Hill Book Company. 1975. pp. 15-19.

4. For a more detailed discussion of the similarities between the insane in Swift's writing and that of Beckett see: Fletcher, John. *The Novels of Samuel Beckett.* Chatto and Windus. London. 1964. pp. 160-161.

5. For an interesting poem on Swift's Hospital see : 'Mnemosyne Lay in Dust (1966)'. *Austin Clarke. Selected Poems. Edited with an introduction by Thomas Kinsella.* The Dolmen Press, Dublin and Wake Forest University Press, North America. 1976. pp. 79-82.

6. Swift, Jonathan. 'Verses on the Death of Dr. Swift.' *Swift. Gulliver's Travels and Selected Writings in Prose and Verse.* ed. John Hayward. Nonesuch Press. London. 1979. p. 824.

7. D'Alton, John. *The History of County Dublin.* Tower Books. Cork. 1976. p. 107. pp. 257-259. D'Alton in fact attributes the derivation of the name Fingal to *Fionn-Gael* meaning 'black foreigner', but if this derivation is correct, the meaning would be 'fair foreigner', a more suitable appelation for a Scandinavian warrior. However, a more likely derivation is *Fine-Gall*, meaning the territory or tribe of the Galls or Danes. (Joyce, P.W. *The Origin and History of Irish Names and Places.* vol. 1. The Educational Co. of Ireland, Dublin, and Longmans, Green and Company, London. 1873. p. 97.)

8. Joyce, Weston St. John. *The Neighbourhood of Dublin. Its topography, antiquities and historical associations.* M.H. Gill & Son Ltd. Dublin. 1912. p. 282. Another explanation for the name 'Hill of Wolves' is that 'this ridge-back hill was the last haunt of wolves in Ireland, and tradition has it that the last Irish wolf was run to earth here at the end of the eighteenth century'. (O'Shea, Tom. 'Feltrim Hill' in: *Old Tales of Fingal.* eds. Condrot R, Hurley P, Moore T. An Taisce Fingal. 1984. pp. 7-11.)

9. The windmill is thought to have been erected at the end of the seventeenth century as a woollen mill by Dutch craftsmen using best quality Dutch bricks. In 1973 it was demolished by vandals. (Flanagan, Noel. *Malahide Past and Present.* Dublin 1984. pp. 59-61.)

10. In 1946 quarrying of the Hill was begun to supply stone for the runway extension at Dublin airport. Numerous archaeological artefacts were revealed, many of which show that Feltrim Hill has neolithic associations. (Hartnett P.J, and Eogan G. 'Feltrim Hill, Co. Dublin; A Neolithic and Early Christian Site.' *Journal of the Royal Society of Antiquaries of Ireland.* 1964. vol. 94. pp. 1-37.)

11. Fourteen beech trees once stood along a path to the hill marking the Stations of the Cross which were performed by pilgrims to the holy well at Feltrim. Nearby the pilgrims left pieces of their clothing on a fairy thorn-bush. It has been suggested that the beech trees were planted to replace fourteen standing stones that may have stood as a lunar astronomical calender in pre-Christian times. (O'Shea. 'Feltrim Hill' in *Old Tales of Fingal.* p. 9.)

12. D'Alton. *County Dublin.* pp. 217-220. For a detailed account of Lambay Island's unique flora and fauna see: Praeger R.L. and Seymour H.J. eds. 'Contributions to the Natural History of Lambay, County Dublin.' *Irish Naturalist,* Jan. and Feb. 1907. pp 1-112.

13. Flanagan, *Malahide.* pp. 24-42. For a history of Malahide Castle see: Wynne, Michael, *Malahide Castle.* Irish Heritage Series No. 22. Eason & Son. Dublin 1978.

14. D'Alton, *County Dublin.* pp. 85-87; see also: Ball, Francis Elrington. *A History of County Dublin. Part 5. Howth and Its Owners.* The University Press. Dublin. 1917. pp. 15-19.

15. D'Alton. *County Dublin.* pp. 242-243.

16. Flanagan. *Malahide.* pp. 161-164.

17. Elaborate plans were circulated - 'To leffen as much as poffible that Confufion which muft neceffarily take Place in cafe of Alarm on the landing of the Enemy, - the following PLAN for the more eafy Removal of the Women and Children, and the aged and infirm, from Villages near the Sea Coaft to the Place of general Military Rendezvous, is recommended.' Thirty-nine Martello Towers are still standing in Ireland, of which twenty-one are in the county of Dublin. Enoch, Victor J. *The Martello Towers of Ireland.* Eason and Son Ltd. n.d. p. 1.

18. I am indebted to Dr. Michael Conway, Clinical Director and Medical Superintendent, St. Ita's Hospital, Portrane, Donabate, Co. Dublin for giving so generously of his time in escorting me around his hospital and for allowing me to read the text of a talk he delivered on the history of the hospital in October 1981.

19. The last of the Evans family to occupy Portrane was George, a Member for Parliament, in whose memory the round tower was erected by his widow in 1844. The structure, often known as Evans' Folly, is without an internal staircase, and access is gained to a chamber through a doorway some fifteen feet from the ground on the side facing Lambay. Here a marble bust of George Evans was placed bearing the inscription. 'To the memory of George Evans, M.P., an honest man, firm friend, and true patriot, this monument, a revival of the ancient architecture of his country is respectfully, affectionately and mournfully dedicated. October 1844'. The bust was removed when the tenancy passed from the Evans family. The folly pays tribute, as the inscription implies, to the ancient round towers of Ireland the origins and uses of which have provided fertile polemic for archaeological scholars over the centuries. Apart from two examples, probably erected by the Irish in Scotland, they are unique to Ireland. It is accepted that they were erected well before the Danish settlements and probably before the introduction of Christianity in 432 A.D. As to their function there are many theories; they may have been used for protection of person or goods, as anchorite towers, or as D'Alton suggests 'as fire houses for the preservation of the sacred fire, at the time when worship of the sun was the prevalent creed in Ireland.' (D'Alton. *County Dublin.* pp. 460-462. See also: Craig, Maurice. *The Architecture of Ireland from earliest times to 1880.* B.T. Batsford. Ltd. London. 1982. pp. 31-34, and Stokes, Margaret. *Early Christian Art in Ireland.* Chapman and Hall. London. 1887. pp. 164-179.) For a photographic reproduction of the Evans bust see: Bates, Peadar. 'Sophia Evans' in *Old Tales of Fingal.* p. 32. Details of the tower may also be found in: Joyce, *Neighbourhood of Dublin.* pp. 298-299.

20. For a biography of Petrie see: Stokes, William. *Life and Labours in Art and Archaeology of George Petrie.* Dublin. 1868.

21. *More Pricks than Kicks,* p. 31.

22. *More Pricks than Kicks,* p. 28.

23. D'Alton. *County Dublin.* p. 214-215.

24. The ruined church of Portrane opposite the entrance to the asylum dates back to the thirteenth century. It is now a roofless ruin surrounded by a housing estate. Within the walls of the church are the graves of the Evans family. Of greater interest is the square tower, a field's distance away, which attracted Belacqua. Known as Stella's Tower, it was built in the early eighteenth century by one named Charles Wallis who is mentioned in a letter from Swift to Stella in 1712

- 'I did not know your country place had been Portrane until you told me in your last. Has Swanton taken it of Wallis? That Wallis was a grave, wise cox-comb.' Marking the site of an old castle, it possesses an angular watch tower (reached via forty-eight stone steps) from which there is a commanding view of the coast and landscape. The tower was in good condition at the time of Belacqua's visit, but the climb to the top is now extremely perilous and the watch tower must surely soon collapse. See: D'Alton. *County Dublin*. p. 158, and Dix, McC E.R. 'The Lesser Castles in the Co. Dublin. IV.' *The Irish Builder*. Jan 1, 1879. vol. 39. p. 2.

25. *More Pricks than Kicks*, p. 33.

26. There is another reference to the witty Dean in *More Pricks than Kicks*, p. 154.

27. Swords, once the site of a leper colony and monastery is one of the oldest towns in Co. Dublin, having been founded in 550 A.D. by St. Columbkille. For a history of this interesting township see: D'Alton, *County Dublin*. pp. 136-145.

28. Beckett told me that he and Jack Yeats often walked from the city to Taylor's pub in Swords. The 'Mr. Taylor', who did not like the manner in which his client was 'drinking and laughing' was Mark Taylor, proprietor of *The Star* in Swords. This long-established public-house was burned to the ground by the Black and Tans in the 1920s as a reprisal for the republican sympathies of the family. Three of Mark Taylor's brothers had been involved in 1916 rising, and one was wounded at Ashbourne. Though it is often assumed that this family is related to 'The Family of Taylor' (D'Alton, *County Dublin*. pp. 145-150), this has never been confirmed. I am grateful to Mark Taylor of Swords for this information.

29. Harvey considers the reference to the 'sad swans of Turvey Swords' to be to one of the several gateways to Turvey House which were flanked with columns surmounted by stone swans. (Harvey, Lawrence E. *Samuel Beckett, Poet and Critic*. Princeton University Press. New Jersey. 1970. p. 140.) William Garner, Director of The Irish Architectural Archive, who photographed Turvey House before its demolition does not recall any such gates, and it is more likely that Beckett is merely referring to the abundance of swans in the area. Beckett often visited the home of his professor T.B. Rudmose-Brown at Blue Bird Cottage, Dublin Road, Malahide and some of the Malahide evocations in the 'Fingal' vignette may originate from his walks along the Broadmeadow Estuary with Rudmose-Brown. (I am grateful to Roger Little for drawing my attention to this association, and providing me with the relevant details from his biographical researches on Rudmose-Brown. See: Little, Roger. 'Valery Larbaud et les lettres Irelandaises: Connaissance de Rudmose-Brown.' *Revue de Littérature Comparée*. 1983. vol. LVII. no. 1. pp. 101-111, and Little, Roger, "Beckett's Mentor, Rudmose-Brown: Sketch for a Portrait". *Irish University Review*. 1984. vol. 14. no. 1. pp. 34-41.) No mention of the swans of Turvey is to be found in accounts of the Barnewalls of Turvey, who resided at Turvey House. (D'Alton, *County Dublin*. p. 151-158; Joyce, *Neighbourhood of Dublin*. pp. 297-306.)

30. The House of St. John of God. Stillorgan, Blackrock, Co. Dublin is entered in *Thom's Directory*, 1927. p. (1304.): 'This institution is devoted to mentally affected gentlemen. For Prospectus apply to the Rev. Prior of the Hospitaller Brothers of St. John of God as above.'

31. Montgomery holds that 'there is no recognizable similarity to connect the *asile* (Asile Saint-Jean de-Dieu) with Stillorgan Castle outside Dublin ...' but in making this statement he ignores the presence of the gate-lodge, pleasure gardens, the extensive view and proximity of the sea and Dalkey Island. (Montgomery, Niall. 'No symbols where none intended.' *New World Writing*. 1954. April 5. No. 106. pp. 324-337).

32. O'Brien, Eoin, 'The Georgian Era 1714-1835' in: *A Portrait of Irish Medicine. An Illustrated History of Medicine in Ireland*. eds. O'Brien, E., Crookshank, A., Wolstenholme, G. Ward River Press. Dublin. 1984. pp. 85-89.

CHAPTER 8: DUBLIN:

A City of Character and Characters

1. The Yellow House was, and still is, a popular public-house in Rathfarnham at the foot of the Dublin mountains. It is mentioned once in *More Pricks than Kicks*, p. 65.

2. Other Dublin newspapers that receive mention in Beckett's work are *The Irish Independent*, which is still in existence (*Eh Joe*, p. 19), and the *Weekly Irish Times*, (no longer in publication) (*Murphy*, p. 147). In *Happy Days* (p. 46) there is reference to a once popular Sunday newspaper - *Reynolds News*. Irish newspapers of the 'thirties voiced conservative sentiments in parochial manner, a characteristic given satirical treatment by Beckett in his reference to the Moscow notes of the *Evening Herald*. (*More Pricks than Kicks*, p. 54). Irish journalists shared with the majority of their countrymen the religious and patriotic prejudices that limited their intellectual perception, but for the greater part they lacked the affectation that Beckett found so offensive in that most notable of intellectual organs, *The Times Literary Supplement*: 'And in winter, under my greatcoat, I wrapped myself in swathes of newspaper, and did not shed them until the earth awoke, for good, in April. The Times Literary Supplement was admirably adapted to this purpose, of a never failing toughness and impermeability. Even farts made no impression on it.' (*Molloy*, p. 30.)

3. *More Pricks than Kicks*, p. 54.

4. Guinness's stout is almost synonymous with Dublin, though it is now available throughout the world. The famous brewery in James Street has been in existence since 1759. This beverage is mentioned in *More Pricks than Kicks*, p. 197, and *Texts for Nothing. Collected Shorter Prose*, p. 80.

5. Only the best Jameson, fifteen-year old acquired 'on tick' receives mention. (*More Pricks than Kicks*, p. 101.) This precious elixir is chosen by Belacqua and Ruby to facilitate their planned suicides, but its effect leads to more pleasurable pursuits. In the French *Mercier et Camier*, Mercier and Camier call for 'une *bouteille de J.J.*,' that is, a bottle of John Jameson's Irish whiskey. (Mercier, Vivian. *Beckett/Beckett*. Oxford University Press. Oxford. New York. Toronto. Melbourne. 1979. p. 42).

6. 'Golden Guinea' was probably a champagne. (*More Pricks than Kicks*, p. 154.)

7. Beamish stout and porter is manufactured in Cork. Beamish's porter gains mention in *Murphy*, p. 63, and in *More Pricks than Kicks*, p. 185 we find a 'Sister Beamish' in the nursing home in which Belacqua dies. The word, as much as the beverage, may have attracted Beckett - 'Come to my heart my beamish boy.' (*Thro the Looking Glass* by Lewis Carroll). In an early draft of *Krapp's Last Tape*, Beckett used the name Miss Beamish for Miss McGlome, the singer. Miss Beamish, a former Dubliner, was a woman Beckett knew during his Roussillon exile. (Gontarski, S.E. *The Intent of Undoing in Samuel Beckett's Dramatic Texts*. Indiana University Press. Bloomington. 1985. p. 63.)

8. Lipton's was a well-known purveyor of high class foods including the best teas in Dublin: 'Perhaps they meet, and sit over a cup of that green tea they both so loved, without milk or sugar, not even a squeeze of lemon ... Personally I always preferred Lipton's.' (*Play*, p. 154) The most popular tea of the period in Dublin was 'Lapsang Souchong' provided by Miss Carridge in London for Celia. (*Murphy* p. 50). Oliver Gogarty uses the assonance of the name in the poem *Ringsend* -

> And up the back garden
> The sound comes to me
> Of the lapsing, unsoilable,
> Whispering sea.'

('Ringsend (After Reading Tolstoi)' in: *Others to Adorn*. Oliver St. John Gogarty. Rich and Cowan. London 1938. p. 37).

9. Irish stew receives mention by way of oblique insult to the nation - 'I peered into the pots. Irish stew. A nourishing and economical dish, if a little indigestible. All honour to the land it has brought before the world.' (*Molloy*, p. 105).

10. There are many studies of Beckett's use of the Irish idiom; for a comprehensive discussion see: Dolan, T.P. 'Samuel Beckett's Dramatic Use of Hiberno-English.' *Irish University Review*. 1984. vol. 14. no. 1. pp. 46-56; Irish dialect in *All That Fall* is discussed in: Cohn, Ruby. *Back to Beckett*. Princeton University Press. New Jersey. 1973. p. 163, and Mercier, *Beckett/Beckett*, p. 148; the preservation of Irish dialect in translation is touched on by: Fletcher, John. *The Novels of Samuel Beckett*. Chatto and Windus. London. 1964. p. 193; that the name of Belacqua's second wife Thelma bbogg's in *More Pricks than Kicks*, (p. 127) might constitute a mockery of 'Irish landscape, orthography, and uniformity' is suggested by: Cohn, Ruby. *Samuel Beckett. The Comic Gamut*. Rutgers University Press. New Jersey. 1962. p. 34; Irish pronunciation, giving to words such as third and fourth, a lavatorial 'turd' and 'fart' is examined by: Beer, Ann. '"Watt", Knott and Beckett's bilingualism.' *Journal of Beckett Studies*. John Calder. London. 1985. no. 10. pp. 37-75. One reviewer is of the opinion that *All That Fall* is 'sited so firmly in a particular milieu, that some of the jokes need for their appreciation a first-class knowledge of the Republic of Ireland today.' (Davie, Donald. Review of 'All That Fall'. *Spectrum*. Winter 1958. pp. 25-31. It is perhaps apposite to note that Davie has written a poem 'Samuel Beckett's Dublin'. Davie, Donald. *Collected Poems. 1950-1970*. Routledge and Kegan Paul. London. 1972. pp. 51-52.)

11. *More Pricks than Kicks*, p. 46.

12. *More Pricks than Kicks*, p. 48.
The use of the common Dublin term 'mot' or 'motte' occurs again in 'Fingal' (*More Pricks than Kicks*, p. 34). For a discussion on the derivation of 'motte' see: Rabinovitz, Rubin. *The Development of Samuel Beckett's Fiction*. University of Illinois Press. Urbana and Chicago. 1984. pp. 52-53.

13. *More Pricks than Kicks*, p. 48.

14. *Endgame*, p. 16.
The word 'smithereen' is used also in *Molloy*, p. 24.

15. *Murphy*, p. 121.

16. *Watt*, p. 239.
Niall Montgomery has written: '... the dialogue of the railway officials at the end of the book (*Watt*) is accurate Dublin, as first noted by Joyce, and subsequently orchestrated in *At Swim Two Birds* by Flann O'Brien...' Montgomery. N. 'No Symbols Where None Intended.' *New World Writing*. 1954. Apr. 5. no. 106. pp. 324-337.

17. *Watt*, pp. 100-102.
For a study of the Irishness of the names in *Watt*, see: Kennedy, Sighle. 'Spirals of Need: Irish Prototypes in Samuel Beckett's Fiction.' *Yeats, Joyce and Beckett. New Light on Three Modern Writers*. eds. Kathleen McGrory and John Unterecker. Bucknell University Press, Lewisburg and Associated University Presses. London. 1976. p. 156. Examples of Irishisms are listed for Beckett's drama in: Fletcher, Beryl S, Fletcher, John. *A Student's Guide to the Plays of Samuel Beckett*. Faber and Faber. London and Boston. 1985.

18. *Molloy*, p. 117.
'What ails you' is a common Irish enquiry used also in *Dream of Fair to Middling Women*, p. 334.

19. *More Pricks than Kicks*, p. 17.
The word 'lepping' conveys a more repetitive action than 'leaping': 'Not that she neglected me, she could never have neglected me enough, but the way she kept plaguing me with our child, exhibiting her belly and breasts and saying it was due any moment, she could feel it lepping already. If it's lepping, I said, it's not mine.' (*First Love*, p. 18). In the erotic poem *Hell Crane to Starling*, in *The European Caravan*, p. 476, we find the word used again: 'But there's a bloody fine ass/lepping with stout and impurée de pommes/in the hill above Tsoar.' (Harvey, Lawrence. *Samuel Beckett. Poet and Critic*. Princeton University Press. New Jersey. 1970. p. 305). The word occurs again in *The Unnamable*, (p. 411): '... there's a story for you, I thought they were over, perhaps it's a new one, lepping fresh ...'

20. *More Pricks than Kicks*, p. 29.
The word 'eejit' is a much used Dublin expression denoting a fool or idiot.

21. 'Dante ... Bruno. Vico ... Joyce.' *Disjecta*. p. 19.

22. See: Fletcher, John and Spurling, John. *Beckett. A Study of his Plays*. Eyre Methuen. London. 1972. pp. 60-61, and p. 39.

23. Joyce, James. *Ulysses*. The Bodley Head. London. 1964. p. 444

24. *Waiting for Godot*, p. 43.
The word 'Camogie' is not listed in the Oxford Dictionary, though possible derivations from the Gaelic *camag* and *camán* for a bent-stick for hurling, shinty, hockey, and a golf-club are given.

25. 'Kapp & Peterson, Ltd. Sole meershaum and briar pipe manufacturers in Ireland, tobacconist, etc.' were situated at 35 O'Connell Street, and 55 and 117 Grafton Street. (*Thom's Official Directory*. 1922. p. 1610).

26. *The Old Tune*. An English adaptation of *La Manivelle* by Robert Pinget. (*Collected Shorter Plays*. p. 178). In this translation Beckett gives to Toupin, the name of his old friend Gorman in *Watt* (p. 237); another example of Irish dialogue in this translation is: 'Grand match, Mr. Cream, grand match, more power to you.' (p. 177).

In 1959, the script editor of the BBC, Barbara Bray, suggested to Pinget that he should write an original play for radio; Beckett translated the work into English, and gave the play a very strong Irish flavour which was accentuated in Barbara Bray's production (Third Programme, August 23, 1960) in which the central characters Cream and Gorman were played by Patrick Magee and Jack MacGowran. (Esslin, Martin. *Mediations. Essays on Brecht, Beckett, and the Media.* Eyre Methuen, London. 1980. pp. 137-138.) Beckett's translation of *La Manivelle,* in Coe's opinion 'is more effective from every point of view - poetically, dramatically, atmospherically ... than it is in the original.' (Coe, Richard, N. 'Beckett's English.' *Samuel Beckett. Humanistic Perspectives.* eds. Morris Beja, S.E. Gontarski, Pierre Astier. Ohio State University Press. 1983. p. 37). Pinget's affection for Beckett is evident in his dedication of a little text 'Sainte Marie-Madelaine', to Beckett for his sixtieth birthday. (*Beckett at Sixty. A Festschrift.* ed. John Calder. Calder and Boyars. London. 1967. pp. 84-85).

27.   *The Old Tune. Collected Shorter Plays,* p. 179.

28.   *All That Fall,* p. 22.

29.   *All That Fall,* p. 34.

30.   *Happy Days,* p. 46.

31.   *Disjecta,* p. 83.
       The word 'jizz' may also be found in *Texts for Nothing.* (p. 78): 'a week will be ample, a week in spring, that puts jizz in you.'

32.   Other examples of encounters with the police may be found in *More Pricks than Kicks,* p 152; *The Unnamable,* p. 330; *The Expelled,* pp. 26-27; *Molloy,* p. 33; *Mercier and Camier,* p. 91; *Enueg II,* p. 13.

33.   *Molloy,* p. 167.

34.   *Home Olga,* p. 8.

35.   *Che Sciagura* written in 1929, takes its title from the lament of the eunuch in Voltaire's Candide, 'Che sciagura d'essere senza coglioni' - 'What a misfortune to be without balls.' (Mercier, *Beckett/Beckett.* p. 210); see also: Cohn. *Back to Beckett,* p. 11.

36.   Giordano Bruno's *Principle of Identified Contraries* recurs throughout Beckett's writing. Bruno (1548-1600), Italian philosopher, entered the monastery of S. Domenico at Naples in 1576 at the age of 15 years, but he was soon in conflict with his superiors and he fled the monastery to spend most of his life wandering throughout Europe, publishing his Latin and Italian writings as he went. He eventually fell into the hands of the Italian Inquisition at Venice in 1592, and refusing to retract his beliefs after many years interrogation in Rome, he was burnt in 1600. 'His importance and attractiveness lie not so much in any particular aspects of his teachings ... as in his unswerving insistance on the freedom of the human mind and his belief that the quest for truth must be forward-looking not backward-looking.' (Rees, D.G. 'Bruno, Giordano.' in: *The Penguin Companion to Literature. 2. European.* ed. Anthony Thorlby. Penguin Books. Middlesex. 1969. p. 146.) For a major study of Bruno see: Singer, Dorothy Waley. *Giordano Bruno, His Life and Thought, with Annotated Translation of his Work, 'On the Infinite Universe and Worlds.'* New York. 1950; and for discussion on the place of Bruno in Beckett's writing see: Kennedy, Sighle. *Murphy's Bed. A Study real sources and sur-real associations in Samuel Beckett's first novel.* Bucknell University Press. Lewisberg. 1971. pp. 44-46.

37.   'Communion' is also referred to briefly in: *Murphy* p. 39.

38.   Another tilt at the sacrament is made in *Watt* (p. 240): 'On Sundays she remained in bed, receiving there the mass, and other meals and visitors.'

39.   The angelus bell broadcast to the nation by Radio Telefis Eireann is a recording of the bell of the Pro-Cathedral, Dublin. See:Liddy, Pat. *Dublin Today.* Irish Times Publication. 1985. pp. 42-43.

       Other references to religious prayer and custom may be found in: *Texts for Nothing,* p. 108; *The Expelled,* pp. 26-27; References to Protestants and Quakers occur in: *More Pricks than Kicks,* pp. 147, 172, 178, 184, and 201, and in *Dream of Fair to Middling Women,* pp. 9 and 90. See also: Montgomery, *No Symbols,* for a discourse on religion in Beckett's writing.

40.   For a discussion on the place of Limbo in Beckett's writing see: Cohn. *Back to Beckett.* pp. 101-102.

41.   *All That Fall,* p. 23.

42.   *Murphy,* p. 55. For a critical examination of the use of the word 'synecdoche' see: Kennedy, *Murphy's Bed.* pp. 288-290.

43.   Mays, J.C. 'Young Beckett's Irish Roots.' *Irish University Review.* 1984. vol. 14. no. 1. pp. 18-23. Beckett's problems with the censor were not, of course, confined to the Saorstat. The Lord Chamberlain insisted on so mutilating the language of *Endgame* that Beckett in exasperation wrote that he was: "tired ... of all this buggering around with guardsmen, riflemen, and huzzars. There are no alternatives to 'bastard' agreeable to me. Nevertheless I have offered them 'swine' in its place. This is definitely and finally as far as I'll go ... If 'swine' is not acceptable, then there is nothing left but to have a club production or else call the whole thing off. I simply refuse to play along any further with the licensing grocers." Lake, Carlton. *No symbols where none intended. A Catalogue of Books, Manuscripts, and Other Material Relating to Samuel Beckett in the Collections of the Humanities Research Center.* The University of Texas at Austin. 1984. p. 99.

44.   *Censorship in the Saorstat. Disjecta,* p. 88.

45.   *Censorship in the Saorstat. Disjecta,* p. 84.

46.   *Censorship in the Saorstat. Disjecta,* p. 84-85.

47.   *Censorship in the Saorstat. Disjecta,* p. 85.

48.   Harvey, *Beckett. Poet and Critic.* p. 418.

49.   Cohn. *Back to Beckett,* p. 11. Beckett's writing is often more anti-fertility than merely pro-contraceptive. In the unpublished *Eleutheria,* Dr. Andre Piouk advocates the termination of humanity by any means ranging from abortion to euthanasia; see: Cohn. *Back to Beckett.* pp. 125-127.

50.   *Censorship in the Saorstat. Disjecta,* p. 87.

51.   In *Film* (p. 31), generally considered to be one of Beckett's few published failures, the early manuscripts provide for the inclusion of more sound than the final, single, 'ssh'. The opening scene was to have included: 'No cars. One cab drawn by cantering nag, (hooves) driver standing brandishing whip. Bicycles.' (Gontarski. S.E. '*Film* and Formal Integrity' in: *Beckett. Humanistic Perspectives.* p. 132.) In other words, Beckett intended that the setting of *Film* should be the world of *Mercier and Camier,* namely Dublin. (Dodsworth, Martin. '*Film* and the religion of art.' in: *Beckett the shape changer. A symposium edited by Katherine Worth.* Routledge and Kegan Paul. London and Boston. 1975. p. 166.)

52. It is also worth noting Thomas MacGreevy's poem on a journey through Dublin in a horse-drawn cab. 'Crón Tráth na nDéithe.' *Thomas MacGreevy. Collected Poems.* ed. Thomas Dillon Redshaw. Foreword by Samuel Beckett. The Belacqua Series. Raven Arts Press/New Writers Press. 1983. pp. 24-25.

53. For a discussion of animals in Beckett's writing see p. 15; For an interesting, but by no means comprehensive, essay on animals in Beckett's work see: Connor, Steven. 'Beckett's animals.' *Journal of Beckett Studies.* John Calder. London. Autumn 1982, no. 8. pp. 29-44.

54. *Molloy*, p. 155.

55. O'Brien, Flann. *The Third Policeman.* Picador. London. 1967. p. 85. For a discussion on the bicycle in the writings of O'Brien and Beckett see: Menzies, Janet. 'Beckett's bicycles'. *Journal of Beckett Studies.* John Calder. London. Autumn 1980. no. 6. pp. 97-105.

56. For an analysis of *Sanies I* see: Harvey. *Beckett. Poet and Critic.* pp. 142-147.

57. 'The Swift' bicycle was advertised regularly in the *Irish Cyclist and Motor Cyclist* in the 'thirties as 'A Lifelong Friend' that combined 'Elegance, strength and speed' as well as safety, a feature highlighted by reference to an event reported in *Cycling*, 17th October, 1891: 'A 'Swift' Safety made by the Coventry Machinists' Co. has recently been in a terrific collision whilst going at the rate of about twenty miles an hour. Luckily the rider was scarcely hurt, but the machine was twisted into fantastic shapes. Although bent about, however, not a single part of the metal was broken.'

58. *More Pricks than Kicks,* p. 33.

59. Findlater's was a long-established firm of victuallers with a number of shops throughout Dublin; there was one branch in Foxrock village from which the van and horse delivered to the locality. The 'frieze of hawthorn' may be a reference to *Cooldrinagh* which was once surrounded by a blackthorn hedge. (Information to the author from Samuel Beckett).

60. In *Watt,* (pp. 23-24) the newspaper vendor, Evans, at Harcourt Street Station is a deformed but competent cyclist.

61. In *Endgame,* (p. 19) it is on a tandem that Nagg and Nell lose their legs, and Mercier and Camier (*Mercier and Camier* p. 20), like Moran and his son, are skilled at using an ordinary bicycle to propel both of them along.

62. The 'rustless all-steel' (*More Pricks than Kicks,* p. 93), and the 'trusty all-steel' (*Sanies I, Collected Poems,* p. 17) are references to Raleigh advertisements of the period.

63. *Molloy,* p. 141.

64. *Molloy,* p. 143-144; p. 156.

65. *Dream of Fair to Middling Women,* p. 64.

66. *Watt,* p. 24.

67. Kenner, Hugh. 'The Cartesian Centaur' in *Samuel Beckett. A Collection of Critical Essays.* ed. Martin Esslin. Prentice Hall. New Jersey. 1965. pp. 52-61.

68. Kenner. 'Cartesian Centaur'. p. 59.

69. *All That Fall*, p. 17.

70. Other references to the bicycle or cycling may be found in *Molloy*, pp. 16, 20; *Mercier and Camier,* pp. 20-21, 85; *Malone Dies,* p. 253; *Endgame,* p. 15.

71. That Beckett continued to take an interest in cycling is suggested by Kenner, ('Cartesian Centaur', p. 56): 'Thus is fulfilled the serpent's promise to Eve, *et eritis sicut dii*; and it is right that there should ride about France as these words are written, subject to Mr. Beckett's intermittent attention, a veteran racing cyclist, bald, a 'stayer', recurrent placeman in town-to-town and national championships, Christian name elusive, surname Godeau, pronounced, of course, no differently from Godot.'

72. Details of this event are reported in the *Irish Cyclist and Motorcyclist.* 11 March, 1925. p. 18. "The smallness of the entry was distinctly disappointing in the open novices' trial held by the Dublin University M.C. and L.C.C. on Saturday. There were only seven starters and two of those failed to finish, while of the surviving five two at least went off the course ...' The finishers were: J.D. Battley, 7 h.p. A.J.S. and s.c.; J. Sutton (Drogheda), 2¾ h.p. Rudge; T.J. Hegarty (Drogheda) 3½ h.p. James; B. Gardiner, 3½ h.p. Norton; and *S.B. Beckett,* 2¾ h.p. A.J.S. The two non-finishers were W. McCulloch, 3½ h.p. Norton, and P. Byrne, 4 h.p. Triumph; both had dropped out before reaching the 'Waterfall of Bricks."

The course for this race was 63 miles much of it through the Dublin mountains so familiar to Beckett. The route included most of the usual trial hills in the south Co. Dublin and north Wicklow area. The start was from Donnybrook, the route passing through Stillorgan, Dundrum, Stepaside, Glencullen, Pine Forest, Glencree, Sally Gap, Annacarta crossroads, down Calary Lane and Red Lane to the Glenview Hotel, then up the 'Waterfall of Bricks', through Delgany, back to Glenview Hotel, by the side road through watersplash to Kilmacanogue, Goat's Pass, Enniskerry, Kilmalin, Devil's Elbow, Stepaside, Dundrum, Stillorgan, and back to Donnybrook.

73. *More Pricks than Kicks.* p. 54.

74. 'Recent Irish Poetry'. First published under the pseudonym 'Andrew Belis' in *The Bookman* (London). LXXVI (August 1934), pp. 235-236. Republished *Disjecta.* pp. 70-76.

75. 'Recent Irish Poetry', *Disjecta,* p. 70.

76. 'Recent Irish Poetry' *Disjecta,* p. 70.

77. James Stephens (1880/82-1950) was born in Dublin. He wrote many novels often based on the symbolism of folklore of which *The Crock of Gold* and *The Charwoman's Daughter* are among the best known. He also wrote many volumes of poetry. (McFate, Patricia, *Dictionary of Irish Literature.* ed. Robert Hogan. Gill and MacMillan. Dublin. 1985. pp. 627-629).

78. Frederick Robert Higgins (1896-1941) was born in Foxford, Co. Mayo. A pioneer of the labour movement, he became a contributing editor to two outstanding, if short-lived, literary papers *The Klaxon* (1923-4) and *To-Morrow* (1924). (Burnham. Richard in: Hogan, *Dictionary.* pp. 295-297).

79. Monk (William) Gibbon was born in Dublin in 1896 and educated at St. Columba's College, and at Keble, Oxford. He has written a number of volumes of poetry and some autobiographic memoirs. (Hogan, *Dictionary.* pp. 260-261). See also: Wright, Barbara. 'The Prose Work of Monk Gibbon.' *The Dublin Magazine.* Autumn/Winter 1968. pp. 51-62.

80. W.B. Yeats (1865-1939), one of Ireland's best known poets, founded, with Lady Gregory, the Abbey Theatre, which was to have a significant influence on Irish drama and literature. For discussion of Yeats's writing see: Bloom, Harold. *Yeats.* Oxford University Press. London. Oxford. New York. 1970.

Beckett wrote 'A Review of the Work by W.B. Yeats' about 1934, which unfortunately cannot be traced. (Federman, Raymond and Fletcher, John. *Samuel Beckett. His Works and His Critics. An Essay in Bibliography.* University of California Press. Berkeley, Los Angles. London. 1970. p. 105).

81. Vivian Mercier (*Beckett/Beckett*, p. 4) has noted Beckett's 'malicious quotation' from Yeats's then-recent lines: 'We were the last romantics - chose for theme /Traditional sanctity and loveliness...' (Yeats, W.B. 'Per Amica Silentia Lunae.' *Mythologies.* Macmillan, London. 1959. p. 328).

82. Yeats, William Butler. 'The Tower (1928),' *The Collected Poems of W.B. Yeats.* MacMillan and Co. Ltd., London. 1963. pp. 224-5.

> The death of friends, or death
> Of every brilliant eye
> That made a catch in the breath -
> Seem but the clouds of the sky
> When the horizon fades;
> Or a bird's sleepy cry
> Among the deepening shades.
> (1926)

It is of interest to note that Beckett's later regard for 'The Tower' was not evident in his critical essay on 'Recent Irish Poetry' written in 1934: "His (Yeats's) bequest in 'The Tower' of his pride and faith to the 'young upstanding men' has something almost second-best bed, as though he knew that they would be embarrassed to find an application for those dispositions."

For a discussion of similarities in the writings of Beckett and Yeats see: Worth, Katherine. 'Yeats and the French Drama.' *Modern Drama.* 1966. vol. 8. no. 4. pp. 382-391; Pilling, John. *Samuel Beckett.* Routledge and Regan Paul. London. Henley and Boston. 1976. pp. 102-103; Cohn. *Back to Beckett.* pp. 180-181.

83. The poetry of Austin Clarke (1896-1974) is uneven, in the opinion of Thomas Kinsella: 'He was capable, at any stage of his career, of writing poorly ... the reading of his poetry demands patience and discrimination to an unusual degree; it is a constant test of one's power of judgement.' (Clarke, Austin. *Selected Poems. Edited with an introduction by Thomas Kinsella.* Dolman Press. Dublin. 1976. p. ix; see also: Craig Tapping, G. *Austin Clarke. A Study of His Writings.* Academy Press. Dublin. 1981).

Many of Beckett's characters have been identified by various writers. However, with the exception of the Foxrock personalities in Chapter 1, whose identity I can accept with confidence, I have not attempted to identify Beckett's fictitious character creations. Dublin of the thirties, prided itself on such a variety of personality that the creative novelist was not likely to be deprived of inspirational material: "Dublin was a town of 'characters' then as now, and I suppose will ever be. A man I knew was taking a stroll down Grafton Street one day when he happened to overhear part of a discussion which three citizens were having outside Mitchell's cafe. The gist of their dialogue was that they were deploring the absence from the Dublin scene of any *real*

'characters'. They appeared to be genuinely aggrieved. They were, in fact, Myles na gCopaleen, Sean O'Sullivan and Brendan Behan." (Ryan, John. *Remembering How We Stood.* Gill an MacMillan. Dublin 1975. p. 42).

'Austin Ticklepenny, Pot Poet from the County of Dublin' (*Murphy*, p. 61, 63) has been identified as Austin Clarke. Neary has been identified as a Trinity philosopher, H.S. Macran, 'a great Hegelian and eccentric; who was often to be found in Neary's pub ...' Mr. Endon has touches of Beckett's friend, Thomas MacGreevy, and Mr. Willoughby Kelly has been likened to Joyce. (Mays, J.C.C. 'Young Beckett's Irish Roots.' *Irish University Review.* 1984. vol. 14. no. 1. p. 23).

84. Also mentioned in 'Recent Irish Poetry', but not discussed because Beckett is unfamiliar with their poetry, are Frank O'Connor, Sean O'Faolain, Niall Sheridan, Donogh McDonagh, Irene Haugh, and Niall Montgomery.

85. Blanaid Salkeld (1880-1959) was born in Chittagong (now Pakistan), where her father was in the Indian Medical Service. Her grand-daughter, Beatrice, married Brendan Behan. (Hogan, *Dictionary.* p. 580).

86. Arland (Percival) Ussher (1899-1980) was born in London into a family with ancient Irish connections. Best known for his philosophical deliberations on the Irish character in works such as *The Face and Mind of Ireland*, he also wrote some fine prose. (Hogan, *Dictionary.* pp. 670-671).

87. John Lyle Donaghy (1902-1947) was born in Ulster and educated at Larne Grammar School and Trinity College. He published a number of volumes of poetry but never managed to fulfill the poetic promise of which he had an abundance. (Hogan, *Dictionary.* pp. 207-208).

88. Geoffrey Taylor was born in England in 1900, brought up in Sligo, and educated at Trinity College. An entomologist by profession, he published many books on this subject. He was poetry editor of *The Bell*, editor of *Irish poets and poetry of the 19th Century*, and published several volumes of his own poetry, and a book on Ireland, *The Emerald Isle*. (Cleeve, Brian. *Dictionary of Irish Writers.* Mercier Press, Cork. 1967. p. 132).

89. 'Recent Irish Poetry'. *Disjecta.* p. 75.

90. For biographical details on Denis Devlin (1908-1959) see: *Denis Devlin Special Issue.* Advent VI. Advent Books 1976, and also Montgomery, Niall, ('Farewells Hardly Count.' *The Lace Curtain. A magazine of poetry and criticism.* ed. Michael Smith, Summer 1971. No. 4.): 'Born in Scotland, educated in Dublin, Munich and Paris, living in New York, London, Washington, Rome, representing, not typifying his fellow-countrymen, Denis Devlin, is perhaps, of the order (of the Order?) of the ideal Irishman, symbol carried before the eyes of the Heroic Generation, a European.' A more recent tribute by Richard Ryan, ('Remembering Denis Devlin.' *Ireland Today.* September 1984. no. 1011. pp. 4-7) outlines his career, and assesses briefly the importance of his poetry. For Devlin's poetry see: *The Collected Poems of Denis Devlin*, ed. Brian Coffey. Dolmen Press. 1964.

91. Both Beckett and Devlin were influenced by the poetry of Eluard, and both contributed to: *Thorns of Thunder: Selected Poems of Paul Eluard.* With a drawing by Pablo Picasso. Edited by George Reavey. Translated from French by Samuel Beckett, Denis Devlin, David Gascoyne, Eugene Jolas, Man Ray, George Reavy, and Ruthven Todd. London:

European Press and Stanley Nott. (1936). Beckett also translated: *Confections*, a poem by Paul Eluard. 'Rendered into English by Samuel Beckett'. *This Quarter*. Sept. 1932. vol. 5. pp. 96-98 -

> The black trees the white trees
> Are younger than nature
> In order to recover this freak of birth one must
> Age
> Fatal son of the quick
> One cannot keep thy heart.

92. Beckett, Samuel. "Denis Devlin'. A review of Intercessions.' *Transition. Tenth Anniversary,* vol. 27. April-May, 1938. pp. 289-294. Republished in *Disjecta*, p. 92. It is, perhaps, relevant to note that it was Beckett's close friend George Reavy who published *'Intercessions.'*

93. Brian Coffey, (1925-) was born in Dublin, the son of Dr. Denis Coffey, the first president of University College, Dublin. He was a close friend and collaborator of Denis Devlin. (Kernsnowski, Frank, in Hogan, *Dictionary*, pp. 163-164).

94. 'Recent Irish Poetry'. *Disjecta*, pp 75-76.

95. For comment on Beckett's associations, literary and otherwise see: Gluck, Barbara Reich. *Beckett and Joyce: friendship and fiction.* Bucknell University Press, Lewisburg and Associated University Presses. London. 1969; Hayman, David. 'Joyce - /Beckett/Joyce.' *Journal of Beckett Studies*. John Calder. London. Spring 1982. no. 7. pp. 101-107; Pearce, Richard. 'From Joyce to Beckett: the tale that wags the telling', *Journal of Beckett Studies*. John Calder. London. Spring 1982. pp. 109-114; Deane, Seamus. 'Joyce and Beckett.' *Irish University Review*. 1984. vol. 14. no. 1. pp. 57-68; Mays. J.C.C. 'Young Beckett's Irish Roots.' *Irish University Review*. 1984. vol. 14. no. 1. pp. 18-33. Before reading too much into this relationship it is wise to take note of Montgomery's caveat - "Samuel Beckett is a Dublin man who lives permanently in Paris; he is a learned and skillful writer. Joyce and he were students of Dante. Both are free of the contemporary literary preoccupation - man hours, output, packaging, and market research. (Will readers please note?) There the 'resemblance' perhaps ends." He goes on to say: 'Certainly the questionnaires in *Molloy, Malone ,and Watt* recall *Ulysses*, as the *Watt* Addenda does *Finnegans Wake*, purely by the form. There is an inventory in *L'Innommable* but none of Joyce's catalogues is traversed by such emotion. Perhaps the dactylic ejaculations in *Watt*: (p. 209) *Exelmans! Cavendish! Habbakuk! Ecchymose!* are a salute to the interminable HCE nonsense in Joyce. That's all.' (Montgomery, *No Symbol*, p. 330). There are also a number of similarities to the Joycean style in Beckett's early writings among which may be included *The Possessed, Sedendo et Quiescendo* and *Dream of Fair to Middling Women*. In *More Pricks than Kicks*, (p. 87) Beckett in describing the 'rather desolate uniformity' of the rain over Ireland parodies Joyce's ending of 'The Dead' (Joyce, James. *Dubliners*. Jonathan Cape. London. 1946. pp. 255-256.)

96. Beckett quoted by Shrenker, Israel, 'Moody man of letters: A portrait of Samuel Beckett, author of the puzzling *Waiting for Godot*.' *New York Times*, May 6, 1956, Section 2, p. 3.

97. *James Joyce: An international perspective. Centenary Essays in Honour of the Late Sir Desmond Cochrane. With a Message from Samuel Beckett and a Foreword by Richard Ellman.* ed. Suheil Badi Bushriu and Bernard Benstock. Colin Smythe, Buckinghamshire, and Barnes and Noble Books, New Jersey. 1982. p. vii.

It was to the Liffey river that Beckett went to fetch a stone for Joyce's fiftieth birthday on which William Hayter etched: 'Taken from the Liffey at Chapelizod'. Hayter, Stanley William. 'Tributes to George Reavey'. *Journal of Beckett Studies*. John Calder. London. 1977. no. 2. pp. 5-7.

98. The punctuation of the essay is important: from Dante to Bruno is a jump of about three centuries, from Bruno to Vico about one, and from Vico to Joyce about two. (Federman and Fletcher. *Samuel Beckett. Bibliography*. p. 4.)

Beckett was actively concerned in the translation into French of the 'Anna Livia Plurabelle' section of *Work in Progress.* (Knowlson, James. *Samuel Beckett: an exhibition.* Turret Books. London. 1971. pp. 26-27).

99. For an analysis of this poem see Harvey, *Beckett. Poet and Critic.* pp. 296-297.

100. Joyce, James. *Finnegans Wake.* Faber and Faber. London. 1939. p. 467. Joyce makes reference elsewhere in *Finnegans Wake* to Beckett: 'You is feeling like you was lost in the bush, boy? You says: It is a puling sample of jungle of woods. You most shouts out: *Bethiket* me for a stump of a beech if I have the poultriest notions what the forest he all means.' (*Samuel Beckett. The Critical Heritage.* eds. Lawrence Graver and Raymond Federman. Routledge and Kegan Paul. London, Henly and Boston. 1979. p. 4.

101. For a short essay on G.B. Shaw (1856-1950) see: Feeney, William J. 'Shaw, (George) Bernard,' in: Hogan, *Dictionary*. pp. 581-601.

102. For a discussion of the conflicts between art and religion in this passage from *Dream of Fair to Middling Women* see: Harvey, *Beckett. Poet and Critic.* p. 280.

103. Leventhal, A.J. *Beckett: an exhibition.* pp. 13-14. For biographical details on A.J. Leventhal see: *A.J. Leventhal. 1896-1979. Dublin scholar, wit and man of letters.* ed. Eoin O'Brien. The Con Leventhal Scholarship Committee. Dublin 1984.

104. 'King Street' is King Street South, the street on which the Gaiety Theatre stands.

105. Yeats. W.B. 'At the Hawk's Well' (1917) in: *The Collected Plays.* pp. 207-220.

106. Synge, J.M. 'The Well of the Saints' in: *Four Plays by J.M. Synge.* Maunsel and Company, Ltd., Dublin 1911. pp. 55-136.

107. O'Casey, Sean. *Juno and the Paycock. The Complete Plays of Sean O'Casey.* Vol. 1. Macmillan. London. 1984. pp. 1-89.

108. For a short essay on J.M. Synge (1871-1909) see: Saddlemyer, Ann. 'Synge, (Edmund) John Millington,' in: Hogan. *Dictionary.* pp. 653-659. For an interesting account of Synge's involvement in the twentieth-century Irish literary renaissance, and of his literary contemporaries see: O'Connor, Ulick. *Celtic Dawn. A Portrait of the Irish literary Renaissance.* Hamish Hamilton. London. 1984. pp. 232-239. For an analysis of Synge's influence in Beckett's writing see: Knowlson, James and Pilling, John. *Frescoes of the Skull, The Later Prose and Drama of Samuel Beckett.* Grove Press. New York. 1980. pp. 259-274; Reid, Alec. 'Comedy in Synge and Beckett.' *Yeats Studies.* Irish University Press. Shannon. 1972. no. 2. pp. 80-90; Worth, Katharine. *Beckett the shape changer. A Symposium edited by Katharine Worth.* Routledge and Kegan Paul. London and Boston. 1975. pp. 5-6.

109. *More Pricks than Kicks.* p. 100.

110. 'Recent Irish Poetry.' *Disjecta*. p. 70.

111. For a short essay on Sean O'Casey (1880-1964) see: Hogan. *Dictionary*. pp. 488-499. As has been remarked by Katherine Worth, it is unfortunate that Beckett and O'Casey never came to know each other better. O'Casey was somewhat antagonistic to what he took to be Beckett's pessimism: 'Beckett? I have nothing to do with Beckett. He isn't in me; nor am I in him. I am not Waiting for Godot to bring me life; I am out after life myself, even at the age I've reached.' (Worth, Katherine. *The Irish Drama of Europe from Yeats to Beckett*. The Athlone Press of the University of London. 1978. p. 251.)

112. 'The Essential and the Incidental.' A review of *Windfalls* by Sean O'Casey. *Disjecta*, pp. 82-83. O'Casey's poetry is mentioned in Beckett's review 'Recent Irish Poetry', but no critical statement is made - 'And I know that Mr. Sean O'Casey does (write verse) having read a poem of his in *Time and Tide*.' In his review of *Windfalls* (*Disjecta*, p. 83) Beckett likened O'Casey's poems to 'the model palace of a dynamiter's leisure moments.'

113. George Russell, (1867-1935) poet, painter, economist and editor, was best known as AE. For a short biographical essay see: Kain, Richard M. 'AE' in Hogan, *Dictionary*. pp. 85-88.

114. A.E. *The Candle of Vision*. Macmillan and Co. London. 1918.

115. *Watt*, p. 227.

116. A.E. *Homeward Songs by the Way*. Whaleys. Dublin. 1894.

117. The statements on Beckett in this paragraph are taken from: 'Interview with Jack MacGowran by Kathleen McGrory and John Unterecker. April 20, 1971, at Western Connecticut State College, Danbury, Conn. *Yeats, Joyce and Beckett. New Light on Three Modern Irish Writers*. pp. 172-182. For other reminiscences by MacGowran see: MacGowran, Jack. 'Working with Samuel Beckett'. *Beckett at Sixty*. pp. 23-24. Jack MacGowran (1918-1973) was born in Dublin. He played at the Gate and Abbey Theatres in Dublin, and went to London in 1953 where he acted with success in a number of West End plays. In the 1950's he commenced his interpretations of Samuel Beckett's writings, and in 1961 he was named British Television Actor of the year for his performance as Vladimir in *Waiting for Godot*, and in 1971 he was nominated the New York Critics 'Actor of the Year' for *Beginning to End*. Jack MacGowran died during a performance of Sean O'Casey's *The Plough and the Stars* at the Vivian Beaumont Theatre, New York, on January 30th, 1973. (Boylan, Henry. *A Dictionary of Irish Biography*. Gill and Macmillan. Dublin. 1978. pp. 201-202)

118. J.M. Mime has been shown to have similarities to *Enough* (Murphy, Peter "The nature and art of love in 'Enough' ". *Journal of Beckett Studies*. John Calder. London. Spring 1979. no. 4. pp. 14-34), and to the geometrically structured *Quad I and II*. (Gontarski, S.E. " '*Quad I & II*': Beckett's sinister mime(s)." *Journal of Beckett Studies*. John Calder. London. 1985. no. 9, pp. 137-138).

119. Federman, Raymond and Fletcher, John. *Samuel Beckett. Bibliography*. pp. 103-104.

120. 'Beginning to End' is composed of passages from *Malone Dies, Embers, Echo's Bones, Molloy, Cascando, Waiting for Godot, Words and Music, Krapp's Last Tape, Endgame*, and *The Unnamable*. MacGowran's one-man show *End of Day* has been recorded by Claddagh Records under Beckett's supervision. For further details on Beckett and MacGowran's collaboration see: Lake. *No symbols where none intended*. pp. 133-135, and Knowlson, *Beckett: an Exhibition*. p. 109.

121. Knowlson, *An Exhibition*. p. 105.

122. Knowlson and Pilling. *Frescoes*. p. 132. The first edition of *All Strange Away* limited to 200 numbered and signed copies and 26 lettered and signed copies was published by Gotham Book Mart. U.S.A. in 1976.

123. For biographical details on Thomas MacGreevy (1893-1967) see: Hogan, *Dictionary*. pp. 403-404. and O'Murchu, Domhnall. 'Remembering Thomas MacGreevy.' *Irish Times*, May 5, 1983. p. 10. cols. 1-6.

124. MacGreevy, *Collected Poems*. p. 41.

125. MacGreevy published the following works on art: *Introduction to the Method of Leonardo da Vinci; Jack B. Yeats. An Appreciation and an Interpretation*. Victor Waddington Publications. Ltd. Dublin. 1945; *Pictures in The Irish National Gallery*. The Mercier Press. Cork. 1945; *Catalogue of Pictures of The Italian Schools. National Gallery of Ireland*. The Stationary Office. Dublin. 1956; An introduction in Italian, Gaelic, French and English for *XXXI Esposizione Biennale Internazional d'Arte. Jack B. Yeats 1871-1957*. Venezia 1962; *Nicholas Poussin*. Dolmen Press. Dublin. 1960; *Some Italian Pictures in the National Gallery of Ireland*, Dublin, 1963; *Concise Catalogue of the Oil Paintings*, Dublin 1963. MacGreevy also published: 'The Catholic Element in *Work in Progress*.' *Our Exagmination Round his Factification for Incamination of Work in Progress*. Faber and Faber. London. 1972. p. 119-127; *Thomas Sterns Eliot*. Chatto and Windus. London. 1931; *Richard Aldington: An Englishman*. Chatto and Windus. London. 1931. MacGreevy translated Montherlant's novels, *Les Célibataires* and *Les Jeunes Filles* (Knowlson. *Beckett: an Exhibition*. p. 37).

126. Recent Irish Poetry. *Disjecta*, p. 70.

127. Recent Irish Poetry. *Disjecta*, p. 74.

128. 'Humanistic Quietism' *Disjecta*, pp. 68-69.

129. MacGreevy. *Collected Poems*. p. 43.

130. MacGreevy. *Collected Poems*. p. 40.

131. MacGreevy. *Collected Poems*. pp. 24-31.

132. 'Recent Irish Poetry.' *Disjecta*, p. 74.

133. MacGreevy, *Collected Poems*. p. 15.

134. MacGreevy. *Collected Poems*. pp. 73-74.

135. It is reasonable to assume that the paintings most prized by MacGreevy were those selected for inclusion in his illustrated book *Pictures in the Irish National Gallery*. (1945). As these would have been well known to Beckett, they are listed (with altered attributions and catalogue numbers in parentheses): *The Attempted Martyrdom of Saints Cosmas and Damian* by Fra Angelico. (no. 242); *The Battle of Anghiari*. Florentine School. (no. 778); *The Story of Lucretia* by Sandro Botticelli. (Master of Marradi. no. 110); *Madonna and Child*. School of Verrochio. (no. 519); *Portrait of a Musician* by Cosimo Tura. (Flippino Lippi. no. 470); *Judith with the Head of Holofernes* by Andrea Mantegna. (no. 442); *Portrait of a man* by Alessandro Oliverio. (no. 239); *Portrait of Baldassare Castiglione* by Titian. (no. 782); *A View of Dresden* by Bernardo Bellotto. (no. 181); *Our Lord Bidding Farewell to His Mother* by Gheerhardt David. (no. 13); *Scenes from the Life of Saint Augustine* by The Master of the Silver Windows. (The Master of St. Augustine. no. 823); *The Flight into Egypt* by Jan de Cock. (no. 1001); *Christ at the House of Martha and Mary* by Peter Paul Rubens and Jan Bureghel.

(no. 513); *Portrait of a Young Woman* by Rembrandt van Rijn. (no. 808); *The Village School* by Jan Steen. (no. 226); *A Wooded Scene with Figures* by Jacob Ruisdal and Thomas de Keyser. (no. 287); *Judith with the Head of Holofernes* by Lucas Cranach. (no. 186); *Portrait of Heinrich Knobhauch* by Conrad Faber. (no. 243); *St. Jerome in the Wilderness* by Luis de Morales. (no. 1); *Portrait of a Young Prince* by Alonso Sanchez Coello. (no. 17); *St. Francis in Ecstasy* by El Greco. (no. 658); *A Concert* by J.B. del Mazo. (no. 21); *A Spanish Woman* by Francisco Goya. (no. 784); *St. Jerome Translating the Bible* by Nicolas Francés. (no. 1013); *The Entombment* by Nicholas Poussin. (no. 214); *The Young Governess* by J.B.S. Chardin. (no. 813); *The Western Family* by William Hogarth. (no. 792); *Mrs. Frances Fortescue* by Joshua Reynolds. (no. 790); *Landscape with Cattle* by Thomas Gainsborough. (no. 796); *Self-Portrait* by James Barry. (no. 971); *Portrait of a Harper* by James Barry. (no. 631); *The Poachers* by James Arthur O'Connor. (no. 18); *Portrait of John O'Leary* by John Butler Yeats. (no. 595); *St. Patrick's Close* by Walter Osborne. (no. 836).

136. Beckett thought highly of MacGreevy's criticism (MacGreevy on Yeats, *Disjecta*, p. 95) and it is surely time for publication of a collection of his essays on art, artists and writers from *Formes, The Studio, The Times Literary Supplement, The Dial, The Criterion, Transition, The Capuchin Annual* and other periodicals in which his writings appeared.

137. MacGreevy, Thomas. *Jack B. Yeats. An Appreciation and an Interpretation.* Victor Waddington Publications Ltd., Dublin. 1945.

138. MacGreevy. *Yeats.* p. 5.

139. MacGreevy. *Yeats.* p. 8.

140. MacGreevy. *Yeats.* pp. 14-15.

141. MacGreevy. *Yeats.* p. 15.

142. MacGreevy. *Yeats.* pp. 22-23. One critic suggests that at least one of Yeats's paintings may have had a specific influence on Beckett's writing: "There hangs in the Tate a picture by Jack B. Yeats, oil on canvas, entitled 'Two Travellers.' The 'travellers' – 'tinkers' as they used to say – are ragged figures on a road in Connemara ... and it seems evident to me that 'Two Travellers' provided at least one point of departure for Didi and Gogo in 'Waiting for Godot'." (Mahon, Derek. 'Enigma of the Western World'. *The Observer.* 13 April 1986. p. 21.)

143. MacGreevy. *Yeats.* p. 35.

144. MacGreevy. *Yeats.* p. 24. Yeats was more aware than most of the mystic suggestiveness of pastoral beauty: 'These blues and purples and pale greens - what crowd ever seemed clad in such twilight colours? And yet we accept it as natural, for this opalescence is always in the mist-laden air of the West; it enters the soul to-day as it did into the soul of the ancient Gael, who called it Ildathach - the many coloured land; it becomes part of the atmosphere of the mind.' Pyle, Hilary. *Jack B. Yeats. A Biography.* Routledge and Kegan Paul. London. 1970. p. 165.

145. *More Pricks than Kicks,* p. 109.

146. 'Humanistic Quietism.' *Disjecta,* p. 68.

147. 'MacGreevy on Yeats' *Disjecta,* p. 95.

148. 'MacGreevy on Yeats' *Disjecta,* p. 95.

149. Pyle. *Yeats.* p. 104.

150. For biographical details on Jack Yeats (1871-1957) see: Pyle. *Yeats;* McGuinness, Nora. 'Yeats, Jack (Butler).' in: Hogan. *Dictionary.* pp. 696-697. For biographical essays and a bibliography of his writings, see: Beckett, Samuel; Caldwell, Martha; O'Doherty, Brian; O'Malley, Ernie; Oshima, Shotaro; Rose, Marilyn Gaddis; De Vere White, Terence. *Jack B. Yeats. A Centenary Gathering.* ed with an introduction by Roger McHugh. Dolmen Press. Dublin. 1971; For a number of interesting essays on Jack Yeats see: 'Theatre and the Visual Arts. A Centenary Celebration of Jack Yeats and John Synge.' eds. Robert O'Driscoll and Lorna Reynolds. *Yeats Studies.* Irish University Press. 1972. no. 2; Pyle, Hilary. *Jack B. Yeats in The National Gallery of Ireland.* The National Gallery of Ireland. 1986.

151. Pyle. *Yeats.* pp. 123-124.

152. The family achievements are summarised in: *Jack B. Yeats and his family.* The Arts Council. Dublin. 1972, but for a comprehensive and scholarly treatise on this remarkable Irish family see: Murphy, William M. *Prodigal Father. The Life of John Butler Yeats. (1839-1922).* Cornell University Press. Ithaca and London. 1978.

153. Pilling, John. "The living ginger: Jack B. Yeats's 'The charmed life' ". *Journal of Beckett Studies.* John Calder. London. 1979. no. 4. pp. 55-65.

154. Yeats's plays are published in: Skelton, Robin. *The Collected Plays of Jack B. Yeats.* The Bobbs-Morrill Co., Inc. Indianapolis/New York. 1971. For a listing of other published writings see: Caldwell, Martha. 'A Bibliography of the Published Writings of Jack B. Yeats.' in *A Centenary Gathering.* pp. 110-114.

155. 'An Imaginative Work.' *Disjecta,* pp. 89-90.

156. Beckett's appreciation of painting and his visual sensitivity to colour and form make friendship with artists inevitable. Among his close friends may be numbered the artists Jack Yeats, Henri Hayden, S.W. Hayter, Avigdor Arikha, and Bram van Velde. He has collaborated in publication with: S.W. Hayter (*Still,* with six etchings by Stanley William Hayter and notes by A.J. Leventhal. A limited printing, large-sized cased edition, published by M'Arte Edizioni of Milan. Limited edition of 160 copies. 1975.); Avigdor Arikha (*Three Plays: Waiting for Godot. Endgame. Krapp's Last Tape.* Frontispiece: Double Study of Beckett by Avigdor Arikha. 1971. Limited edition published by the Franklin Library. Pennsylvania. 1981.); Jasper Johns (*Foirades.* Fizzles. Petersburg Press. London. New York 1976. Limited edition of 250 copies); Edward Gorey (*All Strange Away.* Gotham Book Mart, 1976. Limited edition of 226 copies); Dellas Henke (*Company.* Iowa Center for the Book. University of Iowa. 1985. Limited Edition of 52 copies.)

Beckett has published criticism on Tal Coat, Andre Masson and Bram van Velde in: ('Three Dialogues. Samuel Beckett and Georges Duthuit.' *Transition Forty-Nine.* 5. 1949. pp. 97-103.) Further comment on Bram van Velde may be found in: *La Falaise,* entitled *Pour Bram* (Hansford, James. " 'Imaginative Transactions' in 'La Falaise.' " *Journal of Beckett Studies.* John Calder. London. 1985. no. 10. pp. 76-86); 'La Peinture des Van Velde ou le monde et le pantalon.' 1946; 'Peintres de l'empechement', *Derriere le Miroir.* Paris, Galerie Maeght, Editions Pierre a Feu. nos. 11-12. June 1948; *Bram Van Velde,* Samuel Beckett, Georges Duthuit, Jacques Putman. Le Musee de Poche. Paris. 1958.

For criticism on Jack Yeats see: 'MacGreevy on Yeats'. A review of *Jack B. Yeats. An Appreciation and an Interpretation* by Thomas MacGreevy. *Irish Times.* Sat. Aug. 4. 1945. Cols 6 & 7; 'Hommage a Jack B. Yeats.'

Les Lettres Nouvelles. April 1954. (Translated in *Disjecta*, pp. 148-149). For Beckett's comments on Avigdor Arikha see: *Pour Avigdor Arikha.* Galerie Claude Bernard, Paris. 1967. Translated in Victora and Albert Museum Catalogue February-May 1976). Three tributes from Samuel Beckett to Arikha – 'For Avigdor Arikha', 'Ceiling' and 'Avigdor Arikha' are published with Arikha's etchings of Samuel Beckett in: *Arikha*, texts by Richard Channin, André Fermigier, Robert Hughes, Jane Livingston, Barbara Rose, and Samuel Beckett. Hermann. Paris. Thames and Hudson. London. 1985. pp. 3-9. For comment by Beckett on Henri Hayden see: *Henry Hayden, homme-peintre.* Les Cahiers d'Art-Documents, 22, Ecole de Paris. 1955.

157. 'Recent Irish Poetry.' *Disjecta,* p.70.

158. 'Homage to Jack B. Yeats.' *Disjecta,* p. 149. For an alternative translation see: Mercier, *Beckett/Beckett.* p. 111-12.

159. Much has been written on the influence of philosophers in Beckett's writings; for a selection see: Kenner, Hugh. *Samuel Beckett: a critical study.* Berkeley, U.S.A. 1961; Hesla, David. *The shape of chaos: an interpretation of the art of Samuel Beckett.* University of Minnesota Press. Minneapolis 1971. pp. 57-58; Brienza, Susan. " 'Imagination dead imagine': the microcosm of the mind" *Journal of Beckett Studies.* John Calder. London. 1982. no. 8. pp. 59-74; Mooney, Michael E. "Molloy, part 1: Beckett's 'Discourse on method.' " *Journal of Beckett Studies.* John Calder. London. 1978. no. 3, pp. 40-55; Esslin, *Mediations.* pp. 80-86; Coe, Richard. *Samuel Beckett.* New York, U.S.A. 1964; Cohn, Ruby, 'Philosophical Fragments in the Works of Samuel Beckett'. *Critical Essays.* pp. 169-177; Pilling, *Samuel Beckett* pp. 110-131; Kennedy, *Murphy's Bed.* p. 9; pp. 87-89; pp. 124-150.

160. The Brothers Boet also known as Boate, De Boot, Bootius or Botius. Gerard Boet, M.D. (1604-1650) - a native of Gorcum in Holland, was entered on the physic line at Leyden, 21st June, 1628, being then twenty-five years of age, and graduated a doctor of medicine there, the 3rd July 1628. He was admitted a Licentiate of the College of Physicians on 6th November, 1646. He was appointed doctor to the Military Hospital at Dublin, where he collected the material for his 'Natural History of Ireland' which was published in London after his death in 1650 with a dedication to Oliver Cromwell and Charles Fleetwood, commander-in-chief in Ireland. Arnold Boet, M.D., like his brother was a graduate from Leyden, who came to Dublin where he established a successful practice. He involved himself in translation of the Hebrew text of the Bible and when his wife died published 'The Character of a Trulie Virtuous and Pious Woman, as it had been acted by Mistris Margaret Dungan (wife to Dr. Arnold Boate) in the constant course of her whole life.' In 1641, the Boot brothers published in Dublin a treatise criticising Aristotlian philosophy with the title: *Philosophia Naturalis Reformata. Id est Philosophiae Aristotelicae Accurata Examinatio ac Solida Confutatio et Novae et verioris Introducto. Per Gerardum ac Arnoldum Botios, Fratres Hollandos, Medicinae Doctores.* Dublinis in Hibernia. Ex Officina Typographica Societatis Bibliopolarium. Anno Nati Christi. M.D.C. XLI. Mense Julio. For details on the Doctors Boate, see: *The Compact Edition of the Dictionary of National Biography.* Oxford University Press. 1975. vol. 1. p. 178. For details on Arnold Boate, see: Monk, William. *The Roll of the Royal College of Physicians of London. vol. I. 1518 to 1700.* Royal College of Physicians. London. 1878. 2nd ed. p. 243. For an account of Gerard Boate's Natural History see: Hinch J. De W. *Notes on Boate's Natural History of Ireland 1652.* The Bibliographical Society of Ireland. vol. 3. no. 5. 1928 in the Thorpe Collection of Pamphlets, National Library of Ireland.

In the poem *Whoroscope,* Beckett gives the date of the Boot brothers' refutation of Aristotle as 1640, (*Collected Poems*, p. 5) whereas the date of publication would appear to be 1641. I am grateful to Joseph Collins for drawing my attention to this discrepancy.

161. For a lengthy analysis of *Whoroscope* see: Harvey, *Beckett. Poet and Critic.* pp. 3-66.

162. For a brief essay on George Berkeley (1685-1753) see: Houghton, Raymond W. *The World of George Berkeley.* The Irish Heritage Series. No. 53. Eason & Son. Dublin. 1985. For a discussion on the similarities and differences between *Dean Berkeley and His Entourage. The Bermuda Group* in the National Gallery of Ireland, and *The Bermuda Group* at Yale, see: Houghton, Raymond W., Borman, David. and Lapan, Maureen T. *Images of Berkeley.* National Gallery of Ireland and Wolfhound Press. Dublin. 1986. pp. 53-57.

163. Rabinovitz. *Samuel Beckett's Fiction.* p. 26.

164. Berkeley's writings include: *A treatise concerning the principles of human knowledge* in: *Principles, dialogues and philosophical correspondence.* ed. Colin Murray Turbayne, Bobbs-Merrill, Inc., Indianapolis. Library of Liberal Arts, 1965; *Three dialogues between Hylas and Philonous* in: *Principles, dialogues and philosophical correspondence; Philosophical Commentaries.* ed. A.A. Luce. Thomas Nelson and Sons. London. 1944. Arthur Aston Luce was one of Beckett's teachers at Trinity College. Dublin.

165. For an essay on the influence of Berkeley on *Film* see: Henning, Sylvie Debevec. " 'Film': a dialogue between Beckett and Berkeley." *Journal of Beckett Studies.* John Calder. London. 1982. no. 7. pp. 89-99.

166. This reference to Berkeley is discussed by: Berman, David. 'Beckett and Berkeley.' *Irish University Review:* Spring. 1984. pp. 42-45. 'The sweated sinecure', which precedes the quoted passage, may, in Berman's view, be a reference to a 'Trinity College Fellowship, which involved an arduous examination'.

167. This reference is to Berkeley's *A Chain of Philosophical Reflexions and Inquiries Concerning the Virtues of Tar-Water.* Innys and Hitch. London. 1744.

168. Berman. 'Beckett and Berkeley'. pp. 42-43.

169. For studies of the relationship between Swift and Beckett see: Fletcher, John. *Samuel Beckett's Art.* Chatto and Windus, London. 1967. Chapter. V; Pilling, *Samuel Beckett*, pp. 141-143; Rabinovitz, *Beckett's Fiction.* p. 41; p. 53.

170. Rabinovitz. *Beckett's Fiction.* p. 219.

171. For a biography of Sterne see: *The Compact Edition of the Dictionary of National Biography.* Oxford University Press. 1975. vol. II. pp. 1996-1998. For discussion on the influence of Sterne on Beckett's writing see: Pilling. *Samuel Beckett.* p. 41. pp. 141-145; Muir, Edwin. Review of *More Pricks than Kicks. Listener.* 4 July 1934. p. 42; Pritchett, V.S. Review of 'The Triology'. *New Statesman.* 2 April 1960, p. 489.

172. For an account of Robert Graves (1796-1853) and of the 'Dublin School' see: O'Brien, Eoin. *Conscience and Conflict. A Biography of Sir Dominic Corrigan.* The Glendale Press. Dublin 1983. pp. 107-170. Another reference to Graves may be found in *Murphy*, p. 27.

173. Richard Bright (1789-1858), was a physician at Guy's Hospital in London where he described the kidney disease that now bears his name.

174. For a full account of Billy in the Bowl see: Collins, James. *Life in Old Dublin*. James Duffy and Co. Ltd., Dublin 1913. pp. 77-79.

175. Collins. *Life in Old Dublin*. p. 78.

176. Billy in *Rough for Theatre I (Collected Shorter Plays, pp. 67-73)* plays a fiddle, having once played the harp, and is a fictional fusion of 'Billy in the Bowl', and the painting of *Art O'Neill*, the blind harpist in the National Gallery of Ireland. (p. 150). Dublin's 'Billy in the Bowl' may represent the reality of commencement for many of Beckett's incapacitated, and later immobile characters, for example, Winnie in her mound of sand in *Happy Days*, Mahood in his jar in *The Unnamable*, and the urned protagonists of *Play*.

177. For a further discussion on deformity in *The Unnamable* see: Kennedy, Sighle. 'Spirals of Need: Irish Prototypes in Samuel Beckett's Fiction' in *Yeats, Joyce, and Beckett*. pp. 164-166; Fletcher. *Novels of Samuel Beckett*. pp. 184-185; Cohn. *Back to Beckett*. pp. 104-105.

CHAPTER 9: BEYOND THE PALE

1. For an account of 'The English Pale' see Joyce, Weston St. John. *The Neighbourhood of Dublin*. M.H. Gill & Son. Dublin and Waterford. 1912. pp. 427-436.

   In my research of Irish place-names in Beckett's writing I have not made a detailed study of Beckett's unpublished manuscripts, many of which, for example the 'Kilcool' manuscript (Trinity College. Dublin, MS 4664), and Eleutheria (Reading University Library, MS 1227/7/4/1) contain Irish references. Nor have I studied the earlier manuscripts of published works, many of which also contain references to Ireland that have been deleted in later drafts. For example, in *Watt*, the place names Enniskillen, Sandyford, the Aran Islands, Mullingar and the information that Arsene and Erskine failed to participate in the fight for Ireland's freedom, all present in earlier manuscripts, are no longer to be found in the published work. A similar pattern is evident in *Company*. (Beer, Ann. " 'Watt', Knott and Beckett's bilingualism." *Journal of Beckett Studies*. John Calder. London. 1985. no. 10. pp. 37-75.) Beckett, also deletes reference to Ireland in translations of his writing; for example, the reference to Glasnevin Cemetery in *Malone Meurt* (Les Éditions de Minuit, 1952) does not remain in the English translation. Irish locations may even disappear in revision, for example, in the first edition of *Watt* (Collection Merlin, The Olympia Press. 1953) the Wicklow town of Newtown Mount Kennedy: ('Like the Jerusalem Artichoke, she was born in Newtown Mount Kennedy, and can hardly walk, but she is a true Indian Runner for all that.' p. 46), but this has been removed from the 1972 edition (Calder and Boyars. Ltd.) This feature of Beckett's writing has also been noted by Gontarski: 'Often the early drafts of Beckett's work are more realistic, the action more traditionally motivated, the world more familiar and recognisable, the work as a whole more conventional than the final.' (Gontarski, S.E. *The Intent of Undoing in Samuel Beckett's Dramatic Texts*. Indiana University Press. Bloomington, 1985. p. 4.)

   Irish locations mentioned fleetingly in *Dream of Fair to Middling Women*, are Youghal, Tramore, and Wicklow Town, (p. 127); Meath and Westmeath, (p. 135); and Drogheda (p. 86). The name Capper Quin, alias Hairy, in *More Pricks than Kicks*, (p. 134) is likely to be derived from Cappoquin a small market town in Co. Waterford.

2. For an attractive photographic presentation of this city see: *Cork, City by the Lee*. Corporation of Cork in association with The Mercier Press. Cork. 1983. For historical details see: Killanin, Lord, and Duignan, Michael. *Shell Guide to Ireland*. The Ebury Press. London. 1962. pp. 174-180.

3. Father Prout is mentioned again in *Murphy*, on p. 87.

4. Kent, Charles. 'Biographical Introduction', *The Works of Father Prout (The Rev. Francis Mahony.)* George Routledge and Sons. New York. 1881. pp. vii-xxxiv. For further biographical details see: *The Dictionary of National Biography* (Compact Edition). Oxford University Press. London. 1975. pp. 1297-1298.

5. Kent. *Father Prout*. p. x.

6. Kent. *Father Prout*. pp. xvii-xix.

7. Prout, 'Dean Swift's Madness. A Tale of a Churn' in: Kent, *Father Prout*. p. 78.

8. Prout, 'Dean Swift's Madness' in: Kent, *Father Prout*. p. 82.

9. L.A.G. Strong has written an interesting essay on Prout in which he quotes a pen-portrait of him by Jerrold: 'A short, spare man, stooping as he went, with the right arm clasped in the left-hand behind him; a sharp face with piercing eyes that looked vacantly upwards, a mocking lip, a close-shaven face, and an ecclesiastical garb of slovenly appearance - such was the old Franciscan, who would laugh outright at times, quite unconscious of bystanders, as he slouched towards Temple Bar, perhaps on his way to the tavern in Fleet Street where Johnson's chair stood in the chimney-corner.' Strong concludes his essay: 'there is a lot to be said for being a one-song man ... Yes. Father Prout was lucky in his song, that old, attractive jingle, which so happily crystallises all that was best in his nature and pleasantest in his life. The picture it calls up is not of seminaries and disappointed hopes, nor of Kensington and controversy, nor of a lonely old man toasting a chop in a small, none too-clean apartment in a foreign city; but of smiling waters, of sunshine, and a time as graceful as the ripples and the distant sound of bells.' Strong, L.A.G. 'Francis Sylvester Mahony - Father Prout.' *Irish Writing*. no. 11. May, 1950. pp. 66-72.

10. Prout. 'The Shandon Bells' from 'The Rogueries of Tom Moore' in: Kent, *Father Prout*. p. 100.

11. *The Groves of Blarney* have been celebrated in song by Richard Millikin. (Killanin and Duignan, *Shell Guide to Ireland*) and in verse by Father Prout. (Prout. 'The Groves of Blarney' from 'A Plea for Pilgrimages, Sir Walter Scott's Visit to the Blarney' in: Kent, *Father Prout*. p. 38.)

12. A reference to Ringaskiddy may also be found in *Murphy*, p. 37. Other references to Cork occur in *Murphy*, p. 8, and *Watt*, p. 154.

13. Killanin and Duignan, *Shell Guide*, p. 167.

14. Killarney, Co. Kerry, is Ireland's most celebrated tourist resort by virtue of its romantic lakes and mountain scenery. The Lakes of Killarney, to which the district primarily owes its fame, lie at the foot of the Mangerton Mountains, and Macgillicuddy's Reeks where Carrauntouhill, Ireland's highest mountain (3,414 feet) may be found. (Killanin and Duignan, *Shell Guide*. pp. 329-332.)

15. *Rough for Radio I. Collected Shorter Plays*, p. 110.

16. *Watt*, p. 169.

17. *Watt*, p. 171. Ennis, Co. Clare, is the capital of the county and the cathedral town of the Catholic diocese of Killaloe. (Killanin and Duignan, *Shell Guide*, pp. 269-270.)

18. Keane, Maryangela. *The Burren. County Clare*. The Irish Heritage Series. no. 30. Eason and Son. Ltd., Dublin. 1980.

19. Galway is situated at the mouth of the short Galway River, near the north-eastern corner of County Galway, famed for its beauty. This university town has an interesting history and contains many monuments of note, among which is the ancient Church of St. Nicholas. (Killanin and Duignan, *Shell Guide*. pp. 282-286.)

20. Knoll, Jeri L. "Belacqua as artist and lover: 'What a misfortune' ". *Journal of Beckett Studies*. John Calder. London. Summer 1978. no. 3. p. 25.

21. *More Pricks than Kicks*, p. 136.

22. For an account of Connemara see: Killanin and Duignan, *Shell Guide*, p. 171.

23. Lucky mentions Connemara three times, the first occasion being:

    '... in a word the dead loss per caput since the death of Bishop Berkeley being to the tune of one inch four ounce per caput approximately by and large more or less to the nearest decimal good measure round figures stark naked in the stockinged feet in Connemara in a word for reasons unknown ...'

    (*Waiting for Godot*, p. 44)

24. For analysis of this poem see: Harvey, Lawrence E. *Samuel Beckett. Poet and Critic*. Princeton University Press. New Jersey. 1970. pp. 93-96.

25. Croagh Patrick (2,510 feet) is a beautiful quartzite ridge and cone, rising steeply from the southern shore of Clew Bay. St. Patrick is said to have fasted on the mountain-top for 40 days, and every year thousands of devout pilgrims climb to the summit before dawn on Garland Sunday, the last Sunday of July. (Killanin and Duignan, *Shell Guide*. p. 456.)

26. For an account of Achill and the surrounding areas see: Killanin and Duignan, *Shell Guide*. pp. 39-40.

27. Quoted from a letter of Samuel Beckett to George Reavey, 6 August 1937 in: Bair, Deirdre. *Samuel Beckett. A Biography*. Pan Books Ltd., Picador Edition. 1980. p. 225. p. 567.

28. Quoted from a letter of Samuel Beckett to Mary Manning Howe, 14 November 1936 in:Lake, Carlton, *No Symbols where none intended. A Catalogue of Books, Manuscripts, and Other Materials Relating to Samuel Beckett in the Collections of the Humanities Research Center*, The University of Texas at Austin. 1984. p. 43.

29. Lewis, Samuel. *A Topographical Dictionary of Ireland*. Kennikat Press. New York. London. 1970. vol. 1. p. 119.

30. The Antrim Coast Road is a sixty kilometer stretch of senic road that was blasted out of the cliff-rock by William Bald in 1832; it passes along a coastline rich in obscure names – 'The Black Cave Tunnel', 'The Maiden's Rocks', 'The Madman's Window' and 'The White Lady'. (Storrie, Margaret C. 'The man who built the Antrim Coast Road.' *Geographical Magazine*. London. January 1971. pp. 247-254. Rhodes, P.S. *The Antrim Coast Road with notes and sketches of its geology and scenery*. The Northern Ireland Tourist Board. Belfast. n.d. pp. 1-39.)

31. Federman, Raymond and Fletcher, John. *Samuel Beckett. His Works and His Critics. An Essay in Bibliography*. University of California Press. Berkely, Los Angeles, London. 1970. p. 9.

32. 'The Guard, who had much more of the lion than of the fox, kept him standing until inside his helmet the throbbing of his Leix and Offaly head became more than he could endure.' (*More Pricks than Kicks*, p. 77).

33. Lewis. *Topographical Dictionary*. vol. 1. p. 367.

It is, perhaps, deserving of mention that one exceptionally fine chancel arch at Clonmacnois has a Sheila-na-gig engraved upon it (Killanin and Duignan, *Shell Guide*, p. 162), because of the significance of this grotesque mythical female in Beckett's literature; for a review of the subject see: Kennedy, Sighle. 'Spirals of Need: Irish Prototypes in Samuel Beckett's Fiction' in: *Yeats, Joyce and Beckett. New Light on three Modern Irish Writers*. eds. Kathleen McGrory and John Unterecker, Bucknell University Press, Lewisburg, and Associated University Presses, London, pp. 153-166.

CHAPTER 10: SAINT-LÔ:
'Humanity in Ruins'

1. The late Alan Thompson kindly gave me Beckett's signed copy (S.B. Beckett. Tours. August 1926) of an illustrated book which he used for planning his cycling holiday: Debraye, Henry. *En Touraine et sur les bords de la Loire (Chateaux et Paysages)*. Editions J. Rey. Grenoble. 1926.

2. Knowlson, James. *Samuel Beckett: an exhibition held at Reading University Library, May to July 1971*. Turret Books. London. 1971. p.43.

3. Knowlson. *Beckett: an exhibition*. pp. 25-27.

4. Beckett left the physical safety of neutral Ireland, for the spiritual freedom of wartime France. 'I preferred France in war to Ireland in peace.' Shenker, Israel. 'Moody Man of Letters.' *New York Times*. 6 May 1956. Section 2. p. 3.

5. Knowlson. *Beckett: an exhibition*. pp. 43-44.

6. While at Roussillon, Beckett wrote the novel *Watt*. For an account of Beckett's war-time activities in France see: Bair, Deirdre. *Samuel Beckett. A Biography.* Pan Books Ltd., Picador Edition. 1980. pp. 257-285; Foot, M.R.D. *SOE in France. An Account of the Work of the British Special Operations Executive in France 1940-1944.* Her Majesty's Stationery Office. London. 1966. pp. 319-320; Reid, Alec. *All I can Manage, More than I Could: An Approach to the Plays of Samuel Beckett.* Dolmen Press. 1968. pp. 13-14.

7. This was not the first proposal from Ireland for the erection of a war-time hospital: In 1917 'the War Office ... accepted an offer from the medical Profession of Dublin to staff a base hospital in France for a period of at least a year. The members of the staff will work in relays, no period of service to be less than three months. The selection of the staff has been in the hands of the Presidents of the two Colleges and within the somewhat narrow limits of age set by the War Office - 40 to 55 - they have been able to enlist the services of practically all the hospital surgeons and physicians of Dublin who are not already on service.' "A 'Dublin Hospital' for France." *Dublin Journal of Medical Science.* 1917. vol. CXLIII. p. 383. What became of this proposal is not recorded. Indeed the Irish medical profession had an even earlier association with France; on October 8th 1870, the Irish Ambulance Corps departed Ireland for France: 'In and around the Rotundo Gardens the excitement was intense, as the public flocked thither in thousands to get a view of the Ambulance wagons which were destined, alas to be filled with the victims of destructive war, or to see the noble animals which were to bear them away from the harvest of death.' The adventures and exploits of the rather strange body of men that comprised the Irish Ambulance Corps is recounted by a member of the Corps in a fascinating journal from which the above quotation is taken (p. 12). (Leeson, M.A. *Reminiscences of the Franco-Irish Ambulance; or Our 'Corps' with The Mocquarts and on The Loire. 1870-1871.* M'Glashan and Gill. Dublin. 1873).

8. A newspaper clip from one of the Irish daily papers (in the possession of Miss. M. Crowley) reported: *'Irish Red Cross Hospital Experts leave for Paris.* Headed by Colonel Thomas J. McKinney, Officer in Charge of the Irish Hospital Unit for France, the Irish Red Cross Society's team of expert advisors left Dun Laoghaire by the Mail-boat yesterday morning, on the first stage of its journey to Paris, where the necessary advance arrangements for the units reception will be made. The delegation, which with Colonel McKinney, consists of Dr. Alan Thompson, Mr. Michael Scott and Commandant C.J. Daly, will be met in London and Paris by Eire's representatives and probably will spend a number of weeks in France making a preliminary survey and completing final arrangements.' McKinney wrote of this preliminary visit as follows: "I had the opportunity to visit France in April 1945, when negotiations were in progress between the French and Irish Red Cross societies to determine what help the Irish could give. I saw Brest, which I reached at night. What feelings I had in this city of silence, gloom and ashes. I saw Saint-Lô, a little later. It well deserved its title, 'Capital of the Ruins.' On my return to Ireland, I had the opportunity of addressing my compatriots over the radio on my impressions of France; I ended the programme with the words: 'it is imperative that Ireland help France, her neighbour and friend.' " (McKinney, Col. Thomas. 'Dans nos Ruines ... une Cite blanche. L'Hôpital Irlandais de Saint-Lô. Don de l'Irlande a La Normandie.' *Terre Normande.* No. 3. Mars-Avril, 1946. p. 15. (By courtesy Mr. and Mrs. P. Carey). Ireland responded by providing the staff and equipment for a hospital at Saint-Lô, and 200 French children 'who had for one reason or another suffered, or were still suffering from the effects of war' were received in Ireland. (MacKinney, *Terre Normande,* p. 15).

9. For a dramatic pictorial history of the devastation of Saint-Lô see: Elmer, Marc. *Images - Souvenirs du Debarquement et de la Bataille de Normandie.* Publications D'Arromanches. France. n.d.

10. Lelievre, Raymond. 'Dans nos Ruines ...' *Terre Normande,* p. 14.

11. I am indebted to Miss Mary Crowley for the invaluable assistance she gave me in the preparation of this chapter. She made available to me her albums of photographs from Saint-Lô from which many of the illustrations are taken. I acknowledge with gratitude her paper on Saint-Lô, from which she has allowed to quote freely. (Crowley, Mary F. 'The Hôpital Irlandais St.-Lô.' Address to the Soroptimist Club of Dublin. 23 November 1948.)

12. 'French Unit.' *Irish Red Cross Bulletin.* September 1945. vol. v, no. 9, p. 259. I am grateful to Mr. and Mrs. Carey for a copy of the *Bulletin.*

13. Harvey, Lawrence E. *Samuel Beckett, Poet and Critic.* Princeton University Press. New Jersey. 1970. p. 179.

14. *Irish Red Cross Bulletin.* 1945. vol. v, p. 259.

15. Harvey. *Beckett, Poet and Critic.* p. 218.

16. James Gaffney was born on July 7, 1913, educated at O'Connell Schools, North Richmond Street and at Trinity College, Dublin where he graduated as a doctor of medicine in 1934, at the age of 21 years. After a period of training in pathology in Great Britain, he returned to Dublin to an academic appointment with the late R.A.Q. O'Meara at Trinity College with an attachment to Sir Patrick Dun's Hospital. He was killed tragically in the Aer Lingus aeroplane crash in the Welsh mountains on January 10th 1952. (I am grateful to Maurice Gaffney for these details.)

17. Letter from Dr. Gaffney to his mother from *Hôpital Irlandais.* 31.8.45.

18. Letter from Dr. Gaffney to his sister Maureen, 31.8.34.

19. Letter from Dr. Gaffney to his sister Josie, 7.9.45.

20. Letter from Dr. Gaffney to his brother Maurice, 10.9.45.

In September 1945, Dr. Alan Thompson submitted a confidential report on the difficulties in establishing the hospital. (A résumé of this report is in Miss Crowley's possession): 'It was necessary to find a temporary store in Saint-Lô. We were fortunate in getting a large granary in a Stud Farm near the hospital. When the ship arrived we saw the stores off the ship to railway wagons, and returned to St. Lô. After a few days railway wagons commenced to arrive at St. Lô. We had to move the stores by lorry 1 - 1½ miles to our store. Everything had to be taken upstairs. Some packets weighed over 2 cwts. Stores came in for days and days. All are stored safely now. It was a considerable task... The present position is that stores are safely housed under lock and key and well protected from the rain. The *Storekeeper* (Samuel Beckett) and assistant are making out stock cards for all material ... We borrowed beds and camped out in the hut. No running water - no sanitation of any kind. The water had to be carried in buckets ... Sanitation was held up due to lack of pipes and still consists of a hole in the ground with sacking around it. It is impossible, while sanitation is so primitive, to contemplate bringing out any additional staff ... The climate is very wet and muddy. Facilities for amusement are virtually nil ... The people seem to be very anxious for us to work there. They are asking all the time when the hospital will be open and taking in patients. The Mayor is very keen on the hospital functioning ...'

Recreational facilities were improved when the Countess Kerjorley, wife of the President of the French Red Cross, offered a seaside villa to the staff of the Hospital for use in their off-duty time. (Letter from Dr. Gaffney, to his sister Josie, 9.4.46).

21. Letter from Dr. Gaffney to his sister Maureen, 20.9.45.

22. Some years earlier, Beckett had written a poem drawing on his experiences in Dieppe in the thirties:

> again the last ebb
> the dead shingle
> the turning then the steps
> towards the lights of old
> (*Collected Poems*, p. 51)

For an analysis of this poem see Harvey, *Beckett, Poet and Critic*. pp. 215-219.

23. Letter from Dr. Gaffney to his sister Nora, 2.10.45.

24. Letter from Dr. Gaffney to his sister Nora, 2.10.45.

25. Letter from Dr. Gaffney to his sister Nora, 22.10.45.

26. Letter from Dr. Gaffney to his brother Christy, 28.10.45.

27. The staff complement was as follows:

Staff of the *Hôpital de La Croix Rouge Irlandaise*

1945 - 1947

Administrative

Colonel Thomas J. McKinney (Director)

Miss Dorrie Smith (Administrative Officer)
Miss Clare Olden (Secretary)
Mr. Samuel Beckett (Quartermaster-Interpreter and Storekeeper)
Father Brendan Hynds (Chaplain)
Mrs. Barrett (Receptionist Interpreter)
Miss Agnes O'Doherty (Shorthand typist)
Mr. Tommy Dunne (Assistant Storekeeper)

Medical

Physicians	*Surgeons*
Dr. Alan Thompson	Mr. Freddie F. McKee
Dr. Anthur W. Darley	Mr. Patrick Carey
Dr. Desmond Leahy	Mr. Patrick McNicholas (E.N.T.
Dr. Kitty O'Sullivan	and Ophthalmology)
Gynaecology	*Radiographer*
Dr. Timothy Boland	Miss Julia Murphy

Pathology
Dr. James C. Gaffney (Acting Director)
Mr. Michael B. Killick (Technician)

Pharmacist
Mr. Timothy O'Driscoll

Nursing

Miss Mary Crowley (Matron)

Sister Conroy (Assistant Matron)	Ann O'Leary
Sister Mary B. Murphy (Assistant Matron)	Ann Doherty
Sister Margaret Doherty (Theatre)	Eileen Dunne
Sister Breda O'Rahelly (Theatre)	Moira McGiskin
Sister Ita McDermott	Dilly Fahy
Sister Nora Cunningham	Madge Treacy
M. Martin	Joan Burke
Mary Fitzpatrick	E. O'Driscoll

A.M. O'Reilly	Terry Healy
Maeve McDermott	Margaret Malone
Mary Josephine Cullinan	E. Mulally

Between 30 and 35 nurses were selected in Dublin: 'Nurses salaries will range from £300 a year (for the Matron) to £100 a year (for an ordinary nurse). Staff sisters and theatre sisters will be paid £150 a year. When the nurses have been picked, the Society's team will be almost complete, as already fifteen doctors have been chosen in addition to a number of clerical and technical workers.' (Notice in Miss Crowley's possession).

28. Letter from Dr. Gaffney to his mother, 20.3.46.

29. Letter from Dr. Gaffney to his sister, Josie, 9.4.46.

30. Letter from Dr. Gaffney to his sister, Maureen, 12.4.46.

31. Letter from Dr. Gaffney to his sister, Josie. 9.4.46.

32. Patrick Carey recalls that many of the French, being unfamiliar with Irish whiskey, failed to see the day through.

33. Letter from Dr. Gaffney, to his sister, Maureen. 12.4.46.

34. Crowley. *Hôpital Irlandais*.

35. There was one exception - Beckett's friend Arthur Darley who contracted tuberculosis at Saint-Lô and died from the illness at Our Ladys' Hospice, Harold's Cross, Dublin, on December 30th 1948. He had revisited Saint-Lô shortly before his death. For obituary notices see: Brendan Ryan in: *The Irish Red Cross*. Bulletin. January 1949; T.A. Bouchier Hayes in: *The Evening Herald*. Sat. Jan. 1. 1949; Anonymous. *The Catholic Standard*. Fri. Jan. 7. 1949.

36. Lelievre, 'Dans nos Ruines ...' *Terre Normande*. p. 14.

37. Miss Crowley remembers her thirteen prisoners with affection, as they remember her; she still receives correspondence from some of those who survive. The prisoners were delivered to the hospital each morning by a British Officer, and Miss Crowley immediately restored their dignity by replacing their prisoner-of-war garb with the uniforms of an orderly. None ever attempted to escape and Miss Crowley went so far as to take her clutch to the beaches of Normandy on picnics without a guard! Dr. J. Gaffney also wrote warmly of the German P.O.W.'s, who performed odd jobs for the staff: 'for example, they clean our shoes, brush our clothes, etc. and I have one whole-time in my lab. who is very useful at washing bottles, keeping an eye on my water-distillation plant and so forth.' The P.O.W. camp in Saint-Lô held about 1000 prisoners, among whom was a doctor - Dr. Lippit from Giaz, Austria, who had 'written to his people 84 times without getting a reply'. (Letter from Dr. Gaffney to his mother, 9.10.45).

Patrick Carey recalls that one of the German P.O.W.'s fell on his bayonet prior to his capture, and the tip broke off lodging in his buttock. The wound became infected and the prisoner became seriously ill; Carey located the metal tip and successfully performed a difficult operation to remove it; on presenting the offending piece of weaponry proudly to his patient, he was informed that had a German not invented x-rays, he would have been unable to locate it. (Personal communication).

38. I am indebted to Sean O'Mórdha for obtaining for me a copy of Beckett's typescript entitled 'The Capital of the Ruins.' Dated 10/6/'46, and signed by Samuel Beckett. It is not known if the broadcast took place. It is published here in full with the permission of Radio Telefis Éireann. Beckett had left Saint-Lô to return to Paris at the time of writing the broadcast, though he continued to assist the hospital by performing whatever duties needed attending to in Paris.

39. When functioning fully the hospital had 115 in-patients.

40. Many of the illnesses treated were due to malnutrition and neglect. Patrick Carey recalls two surgical operations, which though minor, earned him lasting gratitude. A middle-aged peasant came to out-patient's with the largest sebaceous cyst that the young surgeon had ever seen; about the size of a melon, it sprouted from his forehead like a second head which he was forced to support with his hands so that he could hold his head up; the misery of years of carrying this mill-stone was relieved by a brief operation. The Chief of the Gendarmerie in Saint-Lô had lost his son tragically in the bombing of the city, and his teenage daughter had had her leg amputated; his wife and he decided to have another child, and this belated arrival was brought to the Irish Hospital after drinking boiling liquid that caused life-threatening oedema of the glottis; death was only prevented by an emergency tracheostomy performed by Paddy Carey. (Personal communication).

41. This would seem to have been the case: 'Looking up at the date I find it two months since I came here; and I must add that I've learned more about humanity and human nature in these two months than I'd learn at home in two years.' (Letter from Dr. Gaffney to his brother Christy, 28.10.45). Colonel MacKinney, expressed similar sentiments: 'We, Irish doctors, and nurses have had the advantage of mixing closely with the French people, and we have been received warmly by many French families. We have learned more from this experience than would have been possible through many years of academic and touristic relations. We have seen the reaction of the people of France in its time of trial, and we have come to love and admire them. I regret departing this land to which I have been so attracted, but in so doing I express for my colleagues and myself, our respect for this noble country. I pay homage to the greatness of France and the courage of its people.' (MacKinney. *Terre Normande*. p. 15.)

42. It has been suggested that some of Beckett's later writings, most notably *Endgame*, are based on his experiences in Saint-Lô. (Gontarski. S.E. *The Intent of Undoing in Samuel Beckett's Dramatic Texts*. Indiana University Press. Bloomington. 1985. pp. 32-39.)

43. This poem has been described as a poem of 'brief and unadorned perfection.' by Harvey (*Beckett, Poet and Critic*. p. 179), and by Fletcher as 'the finest he has written so far in either language.' (Fletcher, John. 'Beckett as Poet'. *Samuel Beckett, a collection of criticism edited by Ruby Cohn*. McGraw-Hill Book Company. 1975. pp. 41-50).

44. For an analysis of the poem see: Harvey, *Beckett, Poet and Critic*. pp. 179-182; pp. 218-220; Fletcher. 'Beckett as Poet' pp. 48-49.

45. Arthur Warren Darley was born on 23 August 1908, and educated at St. Gerard's School, Dublin, and at the Benedictine College, Douai, in England and by private tuition. His father was a famed musician and Arthur Darley was an accomplished violinist, pianist and guitarist often accompanying the celebrated Delia Murphy on record. He studied medicine at Trinity College, Dublin, where he qualified in 1931. He spent some time in the Richmond Hospital and two years working among Dublin's poor. In 1936 he worked as 'assistant' at Portrane Asylum with the intention of specialising in nervous diseases. However in February 1937 'Dr. Arthur Warren Darley shook the dust of Dublin from his feet ... and hied himself off to see the world' as doctor on a Canadian Pacific Liner. (*The Irish Times*. Fri. Feb. 26. 1937.) He went to Saint-Lô in August 1945.

46. I am grateful to Miss Crowley, and Patrick Carey for these personal reminiscences of Arthur Darley at Saint-Lô.

47. I am grateful to Mr. T. Murtagh, Trinity College, Dublin who translated the poem for me. *Mort de A.D.* has been translated in part by: Pilling, John. *Samuel Beckett*. Routledge and Kegan Paul, London. Henley and Boston. 1976. p. 180.

48. For an analysis of *Mort de A.D.* see: Harvey, *Beckett, Poet and Critic*. pp. 230-234.

49. Personal communication from Miss M. Crowley.

50. Following the departure of the Irish, the hospital was taken over by the French and later rebuilt with American assistance to serve as one of the major hospitals in the district.

51. Quotation from 'The Irish Hospital Sweeps' Charitable Achievements,' a document in Miss Crowleys possession.

52. Lelievre, 'Dans nos Ruines ...' *Terre Normande*, p. 14.

53. This medal was awarded to Samuel Beckett in 1947. It was not Beckett's first award from an appreciative French people; on 30 March 1945, he was awarded the Croix de Guerre with a gold star. The citation, signed by General Charles de Gaulle, read: 'Beckett, Sam: A man of great courage, who over the course of two years, demonstrated his effectiveness as an information source in an important intelligence network. He continued this work well past the limit of personal security. Betrayed to the Germans from 1943 he was forced to live clandestinely and with great difficulty.' Bair, *Beckett*. p. 271.

54. Bofin. P.J. Obituary. 'Alan H. Thompson. MA., MSc., MD., FRCPI., FRCP., FACP (Hon).' *Journal of the Irish Colleges of Physicians and Surgeons*. vol. 3. no. 4. 1974. pp. 131-132.

55. Around the same period Beckett wrote expressing similar sentiments to his German friend Axel Kaun: 'And more and more my own language appears to me like a veil that must be torn apart in order to get at the things (or the Nothingness) behind it. Grammar and Style. To me they seem to have become as irrelevant as a Victorian bathing suit or the imperturbability of a true gentleman. A mask.' 'A German Letter of 1947 to Axel Kaun'. Translated by Martin Esslin in: *Disjecta*. pp. 170-173. For further discussion on Beckett's bilingualism see: Beer, Ann. " 'Watt', Knott and Beckett's bilingualism." *Journal of Beckett Studies*, John Calder. London. 1985. no. 10. pp. 37-75; Cohn, Ruby. *The Comic Gamut*. Rutgers University Press. New Jersey. 1962. pp. 260-282; Cockerham, Harry. 'Bilingual Playwright', in: *Beckett the shape changer: a Symposium edited by Katherine Worth*. Routledge and Kegan Paul, London and Boston, 1975. pp. 139-159.

56. The first owner of this delightful house, the Reverend J. Sinclair Stevenson, a Shakespearian scholar named it after the birth-place of Anne Hathaway, Shottery, near Stratford-upon-Avon. *Shottery* in Killiney was built in 1925 and was bought by Frank Beckett in 1935. His daughter Caroline (Murphy) and her family now live there. It is of interest to note that Samuel Beckett has also resided in another house with a Shakespearian association. Beckett's mother moved from *Cooldrinagh* in 1941 to a smaller house, *New Place*, the same name as was attached to one of the finest houses in Stratford, the home of William Shakespeare.

BIBLIOGRAPHY OF
SAMUEL BECKETT'S WRITINGS
CONSULTED IN
THE BECKETT COUNTRY

This listing commences with the date the work was first published, followed by the title in English, details of the first publication, and the publication used for consultation from which page numbers are cited in the text of *The Beckett Country*. Where details of a publication need to be repeated, only an abbreviated entry for that publication is given. (For a full bibliography to 1970 see: Federman, Raymond, and Fletcher, John. *Samuel Beckett. His Works and His Critics. An Essay in Bibliography*. University of California Press, Berkeley, Los Angeles, London. 1970.)

CRITICISM

1929   'Dante ... Bruno. Vico .. Joyce', *Our Exagmination Round His Factification for Incamination of Work in Progress*. Shakespeare and Co. Paris. 1929. pp. 3-22. Republished in *Disjecta. Miscellaneous Writings and a Dramatic Fragment by Samuel Beckett*. ed. Ruby Cohn. John Calder. London. 1983. pp. 19-33.

1931   *Proust*. Chatto and Windus. London. 1931. Repub. *Proust. Three Dialogues. Samuel Beckett and George Duthuit*. John Calder. London. 1965.

1932   'Manifesto. Poetry is Vertical.' *Transition*, March 1932, no. 21, pp. 148-149.

1934   'Ex Cathezra'. A review of *Make it New* by Ezra Pound. *The Bookman*. 1934: vol. 87 p. 10. Repub. in *Disjecta*. pp. 77-81.

1934   'Papini's Dante'. A review of *Dante Vivo* by Giovanni Papini. Translated by Eleanor Hammond Broadus and Anna Benedetti. *The Bookman*. 1934: vol. 87 p.14. Repub. in *Disjecta*. pp. 80-81.

1934   'Recent Irish Poetry.' Under pseudonym Andrew Belis. *The Bookman*. August 1934: vol LXXVI. pp. 235-236. Repub. in *Disjecta*. pp. 70-76.

1934   'The Essential and the Incidental'. A review of *Windfalls* by Sean O'Casey. *The Bookman*. 1934: vol. 87 p. 111. Repub. in *Disjecta*. pp. 82-83.

1934   'Humanistic Quietism.' A review of *Poems* by Thomas McGreevy. *The Dublin Magazine*. 1934: vol. ix. n.s. pp.79-80. Repub. in *Disjecta*. pp. 68-69.

1935   'Censorship in the Saorstat.' Commissioned by *The Bookman,* this essay was written in 1935. After *The Bookman* ceased publication, Beckett sent it to his Paris agent George Reavy for *Transition*, but it remained unpublished. The typescript is in the Baker Memorial Library of Dartmouth College. Published in *Disjecta*. pp. 84-88.

1936   'An Imaginative Work' A review of *The Amaranthers* by Jack B. Yeats. *The Dublin Magazine*. 1936. vol. xi, n.s. pp. 80-81. Repub. in *Disjecta*. pp. 89-90.

1937   'A German Letter of 1937' to Axel Kaun. Addressed from 6 Clare Street. Dublin. IFS (Irish Free State). Dated 9.7.37 This extraordinarily explicit statement on language in writing is in the Baker Memorial Library of Dartmouth College. Axel Kaun an acquaintance encountered during Beckett's 1936 travels in Germany, suggested that Beckett might translate poems by Joachim Ringelnatz, pseudonym of Hans Botticher (1883-1934). Beckett was not interested in doing so. Martin Esslin has translated the letter which is published in *Disjecta*, in German pp. 51-54, and in English, pp. 170-173.

1938   'Denis Devlin.' A review of *Intercessions* by Denis Devlin *Transition*. April-May, 1938: vol. 27. pp. 289-294. Repub. in *Disjecta*. pp. 91-94.

1945   'MacGreevy on Yeats.' A review of *Jack B. Yeats. An Appreciation and an Interpretation* by Thomas MacGreevy. *The Irish Times*. Sat. August 4, 1945. Cols. 6 & 7. Repub. in *Disjecta*. pp. 95-97.

1949   'Three Dialogues' (with Georges Duthuit). *Transition Forty-nine*. 1949. vol. 5, pp. 97-103. Repub. in *Disjecta*. pp.138-145.

1954   'Hommage à Jack B. Yeats.' *Les Lettres Nouvelles*. April 1954. The translation appeared in a catalogue of Yeats' paintings edited by James White. Repub. in *Disjecta*. pp. 148-149.

1982   'Hommage to James Joyce', in *Essays in Honour of the late Sir Desmond Cochrane. With a message from Samuel Beckett and a foreword by Richard Ellman*. eds. Suheil Badi Bushriu and Bernard Benstock. Colin Smyth, Buckinghamshire, and Barnes and Noble Books, New Jersey, 1982. p. vii.

NARRATIVE PROSE

1929 'Che Sciagura'. *T.C.D. A College Miscellany.* Nov. 14. 1929: vol. 36. p. 42.

1929 'Assumption'. *Transition.* June 1929: nos. 16-17. pp. 268-271. Collected in *Transition Workshop*, ed. Eugene Jolas, Vanguard Press, New York, 1949.

1931 'The Possessed'. *T.C.D. A College Miscellany.* March 12. 1931: vol. 37. p. 138. Repub. in *Disjecta.* pp. 99-101.

1932 'Text'. *New Review.* April 1932: vol. II. p. 57. Repub. Cohn, Ruby. *Samuel Beckett: The Comic Gamut.* Rutgers University Press. New Brunswick, N.J. 1962. p. 308.

1932 'Sedendo et Quiescendo'. (Extract from *Dream of Fair to Middling Women) Transition: An International Workshop for Orphic Creation.* ed. Eugene Jolas. Servire Press. Holland. March. 1932: *21.* 13-20.

1932 'Dante and the Lobster'. (Extract from *More Pricks than Kicks.) This Quarter.* December 1932. vol. v, pp. 222-236.

1932 *Dream of Fair to Middling Women.* Beckett's first novel, written in a Paris hotel in 1932, is unpublished, but is in typescript in the Baker Memorial Library of Dartmouth College, New Hampshire, and there is a photocopy in the Beckett Archive, The University of Reading, Reading, England. (MS 122 7/7/16/8). Excerpts have been published from time to time in books on Beckett. e.g. *Disjecta.* pp. 43-50.

1934 'A Case In A Thousand. A short story.' *The Bookman.* 1934; vol. 86. pp. 241-242.

1934 *More Pricks than Kicks.* Chatto and Windus. London. 1934. Repub. Calder and Boyars. London. 1970.

1934 *Murphy* G. Routledge. London. 1938. Repub. John Calder. London, 1963.

1950 *Molloy. Molloy.* Les Éditions de Minuit. Paris. 1951. Repub. *The Trilogy. Molloy. Malone Dies. The Unnamable.* John Calder. London, 1976.

1951 *Malone Dies. Malone Meurt.* Les Éditions de Minuit. Paris. 1951. Repub. *The Trilogy.* John Calder. 1976.

1953 *The Unnamable. L'Innomable.* Les Éditions de Minuit. Paris. 1953. Repub. *The Trilogy.* John Calder. 1976.

1953 *Watt.* Olympia Press. Paris. 1953. Repub. Calder and Boyars. London 1972.

1954 *The Expelled. (L'Expulse. Nouvelles et textes pour rien).* Les Éditions de Minuit. Paris 1954. Repub. *Collected Shorter Prose 1945-1980.* John Calder. London 1984.

1954 *The Calmative. (Le Calmant. Nouvelles et textes pour rien).* Les Éditions de Minuit. 1954. Repub. *Collected Shorter Prose.* pp. 35-49.

1954 *The End. (La Fin. Nouvelles et textes pour rien).* Les Éditions de Minuit. Paris. 1954. Repub. *Collected Shorter Prose.* pp. 51-70.

1954 *Texts for Nothing. (Nouvelles et textes pour rien).* Les Éditions de Minuit. Paris. 1954. Repub. *Collected Shorter Prose.* pp. 71-74.

1956 'From an Abandoned Work'. *Trinity News,* 1956: vol. 3. p. 4. Repub. *Collected Shorter Prose.* pp. 129-137.

1961 *How It Is. (Comment c'est).* Les Éditions de Minuit. Paris. 1961. Repub. Calder and Boyars. London. 1964.

1965 *Imagination Dead Imagine. (Imagination morte imaginez).* Les Éditions de Minuit. Paris. 1965. Repub. *Collected Shorter Prose.* pp. 145-147.

1965 " 'Jem Higgins' Love Letter to the Alba". (Extract from *Dream of Fair to Middling Women). New Durham,* June 1965, pp.10-11.

1966 *Enough. (Assez).* Les Éditions de Minuit. Paris. 1966. Repub. *Collected Shorter Prose.* pp. 139-144.

1966 *Ping. (Bing).* Les Éditions de Minuit. Paris. 1966. Repub. *Collected Shorter Prose.* pp. 149-151.

1968-76 *Closed Place. (Se voir in Pour finis encour).* Les Éditions de Minuit. Paris. 1976. Repub. *Collected Shorter Prose.* pp. 199-200.

1970 *Mercier and Camier. (Mercier et Camier).* Les Éditions de Minuit. Paris. 1970. Repub. John Calder. London. 1974.

1970 *First Love. (Premier Amour).* Les Éditions de Minuit. Paris. 1970. Repub. *Collected Shorter Prose.* pp. 1-19.

1971 *The Lost Ones. (Le Depeupleur).* Les Éditions de Minuit. Paris. 1971. Repub. *Collected Shorter Prose.* pp. 159-178.

1973 *Afar a Bird. (Au loin un oiseau).* Double Elephant Press. New York. 1973 (with etchings by Avigdor Arikha). Repub. *Collected Shorter Prose.* pp. 195-196.

1975 *For to End Yet Again. (Pour finir encore. in Minuit).* Les Éditions de Minuit. Paris. 1975. Repub. *Collected Shorter Prose.* pp. 179-182.

1976 *He is barehead (in Minuit).* Les Éditions de Minuit. Paris. 1976. Repub. *Collected Shorter Prose.* pp. 187-191.

1976 *Horn came always (in Minuit).* Les Éditions de Minuit. Paris. 1976. Repub. *Collected Shorter Prose.* pp. 195-196.

1976 *Still.* M'Arte Edizione. Milan 1974 (with etchings by William Hayter). Repub. *Collected Shorter Prose.* pp. 183-185.

1976 *Old Earth (in Minuit).* Les Éditions de Minuit. Paris. 1976. Repub. *Collected Shorter Prose.* pp. 201-202.

1976 *I gave up before birth (in Minuit).* Les Éditions de Minuit. Paris 1976. Repub. *Collected Shorter Prose.* pp. 197-198.

1976 *All Strange Away.* Gotham Book Mart. U.S.A. 1976. Repub. John Calder. London. 1979.

1979 'Heard in the Dark'. *New Writings and Writers 17.* John Calder. London. Repub. *Collected Shorter Prose.* pp. 203-204.

1979   'Heard in the Dark II'. *Journal of Beckett Studies* 5. Autumn. 1979. John Calder. London. Repub. *Collected Shorter Prose.* pp. 205-207.

1979   *Lessness (Sans).* Les Éditions de Minuit. Paris. 1979. Repub. *Collected Shorter Prose.* pp. 153-157.

1980   'One Evening.' *Journal of Beckett Studies* 6. Autumn 1980. John Calder. London. Repub. *Collected Shorter Prose.* pp. 209-210.

1980   *Company.* John Calder. London. 1980.

1981   *ill seen ill said (Mal vu mal dit).* Les Éditions de Minuit. Paris. 1981. Repub. *ill seen ill said.* John Calder. London. 1981.

1983   *Worstward Ho.* John Calder. London. 1983.

PLAYS

1937   *Human Wishes.* A fragment of a play on the relationship of Dr. Samuel Johnson and Mrs. Thrale. First published in Cohn, Ruby. *Just Play.* Princeton University Press, Princeton. 1980. Repub. in *Disjecta.* pp. 155-166.

1952   *Waiting for Godot. (En Attendant Godot).* Les Éditions de Minuit. Paris. 1952. Faber and Faber. London. 1975.

1956   *All That Fall.* Grove Press. New York. 1957. Repub. *Collected Shorter Plays of Samuel Beckett.* Faber and Faber. London and Boston. 1984. pp 9-39.

1956   *Act Without Words I. (Fin de partie, suivi de Acte sans paroles).* Les Éditions de Minuit. Paris. 1957. Repub. *Collected Shorter Plays.* pp. 41-46.

1956   *Act Without Words II. (Acte sans paroles II).* Manus Presse. Stutgart. 1965. Repub. *Collected Shorter Plays.* pp. 47-51.

1957   *Endgame. (Fin de partie).* Les Éditions de Minuit. Paris. 1952. Faber and Faber. London. 1976.

1958   *Krapp's Last Tape.* Evergreen Review. 1958: 2. 13-24. Repub. *Collected Shorter Plays.* pp. 53-73.

1950s   *Rough for Theatre I.* Repub. *Collected Shorter Plays.* pp. 65-73.

1950s   *Rough for Theatre II.* Repub. *Collected Shorter Plays.* pp. 75-89.

1959   *Embers.* Evergreen Review. 1959: 3. 28-41. Repub. *Collected Shorter Plays.* pp. 90-104.

1961   *Rough for Radio I.* Repub. *Collected Shorter Plays.* pp. 105-111.
        Rough for Radio II. Repub. *Collected Shorter Plays.* pp. 113-124.

1961   *Happy Days.* Grove Press. New York. 1961. Faber and Faber. London. 1973.

1961   *Words and Music.* Evergreen Review. 1961: 6. 34-43. Repub. *Collected Shorter Plays.* pp. 125-134.

1962   *Cascando.* Dramatische Dichtungen. 1963: I. 338-361. Repub. *Collected Shorter Plays.* pp. 135-144.

1963   *Play (Spiel).* Theater Heute: July 1963. Repub. *Collected Shorter Plays.* pp. 145-160.

1963   *Film. Eh Joe and Other Writings.* Faber and Faber. London. 1967.

1963   *The Old Tune. An Adaption of La Manivelle* by Robert Pinget. Les Éditions de Minuit. Paris. 1963. Repub. *Collected Shorter Plays.* pp. 175-189.

1965   *Come and Go.* Les Éditions de Minuit. Paris. 1966. Repub. *Collected Shorter Plays.* pp. 191-197.

1965   *Eh Joe. Eh Joe and Other Writings.* Faber and Faber. London. 1967. Repub. *Collected Shorter Plays.* pp. 199-207.

1970   *Breath.* Gambit. 1970. Vol 4. No. 16. Repub. *Collected Shorter Plays.* pp. 209-211.

1973   *Not I.* Faber and Faber. London. 1973. Repub. *Collected Shorter Plays.* pp. 213-223.

1974   *That Time.* Grove Press. New York. 1976. Repub. *Collected Shorter Plays.* pp. 225-235.

1975   *Footfalls.* Grove Press. New York. 1976. Repub. *Collected Shorter Plays.* pp. 238-243.

1976   *Ghost Trio.* Grove Press. New York. 1976. Repub. *Collected Shorter Plays.* pp. 245-254.

1976   *...but the clouds...* Faber and Faber. London. 1977. Repub. *Collected Shorter Plays.* pp. 255-262.

1980   *A Piece of Monologue.* Faber and Faber. London. 1982. Repub. *Collected Shorter Plays.* pp. 263-269.

1981   *Rockaby.* Faber and Faber. London. 1982. Repub. *Collected Shorter Plays.* pp. 271-282.

1981   *Ohio Impromptu.* Faber and Faber. London. 1982. Repub. *Collected Shorter Plays.* pp. 283-288.

1982   *Quad.* Faber and Faber. London. 1984. Repub. *Collected Shorter Plays.* pp. 289-294.

1982   *Catastrophe.* Faber and Faber. London. 1984. Repub. *Collected Shorter Plays.* pp. 295-301.

1982   *Nacht und Träume. Collected Shorter Plays.* pp. 303-306.

1982   *What Where.* Faber and Faber. London. 1984. Repub. *Collected Shorter Plays.* pp. 307-316.

POETRY

1930   *For Future Reference. Transition.* nos. 19-20. Spring-Summer June, 1930.: pp. 342-343. Quoted Harvey. Lawrence.E. *Samuel Beckett: Poet and Critic.* Princeton University Press. New Jersey. 1970. pp. 299-301.

1930   *Whoroscope.* The Hours Press. Paris. 1930. Repub: *Collected Poems 1930-1978.* John Calder. London. 1984.

1931   *Alba. Dublin Magazine.* VI. n.s. Oct-Dec 1931. 4. Repub. *Collected Poems.* p. 15.

1931   *Casket of Pralinen for a Daughter of Dissipated Mandarin. The Euorpean Caravan. An Anthology of the New Spirit in European Literature.* Ed. Samuel Putnam, Kastlehun Maidal, George Reavy, and J. Bronowski. Brewer, Warren and Putnam. New York. 1931. pp. 476-478. Quoted in Harvey. *Poet and Critic.* pp. 278-283.

1931   *Text. The European Caravan.* pp. 478-480. Quoted in Harvey. *Poet and Critic.* pp. 288-295.

1931   *Yoke of Liberty. The European Caravan.* p. 480. Quoted in Harvey. *Poet and Critic.* p. 314.

1931   *Return to the Vestry. New Review.* I. Aug-Sept-Oct, 1931: 98-99. Quoted in Harvey. *Poet and Critic.* pp. 308-312.

1931   *Hell Crane to Starling. The Europen Caravan.* pp. 475-476. Quoted in Harvey. *Poet and Critic.* pp. 302-205.

1931   *Calvary by Night.* Unpublished. Quoted in Harvey. *Poet and Critic.* p. 275.

1932   *Home Olga. Contempo* (Chapel hill, N.C.) III, no. 13. (Feb. 15, 1934), 3. Repub: *Collected Poems.* pp. 8-9.

1934   *Gnome. Dublin Magazine.* IX n.s. July-September, 1934: 8. Repub: *Collected Poems.* p. 7.

1935   *The Vulture. Echo's Bones and Other Precipitates.* The G.L.M. Press. Paris. 1935. Repub: *Collected Poems.* p. 9.

1935   *Enueg I. Echo's Bones.* Repub: *Collected Poems.* pp. 10-12.

1935   *Enueg II. Echo's Bones.* Repub: *Collected Poems.* pp. 13-14.

1935   *Dortmunder. Echo's Bones.* Repub: *Collected Poems.* p. 16.

1935   *Sanies I. Echo's Bones.* Repub: *Collected Poems.* pp. 17-18.

1935   *Sanies II. Echo's Bones.* Repub: *Collected Poems.* pp. 19-20.

1935   *Serena I. Echo's Bones.* Repub: *Collected Poems.* pp.21-22.

1935   *Serena II. Echo's Bones.* Repub: *Collected Poems.* pp. 23-24.

1935   *Serena III. Echo's Bones.* Repub: *Collected Poems.* p. 25.

1935   *Malacoda. Echo's Bones.* Repub: *Collected Poems.* p. 26.

1935   *Da Tagete Est. Echo's Bones.* Repub: *Collected Poems.* p. 27.

1935   *Echo's Bones. Echo's Bones.* Repub: *Collected Poems.* p. 28.

1936   *Cascando. The Dublin Magazine.* XI n.s. Oct-Dec 1936. 3-4. Repub: *Collected Poems.* pp. 29-30.

1937-9   *they come. Out of This Century.* Peggy Guggenheim. New York. 1946. p. 25. Repub: *Collected Poems.* pp. 40-41.

1937-9   *Dieppe. Les Temps Modernes.* Vol. 2. No. 14. Nov 1946. Repub: *Collected Poems.* pp. 50-51.

1938   *Ooftish. Transition: Tenth Anniversary.* Apr-May 1938. Repub: *Collected Poems.* p. 31.

1946   *Saint Lô. Irish Times.* June 24, 1946, p. 5. cols. 5,6.

1947-9   *Mort de A.D. Les Cahirs des Saisons.* No. 2. Oct. 1955. Repub: *Collected Poems.* pp. 56-57.

1947-9   *My way is the sand flowing. Transition Forty-Eight.* No. 2. June 1948. 96-97. Repub: *Collected Poems.* pp. 58-59.

1947-9   *What would I do without this world. Transition Forty-Eight.* No. 2, June 1948. 96-97. Repub: *Collected Poems.* pp. 60-61.

1947-9   *I would like my love to die. Transition Forty-Eight.* No. 2, June 1948. 96-97. Repub: *Collected Poems.* pp. 62-63.

1962   *Song. Words and Music.* Faber and Faber. 1962. Repub: *Collected Poems.* p. 37.

1974   *Something there. New Departures.* Special Issue No. 7/8 and 10/11. 1975. Repub: *Collected Poems.* pp. 64-65.

1974   *dread nay. Collected Poems.* pp. 33-34.

1976   *Roundelay. Collected Poems.* p. 35.

1976   *thither. Collected Poems.* p. 36.

1979   *neither. Journal of Beckett Studies.* John Calder. London. No. 4. Spring 1979. p. vii.

INDEX

Index

Bold numerals indicate references to photographs and illustrations. References to *Notes and References* are indicated by the page number followed by the reference number with the prefix 'n.'